W9-CFJ-364

INDIA... ...O, MAIN LIBRARY

3 2901 00638 9754

THE LOST ASTRONAUT

Indian River County Main Library
1600 21st Street
Vero Beach, FL 32960

m2-B+T 4/18

THE LOST ASTRONAUT

SEARCH FOR THE GOLDEN THREAD

D. J. CONING

NEW YORK

NASHVILLE • MELBOURNE • VANCOUVER

THE LOST ASTRONAUT
SEARCH FOR THE GOLDEN THREAD

© 2018 **D. J. CONING**

All rights reserved. No portion of this book may be reproduced, stored in a retrieval system, or transmitted in any form or by any means—electronic, mechanical, photocopy, recording, scanning, or other,—except for brief quotations in critical reviews or articles, without the prior written permission of the publisher.

This is a work of fiction. Names, characters, businesses, places, events, and incidents are either the products of the author's imagination or used in a fictitious manner. Any resemblance to actual persons, living or dead, or actual events is purely coincidental.

Published in New York, New York, by Morgan James Publishing. Morgan James is a trademark of Morgan James, LLC. www.MorganJamesPublishing.com

The Morgan James Speakers Group can bring authors to your live event. For more information or to book an event visit The Morgan James Speakers Group at www.TheMorganJamesSpeakersGroup.com.

ISBN 978-1-68350-547-1 paperback
ISBN 978-1-68350-548-8 eBook
Library of Congress Control Number: 2017905750

Cover Design by:
Rachel Lopez
www.r2cdesign.com

Interior Design by:
Bonnie Bushman
The Whole Caboodle Graphic Design

In an effort to support local communities, raise awareness and funds, Morgan James Publishing donates a percentage of all book sales for the life of each book to Habitat for Humanity Peninsula and Greater Williamsburg.

Get involved today! Visit
www.MorganJamesBuilds.com

3 2901 00638 9754

To Andrew, Tim and Abby:
May you always find the golden thread.

TABLE OF CONTENTS

CHAPTER 1
CAPTAIN, WAKE UP!

"Captain, are you awake, sir?" inquired IRIS, the captain's personal android assistant. Expecting to find the captain asleep as he entered the dimly lit quarters, instead IRIS found him sitting up in bed with his eyes wide open, staring off into space, unresponsive to IRIS's presence.

"Captain Marcello, are you awake?" IRIS repeated in a monotone voice, this time at a higher volume.

Getting no response, IRIS quickly performed a bio scan of the captain's vital signs. "Elevated heart rate, increased body temperature, abnormal breathing pattern," IRIS stated as he leaned over and touched the captain's shoulder, jolting him from his trance. Captain Marcello gasped for air.

"Are you alright, sir?" IRIS asked.

"Yes, I'm fine, IRIS. It was just . . ." He paused with an expression of disbelief on his face. "A dream that I hadn't dreamed in a very long time." He wiped the sweat from his brow, took a deep breath, and moved to the side of the bed. "Is there something I can do for you?"

1

"Yes, sir. Commander Corbis has been trying to reach you. We have received a distress signal from an unidentified ship, and he is requesting your assistance on the bridge."

"Inform the commander that I'll be right there," Marcello said as he stumbled to the lavatory to wash the sleep and sweat from his face. He threw on his Royal Celestian military uniform, consisting of tan slacks and a navy blazer with ornate gold buttons and ornamental military epaulettes on each shoulder, symbolizing not only his rank but also identifying him as a prince in the royal family. Then he exited his cabin and walked toward the bridge.

The *Cora Lee* was the pride of the fleet. She was the fastest, most powerful ship in the kingdom, gliding gracefully through space like a sword slicing through the thick morning fog. Her beautiful aerodynamic curves made her look more like an exquisite sea creature than the larger, bulky battleships that had preceded her. Her elegant design made her the perfect ship for diplomacy, but her speed and power made her a formidable foe should diplomacy fail.

Onboard were over three hundred of the finest officers from dozens of planets and species, all sworn to serve the kingdom and protect its vast allegiance of democratic planets from the Murks, a ruthless empire that forced planets into submission or destroyed those that refused. The Murks weren't the only predators in space. Marauding pirates, known as Thorgs, traversed the edge of the galaxy looking for easy prey from which to steal ships, freight, and hostages, which they sold as slaves to border planets on the outskirts of the Celestian Kingdom.

"Attention, captain on the bridge!" Commander Corbis ordered as Captain Marcello entered. Every officer on the bridge snapped to attention.

"At ease," Marcello stated as he navigated to his chair in the center of the command deck. "Status report?"

"Captain, we received what we believe is a distress signal. However, we are unable to interpret the language or identify the species." The ship's communications officer, Lieutenant Beckel, fluent in over a dozen languages, turned to face the captain. "I ran the message through every language database, and there are no known origins for the language. However, we are receiving a universal distress beacon along with the message."

She pressed a button on her station panel, and a distorted video played on the main bridge monitor, initially without sound. The video was fuzzy, and it faded in and out for several moments. Eventually, in the center of the monitor, a humanoid figure appeared and spoke frantically into the camera.

"Is there any sound?" Marcello asked.

"Not yet, sir. The video gets clearer in a moment, and then audio comes in briefly."

A few seconds later, the video cleared up, and it was obvious from the person's uniform that he was the captain or other high-ranking officer. It was also evident that his ship had sustained heavy damage. Thick smoke filled the compartment, and flashes of fire were visible in the background. Then, in a language unfamiliar to everyone on the *Cora Lee's* bridge, his voice faded into the video. Midway through his message, the audio and video ceased. Lieutenant Beckel turned back toward the captain. "That's the entirety of the message, sir. Like I said, the language is unfamiliar."

For several moments after the video ceased, Captain Marcello stood motionless, his jaw slightly dropped, staring at the monitor. The language may have been unfamiliar to Lieutenant Beckel and everyone else on the bridge, but it was certainly familiar to him, though it had been a lifetime since he heard anyone speak English. He had all but resolved that he would never hear his native language again. The message stated: "We have sustained heavy damage to our engines, life support systems, and outer hull. We require immediate assistance. If anyone hears this message, we are on an urgent diplomatic mission of peace and have traveled far to find help to save our planet. We are pleading for your—"

The crew waited for directions from their captain, who was typically decisive and quick to utter a command to enter battle to rescue a stranded ship or defend a helpless planet, but he just stood there staring at the screen.

"Captain, do you believe it to be a trap?" Lieutenant Commander Cho Fe, the ship's security officer, asked. On the edge of space, it was a common tactic for Thorgs to fake distress signals to lure in unsuspecting ships. Marcello still didn't answer, just stood there, frozen.

"Sir, how would you like us to proceed?" Corbis asked, breaking the captain's trance.

"The message is legitimate," Captain Marcello said finally. "Set an intercept course, maximum speed. Commander, you have the bridge. I'll be in my ready room. Notify me when we arrive." Every eye on the bridge watched Captain Marcello as he retired to the adjacent ready room.

"You heard the captain; prepare for battle," Corbis ordered. "Lieutenant, alert Dr. Pandori to have his medical team prepared to receive wounded. Red alert!"

The disciplined, well-seasoned crew sprang into perfectly synchronized action as they prepared for the all-too-familiar battle. Their movements were expedient and decisive but without haste or chaos. After ensuring all the necessary preparations were in place, Commander Corbis rang the doorbell to the captain's ready room and then entered. Captain Marcello was seated behind a large dark wooden desk with his back to the door and his feet propped up on a small shelf that sat beneath the window as he stared into deep space.

"Sir, we are nearing the location of the distress signal, and the crew is prepared for battle." The captain gave no response. Corbis took a deep breath before continuing. "If I may inquire, sir, your behavior has been . . . peculiar. Are you alright? Is there anything I should be aware of regarding this ship and its planet's origin?" Corbis had been a close friend to the captain, serving alongside him in many battles, and he felt he deserved to know the truth.

"I am familiar with this planet and with its people," Marcello said as he turned in his chair to face Corbis. Tears formed in his eyes, and his voice quivered as he continued. "This is my planet. These are my people."

"Sir, that's fantastic news!"

Captain Marcello held up his hand. "The crew must not be informed of this. No one is to know."

"Yes, sir, as you wish," Corbis said and then turned to leave.

The doorbell rang again. Before Marcello could answer, Bayli walked in. Although she was not an official crew member, she was a longtime friend of the captain. They were like brother and sister. She provided both welcome and not-so-welcome advice to him any time she felt he needed to hear it. Of the few friends he had, her opinion mattered more than any other, for she had been there through some of the hardest times of his young life. As an Azurian, her species was nearly annihilated by the Murks, and the Thorgs had captured her and her family. Bayli had beautiful blue skin with long braided black hair and markings up and down her arms.

"It's your planet, isn't it?" Bayli asked.

Marcello's eyebrows rose in surprise. "Yes, how did you know?"

"Lieutenant Beckel forwarded me the distress message to inquire if I was familiar with the language. Don't worry; I told her I wasn't. However, it sounded similar to some of the words I've heard you use when you talk to yourself. Plus, the person on the monitor looks like you." She smiled wryly. "So what are you going to do now?"

Captain Marcello shook his head slowly. "I'm not sure yet. We'll rescue them and then determine what their intent is."

"I see," Bayli replied. "And then you'll reveal yourself to them?"

"No, they must not know that I'm alive."

"Captain to the bridge," Officer Beckel said over the intercom.

"Excuse me," Marcello said as he leaped to his feet and hurried out.

"Sir, we've arrived, and the distressed vessel has sustained heavy damage," Corbis said as Marcello entered the bridge. "They are being attacked by six Thorg predator-class ships."

The Thorgs were neither trained nor disciplined in a military fashion. They operated purely out of greed. Their ships were usually a hodgepodge pieced together from the wreckage of captured ships. Each Thorg ship would alter its attack tactics based upon the culmination of strength from the ships they had previously captured. This particular Thorg ship was using small predator fighters to attack while the mothership hid from harm's way.

After assessing the situation, Marcello ordered the attack, and the *Cora Lee* darted in front of the wounded Earth vessel, blocking the crippled ship from any further shots. Then she fired a single torpedo and struck the underside of a predator ship, detonating it on impact. The remaining predators turned their focus onto the *Cora Lee* and launched a torrent of torpedoes and phasor weaponry against her, lighting up the pitch-black space. The weapons were ineffective against the *Cora Lee*'s advanced defensive shields. In return, the *Cora Lee* launched torpedoes at each of the predators, exploding the small ships.

One predator ship was attached to the outer hull of the Earth vessel, deploying an attack crew to disable the Earth ship from the inside. Precise phasor shots by Lt. Commander Cho Fe sliced the predator from the side of the Earth ship, and then a follow-up torpedo destroyed it.

Only one predator ship remained, and it was fleeing toward its mothership. However, a tractor beam from the *Cora Lee* captured and held the struggling vessel in its grip.

Captain Marcello hailed the predator, and a large, slimy gray creature filled the monitor. His face was contorted with wrath as he spewed insults and curses.

"Silence!" Marcello said to the defiant Thorg in its own language. "I have destroyed your ships and can just as easily destroy you. However, I want you to take a warning to your people. If I find any Thorg ship in this quadrant again, I shall unleash a storm against you that will make today's defeat look minuscule in comparison. There is no distance I won't travel to bring down fire on you. Now leave and deliver this message before I change my mind."

The tractor beam was disabled, and the predator limped back toward its mothership.

"Sir, a team of Thorg scouts made it on board their ship before we could destroy all the predators," Lt. Commander Cho Fe said.

"Scanners are picking up a radiation leak in the engineering section," Chief Engineer Morten added. "If we can't get that under control, the ship could explode, taking us with them."

"We'll need to move quickly," Corbis replied.

"Agreed, but their technology is foreign to us. I'm not sure if we will be able to assist," Morten said.

"Gee, it's a real shame that we don't have someone on board who speaks and reads their language," Bayli whispered loud enough for only the captain to hear.

"Commander Corbis will lead an away team to secure and protect the executive officers," Marcello said. "The chief and I will lead a team to retake the engineering department and determine if we are able to assist them. Bayli, please work with Dr. Pandori to lead the medical teams once we have secured the ship. Lieutenant Commander Cho, you're in charge of the bridge. If things go bad, undock the ship and get clear."

The three teams assembled in the cargo bay to disembark. Marcello was dressed in his full body armor, including a silver reflective helmet that covered his face and a royal insignia on his lapel. He was accompanied by Mahjon, his royal bodyguard, a giant guardian of Mravia. Standing nearly nine feet tall with a muscular frame and smooth, hard skin, Mahjon came from an ancient, powerful species who had sworn long ago to protect the royal family.

Seven elite military personnel from the *Cora Lee* filed into the breached hull of the Earth ship, followed by Mahjon, Marcello, and Chief Engineer Morten. Each crew member wore full body armor and carried a laser rifle with flashlight attached. Emergency lights along the walls of the ship cast a red hue against the smoke-filled halls. The ship's gravitational system was offline, so the team engaged their gravitational boots, allowing them to walk securely down the halls.

Sadly, the first humans they encountered were already dead and floating eerily in place, killed by the Thorgs. As they came to a T in the hallway, signs read "Cafeteria" to the left and "Engineering" to the right. Marcello placed his hand on the shoulder of the security officer in front of him and directed him to the right. They proceeded in military formation, checking each room for Thorgs or survivors, only to find more dead.

The thick security door outside of engineering had been destroyed by a phasor attack, which left a gaping hole. Engineering was made up of three nested, circular chambers. The innermost chamber housed the football-sized power core, while the middle and outer chambers were used for managing and monitoring the core.

Injured and slain engineers in white uniforms, along with security officers, were strewn about the outer chamber. At the rear, three security officers were pinned down and receiving fire from a single Thorg, whose body armor the human weapons couldn't penetrate. Two other Thorgs were in the center chamber, attempting to remove the power core.

After quickly analyzing the situation, the *Cora Lee*'s command force sprang into action. They pushed through the debris and fired a shot, knocking the assailant against the wall. A second shot penetrated his body armor, killing him. As they filed into the middle chamber, the nearest Thorg fired several shots at one of the Celestian soldiers, but his body army deflected them. Several soldiers returned fire from multiple strategic locations, killing the second Thorg. The third Thorg, who had been in the process of extracting the power core, set down his tools, but before he could reach for his sidearm, he was struck several times. The team moved through the chambers in formation, sweeping each room for additional Thorgs.

The security officers who had been pinned down arose with their weapons drawn and pointed at the *Cora Lee*'s command force. Marcello stepped forward and raised his hands to show they meant no harm. After a moment, the humans lowered their weapons and began helping the wounded.

"All clear, sir," said the squad leader of the command force to Marcello after sweeping all the chambers. However, Mahjon's intuition told him otherwise, and he shook his head and listened. Then he walked slowly toward a large electrical panel and paused in front of the door. Suddenly, the panel flew open, and a Thorg who had entered the ship's electrical ducts attacked Mahjon. However, with one powerful blow, Mahjon struck the Thorg's chest, launching him across the room and slamming his body against the opposite wall. The Thorg collapsed and died.

"Now it's all clear," Mahjon said in his deep voice.

Marcello radioed the *Cora Lee* that they had secured the engineering room and were investigating the state of the power core. Commander Corbis reported that his team had secured the bridge and the senior officers while destroying two additional Thorgs. A scan from the *Cora Lee* identified that no remaining Thorgs were on board.

Chief Engineer Morten entered the inner chamber, along with Marcello, to restore the power core. The Thorgs had nearly completed the process of extracting the core and placing it into a transport pod. They reached a large panel in front of the power core and studied the various gauges, switches, and sliders. Morten's radiation meter warned that levels were dangerously high. While their armor suits provided temporary defense against radiation, long-term exposure diminished the suits' effectiveness.

Marcello translated the English labels for Morten, who, out of respect for Marcello's privacy, never inquired how he could read them. Morten pressed several buttons, and two mechanical arms extended. They grabbed the power core and returned it to its stand. A large, thick glass wall lowered, sealing off the power core from the rest of the chamber.

"The core is back in its repository," Morten said, "but it's too hot! If we can't get its temperature down, the entire system is going to blow."

They examined the panel for further options until Marcello read a sign that said, "In case of emergency, use emergency button on the wall." He shone his light around the room, looking for the emergency button. His light landed upon an injured engineer lying on the floor. The engineer, who could barely move, stared at the captain and then pointed at the wall. Moving his light along the trajectory the engineer indicated, Marcello spotted a glass panel labeled "Emergency Only." He ran to the panel, smashed the protective glass with the butt of his light, and then pressed the large red emergency button. Immediately, orange anti-radiation foam filled the inner chamber surrounding the power core. White suds sprayed from overhead sprinklers, soaking everyone and everything. Morten wiped the foam from his meter and watched as the radiation levels diminished until they were undetectable.

Once Chief Morten gave the all-clear, Marcello radioed that the medical team could safely enter the ship and was needed in the engineering department. As the medical team entered, Bayli and Dr. Pandori encountered Marcello and Mahjon as they were heading back to the *Cora Lee*.

"Prepare yourself. It's rough in there," Marcello warned Bayli.

"This is not my first go-around," Bayli replied.

"I know, but it never gets any easier."

"I'll be alright. This is why we're here, is it not?"

Bayli followed the medical team into engineering and began assisting the wounded. She spotted an older man trying frantically to remove a large, heavy beam that had fallen on a young woman, pinning her to the floor. Bayli called for several of *Cora Lee*'s soldiers to assist them in lifting the beam. As soon as the beam was removed, the woman screamed in agony. It was obvious that her leg was broken. Bayli bent down beside her and placed a universal translator device into the woman's ear. Afraid, the woman resisted, but Bayli gently placed her hand on the woman's arm and then, with her other hand, placed the translator into the woman's ear. Bayli spoke slowly, giving the device time to adjust to the woman's biometrics.

"Can you understand me?" Bayli asked.

The young woman nodded as Bayli gave a translator device to the older man.

"It's a universal translator to help us communicate with each other," Bayli explained. "I am Azurian, and I am a medical telepath." Bayli removed the glove from her hand and touched the woman's shoulder. "You have internal bleeding and will require surgery immediately."

The woman tried to sit up on her elbows but then winced in pain and lay back down. Dr. Pandori heard her scream and came over to assist Bayli.

"She has several internal lacerations, a broken leg, and is in shock," Bayli said as the doctor scanned her with his medical hand scanner and confirmed Bayli's diagnosis.

"She will need surgery immediately," Dr. Pandori said. Then he stared at the scanner, perplexed. "This is most odd. She has the same genetic DNA makeup as the cap—"

"Let's prep her for moving to surgery," Bayli interrupted as she applied a sedative.

The older man grabbed her arm. "I'm her father. What are you giving her?"

"It's alright, sir," Bayli said. "I'm giving her a sedative so we can move her. She needs immediate treatment or she may die."

Shocked, he released Bayli's arm and nodded.

"What's your name?" Bayli asked the young woman after she administered the sedative.

"Sara," she replied slowly, already groggy from the medication.

"That's a lovely name," Bayli replied. "Don't worry! You're going to be just fine."

"Your skin, it's . . ." Sara blinked at Bayli's blue skin as she faded in and out of consciousness.

"I know it's blue. It's a bit different, isn't it?" Bayli said, trying to help the woman find her words and defuse the situation.

"No, that's not it. It's . . . beautiful," Sara replied, just before she passed out.

Bayli lowered a floating stretcher and, with assistance from Dr. Pandori and Sara's father, placed Sara onto it. Then the stretcher floated upwards, and Bayli pushed it along the hallway with one hand.

Sara's father touched Bayli's arm. "Where are you taking her?"

"To our ship. We have medical facilities that are quite capable of healing your species. You're welcome to come with us, if you'd like."

Sara's father followed Bayli as she moved Sara over into the *Cora Lee* and prepped her for surgery.

That evening, Marcello gathered his senior officers together in the *Cora Lee*'s strategy room to receive their status reports. Lt. Commander Cho Fe reported that all the Thorgs had either been destroyed or retreated from the area. Chief Engineer Morten reported that they had attached temporary force field generators to contain the hull breaches as they prepared the ship to be towed to Corian for repairs. Dr. Pandori reported 33 human fatalities and 179 injured crewmen that they were helping the human doctors treat. Commander Corbis reported that they had been able to secure the ship's executive officers and gave each a translator to communicate.

"Their ship is called the *Exodus,* and their captain's name is O'Malley," Corbis said. "They come from a galaxy called the Milky Way. They've granted us access to their ship's data and map logs."

A hologram star map appeared over the center of the table, panning in reverse the course the *Exodus* had traveled from Earth, passing through several galaxies until it reached the Milky Way and then Earth's solar system. It moved through Saturn's rings, Jupiter's moons, and then past Mars before it stopped at Earth and began rotating. Then the hologram pulled back, revealing a large formation of battleships surrounding the planet as thick smoke poured from the smaller ships, creating a cloud that encompassed the planet.

"Murks!" Chief Morten exclaimed with disdain.

"That deep in space?" Cho inquired.

"Apparently, they arrived nearly a year ago and began blockading the planet," Corbis replied. "Captain O'Malley mentioned that a team of Corian scientists exploring the galaxy arrived just prior to the Murk blockade and recommended that Earth send a delegation to the closest Celestian planet to request planethood."

"What would the Murks want with such a distant and insignificant planet?" Cho asked. "It can't be strategic. It makes no sense, even for Murks."

"Agreed. It gets even weirder," Corbis replied. "Their captain said something about the Murks demanding that Earth hand over twelve specific kids."

"Kids? What could they possibly want with kids?" Morten asked.

"No idea. What's even more baffling, according to their captain, is that these kids were former classmates and are now gray-haired men. I couldn't quite comprehend what he was saying and wasn't sure the translator was working correctly. When they explained to the Murks that these students were now all older adults, the Murks didn't believe them and demanded they hand over the original twelve so they could pay for some crime they supposedly committed against their emperor, or they would destroy Earth. So the *Exodus* fled with them to Corian to plead for help."

Marcello stood by the window, staring into space as Corbis spoke.

"Tell me, these classmates, are they on board the *Exodus*?" Marcello asked.

"Yes," Corbis replied. "Well, only eleven. Apparently, one of them died a long time ago."

CHAPTER 2
HOME IN INDIANA

"Arise and shine, space campers!" a male deejay's voice blasted from the radio alarm clock with more exuberance than one should possess at that hour of the morning. "It's a bea-u-tiful fall day to have a space launch for Indiana's own Joseph 'Jag' Gabriel."

"As our audience may recall," a female deejay interjected, "Jag was just one of twelve young prodigies selected from around the world to participate in the first ever Space University on board the space station. We'd like to wish Jag Godspeed and safe travels among the stars."

"Well, he couldn't have asked for a better fall day to bid *adieu* to Earth," the male deejay replied. "Today's forecast is clear skies with a high of fifty-eight degrees. In honor of Jag, we'll kick off the hour with a timeless classic from the rocket legend himself, Sir Elton John." The song "Rocket Man" piped through the alarm clock's speakers.

Fall in Indiana was spectacular with its cool, crisp days and vibrant displays of red, orange, and yellow leaves peppering the forest landscape, surrounded by fields of golden cornstalks awaiting harvest. Just outside the small Midwestern town of Mulberry, Indiana, sat a beautiful yellow Victorian-style farmhouse atop a hill, wrapped in white wooden trim, a testimony of the craftsmanship and styles of days gone by. On her right, a round turret stretched up from the first floor through the third floor, coming to a point with a rooster weathervane atop its copper roof. A well-manicured green lawn wrapped around the house, divided by a winding gravel driveway that snaked its way up the hill and around behind the home. Colorful fall flowerbeds dotted the side of the home, leading up to a wraparound porch.

Behind the home, several large white barns stood proudly, the largest barn hosting a basketball backboard and rim. The net had long since worn out as kids pretended to be Larry Bird or Reggie Miller, taking that infamous, last-second fade-away shot, only to miss as an imagined disappointed crowd sighed in disbelief. But, alas, they were inevitably fouled and would be given another chance to sink the shot as the crowd went wild.

Up in the attic of the home was a bedroom that ran the entire length of the house. Jag rolled over to turn off the radio as the last strains of "Rocket Man" faded away. From downstairs came the familiar sounds of his grandmother preparing breakfast, opening the squeaky oven door and pulling out the heavy iron skillet and placing it atop the gas stove. It was Jag's favorite time of the day—lying in bed while enjoying the sounds and smells of breakfast being prepared.

The attic room had several dormers that ran along the front and back of the home. An impressive Celestron NexStar telescope sat near the window, pointing toward the sky, and star maps lined both sides of the dormer's wall, highlighting constellations like Orion, Cassiopeia, and Ursa Major. To the side of Jag's bed stood a large bookshelf filled with tomes on astronomy, math, physics, and engineering, along with several old Calvin and Hobbes cartoon books.

Sitting on a wooden desk was a laptop computer, a gently worn Bible, a leather baseball glove folded over a ball, and a three-foot-high rocket with red stripes. A framed photograph of a naval pilot with his beautiful wife sat upright on the desk beside academic and athletic trophies, ribbons, and medals. A bulletin board was filled with newspaper clippings of amateur rocket competitions, CAD architectural drawings of rockets, and a newspaper story with the headline

"Engine Breakthrough by Young Scientist Has Bright Future." A calendar had all the dates crossed out, leading up to October 24, on which was penciled "T-Minus 0, Lift-off!"

Jag leaped from his bed, removed his plaid flannel pajamas, and threw on socks, a T-shirt, jeans, and a faded Chicago Cubs baseball cap. He grabbed the rocket and ran down the flight of stairs to the second floor, passing by a wall of family photos on one side and a large colorful tapestry on the other. As he reached the kitchen, his grandma was busy slicing, dicing, whisking, and flipping breakfast, which had now filled the entire home with its aroma.

"Good morning, Jag."

"Good morning, Grandma."

"Breakfast will be ready in half an hour."

"Okay. I'll be back by then."

"Grissom is on the porch waiting. You best take a jacket. It's a bit cold this morning."

Jag grabbed his jacket from the coat hook. He opened the back door and pushed open the wooden screen door, which flapped several times against its frame. Sitting on the back porch were two hound dogs with their tails wagging.

"Mornin' Payton," Jag said as he patted the older dog's head. "Come on, Grissom, let's go!" he said to the younger dog. He and Grissom darted down the steps while Payton stayed on the porch, watching them run off.

They ran by an old truck in front of the barn sitting atop cinder blocks with its wheels removed. "Good morning, Grandpa."

"Good morning, Jag!" his grandfather said from beneath the truck.

Jag and Grissom ran past the barn alongside a fence that led toward the back of the property. When they reached the corner fencepost, Jag jumped over the fence as Grissom squatted down and crawled under the lower fence rail. They ran through a patch of trees until they reached a small creek, which Jag leaped over, careful not to get his feet wet. Grissom made no such attempt and ran right through the trickling stream. They reached a hill, at the top of which was a circular cement launch pad with many black stains revealing a history of previous launches. Near the pad sat a small cinderblock shed with Plexiglas windows that Jag and his grandfather had built.

Jag stood the rocket up in the center of the pad while Grissom sniffed the charred remains of earlier launches. He connected a power cable to the rocket that ran into the shed with a sign that read "Mission Control Center." Inside the shed, Jag connected the cable to a salvaged Cessna 182 airplane dashboard, the gauges of which had been rewired to show temperature, humidity, wind speed, and direction. He powered on the dashboard, and the gauges jumped from one side to the other before settling at their appropriate levels. Three monitors flickered on, revealing close-ups of the rocket from various angles fed by cameras installed around the launch pad.

After checking his gauges, Jag counted out loud. "T-minus ten seconds and counting. Ten, nine, eight . . ." When he arrived at eight, a light went out on the dashboard. Jag looked down and saw Grissom had unplugged the launch cable by sitting on it.

"Uh, Houston, we have a problem." Jag bent over and reconnected the cable and then resumed his countdown. Upon reaching zero, he pressed a red button labeled "Launch," and the rocket ignited and lifted off the platform.

"Houston, we have lift-off!" Jag exclaimed. He grabbed a pair of binoculars hanging on a nail by the door, ran out of the shed, and watched the rocket soar into the sky. A digital display in the binoculars tracked the rocket's height. It read 988 feet and continued counting until it reached 1,427 feet. After reaching its apex, the rocket began descending, and a parachute burst out of its tail, allowing the rocket to coast gently toward earth.

"Go get it, boy," Jag said to Grissom, who dashed into the adjacent cornfield as he tracked the falling rocket. Jag shielded his face as he ran through the sharp corn leaves. Locating the rocket hanging from a cornstalk, Grissom stopped and barked.

"Good boy!" Jag lifted the rocket's chute off the cornstalk, careful not to damage the ears of corn. Then he returned to the house, leaving his muddy boots on the porch.

When he entered, his grandfather was already at the table reading the daily newspaper. He always started with the obituary section. He said he wanted to check to see if his name was in there so that he'd know how to plan the rest of his day.

"How high today?" Grandpa asked.

"Fourteen hundred and twenty-seven feet."

"Wow, nice. Apparently, that retooled fuselage helped."

"Yep. And making it lighter on the top also helped balance the rocket better."

"Go wash up; breakfast is ready," his grandmother said. "Oh, and tell Jack, too."

In the dining room, a large table was covered in an ornate tablecloth. Old china dishes with blue flower patterns sat at each seat with coordinating napkins. Jag's grandmother had laid out a smorgasbord of breakfast dishes: fluffy buttermilk pancakes, biscuits and sausage gravy, scrambled eggs, breakfast potatoes, toast, and different jams and fruit. Jag and his Uncle Jack, who was only a few years older than Jag, sat down across the table from Grandpa.

Once everyone was seated, Grandma asked Jag to read the daily Bible verse from the cup of scripture cards at the center of the table. Pulling out one of the cards at random, he squinted as he read from it. "And we know that in all things God works for the good of those who love him, who have been called according to his purpose. Romans 8:28."

After Grandfather prayed over the breakfast, everyone filled their plates.

"So, Jack, what does your day look like?" Grandfather asked.

"I've got some homework I need to finish for my statistics course, and then I need to go into town to get some items before I go back to school. What about you, Dad?"

"I need to go to the auto store and get some new struts for Ol' Betsy. She's been bouncing around like crazy."

At that moment, both dogs barked. Out the window they saw a dark government vehicle drive up the driveway.

"They're early," Grandma said, glancing at her watch.

After parking behind the house, two men dressed in military uniforms stepped out of the car and placed their caps over their "high and tight" military-issue haircuts. Grissom and Payton greeted the two men, their tails wagging in excitement. Grandpa opened the door to welcome them inside.

"Good morning, sir," the younger officer said. "We're here to collect Joseph Alexander Gabriel for transport to Cape Canaveral."

"Come on in, boys, we've been expecting you," Grandpa said.

First to enter was Lieutenant Leon Marks, an average-sized man who sported a tough exterior. He was followed by Chief Master Sergeant David Perez, a behemoth of a man whose six-foot-five-inch frame would have been better suited as an NFL linebacker than a babysitter for space cadets.

"You boys had any breakfast?" Grandma asked as she ferried them to the table.

"No, thank you, ma'am," Sergeant Marks responded. "We've had breakfast along the way and are on a tight schedule."

Sergeant Perez tilted his head back slightly to take in the delightful smells and then stepped around Lt. Marks. "I think we can spare a few minutes." He made his way to an empty seat and sat down, reaching immediately for a biscuit. After a moment's hesitation, Lt. Marks joined him, but he didn't take anything. He just watched as Sgt. Perez loaded his plate with bacon, eggs, and pancakes.

"You must be Joseph Gabriel," Lt. Marks said, turning to Jack.

"No, I'm Jack."

"I'm Joseph, but you can call me Jag; everyone else does," Jag said, smiling at Marks' mistake.

"You're a lot younger than I expected." He looked at his watch. "We need to be ready to go by 0900."

"I'm ready, sir. My luggage is packed and by the door."

"You boys from around here?" Grandpa asked.

"I'm from Alamogordo, New Mexico," Sgt. Perez responded between bites of pancake. "My partner is from Idaho."

"I'm from Iowa, actually," Marks responded indignantly. "Cedar Rapids."

"Well, welcome to Indiana," Grandma said.

"Thank you, ma'am, and thank you for the great food." Sgt. Perez paused to swallow. "I haven't had a spread like this since back home."

"Eat as much as you like," Grandma said. She regarded a hearty appetite as a compliment.

"Say, is that an old '48 Chevy out there?" Perez asked.

"Why, yes, it is," Grandpa replied. "You must have an eye for old trucks."

"Not so much, sir. My papa had one on the farm, but it broke down years ago."

Grandpa walked over behind Grandma. "Sergeant, I find trucks to be a lot like women. The more care, love, and respect you give them, the longer they last, and the more willing they are to return the favor." He gave her a squeeze.

"Oh, Joseph," Grandma replied, smiling with delight at the show of affection.

"If you boys will excuse me, Ol' Betsy is calling my name," Grandpa said, and then he returned outside to work on the old truck.

"Yes, and we must be on our way, too," Marks replied, pushing his chair back.

Grandma told Jag to gather his things and carry them out to the car while everyone else made their way out of the house.

Outside, Sergeant Perez whistled as he approached the truck. "She sure is a thing of beauty. What are you working on?"

"Replacing her shocks and struts. It's been a few years, and she's getting a bit bouncy."

"Well, you've definitely taken good care of her," Perez replied as he looked inside the immaculate engine compartment.

"Thank you, son. I hope to pass this down to Jack some day when he takes over the farm. Who knows, perhaps even my grandson may inherit her someday." Grandpa nodded at Jag as he carried his suitcases to the trunk of the large government sedan.

"Oh, Jag isn't your son?"

"No, he's my grandson."

"If you don't mind me asking, sir, how did Jag get his nickname?"

"He was actually born Joseph Alexander Gabriel, the Third. His daddy was Joe Junior and a naval pilot, so when Joseph came along, his daddy started calling him Jag, and it stuck.

"What happened to his parents?"

"Joe Junior died in the Middle East conflict when Jag was just an infant. Junior was a decorated naval pilot and had flown eighty-one sorties before his jet encountered mechanical trouble over the Persian Gulf. He ejected from the plane but was never seen again. He received the Medal of Honor, posthumously, from the president."

"I'm sorry to hear that, sir. He sounds like a brave and honorable man."

"That he was," Grandpa said, choking up. "After Junior's death, Jag's young mother came down with cancer, and they both moved up here to live with us when Jag was just a toddler. She fought valiantly and hung on as long as she could, but the cancer won in the end."

"That's truly horrible."

Grandpa nodded wistfully. "She was a beautiful, strong woman. She sure did love that little boy. After she passed, we raised Jag the best we could."

"You've done a heck of a job, sir. Space University! Not too many people have that opportunity."

"The credit goes to the missus. After Jag's momma died, Cora Lee retired from teaching high school math. As soon as Jag could talk, she began homeschooling him. He's a sponge, that one is, absorbed anything she taught him: math, science, biology, astronomy. It wasn't long until he outgrew us and started taking classes over at the university. He was the youngest student to ever get his bachelor's degree in Purdue's space program. He's a bright boy."

"Wow, amazing! And what about your other son?" Perez asked.

"Jack? He's in university, too. He's studying to become a mathematician and hopes to become a teacher like his mother someday. Very smart. I'm really proud of him."

"He didn't want to follow in your footsteps and become a farmer?" Perez asked.

"Actually, farming wasn't my primary career. I retired from construction." He nodded at the house. "Built both that home and these barns."

Perez nodded in appreciation as he gazed at them. "Wow, they're beautiful."

"Farming was more of my family heritage. I took the farm over from my parents after I did a stint in the Navy."

"You were in the service, sir?"

"That was a lifetime ago, and the world was a different place than it is now. I was stationed in Asia. After I was discharged, my dad passed and I inherited the farm, which has been in our family for generations."

Over at the car, Lieutenant Marks helped Jag load his luggage into the trunk. Then he walked up to the porch and scratched Payton behind the ears.

"Oh, you'll be a friend for life if you scratch Payton's ears," Grandma said.

"Peyton?" Marks inquired. "Named after the famous football quarterback?"

"No!" Grandma replied. "Gary Payton, the Purdue astronaut. All our dogs have been named after Purdue astronauts. That's Grissom over there. He was named after astronaut Gus Grissom. Our first dog, of course, was named Armstrong, after the first man to walk on the Moon. Then we had, let's see, Wolf, Covey, and Chaffee." She lowered her voice to a whisper, out of respect. "Sadly, both Chaffee and Grissom died in the Apollo accident. Then there's Casper and Cernan," she said a bit louder. "Cernan, of course, was the last of the Apollo astronauts to walk on the Moon."

"Wow, that's a lot of dogs."

Grandma shrugged. "Well, we had a lot of Purdue astronauts."

Lieutenant Marks looked at his watch and then turned to Sergeant Perez. "It's 0920. We have to hit the road."

Grandpa grabbed the rag on the hood of the truck and wiped his hands as he and Sgt. Perez walked over to the government sedan. "If you're ever back in the area, give me a call and I'll take you out for a spin in Ol' Betsy," Grandpa said.

"Will do, sir," Perez replied. "I'd like that very much." He and Grandpa shook hands.

Grandma came out of the house holding a sack of snacks and gave them to Jag, instructing him to share them with Marks and Perez. Then she took Jag in her arms

"I have loved you all your life and couldn't love you any more than if you were my own."

"Thank you, Grandma," Jag said. "I love you, too."

Grandpa put his hand on Jag's shoulder. "I'm proud of you, son, real proud."

"Thanks, Grandpa."

"Did you pack your Bible?" Grandma asked.

"Yes, ma'am."

"You read your Bible every night before you go to bed, and say your prayers."

"Will do."

"I packed some of the memory verse cards in your bag here. You keep those with you as well," Grandma continued.

"Yes, ma'am."

"Now, have fun, and do your best. Remember, God will watch over and keep you. Now, give me one more hug." Grandma reached for him again.

Grandpa turned to the two officers. "You boys have time for a quick prayer?"

"Yes, sir," Marks replied as the two officers removed their hats and bowed their heads.

Grandpa placed his hand on Jag's shoulder and prayed a short prayer of protection and blessing. Afterwards, Sgt. Marks opened the back door as Jag stepped into the sedan. Then the car backed down the driveway, kicking up dust as Grissom ran after it, barking all the way. Grandma and Grandpa stood side by side waving at Jag until the car was out of sight.

CHAPTER 3
LIFT-OFF!

"Welcome back to *The World Today*. I'm your host, Michael Banning," the handsome, suntanned daytime news magazine host said as he faced the camera in his flashy silver suit. As he said his name, he paused to give dramatic emphasis, smiling at the camera with teeth bleached unnaturally white. "We have a very special show today, as we're broadcasting live from the beautiful beaches of Cape Canaveral, Florida, the birthplace of modern space flight."

Several drone cameras buzzed around the host and panned backwards to record the cheering audience.

"I'm with astronaut, author, renowned scientist, architect, and former director of the *Unity* space station and, as if his repertoire wasn't already impressive enough, professor and dean of the Space University. Please give a warm welcome to Professor Petryk Polanski and Assistant Dean Dr. Emily Stevenson."

The audience applauded as Polanski and Stevenson walked out onto the stage, wearing matching blue blazers with a *Unity* space station insignia over the lapel.

"Thank you very much," the distinguished professor said in his thick Polish accent. He and Dr. Stevenson sat down beside a coffee table across from Banning.

"Tell me, what was it like to be the first human to walk on Mars?" Banning asked as video of the historic Mars walk played on the jumbo monitors that stretched across the stage.

"It was life-changing, not only for me but for space exploration. I was privileged to be selected by my peers to be the first human to step out on the red planet. It is my hope that we will have many more opportunities to set foot on other planets in our solar system and beyond."

"It's that very dream that brings you here today, is it not?" Banning asked.

"Yes. I'm more excited today about the launch of the Space University than I was when I stepped onto Mars. No other program will do more to overcome today's technical limitations and propel humanity beyond our solar system."

"Very interesting, professor," the host replied as he leaned forward. "You mentioned today's technical limitations. Can you elaborate on the limitations we face today?"

"No doubt we've come a long way, but every technical advancement humankind has achieved has first had to overcome barriers. For instance, we overcame the barrier of gravity with the invention of air travel. Then we overcame the barrier of sound when we rocketed to the Moon. However, one barrier remains elusive, as we have yet to exceed the barrier of light, which is a prerequisite to achieving our dreams of interstellar and intergalactic space flight.

"Today, scientists are building the next generation of spacecraft, the first of which, the *Genesis,* will be the fastest ship ever built. However, as remarkable as she is, we still can't reach the speed of light and, as such, will be limited in terms of how far we can travel. To go beyond our solar system will require new discoveries that help us overcome the 'big three.'"

"The big three? What are those?" Banning asked. Professor Polanski nodded to Dr. Stevenson to continue.

"Distance, energy, and environment," Dr. Stevenson said. She held up her index finger. "The first and greatest problem we face is distance. How do we travel great distances in a single person's lifetime and return to Earth? Space is so vast that even with the most powerful rockets in existence today, it would take us many human lifetimes to reach the nearest star of Proxima Centauri, which is only four-point-two light years from Earth.

"Our second problem is that even if we could travel at the speed of light, the amount of energy required to power such a vehicle would consume the entire known energy output of Earth for an entire year. Our third problem is how to provide a sustainable and livable environment for humans on such a journey. How do you provide enough water, food, and oxygen for such a long voyage? Until we resolve these three issues, humanity's dream of exploring the stars exists only as a fantasy."

"And it is for this purpose that the university was conceived?" Banning asked. "To solve the big three?"

"Yes," Polanski replied. "A new influx of scientific understanding and innovation must occur if we are to resolve these insurmountable problems. Age brings experience and wisdom, but youth brings new ideas and excitement. Both are needed to break these barriers. The university will marry the passion and ingenuity of youth with the wisdom of experience. Our goal is to bring together today's brightest young minds, the next generation of prodigies."

"You, yourself, were a prodigy," Banning said. "Designing the space station at age seventeen and then walking on Mars when you were only twenty-one! Now you wish to share the same opportunity with some very lucky students. Please, tell us about the school itself."

"Our first school will have twelve students, and we have plans to expand for more students in the future," said Polanski. "Due to construction restrictions on board the space station, our current facility has housing limitations, and, sadly, we've had to restrict the first academy to only male students. Our next program will have facilities for male and female students.

"Our classrooms will be led by professors who are respected leaders in fields like aeromechanics, aerospace design, astrophysics, and astronautics. Students will spend ten months studying, learning, and creating projects that contribute to resolving the big three."

"I've been told that you received thousands of applications from all around the world."

Dr. Stevenson nodded. "Indeed. Seventeen thousand two hundred and eighty-four applications from fifty-seven nations, to be exact!"

"So how were the twelve students selected from such an enormous list?"

"Aside from their educational background, each applicant had to submit a project proposal that fell into one of three categories: propulsion, energy, or environment. A board of professors reviewed each applicant's entry, and after performing interviews with students and their teachers, we selected twelve students who we felt were the most qualified for the program. Each student will develop his project in a state-of-the-art laboratory with input from his peers and professors."

"That sounds fantastic!" Banning said.

"It is a fantastic opportunity," Dr. Stevenson replied. "Even more exciting is that at the end of the school year, we will have the first ever Space Games, where each student will present their projects in front of a panel of guest judges."

"I hear you have a unique and very special reward for the student with the winning project. Is that correct?"

"Well, I don't know how special it is," Professor Polanski replied.

However, Dr. Stevenson's eyes widened as she held up a multicolored flight vest covered in various International Space Agency patches. "This is the flight vest Dr. Polanski wore when he took those historic steps onto the surface of Mars!"

Banning gazed at it in wonder. "This is the actual vest? And the winner of the competition will receive this historic artifact?"

"Yes!" Dr. Stevenson exclaimed.

"Well, that is most certainly an inspirational award! It will be an honor for any of these students to win such a coveted prize."

"I'm not sure about that," Polanski replied. "And that is not the point of the school. The purpose of all this is to propel us toward the goal to expand humankind's reach. If the students achieve that, then we are all winners."

"Thank you, Professor Polanski and Dr. Stevenson," Banning said as he turned to the cameras. "When we return after these commercial messages, we will introduce you to the students of the first ever Space University among the stars."

The red lights atop the floating cameras turned off simultaneously, and stage crew members flooded the stage, moving equipment and furniture from one side to the other. They shuttled the kids onto the stage as tall stools were dragged out and placed in a semicircle facing the audience. Jag was ferried along with several other students to the center of the stage.

"Hi, I'm Jag from Indiana," Jag said as he met a smaller boy wearing a black yarmulke.

"I'm Ben," the soft-spoken boy replied. "I'm from Israel, but I live in France."

As soon as Ben mentioned France, a lanky kid perked up. "Bonjour, je suis Edgard. Quelle partie de la France êtes-vous?"

Noticing the confused expression on Jag's face, and suspecting that Jag didn't understand French, Ben graciously replied in English. "Nice to meet you, Edgard. I'm Ben, and I'm originally from Revobath, Israel, but I currently reside in Le Marais in Paris. This is my friend, Jag."

"What kind of name is Jag?" Edgard asked as he shook Jag's hand then turned back to Ben. "Le Marais! That's a beautiful area. I'm from Leon."

Several more students were escorted onto the stage. A tall redheaded boy interjected in their conversation. "Hi, I'm Sasha from Sochi, Russia, and this is Raj, he's from Mumbai."

"Nice to meet you, Sasha and Raj," Jag replied.

Girls in the audience began screaming as the last student walked onto the stage. Jag and several other students turned to see what all the commotion was about. Two teenage girls broke through the security barrier, jumped onto the stage, and ran toward the last student. They shoved photos of the boy in front of him to get his autograph. Security guards apprehended the girls as they swooned over the boy, but he waved them off.

"Who's that?" Jag asked.

"You don't know who that is?" Edgard responded with surprise. "That's Percy Blackwell."

Jag shrugged, still not understanding what all the fuss was about.

"He's only the son of one of the richest men in the world! The founder of Blackwell Enterprises. It's the largest energy and space exploration company in the world! Percy and his father lead scientific exploration trips, and they have their own TV show. They're celebrities."

"Oh," Jag responded as he watched the security guards drag the girls offstage. He didn't watch much TV.

"Yeah!" Raj said with disdain. "I've seen what their celebrity does. They buy companies to secure land and mineral rights and then fire all the employees. My father was once employed by an oil company in Mumbai until Blackwell came in, bought the company, and fired him and most of the other employees. We had to sell our home and move to another city."

Ignoring Raj's negative comment, Edgard continued. "Blackwell Enterprises subsidized the entire space station and has provided many of the top scientists to the station for research."

"No doubt to steal any discoveries and sell it for a profit," Raj responded.

"Alright, places everyone!" the program manager said. "Please take a seat behind you according to your age, oldest on the left and youngest to the right. We are live in thirty seconds." Stagehands led the students to the correct stools. Jag took the next-to-last stool beside Ben.

"Welcome back," Banning said, flashing his eerily white teeth at the camera. "If you're just joining us, we are broadcasting the launch of the first Space University program on board the *Unity* space station. My guests are Dr. Stevenson and Professor Petryk Polanski. Professor, that sure is a lot of P's" Banning said with a chuckle.

"I hadn't thought about it. Why don't you just call me Professor P for short?"

Banning led Polanski over to the oldest student who, like all the other students, was wearing a stylish red flight jumpsuit with a *Unity* space station logo, consisting of a ship orbiting Earth.

"Our first prodigy is eighteen-year-old Muhammed 'Mo' Ramin from Morocco," Banning said as a video biography played on the large screen, showing clips of Mo's family, his university, and Mo working in a lab on his cryogenic project.

"Mo is majoring as a medical doctor at the prestigious Shahid Beheshti University," Polanski said as he shook Mo's hand. "His class project is to develop a cryogenic solution that will enable future voyages to travel farther by extending the lives of the crew."

"I am sure you must be very excited to be selected for the school," Banning said.

"Yes, sir!" Mo replied. "My family and I are very excited about this opportunity, and I am very honored to study under Professor Polanski."

Next in line was seventeen-year-old Kano Tanaka from Japan. The video background played footage of Kano's hometown, his bio, and the project he had submitted.

Professor Polanski started to reach out his hand but then, seeing Kano bow, lowered his hand and bowed in return. "Kano's specialty is robotic engineering, and he hopes to create robots that will perform tasks deemed too dangerous for humans as we work to build the next generation of spaceships."

"You must be honored to participate in this first class," Banning said.

"Yes," Kano replied.

"Have you ever competed in any robot battles?" Banning asked, trying to draw additional conversation out of Kano.

"No," Kano replied matter-of-factly, followed by a long, awkward pause.

"Well, our next student definitely needs no introduction. He is the seventeen-year-old son of legendary innovator and entrepreneur William Blackwell. As a father-and-son duo, they have built Blackwell Enterprises into the largest global provider of energy, aircraft, and spacecraft. Please welcome Percy Blackwell."

The audience erupted in applause, and girls screamed and held up signs that read things like "Marry Me, Percy," "I Love You," and a few other things that the television network had to blur out.

A video began playing of Percy and his father traveling the globe, meeting with famous dignitaries, delivering aid to refugee camps, and Percy in a white lab coat working with leading scientists to solve energy problems. Then it cut to a global magazine's cover page titled "Expect Perfection! World's Greatest Father and Son Team" with a photo of the two standing on a shore holding surfboards with their long blond hair blowing in the wind. Next they appeared skydiving, BASE jumping, and performing other adventurous exploits.

"It is an honor to meet you, Percy," Banning said.

"Thank you, sir. The honor is all mine," Percy replied.

"I love you, Percy!" a girl screamed from the audience.

"I love you, too!" Percy replied as he waved to the girls in the front row.

"You must be used to the swarm of adulating fans," Banning observed.

"Oh, I don't know if anyone ever gets used to it. It's just fun for my fans and to show them I appreciate them, too. What matters most though is that we are making a difference for humanity. That's why my father has invested so much into this space program."

"Well, I'm sure his gift is greatly appreciated, and I imagine you'll definitely be a strong contender for the vest award."

"Thank you for such kind words. However, there are many talented students in this program, and I can only hope that I'm as talented as they are," Percy said, completely comfortable in front of the camera. "My father's motto is 'Expect to perfect.' He has taught me to reach for excellence in all that I do. I hope to make him proud."

"I'm sure you will," Banning replied.

Banning and Professor Polanski continued down the line, introducing each student and announcing their class project. Next to Percy sat a hefty Lars Klein from Germany, then Niklas Johansen from Sweden, Makalo Zuma from South Africa, Mario Bergoglio from Argentina, Edgard Dubois from France, and then Raj.

"Now the three youngest students in the school, who are, amazingly, only fourteen years old!" Mr. Banning exclaimed as he introduced Sasha Belinsky from Russia. Then they came to Jag.

"Our next student is America's own Joseph 'Jag' Gabriel from Mayberry, Indiana," Banning said with great enthusiasm.

"It's Mulberry, sir," Jag interrupted bashfully.

"Mulberry, Indiana," Banning said. "He has dual graduate degrees from Purdue University in astrophysics and astromechanics." A video of the farm and Jag's rockets played on the screen behind Jag.

"Welcome, Yosef. It's good to have you," Polanski said as he shook Jag's hand.

"Thank you, sir," Jag replied.

"Tell us, Jag, when you're not studying, what are your hobbies and interests?" Banning asked.

"Well, when I'm not flying rockets with my dog Grissom, I like to play baseball and basketball—and go to church."

"Many of our students' projects are attempting to create the next generation of rocket engines," Polanski said. "Jag's project is to create a hyperdrive rocket that will attempt the impossible, to exceed the light barrier."

"Wow, that is ambitious!" Banning exclaimed. "Nice to meet you, Jag, and I wish you the best on your project. Lastly, we have Benjamin Mendelsohn from Israel via France. Tell me what that is all about."

"My father is an ambassador to France from Israel. I have spent most of my life in France," Ben said quietly.

After introducing and greeting each student, Banning wrapped up the newscast by thanking Polanski, Stevenson, and the students. "Before you go, I'm told that anyone who is interested can follow the progress of class and even attend the classes online?"

"Yes, visit us online at spaceuniversity.edu," Stevenson said. "You can follow each student's blog as they share about life on board the space station and what they are learning in class. Feel free to ask them questions and check in often for updates. Open enrollment begins in January, and don't forget, our next school is going to be co-ed."

"We wish you all Godspeed and safe travels on your trip," Banning said. "We'll be back after these messages to view the historic shuttle launch of the first ever Space University class."

CHAPTER 4
THE *UNITY'S* MISSION

The *Unity* space station was the largest manmade object ever built in space and one of the few that was visible from Earth. Resembling a crescent moon, its smooth exterior was made of steel and thick glass rising to fifteen floors high at its center and angling down to six floors at each end. Over twelve hundred astronauts, scientists, and construction crews resided on board, with the ability to expand to three thousand. The *Unity* provided a state-of-the-art facility for studying space exploration and building advanced spacecraft that would propel humankind toward the edge of space.

Mission Control resided in the center of the space station and stood five floors high with an exterior wall of glass reaching from floor to ceiling. Spectacular views of Earth showed massive cloud formations swirling over the North and South American continents. Outside the station was the skeleton of what would eventually become the *Genesis* spaceship, the first ship assembled entirely in space by construction crews working around the clock. Technicians monitored everything from weather patterns on Earth to the precise location of space debris flying around the space station.

Standing in a white vest with a blue tie, a tall, thin man stared out the window with his arms crossed. As soon as Professor Polanski, Dr. Stevenson, and the students entered the room, the man turned around and spoke in a booming voice. "Welcome, Space University students, to Mission Control!"

"Students, this is Director Dr. Harold Reese," Professor P said. "He oversees all activity aboard the space station."

"We look forward to seeing your contributions to our space program!" Reese said. "First of all, you couldn't have a better professor from which to learn. Take every opportunity to glean as much as you can, as I find that even after all these years, I'm still learning from him."

"You're too gracious," Polanski replied. "Dr. Reese and I have been friends for almost twenty years and have served together on many missions." He paused and looked at the large monitors around the room and then turned back to Dr. Reese. "Is everything alright?"

"Actually, we're tracking a category-two hurricane headed toward the East Coast of the United States," Dr. Reese said as he motioned to a technician, who keyed in several commands. The glass windows darkened, and a close-up view of Earth displayed with a large spiral hurricane. Augmented red dotted lines curved out from the eye of the hurricane toward the eastern coast of the United States, projecting a landfall somewhere between the Carolinas.

"Sir, the National Weather Service and the US Coast Guard have been notified, and we have been cleared to disburse the hurricane," technician Emilie Gottschalk said.

"It would appear that your timing is impeccable, as always," Reese said to Polanski. "Your students will be able to see the *Unity* in full swing." He nodded to Gottschalk. "Proceed."

Polanski gathered the students and spoke softly so as not to interrupt the technicians. "The *Unity* doesn't merely monitor the Earth's weather; it can influence it as well."

Red crosshairs appeared on the screen and, using a joystick, the technician maneuvered the crosshairs to the eye of the storm. Panels on the exterior of the space station opened, and a cannon extended into the void. It was nearly ten feet wide and twice that long. Once fully extended, Ms. Gottschalk counted down from ten, pressed a large red "Fire" button, and then the cannon pulsated for several seconds. The lights inside Mission Control dimmed as power was rerouted into the cannon. Energy waves in a tight spiral hit the eye of the hurricane, and after the pulses ceased, the cannon receded and the panels closed.

Over the next several minutes, the hurricane dissipated until it disappeared. Everyone in the control center erupted in applause, congratulating each other.

"Fantastic job, everyone!" Dr. Reese said. Then he turned to the students. "The pulsating beam you just witnessed is one of the many inventions developed here on the space station. It has saved thousands of lives and prevented billions of dollars of damages from hurricanes. Before you go, are there any questions?"

Jag raised his head. "Sir, can it be used against tornadoes?"

"Good question. Where are you from, son?"

"Indiana."

"Ah, yes. Indiana is on the edge of Tornado Alley, with the worst areas being Oklahoma, Kansas, and Texas. We've had limited success against tornadoes, as we have to take more precautions when firing the cannon over populated areas. Also, tornadoes tend to spring up much quicker than hurricanes, giving us less time to position the station over a tornado. We are working on several smaller satellite prototypes that will allow us to monitor various sections of Tornado Alley and be able to fire smaller pulse cannons quicker. Good question. Any others?"

After answering a few more questions, Dr. Stevenson led the students out of Mission Control via a large elevator and down to the second floor, where they walked along the curving corridor toward the end of the hall. They approached two doors with a plaque that read "Dr. Robert H. Goddard Hall." Below in bright letters was the following quote: "It is difficult to say what is impossible, for the dream of yesterday is the hope of today and the reality of tomorrow."

"This hall is named after one of the three fathers of space flight," Dr. Stevenson said. "Can anyone tell me what scientific discovery Dr. Goddard was instrumental in inventing?"

"The liquid-fuel rocket," Percy said after raising his hand.

"Very good," Stevenson replied. "Can anyone else tell me who the other two fathers of space flight are?"

Unlike the previous question, there was some hesitation, and then Kano raised his hand. "Tsiolkovsky and Oberth?"

"Excellent!" Dr. Stevenson exclaimed. "Both Konstantin Tsiolkovsky and Hermann Oberth were instrumental in modern astronautics and rocket propulsion. In fact, Tsiolkovsky envisioned space stations like this one as well as the colonization of planets throughout the galaxy."

Dr. Stevenson led everyone inside the hall as she continued. "Goddard Hall will be your home for the next ten months. The classroom, study hall, and library are on the left, and the dorm rooms and bathrooms are on the right."

The students followed her to the first dorm room. "This is Copernicus and will house our four oldest students: Mohamed, Kano, Percy, and Lars. The middle room is Kepler and will house Edgard, Mario, Makalo, and Niklas. The last room is Galileo and will house our youngest students: Raj, Sasha, Jag, and Ben. The bathroom is the last door on the right. Instructions on how to operate the shower and toilets are posted in each stall. Please go ahead and unpack your things. I'll meet everyone back here in one hour to take you to the cafeteria for supper."

As the students selected their luggage from the baggage cart and filed into their respective rooms, Percy stopped and spoke with Dr. Stevenson. "Excuse me, Dr. Stevenson, it was my understanding that I would have my own room."

Stevenson looked down at her tablet and made several swipes. "Hmm . . . the list I have shows that you're sharing the room with three other students."

"There must be some kind of mixup. Considering how much my father has contributed to the program, we expected that I would have private accommodations."

"I'm sorry, but you'll have to take that up with Professor Polanski. These three rooms are all that are available to us. If you'd like, I can take you over to his office now."

"No, this will do for the time being." Percy snatched his suitcases from the baggage cart and entered the room.

In addition to being named after a scientist who had made significant contributions to science, each dorm room had a different color scheme. Copernicus was blue, Kepler was red, and Galileo was green. Each door was painted in corresponding colors to allow the room to be identified easily. Inside the room, lockers lined both sides of the door. A narrow window was in the center of the wall opposite the door, and two bunkbeds were on both sides of the room. At the foot of the bunkbeds were desks that the students would share. Built-in dressers were allocated for each student. On the floor was a beautiful mosaic of Galileo as a young man with a quote that read: "All truths are easy to understand once they are discovered; the point is to discover them."

The four boys filed into the room and began calling dibs on bunkbeds. Jag and Ben gravitated toward the right side of the room and set their luggage down.

"Well, I guess we'll be bunkmates," Jag said.

"If you don't mind, I'd like to take the bottom bunk, as I have to get up sometimes in the night to go to the bathroom," Ben said.

"Don't mind at all. I actually prefer the upper bunk," Jag said as he jumped onto it. He noticed several straps that ran across the bed and a small sign on the wall that read "To prevent injury, please wear straps while sleeping."

"What do you think the straps are for?" Jag asked.

"They keep us from falling out of bed in the event the station loses gravity during the night," Sasha said, overhearing the conversation. "You'd start to float away, only to be in for a rude awakening when the gravity came back on."

"That'd be a bummer," Ben replied.

"Especially for me," Jag said. "I'd have farther to fall after the gravity came back on!"

"Yeah, but you'd land on me," Ben said, and they all laughed.

Each student had plenty of storage with cubbyholes surrounding the bed. A small monitor near the pillow displayed the current time, and several buttons with lit icons were next to the clock. Jag pressed one of the buttons, and a light shone down from the ceiling.

"Ah, a reading light," Jag said. After turning the light on, he noticed an air vent above his bed connected the Galileo room with the Kepler room next door, as he could faintly hear voices from the next room. After examining all the compartments and features around his bed, he jumped down and unpacked his clothes. On top of the dresser was an empty shelf on which students could place family photos and other personal items. Ben had placed a picture of his mother and father on the dresser. Jag commented that they were a nice-looking couple. Then he retrieved a photo of his grandparents and another one of Grissom and Payton.

"Who's that?" Ben asked.

"That's my grandparents and my dogs, Grissom and Payton. They raised me from when I was little."

"Who, the dogs?" Ben asked with a grin.

Jag smiled. "Very funny."

After Jag unpacked all his clothing and belongings, he found the cup of scripture verses that his grandmother had packed and placed it on the dresser in front of his grandparents' photo.

"What are those?" Ben asked, nodding toward the dresser.

"Daily Bible verses that my grandma packed for me. Does it bother you for me to have them up there?"

"Not at all," Ben said.

Just then, Dr. Stevenson stuck her head in the door. "Hurry up and finish unpacking your belongings so I can show you the most important thing of all: the cafeteria! I also want to give you a tour of the classroom, library, and gymnasium."

Once everyone gathered in the hallway, Dr. Stevenson led the students to the cafeteria to experience their first processed space meal. The small cafeteria had only five tables that sat four people per table. The atmosphere was youthful and fun with cool tables and tall stools. Mounted on the wall was a television that played news stories continuously from around Earth.

Along the back wall stood eight vending machines containing everything from snacks to full entrées and desserts. The entrée selection had sixteen types of meat and vegetarian dishes. Jag, Sasha, Raj, and Ben stared at the options, waiting for someone else to make the first selection. After a period of indecisiveness, Jag pressed a button beside a photo of Salisbury steak, mashed potatoes, and gravy. A robotic arm lifted a pouch, and then a giant needle jabbed into the top of the pouch and injected steaming hot water to rehydrate the contents. Then the needle retracted, and the arm lowered the pouch into a bin. A small sign flashed "Contents Hot!" as a small glass door slid open.

"Wow, that is hot!" Jag said, blowing on his fingertips after picking up the pouch.

Each student selected a different entrée. Ben selected fish and rice, Sasha beef stew, and Raj ordered a vegetarian biryani rice dish. They sat near some of the older students. Jag pulled back a tab that read "Pull," and the pouch opened, making a bowl. Piping hot steam billowed out as Jag picked up his fork. After smelling the dish, he took a cautious bite. His roommates waited for him to be the Guinea pig and, to their consternation, Jag acted as if he was choking. Then he smiled. "Not bad. It's not Grandma's but not bad."

The others dove into their pouches, and soon everyone was eating, telling stories, and laughing about their experiences.

After supper, the students toured the rest of the facilities, starting with the classroom and then the recreation room, where they all played video games, foosball, ping pong, and some type of 3D space billiards game with holographic balls on different dimensions. After about an hour, the students returned to their dorm rooms, where, in each closet, they found fitted pajamas with a *Unity* logo on the chest. After brushing his teeth and putting on his pajamas, Jag climbed into bed. The lights dimmed automatically to a soft glow.

Jag rolled over onto his elbows with his hands holding his head up as he gazed out the small window. The stars seemed so much larger and vibrant in space. He thought about the incredible day and couldn't believe he had made it into space. All his young life he had dreamed of being an astronaut. Every book he read, every subject studied had led to this incredible moment.

"Isn't it unbelievable?" Ben asked as he looked out the window from his bed.

"It sure is," Jag said.

"My dad used to take me camping, and we would lie beneath the stars," Sasha said as his feet dangled from the top bunk. "This view is so much better."

Jag yawned, rolled over in his bed, pulled up his blanket, and followed the instructions for strapping himself in.

The next morning, at exactly 5 a.m., the lights brightened as an alarm beeped several times. Raj yawned and then rolled over and pulled his blanket over his head. The small screen on the wall beside each student flashed and beeped. "You've got a message!" appeared on the screen. When Jag touched the screen, it read: "Rise and shine! It's time for exercise! Put on your gym clothes, and meet me in the gym in twenty minutes." It was signed "Professor P."

The students arrived at the gymnasium yawning and barely awake. The gym was windowless, and the floor, walls, and ceiling were lined with a thick, heavy padding that felt like walking on a giant sponge. On both ends of the gym were basketball goals that had to be nearly two times taller than a normal basketball goal. Several basketballs sat on the floor. Raj went over, picked one up, and shot it with all his might toward the goal. It went up about halfway and fell to the floor. Several students laughed.

"Let me try!" Sasha said. His shot went higher but still nowhere near the backboard. It hit the wall and rolled over in front of Ben. Walking toward Ben and Jag were Edgard and Lars, who had the unfortunate nickname of "Tank" due to his enormous size.

"*Bonjour à tous*," Edgard said.

"Good morning," Ben replied as he picked up the basketball.

"Let me try shooting," Tank said as he ripped the ball from Ben's hands. Then he hurled the ball at the goal. It bounced off the rim and ricocheted about forty feet into the gym. Embarrassed, Tank shoved Ben as he walked by. "At least mine hit the rim."

"What type of gymnasium is this?" Mario asked.

"It's a gravity-regulated exercise room," Professor Polanski said as he entered. Then he pressed a button on a remote attached to his wrist, and all the students, not to mention the professor and the basketballs, began floating.

"Hey, look at me," Raj said as he performed a back flip in midair.

As soon as Mo saw Raj complete the backflip, he started performing a series of backflips, laughing as he flew gently across the room.

"As you can see, we are able to control the force of gravity in this room and simulate the gravitational environment on any planet or moon. This is an ideal environment for training for moonwalks and testing equipment, but most importantly, for playing space basketball! Right now, gravity is set to one-tenth of what it is on Earth. Feel free to bounce around," Polanski said as the students began jumping, flipping, bouncing, and bounding around the room. He nodded at Raj. "Now take a shot."

Raj grabbed the ball beside him and shot it, sending it nearly forty feet high. Throughout the gym, students began jumping and springing themselves up as high as the basketball rim. Jag grabbed a ball and, leaping thirty feet in the air, dunked the ball into the basket.

"Hey, let me try!" said Ben, who was the smallest of all the students. Jag threw him the ball, and he took several steps before leaping with all his might toward the goal, only to have the ball hit the rim and bounce off as he fell backwards, landing on the soft floor. Determined, Ben attempted two more times before dunking the ball.

The class split into two teams of six players, divided equally by age. They played space basketball for an hour, working up a sweat. After the game was over, Polanski informed them that the activity was about more than just having fun. In space, muscle deterioration can occur due to lack of gravity, and they had to exercise twice a day to offset the effects. Then he increased the gravity to three times that of Earth.

"This is now the same gravity level as Venus. We use this for strength conditioning. For the next five minutes, each of us will perform calisthenics to strengthen our bones and muscles."

They followed the exercise regimen twice a day, and it became their favorite time of day. For Jag, nothing was more fun than dunking a basketball on a thirty-foot basketball hoop.

Then the students returned to their rooms to shower and clean up for class. After getting dressed, Jag selected one of Bible verses sitting atop the dresser. After reading the verse to himself and committing it to memory, he placed it back in the cup.

"What did it say?" Ben asked.

"Uh," Jag said, not knowing anyone was watching him. "It was Proverbs 3:5: 'Trust in the Lord with all your heart, and lean not on your own understanding.'"

"I know that verse," Ben said. "Can I read one?"

"Sure," Jag said, holding out the cup of cards.

Ben read his card to himself while Sasha and Raj watched from across the room.

"What did yours say?" Sasha asked.

"For there are three things that endure: Faith, hope, and love, but the greatest of these is love."

"Cool," Sasha said. "Can I have one, too?" He selected a card and read it. "'I know the plans I have for you,' says the Lord. 'Plans to prosper you and give you a hope and future.' Awesome! I got a good one. Everything good is going to happen to me!"

"I'm not sure that's what it means," Jag said.

"My turn," Raj replied. He took his card and read aloud: "'He who overlooks an offense promotes love; but he who repeats a matter separates best friends.' Aw, man, I got a bad one."

"I don't think any of them are bad. They just might apply at different times in our lives," Jag said. Ben started to hand his card back to Jag, but Jag told them all that they could keep their card or, if they liked, pick a different one.

After breakfast, each student reported for class. Like everything on board the *Unity*, the classroom was technically advanced. Each student's desktop was a touchable computer screen linked to an intranet, where students could comb through mountains of research, studies, and reports. At the front of the classroom, a large screen that extended from the floor to the ceiling was used for video-conferencing adjunct professors. Web cameras mounted throughout the classroom allowed students to interact with the professors as well as students following from Earth.

Professor Polanski welcomed the students to their new classroom and then gave a brief overview of the space station's history. Then they reviewed their syllabus, their daily schedules, and project plans. Every day they had two classroom sessions, with Polanski typically teaching the first class while the afternoon classes were taught remotely by adjunct professors on everything from physics to rocket engineering.

After the morning class, they visited the laboratory, which was still under construction. Their first project would be a group assignment to build a long-range satellite to explore deep space and collect planetary information for possible future explorations. Polanski explained how each class from that point forward would mark the start of their school by sending out satellites in different directions to find other habitable planets or, better yet, intelligent life.

Of all the professors to speak, Professor Polanski was Jag's favorite. He brought such excitement and wonder to his subjects. He was so vibrant and funny. While his jokes didn't always translate well into English, his humor and passion for life were contagious. Jag loved his stories about his trip to Mars, building the *Unity* station, and of previous scientists and astronauts. Frequently, Professor P would start out telling one story, only to launch into another before completing the first, but nonetheless his stories were what made the subject matter come alive.

After their first week on the station, each student was given a weekly timeslot to place a video call home. Jag was scheduled after Niklas but before Percy. The calls were made from a video conference room near Mission Control. The conference room was small with a full-height video screen mounted on one wall and a bench on the opposite side.

As Jag sat waiting for his turn, he noticed that it was nearly impossible to avoid listening in on Niklas speaking with his father, because only a thin black curtain separated the two rooms. However, they were speaking Swedish, so Jag couldn't understand anything said. A few minutes later, Niklas slid the curtain back.

"It's your turn."

"Thanks," Jag replied as he entered the video booth and pulled the curtain closed. He took his badge and swiped the reader. Immediately, a message appeared on the screen: "Welcome, Joseph Gabriel. You have ten minutes of video conferencing available." Below the message was a contact menu showing an image of his grandparents. He tapped their image, and the system attempted to contact them as the words "Connecting, please wait . . ." flashed on the screen. After the message disappeared, a video image of his grandparents appeared.

"Hi Grandma and Grandpa!" Jag said.

"Hello, can you hear us?" Grandma asked as Grandpa fidgeted with the camera.

"Yes, loud and clear."

"Good. I wasn't sure that I got this contraption setup correctly," Grandpa replied.

"So how is your school going?" Grandma asked.

"It's awesome. We've had three different professors just this week. I'm learning so much. Astrophysics is my favorite class, and that's taught by Professor Polanski. He's so funny!"

"That fantastic," Grandma said. "Do you guys have any time for recreation?"

"Do we ever! We exercise twice a day to prevent muscle atrophy by playing space basketball!"

"Space basketball?" Grandpa asked. Jag explained how the game was played.

"How's the food?" Grandma asked.

"It okay, but it's nothing like yours. Everything is packaged in these little containers that inject water to rehydrate the food. The food is bland, and the water is nasty. It tastes like chlorine." From the waiting room, Jag heard Percy chuckle at this comment.

"Are you sleeping alright?" Grandpa asked.

"It's different sleeping in space. We have to strap ourselves in at night, or we could float away if the gravity fails."

Grandpa chuckled and shook his head. Then they talked about the farm and how everyone was doing. On the upper right of the video display, a countdown clock showed twenty-eight seconds remained.

"I have to go," Jag said. "The video will stop in a few seconds. Tell Jack hello for me and that I miss him."

"Will do, son," Grandma said. "He has a girlfriend now. Her name is Rachel, and she's real cute. We love you, son," she said, tearing up. "Stay safe."

"Will do," Jag replied.

"We're proud of you, son," Grandpa said again. He was also a bit choked up.

"I love you, too," Jag said as a message flashed that communication had been terminated.

As Jag left the room, Percy was waiting to enter the video booth. "Your parents sound nice," Percy said.

"Thanks. They're my grandparents, and they're the nicest people I know."

"Well, you sound close to them."

"I am. They raised me. You seem close to your dad, too."

"Hmph. Yeah, we're real close, especially when there's a camera around," Percy said sarcastically as he stepped into the video booth.

Makalo Zuma arrived early for his scheduled call as Jag was collecting his bag and other items. Since Jag hadn't had a chance to speak with him yet, he sat down and introduced himself. From the video room, they heard the audio start piping in.

"Ms. Walker, how many times must I tell you that I'm not to be interrupted when I'm in a meeting?" Mr. Blackwell said to his secretary.

"Yes, sir. But it's your son calling from the space station."

"I don't care if it's the pope himself. When I'm in conference with a customer, I am not to be disturbed!"

"Yes, sir. I understand."

"Hi, Dad," Percy said softly.

"Percy, I'm meeting with the prime minister of Russia. Is there something you need?"

"No, sir, just calling to say hi."

"I can't be bothered right now. Please work with my secretary to schedule this better in the future," Mr. Blackwell replied as he disconnected the video link.

"Boy, that's rough," Makalo whispered.

"Yeah," Jag said as he snuck out of the room before Percy left the video booth.

The class worked together for several weeks on building the satellite's propulsion, navigation, and computer systems. As satellites go, it was small, about the size of a desk. It had many cameras for gathering images and data to be transmitted back to Earth. It was designed to change its trajectory and navigate toward any mechanical objects moving in space to make first contact.

The students had to select a name for the satellite and chose Nik's suggestion of *Stargazer*. The professor had the students pose for a class photo. Then he uploaded the photo onto the *Stargazer*'s computer system, which would be part of a hologram greetings protocol upon encountering any objects in space. Aside from the class photo, the program would also display a star map revealing the course the satellite had taken from Earth.

They launched the *Stargazer* from a bay, and the boys crowded around a monitor to view the images sent back every sixty seconds from its rear camera. Its high-resolution video displayed the *Unity* as it grew smaller in the background.

"Fantastic work, everyone," Professor P said. "Now we begin preparing for our field trip to the Moon!"

CHAPTER 5
FLY ME TO THE MOON

"Before setting you lose on the surface of the Moon, you need to learn how to walk. The gravitational field has been set to equal that of the Moon. Spread out, and give yourselves plenty of room," Dr. Stevenson said. "At only one-sixth our gravity, the first astronauts found walking on the Moon very cumbersome. They learned that hopping was a more efficient way to get around. Let me demonstrate the technique." Dr. Stevenson demonstrated by placing two feet together and leaping forward in a single bound. "Now you try."

Everyone began hopping around the gym, with many stumbling over their own feet. Jag tried leaping, and when he landed he nearly fell over. He learned quickly not to land with his feet too close together or he'd lose his balance. Ben followed Jag but lost his footing and fell forward into Tank who, in turn, bumped into Edgard, and both fell to the floor.

"Hey, watch it, twerp," Tank growled.

"Sorry," Ben said as he and Jag laughed at their awkward movements across the floor.

"Just watch what you're doing."

"He said he was sorry," Jag interjected. "It was an accident."

"Go have your accident over there," Tank replied, pointing toward the side wall.

After practicing all week on bouncing and maneuvering in low gravity, they were fitted with custom spacesuits and repeated the exercise of hopping around the gymnasium. They found the restrictive suits made it much more awkward to maneuver.

The night before they were to leave for their trip to the Moon, Raj, Sasha, Ben, and Jag were sitting in their room discussing their plans for the approaching holiday break.

"I can't wait to get home," Raj said. "My older brother, Satish, is getting married! Indian weddings are quite spectacular, often taking many days and sometimes an entire week, but the greatest thing about an Indian wedding is the food! My mother will make her famous Navrattan curry with potato Dam Alu Kashmiri. Then we will have desert: pistachio ice cream and Jelebi, which is like donuts in honey and syrup. And then we dance. It's fantastic."

"Wow, that sounds great," Jag said. "Where are you going, Sasha?"

"My family goes each year to the Sochi Mountains, where we stay in a resort. We spend the weeks skiing, eating, and playing games. How about you, Jag?"

"I'm going home to Indiana to spend time with my family. What about you, Ben?"

"I'm not sure now. The embassy is sending my dad back to Israel on urgent business, and my parents don't know how long they will be gone. So I'm not sure what I will be doing."

"Why don't you come with me?" Jag asked. "My grandparents would love to have you!"

"Oh, I don't know."

"Yes, you have to come. We'll have so much fun. We can go sledding, shoot rockets, eat my grandma's delicious cooking, build snow forts, and open Christmas presents."

"Uh, we don't really celebrate Christmas, only Chanukah," Ben replied.

"No worries! We'll celebrate that with you."

After thinking for a moment, Ben nodded. "Alright. Let me ask my papa."

After dinner, they spoke with Ben's parents, who asked Jag several questions before giving Ben permission to go to Indiana. As they waited to speak with Jag's grandparents, Percy arrived early and swapped places to accommodate his dad's demanding schedule.

"Hi Dad," Percy said.

"Percy," Mr. Blackwell replied without turning toward the monitor.

"We launched the satellite I told you about."

"Um-hmm."

"Now we're scheduling our holiday trips."

"Oh, about that, I wanted to speak to you. I have an important meeting with an Asian energy company to discuss running oil pipelines through northern China and Mongolia. I'm unable to join you for Christmas, as our stocks have dropped due to recent slowdowns in technology and energy markets, and our shareholders demand we take aggressive action."

"That's okay," Percy replied.

"Your stepmom will be vacationing on the Riviera, and you can join her and the kids."

"Oh, joy, Christmas with the babies," Percy mumbled. His two stepbrothers were nearly thirteen years younger than him. After divorcing when Percy was young, Mr. Blackwell had remarried a supermodel twenty years his junior.

"I didn't hear what you said; you're mumbling. What have I told you about mumbling?"

"That will be fantastic. I look forward to it," Percy replied with false enthusiasm.

"Good," Mr. Blackwell said. "I have to go now. Is there anything else?"

"No, that's it, sir," Percy replied. Mr. Blackwell disconnected the video feed. Percy sat there for a moment and then opened the curtain and exited the room.

"I couldn't help but overhear your Christmas plans," Jag said. "Ben is joining me in Indiana. You're welcome to join us, too."

"Indiana? Why would I go with you two? I'm not an orphan, I have a family," Percy sneered, offended by the offer.

"Sorry, it's just that you don't seem too happy about your Christmas plans," Jag said.

"Why don't you just mind your own business?" Percy asked as he stormed away.

Jag and Ben entered the video conference room. When the video came up, Jag's grandma was removing her apron, having just finished washing the dishes. Grandpa stood by wearing overalls and a Purdue Boilermaker hat. Elated to see them, Jag started talking a mile a minute about the satellite they had launched and their preparations for the trip to the Moon.

"Well, son, I have some sad news," Grandma said. "Payton passed away last night. We buried him over by Cernan."

"Oh, I'm sorry to hear that," Jag replied.

"Poor Grissom sits out on the porch whining for Payton," Grandma said.

"He was a good dog. He had a good life," Grandpa said as he put his arm around Grandma.

"Who's your friend?" Grandma asked, nodding at Ben, who had been hiding behind Jag.

"This is Ben Mendelsohn," Jag said, pushing him toward the monitor.

"Pleasure meeting you, Ben," Grandma said.

"Pleasure meeting you, Mr. and Mrs. Gabriel," Ben replied.

"Ah, just call us Grandma and Grandpa. Everyone does," Grandpa said.

"I, uh, we wanted to ask if it was okay for Ben to come to Indiana during Christmas break. His parents have to go back to Israel on an emergency, because his dad is an ambassador."

"Why, of course," Grandma said. "Have you asked his parents?"

"Yes, ma'am," Ben replied. "My papa said it was alright if it's alright with you."

"Then it's settled," Grandpa said. "We have plenty of space for him to sleep in the barn."

Grandma chuckled. "Oh, Joseph . . . He's just kidding, Ben. We have plenty of room for you, and I'll make Grandpa sleep in the barn."

"Son, if you have any other friends who need a place to stay, they are more than welcome," Grandpa said, smiling.

"That's right," Grandma added.

"Nah, just Ben at this point. Oh, by the way, he's Jewish and doesn't celebrate Christmas. He celebrates something called 'Honey Cow,'" Jag said, slaughtering the pronunciation.

"Chanukah," Grandma corrected him.

"That's correct, ma'am. Chanukah," Ben replied.

"So I promised we would celebrate that with him," Jag continued.

"I seem to recall that the Kaplans down the road are Jewish," Grandma replied. "I'll ask them how we should celebrate and invite them over. We look forward to meeting you, Ben."

On the morning of the trip to the Moon, the class reported to the loading docks, where an impressive black shuttle sat with a gold Blackwell Enterprises logo printed on its side. Jag had noticed that just about everything on the space station had a Blackwell Enterprises logo on it; even their spacesuits.

Everyone boarded the extravagant DreamCraft luxury-class shuttle equipped with the latest technology. Stewardesses in nostalgic light blue skirts welcomed the students on board and offered espressos, lattes, or cappuccinos while Frank Sinatra's "Fly Me to the Moon" played in the background through surround-sound speakers.

Jag sat in one of the thickly padded, oversized beige leather seats as a video display console attached to the arm of the seat turned on. A Blackwell commercial played as audio piped through speakers embedded in the seatback: "Imagine walking where our forefathers could only dream of walking, playing golf or spending the night sleeping on the surface of the Moon in one of our lavish, fully automated hotel pods. Blackwell Enterprises, making dreams a reality." It was followed by a large, rotating Blackwell Enterprises logo.

A menu bar floated onto the screen, listing items that included the history of Blackwell Enterprises, news magazines, music, or the option to place an order for snacks or drinks. Jag tapped the news category, and a dozen magazine covers filled the screen. One caught Jag's eye immediately. It featured a large photo of Percy standing in Mission Control with Earth behind him. The text over the photo read "The Future of Space Explorers and Inventors." A small subtitle read "Students of the First Ever Space University Reach for the Stars." Jag wondered when they had taken the photograph, as he didn't recall any mention of it.

He navigated through several advertisements in the digital magazine to the main story, which was supposed to have been about the class but was primarily a bio on Percy, his exploits, and his family background. It discussed how Blackwell Enterprises subsidized the space station by providing tours to the Moon to anyone who could afford the million-dollar price tag. Ben came over and plopped down on Jag's right, Raj and Sasha to his left.

"Wow, this is nice!" Ben exclaimed as he looked around the egg-shaped cabin.

"I know," Jag agreed.

"Hey, that's Percy!" Sasha exclaimed, pointing to the screen on Jag's armrest. Raj and Ben leaned in to see what Sasha was talking about.

"Yep, it was supposed to be a story about our class," Jag replied, "but somehow it became a bio on Percy."

"No doubt his father bought the magazine and made them do the story," Raj said.

"You don't know that," Ben objected.

"Maybe not, but it fits the pattern," Raj retorted.

A stewardess carrying a silver tray of assorted chocolate truffles stopped and asked if they'd like one before take-off. After making several selections, the boys stuffed their faces with the delicacies.

When Percy entered the shuttle, each stewardess greeted him personally. "Good morning, Mr. Blackwell." He took a seat away from the rest of the class. Most days Percy kept to himself. Every once in while he hung out with Tank and Edgard (who was all too eager to spend time with his idol). Most of the time Percy was friendly enough, but once in a while his attitude darkened, and he became sullen and moody. Most people learned to give him space during those times or else face the wrath of his sharp tongue. Jag noticed Percy's mood seemed to darken the most after speaking with his father.

After a pre-flight safety video, the shuttle glided effortlessly out of the *Unity's* dock, and in less than an hour it reached lunar orbit, where it rotated on its axis so that the ceiling faced the Moon. The roof opened, and a large glass window revealed a fantastic view of the Moon. Each seat leaned back gently, allowing the students to observe the Moon's surface. A prerecorded narration performed by a well-known actor told the history of humankind's fascination with the Moon, starting with Aristotle and spanning through time up through Galileo, who discovered that the Moon wasn't perfectly smooth but that it had mountains and craters.

The narration described various Moon landings by both Americans and Russians, and on the glass ceiling, small pinpoints highlighted the precise location of each landing in chronological order. The students felt like they could almost reach out and touch the Moon. After the narration ceased, the roof closed, and the shuttle rotated and landed on a large lunar landing pad. The students were transitioned to the shuttle's bay, where they helped each other put on their suits and made sure everything was snug. Dr. Stevenson checked each suit's oxygen and communication system, which allowed the students to speak to people in their immediate vicinity or broadcast to everyone in the group. The back end of the shuttle bay lowered, forming a ramp down to the Moon's surface. Then Professor Polanski and Dr. Stevenson boarded a two-seat rover with six fat wheels and a cargo box for hauling equipment.

"Follow us down the ramp. When you reach the surface, use the hopping method you practiced," Polanski said.

Once the students reached the surface, Jag, Raj, Ben, and Sasha began competing to see who could hop the farthest. Sasha, being the tallest, had the longest hop. Ben and Jag hopped over to a tall dune to get a better view of the area. From atop the dune, they could see both Earth and the *Unity* in the distance. Jag pressed a button on his wrist pad and took several photos with his helmet-mounted camera.

"Wow, what a view. Isn't this incredible?" Raj exclaimed as he and Sasha joined them.

"Yes, it's beautiful," Sasha replied as Ben hopped down the dune.

Ben had made it halfway down the dune when he crossed paths with Tank and Edgard as they were bouncing up. As Ben passed Tank, Tank stuck out his boot and caught the toe of Ben's boot, sending him tumbling down the dune. Jag turned just as Ben's foot hit Tank's, and he hopped as fast as he could down the dune to help Ben up.

"Are you alright?" Jag asked as he held out his hand.

"Yeah, I must've hit something."

"You hit something alright," Jag said, scowling. He moved over to where Tank was standing. "That was uncalled for."

"It was an accident," Tank replied sarcastically, echoing Ben's words from their encounter in the gym.

"That was no accident. You did it on purpose!"

"How do you know? Can you read his thoughts?" Edgard asked.

"It doesn't take a mind reader to know he did it on purpose," Jag said.

"It doesn't matter; we're even now," Ben replied as he stepped between Jag and Tank to defuse the situation.

"Everyone gather over by the memorial wall," Polanski announced as the students hopped over to where he was standing in front of a tall glass wall. It had been erected by Blackwell Enterprise to satisfy the concerns of the International Space Society to keep Moon tourists from disturbing the historical landing areas and to preserve the site for future generations.

"I see that someone has already become familiar with the Moon's surface," Polanski said, referring to the gray Moon dust all over Ben's suit. Ben chuckled but didn't say anything in reply.

"Welcome to Statio Tranquillitatis, otherwise known as Tranquility Base! This is where astronauts Neil Armstrong and Buzz Aldrin landed their *Eagle* lunar module over a century ago. The metal structure you see behind me is the actual base of the *Eagle* lander."

A plaque on its frame read: "Here men from the planet Earth first set foot upon the Moon July 1969 AD. We came in peace for all mankind."

The professor pressed a large button on the glass wall that read "Play" in English as well as several other languages, causing the site to come alive as light beamed across space, recreating a 3D holographic version of the original landing. Corresponding audio streamed into their helmets, sharing the recorded conversation between Armstrong, Aldrin, and Mission Control on Earth.

Aldrin: "Drifting forward just a little bit; that's good."

The *Eagle* adjusted its course in the glass window in front of them. Then it slowed its descent with bursts from its rockets. It touched down on the surface with holographic dust blowing everywhere

Aldrin: "Contact light."
Armstrong: "Shutdown"
Aldrin: "Okay. Engine stop."
Armstrong: "Houston, Tranquility Base here. The *Eagle* has landed."

Sounds of cheering from Houston piped through their speakers as the engines were disengaged and dust particles kicked up by the exhaust floated down.

Professor Polanski raised his voice over the audio. "Neil Armstrong reported later that they had projected only a 50 percent chance that they'd succeed. In fact, so precarious was their landing that the *Eagle's* on board computer had inadvertently directed them to a crater filled with rocks. Seeing that they were dangerously off course, Captain Armstrong took over the navigation and used what little fuel was left to maneuver over the large crater just to the left of us. When they touched down, they had only seven seconds of fuel remaining or else they would have had to abort the mission and forego landing on the Moon. By today's standards, this ship was primitive at best, but what they lacked in technology they more than made up for in passion and courage."

Aldrin: "Okay. About ready to go down and get some moon rock?"

A moment later the hatch on the holographic *Eagle* opened, and Armstrong and Aldrin exited the *Eagle* module and climbed down the ladder. Then, as Armstrong stepped down onto the Moon's surface, he said: "That's one small step for man; one giant leap for mankind."

The two holographic astronauts walked around the area in front of the students. Incredibly, the video footsteps aligned perfectly with the actual footprints still preserved on the Moon's surface, seeing as there is no wind or rain on the Moon to erode them. After they planted the American flag next to the lunar module, Neil took a photo of Buzz saluting. Then they began unloading equipment.

"Can anyone tell me what device they are installing?" Dr. Stevenson asked as the astronauts set up scientific equipment in front of them. After no one replied, she answered her own question. "It's a lunar laser ranging retroreflector array."

"I was going to say that," Sasha joked.

"What's it for, smarty pants?" Dr. Stevenson asked.

Sasha shrugged. "I have no idea."

Dr. Stevenson looked around. "Anyone?"

"Is it for measuring the distance from the Earth to the Moon?" Niklas asked.

"Very good," Dr. Stevenson said. "By reflecting light particles back to Earth, it allowed us to measure the precise distance between Earth and the Moon. Which is how far?"

"Three hundred and eighty-five thousand kilometers," Makalo replied.

"That's correct, or two hundred and thirty-nine thousand miles, for our non-metric students," Dr. Stevenson clarified.

Next the astronauts loaded moon rocks into the *Eagle*. After leaving their backpacks on the Moon to counter the additional weight of the rocks, they reentered the cockpit.

Aldrin: "Nine, eight, seven, six, five, abort stage, engine arm, ascent, proceed."

The *Eagle*'s rocket ignited, and it lifted off.

Aldrin: "We're off."
Armstrong: "The *Eagle* has wings."

"We stand here today on the zenith of humankind's dreams to reach the stars," Professor P said after the video had finished. "Until this landing, the dream was a mere fantasy. However, through the mandate of President Kennedy and the culmination of hundreds of thousands of people working in unison, that dream was made a reality on this very spot. The journey was costly, paid ultimately by the sacrifices of courageous astronauts and cosmonauts. To reach our dreams, we must follow their example, reaching beyond our technical limitations and what we think is possible, never giving in to fear or doubts about the difficulty of the vision."

He paused and smiled. "With Christmas and the holiday season upon us, I can think of no greater gift to give your loved ones than a moon rock. Feel free to gather as many rocks as you can fit into these bags."

Dr. Stevenson handed each student a small pick and a nylon bag. Then they headed off into the dunes. Jag dug up a football-sized rock as Ben continued a bit farther, where he spotted a large rock. He ran his pick along its perimeter, trying to free it from the ground. As he bent over to pry up the rock, something hit his shoulder. He looked around him but didn't see anything, so he bent down again and continued working at the rock. As he was about to clear the rock from its berth, something hit him hard in the side of his helmet. Out of the corner of his eye he saw a rock about the size of a baseball fall to the ground. Turning, he saw Tank and Raj pointing and laughing, both holding rocks in their hands.

"Real funny, guys. Knock it off!" Ben yelled through his microphone.

As he turned back to pry up the large rock, he heard a cracking sound in his helmet. He spotted a small crack form at the base of his helmet, where the glass and the frame met. Then the glass splintered.

"That can't be good," Ben said. "Uh, Jag? Can you come here quickly?"

"Be right there," Jag said. He bounced over the dune, where he found Ben with his hand pressed to his helmet. "What's up?"

"Can you look at this and tell me how bad is it?"

When Ben removed his hand, Jag's eyes went wide. "That's a crack! How did that happen?"

Ben glanced at Tank but didn't say anything.

"We have to get you back to the shuttle immediately!"

The two of them hurried toward the shuttle, with Jag carrying their bags of rocks. About halfway to the shuttle, the crack in Ben's helmet fractured and split. Within seconds, the crack turned into a small hole, and oxygen began seeping out of his helmet. Warning alarms sounded inside Ben's suit, and lights flashed on his vest and wrist pad.

"We need to move it!" Jag exclaimed as he dropped the rocks and grabbed Ben's arm. They climbed several dunes as the oxygen monitor on Ben's wrist flashed "39%." They hopped over several more dunes as oxygen continued to spew out of Ben's helmet. The oxygen monitor showed "15%" accompanied by the warning "Take immediate action!"

"We're not going to make it," Ben gasped.

"Don't say anything!" Jag replied. "Conserve your oxygen. Keep going!"

Raj and Sasha were coming up from around the shuttle when they saw Jag assisting Ben. Though they weren't sure what was happening, they knew something was terribly wrong. Raj went up the shuttle's ramp and threw open the airlock while Sasha grabbed Ben's other arm, noting that the oxygen panel flashed "0%" in large red letters.

"He's out of oxygen!" Sasha exclaimed as he and Jag carried Ben up the ramp.

"I know! We have to get him inside immediately!" Jag replied.

Upon entering the airlock, they closed the door, and Ben collapsed to the floor. Raj pressed a button, and oxygen flooded the compartment. They pulled off Ben's helmet, and after several seconds he finally took a breath. His face was pale and his breathing shallow.

"What happened?" Raj asked.

"Tank," Jag said with disdain.

The three carried Ben into the shuttle's main transport area and laid him on one of the large seats. A stewardess grabbed an oxygen mask and put it over his head to help him breathe. Color returned to his face as he took deep breaths. Jag sat down on the floor next to him and sighed. "That was too close."

The doors opened, and in walked Tank and Edgard, carrying Ben's and Jag's rock bags.

"Is he alright? We brought your rocks," Tank said in a soft voice as he approached.

"What were you thinking?" Jag yelled, leaping up and pushing Tank against the wall. Raj maneuvered in front of Edgard to prevent him from intervening.

"I was just messing with him," Tank said.

"You could have killed him!"

"I didn't mean to hurt him."

"You apologize now!" Jag insisted.

"I was just having a bit of fun."

"The next time you want to have fun, you can have it with me!" Jag said, his fist raised. Although smaller than Tank, growing up with an uncle to wrestle with made Jag scrappy and a tad bit fearless.

"I'm sorry, man. I was just playing around," Tank said, grimacing in anticipation of a punch from Jag.

At that moment, the rest of the class returned. Percy was the first to enter. Seeing Jag holding Tank against the wall with his fist raised, he stopped short. "What's going on, guys?"

"Nothing," Sasha said. "We're just having a conversation."

"With your fists?" Percy asked.

Jag lowered his fist, and then Tank and Edgard stepped away.

"I really am sorry, man. I didn't mean for this to happen. Please don't tell the professor," Tank said.

After a short stay on the *Unity* to gather their luggage, the students made their way back to Cape Canaveral, where each one was met by his own personal security team, which escorted them home. Lieutenant Marks and Sergeant Perez were waiting for Jag.

"Hey, squirt, I think you've grown since the last time we saw you," Lt. Marks said.

"Who's your friend?" Perez asked.

"This is Ben. He's a classmate, and he's coming with me."

"Nice to meet you, Ben," Sergeant Perez said. Then he and Marks escorted Jag and Ben to the farm. Of course, they found the time to stay for supper before heading back to base.

Each day Jag and Ben spent every waking hour running around the house and outdoors. As Chanukah arrived, they celebrated with the Kaplans, who brought over a Menorah and explained the Festival of Lights. Afterwards, they feasted on all sorts of fried foods and filled donuts. On Christmas, Jag met Rachel, Uncle Jack's girlfriend, and Ben participated in his first Christmas. Everyone took turns reading the Nativity story and opening gifts. Jag gave his grandparents the large moon rock he collected, and he gave a smaller rock to Jack. Then Jag and Ben unwrapped two rockets, which they darted outside to launch, with Grissom barking as he ran behind.

After Christmas, they received additional snowfall, so Grandpa hooked up a large tire tube to the back of Ol' Betsy and pulled Jag and Ben down an empty, snow-covered Mulberry Street. Every night after supper, Grandpa lit a fire in the fireplace, and everyone sat and listened to Jag and Ben tell stories of their experiences on board the *Unity*.

Before they were ready, vacation had ended, and it was time to return to begin work on their school projects. Lieutenant Marks and Sergeant Perez arrived to escort the boys back. Grandpa asked Lieutenant Marks to take a photograph as Sergeant Perez was busy eating waffles at the table. They all gathered in front of the fireplace with the Christmas tree on the left side and the Menorah sitting on the fireplace mantel. Grandma and Grandpa stood with their hands on the boys' shoulders, and Uncle Jack had his arm around Rachel. The camera printed out several wallet-sized photos, which Grandpa gave to each of the boys.

As the government sedan pulled down the drive, Grandma and Grandpa stood on the porch waving. It had been the best Christmas ever.

CHAPTER 6
FAILURE AND MORE FAILURE

A dark cloud the size of a man's hand appeared and grew slowly until it enshrouded Earth. Powerful explosions illuminated the sky, shaking the planet's foundations. Then a fiery metal object fell through the ominous cloud, crashing into the ocean and creating a tsunami that covered portions of North America and Asia. Without light, plant and animal life soon died, followed by humans. The air became stagnant with the stench of death as chaos reigned and life on Earth, as we know it, came to an end.

Jag lay in his bed on board the *Unity* tossing and turning as the terrifying dream flooded his mind. He convulsed violently, shaking the bed as sweat poured out of his body, drenching his pajamas.

Alone in his dream, surrounded by darkness and silence, he saw a small light move toward him. Turning, he ran away in slow motion, but the approaching light overtook him and grew until it became as large as the Sun itself. Close behind was the Moon, followed by eleven smaller stars, all in alignment. The lights encircled and revolved around Jag, spinning faster and faster. Suddenly they came to a halt and, one by one, each light bowed before Jag and then faded away.

Awakened by Jag kicking the wall, Ben rolled out of bed to find him convulsing in his bed.

"Jag, wake up," Ben said, touching Jag's hot, clammy arm. As Ben turned to go get help, Jag sat up in his bed with the strap still around his waist, staring out into space. Again, Ben touched Jag, startling him awake. He looked down at Ben in confusion.

"Are you alright?" Ben asked.

Jag nodded. "Yeah, it was just a dream. A very real and terrifying dream."

"I've never seen anything like that! You were tossing all over the place and kicking the bed. Then you sat straight up. Scared the tar out of me. Are you sure you're alright?"

"Yeah, I think so, though I have a whopper of a headache. Sorry for waking you," Jag said. Then he lowered himself from the bed in his sweat-soaked pajamas and went to shower.

After their morning class with Professor P, the students gathered in the newly finished state-of-the-art laboratory, which was stocked with every imaginable piece of scientific equipment. The lab had been designed with safety in mind. The walls were covered in a thick fire-retardant, coating, and the ceiling had an integrated sprinkler system to contain and extinguish various hazards.

"Welcome to your new laboratory!" Professor P said. "Our thanks to the construction crews and to Blackwell Enterprises for the generous donation of equipment. Everyone, please find your station." The students weaved through the maze of workstations to find their personalized stations with their nameplate attached.

"We are now starting the project phase of our class," Professor P continued. "From this day forward, you will spend most of your time working on your class project. You have two months to complete a working prototype to be presented in our first ever Space Games. Your overall score will be a culmination of your homework assignments, exams, and the final project presentation."

"Don't forget, the winner of the competition will receive Professor Polansky's flight vest, which he wore as he stepped onto Mars," Dr. Stevenson said, holding up the colorful vest.

"Oh, Dr. Stevenson," Professor P scolded, disapproving of the attention. "Remember, students, the reason for all of this is to help us take that giant leap forward in propelling humankind deeper into space."

The students' projects were grouped in the following categories: Environment, Robotics and Computers, Food, and Propulsion. Environment consisted of Mo, Tank, and Sasha. Mo was developing a cryogenics machine to freeze and then reanimate humans so they could travel farther into space. Sasha was working on a tractor beam that could lock onto an object the size of a satellite and pull it into a vessel. Tank (whose family owned a line of waste-management companies in Germany) was developing a device to process waste and convert it into fuel.

Robotics and Computers consisted of Kano, Ben, and Edgard. Kano was creating a small android that could maneuver outside a ship to perform repairs. Ben was creating miniature bots designed to travel through plumbing, ductwork, or ventilation to detect and repair problems. Edgard was working on an artificially intelligent system to manage all the environmental, propulsion, and personnel systems throughout a ship.

The Food category consisted of Makalo, Raj, and Mario. Makalo was designing a hydroponic environment to grow plants without the use of soil while significantly reducing the amount of water needed. Raj was creating a food synthesizer using 3D printing technology to merge proteins with nutrients to replicate food. Mario's design was an encapsulated greenhouse that could be rocketed to distant planets while astronauts were still inflight to provide a fully sustainable environment of air, food, and water once they arrived.

Finally, Propulsion consisted of Percy, Nik, and Jag. Percy's project was to improve the output of the best Blackwell rocket by 300 percent by redesigning fuel flow. Nik was creating an ion thruster rocket that was propelled by electrically charged particles instead of hot gas. Jag was developing a hyperdrive that could bend space around a vehicle, allowing it travel through space at speeds faster than light.

The students examined their workstations and the different tools and equipment. Each station was separated by moveable whiteboards for drawing and designing their projects. Sitting to the side of Mo's station was a mysterious covered cage.

"What's in your cage?" Sasha asked as he reached to peek inside.

"It's a lagomorph," Mo replied, causing Sasha to yank his hand back in fear.

"It's a rabbit, ya dummy," Raj clarified.

"A rabbit?" Sasha exclaimed, lifting the cover to reveal a brown, long-eared hare. "Hey, everyone, Mo has a rabbit!"

"He's cute. What's its name?" Ben asked.

"Name? It doesn't have a name; it's a rabbit."

"He has to have a name," Raj replied.

"Do you name your food?" Mo asked. "Because in Morocco, we eat rabbit."

"Are you going to eat him?" Ben asked, concerned.

"No, he's my test subject for the cryogenic chamber."

"You're going to freeze him?" Jag asked.

"Well, unless *you* want to be my test subject. I have to freeze something."

"Uh, no thanks," Jag replied. "That doesn't sound like much fun."

"He still needs a name," Ben said. "How about Harvey? I've always liked that name."

"No, that's a terrible name," Sasha replied. "How about Laika? She was the first animal in space, a Russian dog."

One by one, various names were called out, like Thumper, Orion, and of course Bugs.

"Don't be ridiculous," Kano said. "He needs something more masculine and powerful."

"Okay, how about Goliath?" Ben suggested.

"Nah, how about Godzilla!" Sasha said.

"Now, that's a good name!" Kano replied, and everyone agreed that it was fitting.

"Will it hurt him?" Ben asked.

Mo looked at Ben. "Will what hurt him?"

"The freezing."

"If my calculations are correct, he shouldn't feel a thing, and hopefully he will be fully reanimated after it's done."

"Hopefully?" Raj asked.

"Yeah. Hopefully, he turns about better than the first two test subjects."

The students spent most of their time working on their projects. Jag continued his research on creating an Einstein-Rosen Bridge or wormhole. To travel faster than light, a hyperdrive was needed to propel an object through hyperspace. Jag used high-intensity lasers and field generators to create a displacement emitter for creating wormholes. Over the next few weeks, he ran hundreds of tests, but every attempt failed.

The class grew attached to Godzilla, though to Mo he was nothing more than a lab specimen. Ben and Sasha convinced Mo to allow them to take care of Godzilla in their dorm room until Mo needed him. He stayed in his cage during the day, but in the mornings and evenings, they let him out to roam around the room.

One morning as Raj was leaving to take his shower, Sasha realized the door had been left open. "Where's Godzilla?" Sasha asked as he took off his pajama shirt.

Sasha, Ben, and Jag looked around the small room, searching every crevice into which the rabbit might be able to squeeze. Finding nothing, they darted out the room.

"Have you seen Godzilla?" Ben shouted at Raj.

"Huh?" Raj asked. He turned just in time to see the tail end of Godzilla hopping down the hallway. He pointed at the retreating bunny. "There he is!"

The four boys ran toward the elevator, half clad in their pajamas. As they came in sight of the elevators, Dr. Stevenson stepped out.

"Stop Godzilla!" Raj yelled.

"What?" Dr. Stevenson asked, looking around.

"The rabbit!" Sasha yelled.

Before she could react, Godzilla had scurried into the back of the elevator as its doors closed.

"Where's the elevator going?" Jag asked.

"Most likely Mission Control. That's where I came from," Dr. Stevenson said.

Raj jabbed the elevator button repeatedly, with no response.

"That'll take too long," Ben said. "Come on, let's take the stairs"

"Ah, man," said Sasha, still shirtless.

All four boys ran up six flights of stairs. They made quite a commotion when they entered Mission Control. Everyone turned to see them running around in their pajamas searching under desks and chairs for Godzilla.

As luck would have it, that morning a news crew had set up cameras in Mission Control, filming an interview with Percy about the school.

"Can I help you boys?" one of the Mission Control officers asked.

"You haven't seen a rabbit, have you?" Raj replied.

"Um, no."

"Our rabbit escaped, and we believe he took the elevator up here," Ben said.

"Taking the elevator would a very logical thing for a rabbit to do," the officer quipped.

"You boys have a pet rabbit on the station?" Dr. Reese asked as he approached to investigate the commotion.

"Nah, Godzilla is Mo's lab animal," Jag answered.

"He's going to freeze him!" Ben interjected.

"Ah. Okay, everyone, let's help them find their rabbit," Dr. Reese ordered as everyone began looking around stations and under desks and chairs.

"I think he's over here!" one of the crewmen yelled.

Everyone ran over to where the ventilation pipes fed oxygen into the room. The bars on the ventilation grille were too small for a boy to fit through, but they were large enough for a rabbit. After removing the cover, Ben crawled into the shaft and found Godzilla nibbling on electrical wires. He grabbed the rabbit and then checked the wires to ensure the insulation had not been damaged. After he crawled out, the boys received an earful from Reese about safety and the need to more closely supervise their pet.

Later that morning, as the students gathered in the cafeteria for breakfast, the morning news played on the cafeteria television. Nik looked up and then pointed at the monitor. "Hey, that's Percy!"

"Turn it up," Makalo said. Nik turned up the volume as a reporter interviewed Percy. Beneath his image, a caption read, "Exclusive! Percy Blackwell interviewed on the *ISS Unity*."

"Percy, can you tell us what school is like in space?" the attractive young reporter asked.

"School has been phenomenal, and the instructors are first rate. The lessons are all designed to prepare us to impact the next generation of space exploration."

"So I've heard there's an upcoming competition that each student must submit a project for," the reporter said.

"Yes, that's correct. We work each day on our project in a fabulous laboratory donated by Blackwell Enterprises."

"Rumor has it that you're a sure win in the competition."

"Well, you're as intelligent as you are beautiful," Percy said, "but I'm surrounded by very capable and brilliant students, who I consider my equals."

Ben leaned over the table. "Wow, I could never do that!" he said softly.

"Do what?" Jag asked.

"Answer her as well as Percy does. He's so at ease in front of a camera."

"At ease?" Raj replied. "It's called being slick."

"We discovered that life aboard the *Unity* is not all work and no play," the reporter continued. "Several students found time this morning to interrupt Mission Control to chase a rabbit. Yes, that's right, a pet rabbit in space! The entire station searched for this 'wascally wabbit.'" A video clip showed the boys busting into Mission Control in their pajamas.

Everyone in the break room burst out in laughter as the four red-faced boys sank down in their chairs. The video ended with a freeze frame of them disheveled from the chase as Ben held Godzilla and Sasha crossed his arms in attempt to cover his shirtless chest.

After breakfast, everyone assembled in the classroom, where Dr. Stevenson was updating the leaderboard. After the first week of reports and assignments, Jag was in first place, Percy in second, and Mo and Ben were tied for third. Jag's roommates patted on him on the back. However, Tank and Edgard booed the results as Percy looked away from the board.

That evening as the students were placing their weekly calls, Jag overheard Percy talking with his father and thought that their conversation sounded more like a board meeting than a conversation between father and son. Mr. Blackwell inquired about Percy's standing in the competition and wasn't pleased when he found out Percy was not in first place.

"Second place is not winning!" Mr. Blackwell said.

"I know, sir," Percy replied, "but the boy who is leading is very bright and has a great idea for a hyperdrive propulsion rocket that we should consider."

"Hyperdrive? That's just fictional nonsense," Mr. Blackwell said. "Our shareholders are counting on your rocket design, and we have reporters ready to editorialize on how it will revolutionize propulsion design for Blackwell Rockets. I can't stress enough how important it is for the future of this company that you win this competition."

"I'm trying as hard as I can, sir," Percy replied.

"Trying? Trying is not winning! Now close your eyes."

"Oh, Dad . . ."

"Close your eyes and stand up straight," Mr. Blackwell said. Percy reluctantly closed his eyes and halfheartedly straightened his posture in a manner that seemed to communicate that he had gone through this routine many times before.

"Now envision your goal in your mind. Can you see it?"

"Yeah."

"Can you see it?" Mr. Blackwell repeated impatiently.

"Yes, sir," Percy said. "I can see it."

"Now repeat after me: 'Expect to perfect every challenge, every defect. Though trials and obstacles resist, I shall persist to climb the highest of heights, for winning is my birthright.'"

Mr. Blackwell proclaimed the statement several times, becoming louder and bolder with each rendition as Percy joined in halfheartedly.

"If you believe this and stay focused, nobody can keep you from reaching your goal. I have used this exercise every day to become one of the most powerful men in the world."

"I know, sir. I will," Percy said.

"Well, just to be sure, I'll have Dr. Lackey stop by to help," Mr. Blackwell replied.

"Sir, I don't need his help. I can do this on my own."

"Either way, you will win this," Mr. Blackwell said.

Later that week, Jag and Ben joined Raj in the break room for lunch, where Raj was giving out samples created by his food synthesizer.

"Try this, and tell me what you think. It's applesauce. It has the same nutritional benefits but is made from my synthesizer, and be honest."

Ben and Jag took a bite of something that looked like applesauce, except that it was bright yellow.

"I have to be honest," Jag said a moment later, "it's not very good, and it doesn't taste—or look—much like applesauce."

"Yeah, it's awful," Ben said, spitting it out and grabbing something to drink.

"Okay, try this one. It's tapioca pudding." Raj slid over a dish of runny pudding.

"This tastes like the applesauce," Ben replied, nearly gagging from the taste.

Just then, Sasha ran in and sat down at the table. "You guys aren't going to believe this. I just came from the lab, and the doors were locked. So I looked through the window and saw people in the back. When I knocked on the door, someone I've never seen came over and asked what I wanted. I told him I was there to work on my project, but he said the lab was closed for cleaning. However, before he closed the door, I saw Percy in the back working on his project, and several adults wearing white lab coats were standing around his rocket!"

Raj slammed his hand on the table. "He's cheating!"

"We don't know that," Jag replied. "He could be demoing his project to his father's friends."

"Yeah, or perhaps they were just janitors wearing white lab coats cleaning up?" Raj retorted sarcastically.

"Right, and they all just happened to have tools in their hands," Sasha added.

"I think they're probably right, Jag," Ben said.

"So what are you going to do?" Sasha asked.

Jag shrugged. "Nothing."

Sash looked at him, aghast. "Nothing? Why? We should at least tell Dr. Stevenson or Professor P."

Jag shook his head. "No, because none of this matters. It's just a game. The purpose of all this is to help us advance technology. If Percy and his 'janitors' get us there quicker, then we all win."

That night Jag fell into a deep sleep and dreamed. Ben awoke and rolled out of bed just as Jag sat up and stared into space. Ben startled Jag from his sleep by touching his arm.

"You were dreaming again. Are you alright?"

"Yeah, I just got a headache," Jag said, out of breath and sweaty.

"I think you need to visit the nurse."

"Nah, I'll be alright. It was just a dream," Jag replied, wiping his forehead.

"If it happens again, I'm getting an adult!" Ben insisted as Jag lay back down.

With his project continuing to fail and the competition approaching, Jag worked tirelessly each night long after all the other students had gone to bed. His status on the leaderboard dropped due to his failing project. Unlike Percy, whose tests results were doubling the speeds of the fastest rocket in existence, Jag was unable to create a wormhole for his hyperdrive. He tried everything, adjusting his equipment and recalculating his findings, only to experience repeated failure— until late one evening it happened without him realizing it.

Exhausted from lack of sleep, Jag adjusted his equipment one more time, fine tuning the arrays ever so slightly. Barely able to keep his eyes open, he set his screwdriver on the desk and then rested his head on his hands for a moment to rest his eyes. As he fell asleep, he accidentally pressed the array's power button with his elbow.

"Have you been here all night?" Ben asked as he tapped Jag on the shoulder.

"Why? What time is it?" Jag asked as he wiped the drool off the back of his hand.

"It's five in the morning."

"Oh, man. I got to get this working!"

"Why don't you just go to bed and worry about this later?" Ben asked.

"I can't. I have to get my displacement emitter working for the hyperdrive," Jag said, yawning as he looked around. "Hey, have you seen my screwdriver? It was right here on the desk."

Ben looked around. "No. Did it fall on the floor while you were asleep?"

Jag looked on the floor and under his desk but couldn't find it anywhere. "It has to be here! I laid it down on the desk just before I fell asleep."

While helping Jag look for the screwdriver, Ben noticed that a strange light was hovering above the desk. It looked distorted, like a broken mirror fragmenting light. Ben tilted his head back and forth to examine the area. Just as he was about to reach out and touch the anomaly, Jag caught Ben's hand.

"Wait!" Jag reached over and powered off his emitters. A second later, the screwdriver appeared where the anomaly had been. "There it is!" Then he set the screwdriver down in the exact location and pushed the power button again. A blue glow enveloped the screwdriver until it became invisible.

Ben looked around. "Where did it go?"

"Well, if my calculations are correct, it went into hyperspace!"

"Awesome, congratulations!"

"Don't congratulate me yet. Now I have to learn how to control its location. Getting to hyperspace is only half the problem. Now I have to move the object through hyperspace."

Doing so proved to be more difficult than Jag imagined. During one attempt, a small hole opened in the outer wall of the lab, causing the vacuum of space to start sucking all the oxygen and anything not attached to a table out through the hole. Sensing the hull breach, the lab's safety system's alarms began screaming.

"Everyone, out of the lab!" Dr. Stevenson yelled.

As soon as everyone was out, the lab doors closed and locked behind them. Emergency arms descended from the ceiling, and a nozzle sprayed thick foam at the hole in the wall. The foam expanded and hardened rapidly, sealing the breach.

Afterwards, the alarm fell silent, and the doors to the lab unlocked. The students walked back into the disheveled room. The vacuum had been so intense that equipment was strewn all over the floor. Jag and the rest of the students began putting the room back in order and identifying missing equipment that had been pulled into space. They looked out the window and saw the equipment floating outside.

"Nice job, Jag!" Percy snarled as he walked by.

"Destroy the whole station, why don't you," Edgard added.

Jag's face fell. "Sorry, everyone."

Dr. Stevenson came over and helped Jag put his station back in order. They picked up the displacement emitter and set it back on the table.

"I don't understand," Jag said. "I checked my calculations at least three times. I'm not sure why the wormhole formed over there. If I can't control where the wormhole forms, then I won't be able to control the trajectory of the drive."

"Don't give up; keep working at it," Dr. Stevenson counseled. "Just be more careful, and next time give everyone a heads-up when you're going to test it. I'll see if Dr. Reese can have one of the shuttles fly by and pick up some of the equipment that escaped."

News about Jag's experimental failure traveled quickly throughout the space station until it reached Professor P. He saw the discouragement on Jag's face when Jag arrived for class. He had heard what some of the students were saying.

"So I heard we had some excitement in the lab yesterday," Professor P said.

"Yeah, Jag almost killed us," Edgard replied.

"No, he didn't. It was just an accident," Ben said.

"Did you know that when Thomas Edison was tackling the daunting task of creating the first light bulb, he failed miserably many, many times?" Professor P asked. "For thousands of years, the only way to get light was by fire. However, Edison dared to envision a new reality in which we could create illumination through electricity. In his attempt to create the first light bulb, he failed so many times that he once said, 'I have not failed. I've just found ten thousand ways that won't work.' Jag has just succeeded in identifying one way *not* to create an Einstein-Rosen Bridge."

"Unfortunately for us, he has nine thousand, nine hundred, and ninety-nine more tries to go," Edgard replied, getting a laugh from the other students.

"I have failed more than I have succeeded, as is the case for anyone who reaches for the impossible," Professor P said. "Jag, if I recall from your introduction, you like to play baseball. One of the greatest players ever was Babe Ruth, who, for the longest time, held the home run record. However, he simultaneously held another record, and that was for strikeouts. He struck out nearly twice as much as he hit homeruns, and yet he said, 'Never let the fear of striking out get in your way . . . for every strike brings me closer to the next home run'."

Professor P pressed a button that caused the tall whiteboard to retract into the ceiling, revealing a large window filled with an array of stars. "My dream is to travel to Alpha Centauri. Though it's the closest solar system to us, it is over four light years from Earth. Even with the most powerful rockets available today, it would take nearly eighty thousand years to reach it. So, if something is impossible to reach, why do we reach for it anyway? We reach because we are explorers, because it's in our DNA. If I truly felt that the stars were forever out of reach, I'd be the first to throw in the towel, buy a Winnebago, and explore Earth."

"Excuse me, professor, but what's a Winnebago?" Mo asked.

"Why, Mo, it is the finest recreational vehicle made by humankind to roam God's green Earth. If I could not explore the stars, then I would explore Earth, only I'd do it in style."

Inspired by the professor's encouragement, Jag modified and redesigned several components. The prototype was no larger than a small cell phone. To test it, he strapped it to a Nerf football he had retrieved from the gym.

After Jag announced he was ready to test his hyperdrive, Dr. Stevenson suggested that everyone take their supper break. Then she, Ben, Raj, and Sasha watched from the hallway through the lab door's window. Jag drew a bullseye on his whiteboard and then dragged it into the aisle. Then he backed up with the football in his hand and his finger on the emitter's trigger. He had designed the hyperdrive to engage as soon as he released the trigger.

"Here goes nothing."

Ben gave a thumbs-up through the window as Jag pulled the football back and threw it at the bullseye on the whiteboard. With his finger no longer pressing the trigger, a blue glow formed around the ball, and it disappeared. Then, on the opposite side of the room beyond the whiteboard, the football reappeared and flew into the wall, bouncing to the floor.

"That was incredible!" Ben yelled as he, Raj, Sasha, and Dr. Stevenson rushed into the lab.

Jag stared at the football in disbelief. "It actually worked!"

"I want to try!" Sasha said.

Sasha stood where Jag had thrown the ball. As soon as he released it, it disappeared, went through the whiteboard, and reappeared on the other side of the room. One by one they took turns throwing the football. Even Dr. Stevenson had a try. Soon, some of the other boys returned from supper and wanted to try it as well.

"A football is one thing, but can it transport something larger?" Percy asked.

"Not sure. That will be my next step," Jag said.

Just then, Mo showed up with Godzilla. It was time to test his cryogenics chamber on a live subject. Seeing Godzilla, the other students followed, concerned about the rabbit's fate. Several reached out to pet the rabbit before Mo placed him inside the modified fridge with the see-through glass door. A display screen mounted on the outside of the chamber displayed the interior temperature of 72°F and the rabbit's heart rate of 271 beats per minute with a red flashing heartbeat glowing beside it.

"He's not gonna die, is he?" Ben asked.

"I hope not; I only brought one test specimen," Mo replied as he engaged the door's lock.

"Why is there a lock?" Nik asked.

"The first door I had flew open during one of my experiments, which turned out rather dismally for the test subject, so I had to add a latch."

After checking the instrument panels, Mo nodded. "Alright, I'm ready to begin." He pressed a button, and the temperature readout descended from 72°F down to 238°F. As the temperature lowered, Godzilla stopped hopping and lay down on the floor. Frost and ice crystals formed around the edges of the glass door. Simultaneously, Godzilla's heart rate dropped from 271 to 0.

As soon as the temperature target was reached and Godzilla no longer showed a heartbeat on the monitor, Mo started his stopwatch. "We have to wait sixty seconds for the test to be successful."

Everyone stared in dread at Godzilla's lifeless form. The moment the stopwatch hit sixty seconds, Mo pressed another button to begin reanimation, and the temperature climbed from 238°F to 72°.

"It'll take a minute or longer for reanimation to occur," Mo said, "if it's going to work at all."

The panel continued to display a heartbeat of zero as they all waited. They mentally counted off the time: ten seconds, twenty seconds. After several minutes had passed, Ben cried.

"He didn't make it," Raj said.

"Why don't we get a towel to cover his body?" Dr. Stevenson suggested.

"No, wait," Mo said. "This has to work! Come on, Godzilla, live!" It was the first time Mo had called his test specimen by name for he, too, had grown fond of the rabbit.

Just then the panel beeped and displayed a heartbeat of one. A few seconds later, another beat. Slowly, it continued to increase. Then Godzilla's foot twitched.

"He's alive!" Ben yelled. Everyone cheered and patted Mo on the back.

Several minutes later, the display showed Godzilla's heartbeat had returned to normal, and the rabbit was up moving around slowly, but he kept leaning to one side and bumping into the fridge walls.

"What's wrong with him?" Sasha asked.

"The cryo-freeze must have impacted his eyesight and motor functions," Mo said.

"It may take a while for the effects to wear off," Dr. Stevenson remarked.

Sure enough, about thirty minutes later, to the relief of the entire class, Godzilla was back to his normal self, hopping around without hitting the wall. That night, the students gave Godzilla an extra portion of food, with several even sharing some of their treats with him.

The leaderboard now listed Mo in first place, followed by Percy, Jag, and then Ben. While Jag continued to make progress on his hyperdrive, both Percy and Nik's rockets were proceeding very well, especially Percy's. His rocket was recording test numbers nearly three times faster than any rocket his father's company manufactured. News of his progress reached shareholders, and stocks climbed as interest in Percy's rocket soared.

CHAPTER 7
SPACE GAMES

The morning of the Space Games finally arrived. Dignitaries from all over the world arrived at the station to watch the students compete against each another. Professor P welcomed everyone, including several reporters and camera crews from popular news stations. Then he introduced each of the guest judges.

"It is my privilege to welcome our panel of distinguished judges. First, most of you already know him, Dr. Harold Reese, director of the *Unity*."

Dr. Reese nodded to the students as they cheered for him.

"Please welcome renowned rocket engineer, Dr. Gordon Lackey," Professor P continued.

Sasha leaned forward to Jag and Ben. "That's him," he whispered. "That's one of the guys I saw working with Percy on his rocket!"

"Next, please welcome Dr. Alenka Curie, who is the leading expert in environment systems and cryogenics. She is also a fellow Pole. Next we have Dr. Noah Lehman, who wrote the book on agriculture and food systems in space. Lastly, please welcome Dr. Iroh Sokka, who specializes in computers and robotics." Everyone applauded as the judges took their seats.

The judges determined the order of events. Within each category, the judges had the students draw numbers to determine their order. Each student had fifteen minutes to present his research, followed by up to twenty minutes to demonstrate his project.

Kano was first and impressed the judges when his android exited the space station, flew to a test site, and assembled several complex components before returning.

Throughout the day, most of the students' projects succeeded without any hitches—except for Tank's garbage-disposal system, which was supposed to convert garbage into energy. He had loaded his invention with an assortment of garbage, but a clogged pipe caused it to backfire, exploding a barrage of garbage throughout the room.

After cleaning things up, it was time for the much-anticipated rocket presentations. Nik was first, followed by Percy, and Jag was last. Everyone transitioned to Mission Control to give their presentation and then track their rockets on the large monitors.

"Welcome to our final competition," said Dr. Lackey, who was overseeing the final demonstrations. "In today's challenge, each student will have twenty minutes for their rocket to travel in a trajectory toward Mars. Now, keep in mind that Mars is well over one hundred and fifty-eight million miles from Earth. It took Professor Polanski's crew one hundred and thirty-seven days to get there, traveling at speeds of 48,000 miles per hour! While we don't expect any of these rockets to hit even one one-thousandth of that distance, we are looking for a rocket that can get us there faster. Each rocket has been transported to a location about a mile away from the *Unity* to prevent any mishaps. I personally have attached a small beacon to each rocket that will emit a unique signal allowing us to track its precise location."

After presenting his research, Nik typed in his launch code. A countdown appeared on the large monitors. When it reached zero, a video feed from a nearby shuttle displayed his ion thruster rocket igniting and moving slowly. A dot on the monitor tracked the rocket as it increased exponentially in speed. A clock on the screen counted down from twenty minutes.

Once it reached zero, the clock stopped, and they recorded the distance as 19,828 miles.

"Fantastic!" Dr. Lackey said. "If we extrapolate the twenty minutes this rocket flew to an hour, we project that it would reach 59,480 miles per hour! For everyone to understand its relevance, if Mr. Polanski's crew had Mr. Johannsson's rocket, the journey that took them one hundred and thirty-seven days could have been completed in just one hundred and ten days, saving Professor Polanski almost an entire month. How does that sound, professor?"

"That would have been fantastic! Well done, Nik," Professor P replied.

As Percy stepped up to speak, all the cameras flashed throughout the room in anticipation of his rocket beating his father's record. After presenting his research, Percy launched his rocket. Unlike the ion thruster, which gradually increased in speed, Percy's rocket shot out with incredible force and reached its maximum speed within seconds. It easily soared beyond Nik's beacon on the map. After twenty minutes, the rocket shut off, and they recorded a record-setting 49,117 miles. Applause and cheers broke out in Mission Control, and everyone patted Percy on the back as camera flashes lit up the room.

"Absolutely outstanding work, young man," Dr. Lackey said. "Your father will be pleased to know that the family business is in safe hands. Again, if we extrapolate the speed into miles per hour, Percy's rocket would hit a mindboggling 147,351 miles per hour! Professor Polanski, this would cut your trip down to only forty-five days! What took you twenty weeks could now be done in six weeks. What do you think about that?"

"Excellent job, Percy! I may have to schedule another trip to Mars," Professor P quipped.

A reporter stepped forward to interview Percy. "This is truly a monumental occasion. Congratulations, Percy. You've not only exceeded your father's rocket capabilities but have broken all current rocket records. How do you feel?"

Before Percy could answer, Dr. Reese tried to get everyone settled down so that the rest of the competition could continue. "Everyone, please take your seats. We have one more presentation before we can decide the winner of the games."

Jag stepped forward and gave his presentation to a mostly disinterested audience, who were distracted by Percy's record and were ready for the day's celebration to begin. After finishing his presentation, Jag went to the control panel and typed in the command to launch his rocket. The countdown began at ten seconds. When it reached zero, the twenty-minute timer appeared on the screen. Everyone turned to watch the monitors with great expectation, but nothing happened. Jag's hyperdrive rocket just sat there, motionless. Jag sat back down at the terminal and began typing frantically.

"I don't understand," Jag said. "I tested the launch sequence yesterday, and everything worked."

As soon as Jag spoke, Edgard chuckled and then glanced at Tank and Percy.

"What did you do?" whispered Percy, who was standing off to the side of the room beside Edgard and Tank.

"Nothing," Edgard replied unconvincingly. "Well, nothing much."

"Why did you do that? I don't need your help to beat him!"

Edgard shrugged. "I was just making sure."

"Let me check," suggested Ben, who was more proficient with computers. He searched through the launch directory files and looked at the system logs. The clock on the wall indicated 16:52 remaining. Sasha, Raj, and several other students gathered around and shouted different suggestions as precious seconds ticked away. Ignoring them, Ben plodded through each directory until he noticed something of interest.

"That's interesting," Ben said. "This configuration file has a different timestamp than the rest. It seems it's been modified."

"I wonder who would have done that," Raj said, glaring at Percy.

Ben quickly replaced the errant file with a copy from Jag. Then Jag restarted the launch sequence. The clock on the wall read 12:42. The hyperdrive came online, and the display in the terminal showed that the batteries where depleted. Panels on the rocket opened automatically, and solar panel wings stretched out.

"Is everything alright?" Dr. Lackey asked.

"Yes, but the batteries need to be charged before the hyperdrive can kick in," Jag said.

Dr. Reese frowned with concern. "How long will that take?"

"Just a couple of minutes."

"Well, I hope you can get it to work. Your time is slipping away," Dr. Lackey said, looking worried.

As the clock reached 7:25, the solar panels folded in, and the rocket moved, slowly at first, and then it picked up speed as everyone remained glued to the monitors. Then a glowing blue field surrounded the rocket, and within a matter of seconds—*poof!*—it was gone.

"Sir, I've lost it. The rocket isn't on my radar," Mission Control agent Gottschalk said. The monitor above her showed two blinking dots, one for Nik's rocket and the other for Percy's.

"Keep looking," Dr. Reese said as he went over to investigate. They made several adjustments to expand the range to other sectors outside the rocket's path.

"Perhaps the rocket exploded," Dr. Lackey suggested.

"No, sir," Gottschalk replied. "If that were the case, radar would pick up debris. However, it's not picking up anything. It's simply not there."

Dr. Lackey placed his arm on Jag's shoulder. "A very admirable attempt. I want to commend Jag for a great presentation, and I want to challenge our students to look at this not as a failure but as a teachable opportunity. It has been a long and phenomenal day, and I think we now have the information we need to determine today's winners."

"Dr. Lackey, I think it may be a bit premature to announce any winners. We should at least wait until the clock finishes its countdown," Dr. Curie said, nodding at the clock, which indicated 2:15 remained for Jag's project.

"I see no reason to delay the inevitable," Lackey replied. "It's getting late, and we should commend all of the students for their great demonstrations . . ."

"Uh, sir," Ms. Gottschalk said.

". . . and I believe that we now have enough information to make our decisions and award our clear winner."

"Sir, one second," Ms. Gottschalk said.

"What is it?" Dr. Lackey replied impatiently.

"I found it."

"Found what?"

"Jag's rocket. I found it!"

"Where?" Dr. Reese asked, stepping closer to Gottschalk's monitor.

"Well, you're not going to believe this, but I expanded the range to use all of Earth's satellites to search for the beacon, but I couldn't find anything. Then, on a whim, I connected to one of Mar's satellites, and, well, there it is."

"There what is?" Dr. Lackey asked, his irritation growing.

"Jag's rocket. It's in Mars orbit."

"Don't be ridiculous," Dr. Lackey said. "That's impossible."

"Let me check," Dr. Reese said as Ms. Gottschalk moved over. He typed a command, bringing up radar from the Mars satellite onto the large monitor for everyone to see. Displaying in the center of the screen was a blinking dot orbiting Mars.

"Oh my gosh!" Dr. Lehman exclaimed. "The lad did it!"

"No," Dr. Lackey protested.

"Yes, he really did it!" Dr. Curie replied, holding her hand over her mouth in amazement as the rest of the judges stared at the dot on the screen.

"No, it's theoretically impossible," Dr. Lackey retorted.

"What's impossible? What did he do?" a reporter standing by Dr. Reese asked.

"Jag created a hyperdrive," Dr. Sokka exclaimed.

"*Supposedly* created," Dr. Lackey corrected. "We need to be very cautious in our determination here. We'll need to verify the data is accurate."

"Is that not the beacon flashing on the map?" Dr. Sokka asked.

"Well, I'm not sure," Dr. Lackey said. "There could be a myriad of explanations, not to mention fraud and deceit."

"Dr. Lackey, did you not install the beacon yourself?" Dr. Reese asked.

"Yes, but we will need time to verify this!"

"Can you explain what a hyperdrive is?" the reporter asked as she extended her microphone toward the judges.

"A hyperdrive is an engine that travels through hyperspace, which is another dimension that allows for faster-than-light travel," Dr. Sokka replied.

"How do I write that in a way that readers will understand?" the reporter asked.

"Tell them that what took Professor Polanski's crew one hundred and thirty-seven days to travel took Jag's rocket only five minutes, which places us at the dawn of intergalactic travel," Dr. Reese explained.

"Oh my, they'll definitely understand that," the reporter said, already scribbling.

Dr. Curie turned to Jag and began clapping. One by one all the judges and then everyone in the room gave Jag a standing ovation as camera flashes captured the moment.

"Now, Dr. Lackey, I think we are ready to determine the results of today's competition," Dr. Reese said.

The judges gathered to the side of the room and spoke softly as they discussed each student. Occasionally, Dr. Lackey could be heard voicing his objection. After several minutes, the judges returned to announce the winners.

"Congratulations to all of today's participants," Dr. Curie declared. "We are impressed with each of you and the projects you presented today. We believe that the future of space exploration is in great hands. Without further ado, the winners of the first ever Space Games are as follows. Coming in third place for his extraordinary android is Kano Tanaka. Our second-place winner, for showing incredible rocket design improvements over current designs, is Percy Blackwell, and today's first place winner for his revolutionary rocket is Joseph Gabriel."

Everyone broke out in applause, except for Percy, Edgard, and Tank.

"Today's win," Dr. Stevenson said, "places Jag securely in first place and makes him the winner of our leaderboard. If Professor Polanski would be so kind as to come forward and present the award."

Professor P helped Jag put on his flight vest, which happened to be several sizes too large, and then put his arm around Jag's shoulder. Ironically, Jag was standing and being photographed in the same location in which Percy had been interviewed only weeks prior.

As everyone celebrated, Percy slipped out of the room. Dr. Lackey followed him into the corridor.

"I'm sorry, Percy. I tried everything!" Dr. Lackey said.

"Apparently not," Percy replied. "You're fired."

"You can't fire me. I don't work for you; I work for your father."

"Then my father will fire you, which I assure you will be less enjoyable. Failure is not an option with him. He expects perfection, not excuses!"

"This is outlandish," Lackey said as he walked away from Percy.

The next day, news reports spread around the world about the mysterious rocket that reached Mars in only five minutes. From that moment on, all interview requests that normally went to Percy went to Jag. Reporters weren't the only ones vying for Jag's time. Companies were in a bidding war to win the rights to patent and produce his hyperdrive rocket. He received numerous emails containing multimillion-dollar offers.

Mr. Blackwell was outraged over Percy's defeat. His exact statement to the school was, "Blackwell Enterprises funded this entire experiment of a school, and this is how you reward me, by awarding this flawed technology first place?"

Almost overnight, Blackwell Enterprises stocks plummeted as sales in their rocket division went stagnant. Many potential customers withdrew their orders to see if hyperdrive technology would be the trend of the future. As a result, Mr. Blackwell ostracized his own son by declining his weekly calls.

CHAPTER 8
DISUNITY

Following the competition, life returned to a semblance of normality. Dr. Stevenson gathered the students into a small shuttle bay to review their final class project.

"You will be divided into three teams, and each team will select one of the shuttles standing behind you into which you will incorporate your individual projects."

The students looked at the three retired shuttlecrafts as Dr. Stevenson announced that the team captains were Jag, Percy, and Kano. On Jag's team was Ben, Mo, and Makalo. Percy's team was Edgard, Tank, and Raj. Kano's team was Mario, Nik, and Sasha.

Each team selected and named their shuttle. Jag's team liked Mo's suggestion of the *Winnebago*. Kano's team chose *Lightrider*. Percy said he didn't care what they named their heap of junk, because his father had "better shuttles in his garage than these," so they named it *Heap of Junk*. Hoping to inspire his team, Jag hung Professor P's vest inside the shuttle. While honored to have won the vest, he didn't feel he deserved all the credit he was receiving.

Several voices within the scientific community were questioning the legitimacy of Jag's experiment, and anonymous bloggers challenged whether the experiment could work with a full-sized ship. Some even suggested that Jag had cheated. Sasha and Raj suspected Dr. Lackey was behind some of the blogs, because they were written in a style that was similar to his published works.

One morning as the students dined in the cafeteria, a news program aired some pundits who argued that Jag's project was a hoax. Having had enough, Jag stormed out of the breakroom.

Ben ran after him. "Jag, wait up!"

"I can't take it anymore," Jag replied.

"Just ignore them!"

Jag whirled to face him. "Ignore them? They say I cheated! My grandparents watch that show."

"Don't worry. Your grandparents know the truth. Let's finish connecting your hyperdrive to the *Winnebago,* and then we'll silence them all."

Jag's shoulders sagged, the fire gone out of him. "I guess you're right."

Ben punched him in the arm in a friendly manner, and they headed for the lab.

From that point on, Jag and his team spent every waking moment building and connecting a larger hyperdrive to the *Winnebago.* They also attached solar panel wings for charging the drive and powering the rest of the shuttle.

That night as the boys lay in bed, they discussed each other's plans after school completed the following month. Raj had been offered an assistant professorship at a prestigious university. Sasha had applied to serve on board the *Unity.* Ben had no idea what he wanted to do, but he thought about going back to Tel Aviv or Paris. He didn't know which.

"How about you, Jag?" Raj asked. "What are your plans?"

"I don't know. Right now I'm just focusing on getting the *Winnebago* working."

"Are you kidding? You can sell your hyperdrive, buy an island, and retire," Sasha said.

"That's true," Raj agreed. "You're sitting pretty. It's the easy life for you from here on in."

"Not according to the news media. I've got a lot to prove before I can go buy my island."

After everyone fell asleep, Jag once again dreamed the vivid and terrifying nightmare that had haunted him twice before. As he tossed and turned, Ben awoke and turned on the lights.

"Hey, what's going on?" Sasha asked, squinting in the unexpected brightness.

"Jag's having another dream," Ben said.

"He's done this before?" Raj asked as they walked over to awaken Jag.

"Wait, don't touch him! The last couple of times when he was done dreaming, he sat up in bed," Ben said.

Sure enough, within a minute, Jag sat up with his eyes wide open and staring into space.

"Wow, that's freaky," Sasha said.

"Jag," Ben whispered, touching his arm. Jag startled and blinked several times. After wiping the sweat from his forehead, he turned and faced his roommates.

"What was that all about?" Sasha asked.

"It's nothing," Jag said, embarrassed by the ordeal. "Just a dream."

"Just a dream?" Raj said. "Is it the same dream or a different dream each time?"

"The same stupid dream each time."

"And this is the third time, correct?"

Jag nodded.

"Three times," Sasha mused. "That's an omen, right?"

"Can you tell us what the dream is about?" Raj asked.

"I don't know if I can. It's so intense." Jag took a deep breath. "In my dream, I'm standing on Earth looking up at the sky when I see a small cloud appear. It grows and becomes this thick, black cloud covering the planet in darkness."

Raj nodded. "Interesting."

Sasha looked at Raj. "Interesting? Sounds creepy to me."

"Then I feel a terrible sense of doom, as though something horrific is about to happen. Explosions occur above the clouds, and then a large, flaming metal object crashes into the ocean, creating a huge tidal wave that covers much of Earth. Then I'm floating all alone in space as small lights head toward me. The lights turn out to be the Sun, the Moon, and eleven stars. They revolve around me, going faster and faster until they stop and, one by one, bow before me."

"Then what?" Ben asked.

Jag shrugged. "Then I wake up."

"That's it?" Sasha asked. "What happens to Earth?"

Jag shook his head. "I don't know."

"You don't know? Maybe you should go back to sleep to see if there's more!"

"It's just a stupid dream," Jag replied.

"It means something," Sasha said. "It means we will all bow before you, and then Earth will be destroyed."

"Guys, it was just a dream. Forget I said anything and go back to sleep," Jag said as he lay back down and pulled his blanket over his head, trying to forget what had just happened.

Little did Jag know that his roommates weren't the only ones listening to his dream. Edgard had been awakened by the commotion and heard the entire conversation through the connecting vent that joined the two rooms. The next morning in the cafeteria, he was all too eager to share the revelation with Percy and Tank.

"That arrogant jerk," Percy said. "The audacity to think I'll bow before him."

"I'll never bow before him," Edgard said.

"Me neither," Tank said halfheartedly. Ever since the incident on the Moon with Ben's helmet cracking, Tank pretty much left Ben and Jag alone, feeling truly remorseful.

"Well, if he gets that hyperdrive working, we'll all be bowing to him for the rest of our lives," Percy said.

When Jag arrived for breakfast, Edgard and Percy stared at him, laughing and talking about him. After placing his breakfast on a tray, Jag walked past them toward an empty table.

"Let me get that for you, your majesty," Edgard said as he pulled out the chair for Jag. "Please, enjoy your breakfast, your grace."

"Knock it off!" Ben said.

"I suppose you overhead our conversation last night. It was just a stupid dream," Jag replied.

"Just know that I'd rather die than bow to you," Percy said. "Oh, and by the way, I've met real royalty before, and you're nothing like the real thing."

Later that evening, Jag and his team continued working inside the *Winnebago*, connecting the hyperdrive and the cryogenic chamber to the *Winnebago's* electrical system.

"I'm exhausted," Mo said. "The cryogenic chamber is finished and set to initiate when the power comes on. I'm going to bed. I'll test it tomorrow."

Makalo yawned. "I'm tired, too."

"Yeah, it's late," Ben agreed. "We can complete the rest tomorrow."

"You guys go ahead. I'm not tired yet, and I want to finish connecting the hyperdrive's remote navigation system," Jag said.

"Are you sure?" Ben asked.

"Yeah, I just want to get it done tonight so I can sleep in tomorrow."

After the others left, Jag was wiring the system that controlled the shuttle's navigation remotely when he heard a noise from the rear of the shuttle.

"I thought you guys were going to bed," Jag said, not looking up.

"Well, well. What do we have here?" Percy asked, Edgard and Tank behind him.

"Hi, Percy," Jag said. "What brings you here?"

"Oh, just came to pay my respects."

"Percy, those dreams don't mean anything."

"You're right. However, you've caused me and my dad's company a lot of problems. Seems the only thing people can talk about is your stupid hyperdrive. I think it's time you learn your place. Everything you think you've accomplished and care for will soon be undone."

Jag stared at him in disbelief. "What are you talking about?"

"The Space University and Professor P are under review by the school board. My father is pulling his funding, and the school will fail, all because of you. Unless, of course, you tell everyone you cheated. Then you can save this precious school and Professor P's career."

"I didn't cheat, and you know it," Jag said. "You're the one who cheated. You were using scientists to help you build your rocket, and your stooges tried to sabotage my launch."

Percy nodded at his companions. "Grab him." Tank reluctantly grabbed Jag's left arm. As Edgard went to grab his right arm, Jag pulled back and punched Percy in the eye.

Percy yelled in pain as he clutched his face. "I said hold him!"

Edgard grabbed Jab's right arm with both hands as Percy punched Jag in the gut, causing Jag to hunch over in pain.

"If it's the vest you want, you can have it," Jag gasped, nodding to the vest on the wall.

"I don't want a filthy vest from a washed-up, has-been astronaut," Percy said.

"So what are we going to do with him? Throw him out a space hatch?" Edgard asked.

"We could attach him to one of my rockets," Percy suggested. "That would be fun."

"Hey, how about we throw him into the cryogenic chamber?" Tank suggested, hoping to buy enough time so he could get Dr. Stevenson to calm everyone down.

Percy grinned wickedly. "Great idea. I think he needs some time to cool off."

"No, don't do this!" Jag pleaded, screaming as they pushed him into the freezer. Edgard flipped the lock as Jag pounded against the glass door.

"Now I think he's ready to learn his lesson," Percy said. "Let's see, how do I start this contraption?" He looked around for the "start" button.

"Wait," Tank said. "We aren't actually going to freeze him, are we? That could kill him."

"Why, Tank, is there a coward under all that blubber?" Percy asked, poking him in the gut.

"I thought we were just going to mess with him. I didn't sign up to kill anyone," Tank said. Then he turned and stormed out of the shuttle.

"You know, he's probably going to get Dr. Stevenson or the professor," Edgard said.

"Go after him. Tell him I was just kidding and only wanted to scare Jag," Percy ordered.

"And what are you going to do with Jag?" Edgard asked, turning to look at him.

"Let him out, of course," Percy said.

Edgard ran after Tank. However, Percy didn't let Jag out. Instead, he went to the front of the shuttle and programmed the shuttle's computer to auto launch in sixty seconds. Hurrying down the aisle, he paused at the chamber to watch as Jag pounded on the glass door.

"You know, we could have been friends," Percy said, "but you didn't know your place. I was supposed to win that competition. I would have made my dad proud, but you took that from me, and now I'm going to take everything from you."

As Percy turned, his eye caught the vest on the wall. "Guess you won't need this where you're going." He grabbed the vest, but it didn't budge due to the clips that Jag had screwed into the wall. He pulled hard with both hands, but it still didn't give. Placing a foot against the wall for leverage, he pulled with all his might. The vest ripped in two, causing him to fall backwards and hit his head against the corner of the freezer. Blood flowed from the wound. Disoriented, he stumbled out of the shuttle and fell to the bay floor just as the shuttle's door closed and its thrusters ignited, maneuvering the shuttle toward the large docking bay door.

An alarm went off as the shuttle reached the bay doors, and they opened automatically, allowing the shuttle to enter an exterior chamber that separated the bay from outer space. Once the doors closed behind it, the outer doors opened, and the shuttle maneuvered into space for its countdown. At that moment, Tank and Edgard returned with Dr. Stevenson.

"What's going on?" Dr. Stevenson demanded when she saw Percy bleeding.

"It's Jag!" Percy said, putting a hand to his wound. "He's gone crazy! I tried to stop him, but . . ." He held up his hand, revealing fresh blood.

"What happened to your head?" Tank asked.

"Jag hit me when I let him out of the freezer," Percy said. "Then he said something about proving me wrong. I tried to stop him. It's all my fault. I'm so sorry, Dr. Stevenson."

"There will be plenty of time to sort this out later, but first we need to stop that shuttle. I need to contact Mission Control," Dr. Stevenson said.

Mission Control was in full emergency mode when Professor P and the rest of the class entered.

"What's the situation?" Professor P asked.

"We have an unauthorized launch by one of your students," Director Reese replied.

"Who's on board?" Professor P asked as he scanned the students' faces to see who was missing.

"It's Jag. He initiated the launch sequence and is testing his rocket," Percy replied.

"What?" Ben exclaimed. "He would never do that!"

"It's true," Edgard replied. "He punched Percy in the face and said he was going to prove to the world that his hyperdrive works."

Everyone turned to look at Percy's face.

"That's preposterous!" Sasha said. "He would never do such a thing!"

"Can another shuttle intercept?" Professor P asked.

"We already have the *Pytheas* en route," Dr. Reese replied.

"Has there been any communication with him?" Professor P inquired.

"We've paged him many times with no response. Perhaps he will respond to you," Ms. Gottschalk said.

"Jag, this is the professor. Son, you need to turn your ship around and return. I believe your rocket will work. You don't have to prove anything to anyone."

After a moment, Ms. Gottschalk shook her head. "No response, sir."

"Can we initiate the remote-control navigation to bring him back?" Professor P asked.

"We've already tried," Dr. Reese said. "It's not accessible."

"It wasn't connected yet," Ben informed them. "Jag was wiring it when I left to go to bed."

At that moment, the solar wings on the *Winnebago* expanded to charge its batteries.

"How long will it take to charge?" Dr. Reese asked.

"About five to eight minutes," Ben said. "How long until the *Pytheas* arrives?"

"Probably after that," Dr. Reese mumbled.

Ben ran over to the microphone and pressed the talk button. "Jag, come back! Don't do this! Please, come back!"

As soon as the batteries were charged, the *Winnebago's* wings folded back, and the shuttle began moving, slowly at first, and then picking up speed. Just like before, a blue glowing force field appeared. Once it surrounded the *Winnebago*, it was gone.

"Can you track it?" Professor P asked.

"No, sir," Ms. Gottschalk replied. "There's nothing to track. It's just . . . gone."

"Send out all the shuttles to track along its trajectory," Professor P said. Then he turned to the other students. "What happened!"

"It was Jag. He was out of control!" Edgard said.

"That's not true!" Ben replied.

"We were arguing, and I said his rocket could never actually fly," Percy said. "He said he would prove it to everyone. I tried to stop him by grabbing his vest, but it ripped. That's when he punched me. I'm so sorry." Percy held up a fragment from the vest. Professor P took it and held it to his chest.

"Alright, you should have the nurse look at that cut. You may have a concussion," Dr. Stevenson said.

All night long, every available shuttle searched for the *Winnebago* as Professor P and the class kept vigil. After hours of searching, the shuttles were ordered back to the station.

"Professor, unless Jag turns the shuttle around, he is most likely out of reach," Dr. Reese said.

"I know," Professor P replied. He clutched the fragment of the vest as he told the students that their only hope was for Jag to turn the shuttle around. Then he turned to Dr. Stevenson. "Emily, please prepare a shuttle for me to visit Mr. and Mrs. Gabriel to report the news."

"Right away, sir," Dr. Stevenson said. Some of the students were already sobbing.

"Sir, would it be alright if I accompanied you?" Ben asked.

"I think that would be very nice," Professor P replied.

CHAPTER 9
DARKNESS COMES

Space, infinitely dark, silence filling the vast void, allowing nothing to escape its cold, lifeless abyss. But there, in the depths of the darkness, a lonely vessel dared to traverse. Traveling beyond the speed of light, a small shuttle dropped out of hyperspace long enough to recharge its batteries, its unwilling occupant frozen in time and thought. Unaware of the future ahead, indeed, seemingly without a future or a hope, it journeyed aimlessly through space, moving farther and farther from Earth.

In the vacuum of space, time was meaningless as minutes turned into weeks and weeks into years. All would have been lost, had it not been for a fortuitous event directed perhaps by an unseen hand that changed the course of the tiny ship and its occupant, and perhaps humanity itself, forever.

While recharging its batteries, the shuttle was intercepted by a large and foreboding ship. It cast an ominous shadow upon the *Winnebago* as it unleashed a claw that pulled the shuttle into its iron belly. Strangers boarded the defenseless shuttle, searching, scanning, and scavenging, finding nothing of value except the small, frozen occupant locked inside his frigid coffin.

CHAPTER 10
SPACE PIRATES

Jag's lifeless body lay on a cold metal table in a dimly lit room on an alien ship. A stranger in white clothing approached and began prodding, exploring, and examining him. Tools and equipment surrounded the table. Lights blinked, machines beeped, and a monitor showed X-ray scans of Jag's body. The stranger left the room, returning every so often to check on his subject. After hours without any response, he noticed a twitch in Jag's index finger.

"*Usk Vignorgan Mit Nogginsnicker,*" the stranger said with a baffled expression.

As he lay thawing on the table, Jag heard a thud, which was followed by an enormous pain in his ear.

"Well, hello, my friend, you have been on a long journey," the stranger said. "Seems you've been in stasis for a long time. Your body is slowly beginning to awaken. Rest now. I will check on you again soon."

Hours passed before the stranger returned and examined Jag again. "Your body temperature is rising. It is good that we found you, or you may have spent eternity in that primitive ship. You are most peculiar. What type of species are you, and why were you in that contraption? Rest now, for there will be many questions when you awaken. Hopefully, there won't be any side effects or mental defects from being in stasis for so long."

Eventually, the color returned to Jag's face. He grimaced and slowly lifted his hand and grabbed at his ear.

"Oh, I do apologize for that," the stranger said. "The discomfort you feel in your ear is my fault. These dreaded outdated cortex translators sometimes get stuck in the ear canal, and we have to give them a little tap to dislodge them."

"Where am I?" Jag croaked.

"You are on board the *Killclaw*, a Thorg pirate ship."

"Why can't I see?"

"The effects of stasis are still wearing off. Your eyesight will probably be the last sense to be restored, if it is restored at all."

"Why can't I move my legs?"

"You are strapped down until we can determine if you are a threat."

"How did I get here?"

"We were hoping you could tell us that. But first, what's your name?"

"My name is . . . I can't remember."

"Don't worry. Your memory will most likely return eventually. Hopefully, you will prove to be of some use to the Thorgs or this, my friend, will be a very short trip for you."

"I can see something, a dim, blurred light," Jag said. He blinked several times and squinted.

"Good, your eyesight is returning. That is a good sign."

Just then, the door opened, and in walked an enormous alien. "Dr. Neebo, how's our captive? Has he said anything about his ship, where he was headed, or where he came from?"

"Not yet. Not all his functions have fully returned," Dr. Neebo said as he checked the monitors. "He truly is a peculiar being; I've never seen this species before."

"Remember, he is not a science specimen, doctor. You'll need to determine quickly if he has any use to us. If not, Rahuke says to discard him and not to waste any more resources."

"I won't have an answer for several more days," Dr. Neebo said.

"You have until tomorrow," the alien said as he left the room.

Jag struggled to listen to their conversation but found he couldn't stay awake any longer.

Hours later, he awoke to find that his eyesight had been restored and that he was constrained to a large metal table in a medical facility. Then he saw what he thought was a tall man headed toward him. However, the creature was not human. His eyes were larger than a human's, and his eyebrows were angled upwards from the center of his face. He had a multicolored beard and fair skin. Jag blinked several times, thinking his eyesight was playing tricks on him. As the man approached with a metal object in one of its hands, Jag pulled back.

"Good! Your eyesight has returned," Dr. Neebo said. "Don't be alarmed. I am Dr. Neebo, and I am Auloran. Based on your reaction, I must look as strange to you as you do to me. Now then, do you recall your name?"

"I . . . I'm Jag," he said, relieved at being able to remember it.

"Excellent. Can you tell me where you're from and where you were headed?"

"The last thing I remember, I was working on the shuttle," Jag said. Then a wave of memories flooded his mind, and he remembered his fight with Percy. Overcome with anger, Jag tried to sit up, but he was still restrained. "I must get back on my shuttle and return home, to Earth!"

"Home?" Dr. Neebo said. "I'm afraid you don't understand the predicament you're in. You, my friend, are on a pirate ship and are now the property of the Thorgs."

"I'm nobody's property! I'm a student training to explore space."

"Well, then, consider your training complete!" Dr. Neebo said sarcastically. "However, you must realize that you are now the property of the Thorgs, who found you. If you wish to stay alive, you best prove yourself useful. Otherwise, once they no longer have a need for you, they will jettison you into space or, worse, feed you to their pets."

"This whole thing is a misunderstanding," Jag pleaded. "Surely I can speak to their captain, and he will understand."

"The *Killclaw* has no captain. It only has a master Thorg named Rahuke, who you'd do well to steer clear of. Now, let's get you stood up."

Dr. Neebo unfastened the straps and assisted Jag as he sat up. Just then, the medical facility's door opened, and in walked a large and terrifying creature. He wore a dingy, loose-fitting spacesuit and was well over seven feet tall with grey, slimy skin. He reeked of a pungent odor, and beads of sweat dripped down his scalp.

"Good, he's awake," the Thorg said. "Rahuke wants to see him."

"Good morning to you, too, Maruke. By the way, this is Jag, and he says he's from a planet called 'Hurth'."

"Earth," Jag corrected.

Maruke raised a large device resembling a cattle prod and sent a shock through Jag's body that knocked him to the floor.

"Don't speak unless spoken to, Mut-yut!"

"He will be of no service to Rahuke if you damage him. He needs to rest," Dr. Neebo said.

"He has one night, and then we will determine if he is of use," Maruke replied as he left the room. Dr. Neebo assisted Jag back onto the table.

"If you wish to stay alive, you will need to learn quickly to keep your head down, do what you're told, and speak only when spoken to. Here now, eat this. It will help restore your strength; you're going to need it."

He handed Jag a bowl of what looked like grey, lumpy Cream of Wheat. It tasted as bad as it smelled, and Jag struggled to swallow the foul substance.

"You best get used to it. It's all you'll eat on this ship. It has all the proteins and nutrition that your body needs. It may not taste like what you are used to, but it will keep you alive."

Maruke returned the next day and ordered Jag to come with him. Jag staggered behind him, using the walls to balance himself. Everything was still a haze, and his body hadn't fully recovered.

They entered the bridge, where several Thorgs were monitoring and navigating the ship. In the center stood an enormous Thorg. Seated at his feet were three large, fierce-looking wolf-like creatures that glared at Jag with dark, piercing eyes. Their thick, coarse hair stood up straight on their back as they lunged at Jag, restrained by heavy chains.

"This is Rahuke, the master of this ship," Maruke said.

"Dr. Neebo says you may be of use on board my ship," Rahuke said, turning to Jag. "If so, I'll let you live."

He reached into a metal cage and threw a squealing rodent onto the floor. The wolf creatures fought over it, and then the female growled and snapped at the two smaller males, who cowered and released it to her. She devoured the poor creature with one bite.

Rahuke smiled at the look of disgust on Jag's face. Then he raised his right hand up high. "Thorgs." He lowered his hand a couple of feet. "My wolves." Finally, he moved his hand even lower and looked at Jag. "Mut-yut."

Jag understood that his place on the ship was below the wolves. Later, he discovered that Mut-yut was their word for wolf feces.

After Rahuke dismissed him, Maruke led Jag from the bridge down a maze of dimly lit corridors that were filthy compared to the pristine *Unity*. The *Killclaw* was a disorganized hodgepodge of winding, twisting hallways with seemingly little intelligent design in the structure. As they neared their destination, Jag got a whiff of the foulest stench he had ever smelled. Upon opening the door, he saw the source of the odor: a garbage room with mounds of waste in large metal containers.

"Strip off your clothes," Maruke said as he led Jag to one of the external vents.

"What?" Jag asked. In response, he received another shock from Maruke's prod.

After picking himself off the floor, Jag stripped down. Maruke placed a metal cuff around his ankle attached to a long cord. He also gave Jag an oxygen mask that was too large for his face, but nevertheless oxygen flowed. He also handed Jag a long-handled scraper, and then Maruke opened the door leading to the large pipe.

"Scrape!" Maruke demanded. "It's clogged."

"You want *me* to go into *that*?" Jag asked. Maruke lowered the prod again, but Jag ducked out of the way. "Okay, okay, I'm going."

"Knock on the door when you're finished," Maruke said. "And you're not finished until you've scraped the entire pipe."

Jag climbed into the foul pipe, and Maruke secured the door behind him. The light on Jag's facemask emitted just enough light for him to see. As Jag began scraping the top of the pipe, a pile of filth fell onto him. The stench was so offensive that he had to remove his helmet as he vomited what little breakfast he had eaten that morning.

As he got tangled in the cord strapped to a cuff on his leg yet again, Jag wondered what purpose it served. However, just as he asked himself that question, the pipe slanted downwards, and, losing his footing, he slid through the thick filth that covered his body. As he slid, he headed straight toward the sharp point of a large metal auger used to push the waste through the pipes. Just as he was about to hit the tip, the cord attached to his leg drew tight, yanking his body with such a tremendous jerk that it caused his mask to fly off. Jag scrambled to find the mask and put it back on. He took several deep breaths as his heart nearly pounded out of his chest.

Then Jag saw the cause of the blockage: a metal object was stuck between the auger and the side of the pipe, preventing the auger from spinning. Jag stood and, using his scraper, struck the object several times until it broke free. The auger began spinning and crushed the object, pulling it and waste through the pipe. Had it not been for the cord, Jag would have also been crushed and pushed through the pipe. It took several attempts before he managed to pull himself back up the slanted pipe, his hands slippery from the filth.

After finishing, Jag knocked many times before Maruke opened the door. As he stepped out of the pipe, covered from head to toe in filth, Maruke belted out a hearty laugh. Then he took a hose and blasted Jag with ice-cold water. There was no soap, only the water to wash off the filth. In fact, in all his days on board the *Killclaw*, Jag never saw any soap except for what Dr. Neebo used to clean his hands.

Shivering, Jag put his clothes back on and followed Maruke from the garbage room down several corridors to the far side. They entered a section of the ship that was structurally quite different. The walls, floor, and ceiling were unlike the rest of the ship. It looked as if they had spliced two ships together to form one massive ship.

Doors lined both sides of the dark hallway. The only light came from Maruke's spacesuit. Maruke motioned toward the rooms. "Welcome to your home. All the rooms are empty here, Mut-yut. So feel free to take whichever one you'd like."

Jag stepped toward one of the rooms in the middle of the hallway, expecting the door to open automatically, but nothing happened. Maruke grabbed the door and slid it open. There was no light in the room except for what little starlight shone through a window. In fact, all the electrical systems in the room appeared to be offline, including, most importantly, the heater. Jag shivered.

"I'll be back for you in the morning, Mut-yut," Maruke said as he closed the door. Jag strained to look around the room and made out an outline of a bed and a desk. He walked over to the window and saw that the *Killclaw* was indeed a hodgepodge of different vessels attached to each another without any apparent rhyme or reason.

Jag felt his way over to the small bed. It had a thin, hard mattress, barely thicker than a pancake. The bed was so small that Jag wondered what type of creature it had been designed for, obviously not a Thorg. He lay down on the blanket-less bed, the stench still lingering on his skin. His atrophied muscles were sore from scraping the pipe. The room was so cold that, as he exhaled, he saw his breath. Jag looked out the window and stared at the stars. None of the constellations were familiar to him.

Jag's thoughts ran to his grandparents. Oh, how he wished he were in his bed back home listening to his grandmother preparing breakfast. He recalled how tightly she had held him at Christmas as she said, "I am so proud of the young man you are becoming. I couldn't love you any more than if you were my own son."

Tears flowed down his cold cheeks. "Grandma and Grandpa, I miss you both so much," he whispered. "Pray that I might find my way home."

All night long, Jag tossed and turned, trying to get warm. He pulled his knees up to his chest and placed his arms inside his shirtsleeves, but it was not enough to counter the bitter cold. Each time he fell asleep, he awoke minutes later due to his aching muscles or the freezing cold. After several hours, Jag couldn't take it any longer, so he went to the door and forced it open. It was dark in the hallway, and he had to feel his way along the wall to the large doors that led into the ship's main compartment. The doors opened automatically, and lights illuminated his path as he retraced his way back to Dr. Neebo's medical facilities.

As he turned down one of the corridors, he ran into the two male wolves, which were out roaming the halls. Seeing him, the hair on their backs shot straight up as they crouched in an attack stance, growling as saliva dripped from their mouths. Jag backed up slowly, careful not to make any sudden or threatening movements. The wolves matched him step for step. Then Jag turned and ran as fast as he could while the wolves closed in, nipping at his heels. As he made yet another turn, he came face-to-face with the larger female wolf.

Trapped, Jag stood frozen in fear as the wolves closed in, growling. Out of the corner of his eye, Jag saw a metal ladder about six feet up from the ground that led to a hatch in the ceiling. Jag leaped toward the ladder, grabbed its lowest rung, and pulled himself up just as the female wolf lunged and grabbed his foot, biting through his shoe. Jag screamed, and with his free foot, kicked the wolf repeatedly in the face until she released him. Pain shot through his foot, and his shoe filled with blood.

Adrenaline pumping, Jag pulled himself up to the top rung, where he tried to open the hatch, but it wouldn't budge. As he hung from the ladder, the wolves took turns leaping for him. He wrapped his arms and legs around the ladder's rungs, interlacing them so he couldn't fall. He hoped the wolves would become bored eventually and give up, but instead they lay down, evidently waiting for him to come down. Any movement he made, they perked up and began growling again.

After several hours, Jag heard someone approaching. It was Maruke. He laughed when he saw Jag up the ladder. He ordered the wolves to leave, but they ignored him. They obeyed only Rahuke. One of the males growled at Maruke, who zapped it with his prod, sending the wolf yelping down the hallway. The other two wolves tucked tail and ran off.

"You can come down now, Mut-yut," Maruke said. "You should never roam the ship on your own, especially when Rahuke's pets are on the prowl."

Jag followed closely behind Maruke, limping as he walked, his blood-soaked shoe leaving a trail of red footprints behind him. As he entered the medical facility, Dr. Neebo was elated to see him.

"You survived!" the doctor said as he looked down at Jag's injured foot. "Well, most of you." He helped Jag over to the table and then turned his head as he got a whiff of Jag. "No need to ask what the Thorgs had you doing yesterday. I can smell it!" He helped Jag up onto the table and gently removed his shoe, which had impressions from the wolves' teeth embedded in it.

"Those confounded wolves!" Dr. Neebo said as he sterilized and bandaged the wound. Then he gave Jag a shot. "This will protect you against the bite."

"Why are they even on the ship?" Jag asked.

"They're used to keep the rodent population under control from the freight the Thorgs confiscate. Plus, we get the occasional stowaway, and the wolves seem to find them pretty quickly."

"Stowaways?" Jag asked. "What would possess someone to stow away on this ship?"

"Believe it or not, there are things worse than a Thorg ship."

"Where do the Thorgs come from?"

"From Krygos, a distant, dying planet long depleted of any natural resources. As their population dwindles, they seek only one thing: credits."

Jag frowned. "Credits?"

"Money, currency, wages. You do have that where you come from, don't you?'

"Yeah, we do, and a lot of humans are just as consumed by that as well," Jag said as he thought of Percy and his father. "Do the Thorgs have families?"

"Of course, if they live long enough, that is. Each Thorg must prove himself and earn his wealth before he can settle down. Most of them live a life of piracy and thievery. Once they amass enough wealth, they head home, take up several wives, and have lots of children, who grow up and replace them on board the family ship."

"Family ship? You mean these guys are related?" Jag asked.

Dr. Neebo nodded. "Yep. You already met brothers Rahuke and Maruke Binok. They have a baby brother on board as well." He chuckled. "Kavin isn't quite so little anymore. You may not have met him yet. He works down in the parts bay."

"No, I don't believe I have."

"Oh, you would know if you met Kavin; there's no way to miss him. Here, try to put your shoe back on over the bandage now," Dr. Neebo said as he handed Jag's bloody shoe back to him. Jag winced as he pulled it back on.

"Then there are the cousins, Lamka, Kuirk, Taruke, and Mikelle. They work in the bridge and in the bay area. Except for Mikelle. He works with Uncle Lorka in the engine room. Uncle Lorka is the elder of the group and actually retired several years ago. However, he had a falling out with the family, so he was exiled back to pirating."

"If he's the elder, why isn't he in charge?"

"The master of the ship is determined by family members back on Krygos, and the pick usually goes to whoever they think can make the most credits for the family."

"Are there any other slaves like us on board?"

"Like us?" Dr. Neebo asked, a look of confusion on his face as he handed Jag his morning sludge for breakfast. "You're the only slave on board."

"You mean you're not a slave, too?"

"Oh, heavens no. I get paid for my services, and rather nicely, I must confess."

Jag raised his eyebrows. "You do this for money?"

"I'll collect a cut of everything they sell. All I have to do is keep them healthy so they can retire when their service is over."

"Oh," Jag said, disappointed at the doctor's lack of integrity.

"Truth is, the Thorgs don't take slaves as often as people think. Not enough crew to secure them or food to feed them. Plus, it's too risky, because it's outlawed in most places now."

"So why did they keep me?" Jag asked.

"Well, you were so small they figured you couldn't eat much. Plus, if you cause any problems, they'll just jettison you out the garbage port."

"So that's why they had me cleaning it," Jag said.

Just then, the doors to the medical facility opened. "How's the foot?" Maruke asked as he entered.

"He'll live, but he's lucky he has a good doctor available to patch him up."

Maruke smirked. "Let's go, Mut-yut. You'll be cleaning the kitchen today."

The kitchen looked as though it had never been cleaned. It was filled with piles of leftover food and dirty dishes. After Jag spent all day scrubbing, Maruke led him to an adjacent food storage room. As soon as Maruke turned on the lights, rodents scurried from the food containers to holes in the walls that led to other rooms on the ship. Scattered around the floor were large metal traps. However, the traps filled quickly, and cleaning the traps became one of Jag's many daily duties. He dumped the rodent carcasses into a barrel for the wolves' daily feedings.

After working all day, Jag returned to his cold room, where he tossed and turned once again while trying to fall to sleep. Just as he finally dozed off, he awoke to the sound of the wolves scratching at his door. He heard them breathing as their noses pressed against the gap beneath the door, smelling him. With nothing to protect himself if they got in, he sat up in bed with his back against wall and his eyes on the door, trembling with terror. After a while, the wolves gave up and moved on.

When Maruke arrived later that morning and slid the door open, he found Jag asleep sitting up against corner of the wall. Startled, Jag jumped as Maruke entered. "Let's go, Mut-yut," Maruke said.

He led Jag to the engine room. Six large, powerful engines standing nearly five stories tall pumped out thick smoke, which filled the room. Like everything else aboard the *Killclaw*, the engine room was poorly kept. Everything was covered in a black layer of grease and grime. However, out of all the places he had worked on the ship, Jag preferred the engine room, because at least it was warm. The rest of the ship had little to no heat, because, as Dr. Neebo explained, the Thorgs overheated easily. Their bulky bodies didn't regulate temperature well, so, they wore their spacesuits at all times just to stay cool.

In the engine room, Mikelle and Uncle Lorka pretty much left Jag alone as he cleaned. Uncle Lorka spent most of his time asleep on a cot. Whenever an engine acted up, he grabbed a sledgehammer and pounded on the wall of the engine and yelled until it relented. The many dimples in the engine walls served as historic markers of his methods.

One night Jag determined that he couldn't take the cold or the nightly sounds of wolves scratching at his door any longer, so he snuck through the hallways, keeping an eye out for the wolves. He made his way into the engine room, where he slipped past Uncle Lorka, who was snoring, and climbed the ladder on the side of one of the engines. When he reached the walkway at the top, he laid down beneath an exhaust pipe, even as smoke poured from its many leaks. Lying down on his stomach, Jag stuck his head through a metal railing so he could breathe the fresher air from below as the warm exhaust poured over his back. Warm and away from the wolves, he closed his eyes and quickly fell asleep.

The next morning, Jag awoke as Mikelle arrived to replace Uncle Lorka. Jag's hair stood straight up from the exhaust fumes that had poured through his hair as he lay with his head dangling between the rails. He didn't know which would kill him first: the cold, the wolves, the dangerous work, or the fumes.

As he descended the ladder, something caught his eye. It was a tool that one of the Thorgs had dropped from the walkway. He grabbed it and, after wiping it off, saw that it was an assortment of different tools all in one: screwdrivers, plyers, a pronged device, probably for testing electrical current, and a flashlight. Jag snuck the tool into his pant pocket and made his way to the medical bay for his morning sludge.

That night after Jag returned to his room, he removed the tool and turned on the flashlight. He shone it around the room and saw an electrical panel on the wall. Using one of the screwdrivers, he removed the screws and then the panel. He placed the pronged end of the tool against various wires inside, but nothing happened. Jag reasoned it could mean one of two things: either no electricity was coming into the room, or the tool was broken, which was why the Thorg had not retrieved it. However, knowing what he knew of the Thorgs, it was a safe bet the Thorg had just been too lazy to retrieve the dropped tool.

Jag opened the door from his room and shone the light down the hallway, checking for wolves. Then he crept down the hallway to a panel at the entrance of the wing. He opened the panel and touched the pronged device to various wires, and the tool lit up.

"So power is flowing into this wing," Jag said. He saw that one of the computer boards had scorch marks all over it and figured it was probably fried. Jag spent the better part of an hour walking from room to room in the wing until he found a similar computer board in an unused room. As soon as he replaced the computer board, the lights on the hallway came on.

He returned to his room. As he approached his door, it slid open, and his room's light came on. Normally, automatic doors would be a convenience, but not with a pack of ravenous alien wolves scavenging throughout the ship. Jag examined the door and found a button that he guessed was for locking the door. After enabling the button, he tested the door several times by waving his hand over a sensor. The door didn't budge.

Jag went to the electric panel in his room. Along the top were buttons with what looked like hieroglyphics imprinted on them. Jag made an educated guess and, after selecting an icon, warmth radiated up from the room's floor. Jag was relieved that he would be able to spend the night in warmth without the fumes from the engines.

Hours later, he awoke once again to the sounds of the wolves growling and scratching at his door. Immediately, fear gripped him as he imagined the door opening automatically, even though he knew it was locked.

"One problem down, one to go," Jag said as the wolves gave up.

CHAPTER 11
FLOATING WOLVES

With nightly threats from the wolves, Jag was determined to do something about them. He roamed through the wing looking for something with which to defend himself. At the end of hall were two large doors with an illegible sign posted above. The doors didn't open as he approached, so he forced them open and shone his light around the large dark room. As soon as he stepped into the room, he felt the gravity change and his forward momentum propel him toward the ceiling. He flailed his arms and legs trying to grab the door. However, it was too late, as he was already floating toward the center of the room.

Jag, you fool, he thought. He had walked into a large room in which the gravity had not been enabled. Shining his light around the room, he saw that it was a cafeteria with tables and chairs attached to the floor. Debris floated around, and lights hung evenly spaced from the ceiling. As Jag floated near one of the lights, he grabbed it. Pulling himself to the ceiling, he "walked" hand over hand toward the wall. When he reached the wall, he grabbed different objects and maneuvered himself down to the floor.

Jag made his way to a large electrical panel near the entrance. After making a few tweaks, the room's power and gravity was restored. Debris that was floating around the room fell to the floor with a thud. The Thorgs had ransacked the room and extracted anything of value. However, they had left large gaps in the walls, exposing pipes and wires. Jag removed several pieces of pipe that he could use to defend himself.

Jag realized how fortunate he was that he had been moving fast enough when he had entered the room or else he could have remained floating in the center of the room for days. Then a mischievous thought entered his mind, followed by a large grin. It might work, or it might just get him killed. Either way, his problem will be solved.

Jag collected long strands of wire that he twisted into a rope. He tied one end to the sign above the doors going into the cafeteria and then tied a small pipe to the bottom so that it dangled halfway down the door. Next, he disabled the gravity field, the lights, and the automated doors. Then he stood behind the doors and waited for the wolves to return.

Like clockwork, the wolves came sniffing at his bedroom door. However, because Jag hadn't locked the door, it opened automatically, and they entered his room. After several minutes, they exited, the two males wrestling with his mattress, as they could smell Jag on it. They tugged back and forth, fighting over their prize. As they moved toward the doors at the far end of the hallway, Jag pushed the cafeteria doors apart as wide as he could, stepped into the hallway, and then whistled to get their attention. Seeing him, the wolves dropped the mattress and darted toward him.

Jag raced toward the open door and grabbed the dangling pipe. With the gravity disabled, his momentum propelled him into the room. Once the rope drew tight, it pulled him upwards over the door and back toward the wall as the three wolves leaped into the cafeteria. They floated past Jag, kicking and twisting their bodies as they tried to reach him, but it was too late. Their momentum launched them into the weightless cafeteria. Jag pulled himself down, closed the doors, and looked through the window to see the wolves running as fast as they could in midair but going nowhere.

Jag walked down the hall bursting with satisfaction. After finding a replacement mattress, he had his best sleep since arriving on the *Killclaw*. The next morning, before Maruke arrived, Jag checked on the wolves. The female wolf saw Jag through the window and growled at him, baring her fangs. Each morning and night, Jag checked on the wolves and saw them floating around the room.

One morning when Jag was finishing his daily sludge, Maruke came by and asked him and Dr. Neebo if they had seen the wolves.

"No, not recently," Dr. Neebo said.

"I haven't seen them in the hallways," Jag said, struggling to hold back a grin.

Later that day, Jag initiated phase two of his plan. As he was cleaning the rodent traps, he took three dead rodents from the barrel. When he verified that the wolves were still floating, he entered the cafeteria and re-engaged the gravity. The wolves fell, and as soon as they hit the floor, they turned and started toward Jag, growling.

"No!" Jag shouted as he raised his hand. Then he disengaged the gravity, which sent them floating again. He repeated the process several times, each time raising his hand and saying "No." Afterwards, he left the gravity disengaged and then threw each of the wolves a dead rodent, which floated toward them. Every day he repeated the exercise until they stopped growling and darting at him when he engaged the gravity.

About a week later, as Jag was working in the engine room, Maruke arrived, followed by Rahuke and his three wolves. The wolves stood quietly at Rahuke's side.

"Guess who I found this morning locked in your wing?" Rahuke asked.

"Who?" Jag asked as innocently as he could muster.

"My wolves. They were trapped in the cafeteria near your room."

"Oh, are they alright?" Jag asked, acting surprised. "They do look a bit thinner."

"I don't suppose you know anything about how they got in there?" Rahuke asked. "I also noticed that your room has heat and light. What else can you fix?"

"Just about anything, if I have the right tools and parts," Jag replied.

Rahuke turned to his brother. "Hmm . . . seems our Mut-yut has some smarts. Take him to Kavin and see if he can be useful as a maker." A "maker" was the Thorg term for any type of engineer.

"Follow me," Maruke said. As Jag walked by, one of the male wolves growled.

"No," Jag said softly as he lifted his hand. The wolf cowered, and all three wolves sat down. Rahuke stared at Jag as he left the room, pondering what he had just witnessed.

The storage bay was filled with mountains of parts they had acquired over the years. It was the largest and most chaotic bay Jag had ever seen. Mound after mound of parts lying on top of each other, reaching up to a ceiling that was nearly one hundred feet tall. They maneuvered through the meandering paths around piles of miscellaneous parts until they reached the center of the bay, where several tables were aligned with various tools for repairing parts.

"Kavin!" Maruke yelled as he looked around. "Where is that moron?"

Then, flying above the piles, they saw an enormously fat Thorg seated in a large rocket-propelled chair, a trail of smoke pouring out behind it. He careened through the piles, nearly hitting Maruke in the head with his foot as he landed in front of them.

"What can I do for you, brother?" Kavin asked as he arose from his chair.

Jag recalled Dr. Neebo's description of Kavin. The shortest of the Thorgs, he was nearly as wide as he was tall. When he walked toward them, his belly bounced with each step.

"Rahuke wants you to use Mut-yut to clean up, organize, and repair parts," Maruke said.

"Why?" Kavin asked. "It's organized."

Maruke shrugged. "It's Rahuke's orders, not mine."

"Boy, there sure are a lot of parts," Jag observed.

"Oh, this is just one bay," Kavin said. "We have four more, but this is the largest. We have everything from power cores and generators to tables and toilets. You name it, we got it."

"How do you keep track of it all these parts?"

Kavin tapped his head. "It's all in here. I remember where everything is."

"He likes to think he does," Maruke said.

"Well, I do. Sometimes it takes me longer to remember, but I never forget."

"Rahuke wants this organized so we can find parts quicker for customers."

"Yeah, yeah," Kavin said as Maruke left.

Kavin gave Jag a tour of the bay, floating above the path as he pointed out the various contents of each pile. Kavin moved parts throughout the bay via a remote-controlled lift that ran along tracks attached to the ceiling. Long mechanical arms with retractable hands grabbed a part and moved it. If Kavin had a system for organizing his parts, it wasn't obvious. Jag began organizing, sorting, and cataloging them. Most of the parts were junk, but the Thorgs never threw out anything in the event it might prove useful one day.

Jag helped Kavin build shelves from the metal frames of old ships to store the parts. Afterwards, Kavin had Jag catalog all the products on a tablet computer with a photo and location of each part.

After organizing and cataloging the large bay, Kavin sent Jag into one of the smaller adjacent bays. As Jag entered, something immediately caught his attention and he froze. Sitting atop a mound of junk was the *Winnebago*! Its rocket, which was probably the only thing of value to the Thorgs, had been removed, but the rest of the shuttle appeared to be intact.

Jag dashed up the pile of parts, opened the door, and entered the shuttle. Shining his flashlight around, he sighed, comforted to be in something so familiar. He saw the components that his team had had worked on as well as half of the torn vest still attached to the wall. When his flashlight landed on the cryo-chamber that had been his prison, a chill went through him.

He went to the cockpit's command console, hoping there would be enough power in the batteries so he could at least see the logs to determine how long he had been in stasis. Not knowing how long he had been frozen haunted Jag. Had it been five years? Ten? A hundred? A thousand? Not only could the *Winnebago's* logs answer that, they could also tell him how far he had traveled from Earth. However, when he pressed the power button, nothing happened. The main batteries were dead. Jag would have to get power to the ship to enable the shuttle's computer to boot up so he could view the logs.

When he exited the *Winnebago* to look for a power source, Jag was immediately grabbed by the large lift. It pulled him straight up and barreled him back toward the main bay, weaving between the piles of parts. His feet dangled as he floated over the piles, hitting several pieces. He came to an abrupt halt over a bin of nuts and bolts as Kavin flew in and hovered face to face with him.

"Caught you trying to escape!" Kavin said, furious.

"I wasn't trying to escape," Jag gasped, the lift's arm squeezing him so tightly he couldn't breathe.

"Do you know what Maruke—not to mention Rahuke—would do to me if you escaped?" Kavin asked, his chair flying back and forth in front of Jag.

"I wasn't escaping," Jag insisted. "I was just trying to see my ship's computer logs to determine how long I was in stasis. I wanted to know how long I was frozen."

"Why does that matter?"

"I want to know if my family is still alive. I don't know if I've been gone one year or a hundred years."

"Hmm . . . Why would you care about your family?"

"Unlike Thorgs, humans usually love their family and enjoy being around them."

"Love? Absurd!" Kavin said as he pressed a button, releasing Jag. He crashed into the bin fifteen feet below him.

"Ow!"

"I won't report you this time. Just don't ever visit your ship again," Kavin said.

Jag pulled himself out of the bin and returned to his room. The next day, he continued cataloging parts, but he noticed the *Winnebago* was gone.

After all the parts were organized, Kavin had Jag fabricate new parts out of existing components. Given enough time, Jag could fabricate just about any part. It was the one thing that brought enjoyment to his abysmal life on board the *Killclaw*, because it took his mind off his situation.

Rahuke grew fond of Jag's abilities, as he could charge exorbitant prices for specialized parts and repairs. In the deepest recesses of space, spare parts were hard to come by, and having a maker who could fabricate parts was a godsend. Frequently, Jag's assistance was outsourced to another ship or station. Before allowing Jag to leave the *Killclaw*, Maruke secured a shock collar around his neck. The collar was tamper proof with a built-in locator for tracking and could be activated remotely. Whenever Maruke tightened the collar, the metal prongs dug painfully into Jag's neck until he winced, at which point Maruke would guarantee that the pain from the shock would far outweigh anything Jag had felt before.

One morning as Jag was consuming his morning sludge with Dr. Neebo, the lights dimmed in the medical room, and a red light came on overhead.

Jag looked around. "What's going on?"

"Must be a Celestian ship in the area" Dr. Neebo replied.

Then the *Killclaw* powered down all systems except for life support. Jag was about to ask another question, but Dr. Neebo held his finger to his lips. "You must whisper!" he said as he looked out the window to see what was going on. "It's a Celestian battle cruiser!"

"What's that?" Jag asked, struggling to get a look at it.

"Celestia is a large federation of planets in the area. They govern most of this galaxy, and they aren't too fond of pirates."

"Can't they see us?" Jag asked.

"Oh yeah, they see us. However, the Thorgs fashion their ship to look like large, floating piles of junk, when powered down."

"That explains the random pieces of ships attached without any apparent design," Jag replied.

"Exactly," the doctor said. "You know that I'm Celestian?"

Jag looked at him in surprise. "Really? Why did you leave?"

"I grew up on the capital planet of Aulora. However, a few years ago, I got myself into a bit of legal trouble and can never go back home, or it's off to Darkside Prison for me."

"How long since you've been home?" Jag asked.

"At least a decade. But I don't have any desire to go home. My dream is to own my own piece of paradise. Just one more big score, and then I'm out of here."

"Oh," Jag said sadly. Dr. Neebo was the only person on the ship who actually cared for anyone. "I don't think I'll ever get off this ship."

"Perhaps you might once you are no longer of any use to then. Then they'll sell you or trade you to one of the colonies."

"Yeah, but how long will that take?"

Dr. Neebo shrugged. "Don't know. Perhaps never if you keep fixing everything and making them credits."

"And you, too?" Jag replied.

Dr. Neebo frowned. "What do you mean?"

"I'm making you credits, too."

The doctor chuckled nervously, realizing that although he despised slavery, he was profiting from it. "Yeah, I guess so."

One day as Jag was repairing a part in the main bay, the lights dimmed again, but instead of a red light, a green light flashed. He hurried out and ran into Maruke.

"Come with me," Maruke said.

Jag followed him to a room, where Maruke secured the shock collar around Jag's neck. Then he told Jag to put on the smallest spacesuit available, though it was still nearly two sizes too large. They entered a small circular room, where they were joined by several family members, all clad in armored suits and holding weapons. The room descended slowly down a shaft outside. That's when Jag understood how the *Killclaw* got its name. Its giant claw had captured a ship. Once the elevator reached its hull, Jag felt the jarring vibrations of metal grinding beneath his feet as a large drill cut a hole in the captured ship.

Maruke and his cousins stepped off the elevator as Rahuke followed, shouting orders. Immediately, they took fire from the captured ship's crew. However, their armored suits deflected the attacks, and within minutes, the Thorgs had disabled the ship's defenses.

"Take anything of value," Rahuke ordered as Maruke motioned for Jag to follow him into the engine room. Maruke and Mikelle removed various components with a laser cutter.

"Do you see anything of value here?" Maruke asked.

Jag stood gaping as he looked around in disbelief. They were destroying the ship and the lives of the people on board just to make a profit. The crew continued to cut out components: a converter here, a transformer there, and many computer devices. Then Maruke went to the ship's power core and began cutting it out. Jag realized it would leave the poor people without any power for life support.

"We can't take the power core. These people will die," Jag said.

"It's not my problem, Mut-yut," Maruke replied. "Now grab the end of this power core."

"I can't be a part of this!" Jag exclaimed. Immediately, a shock unlike anything he had felt before pulsated through his body. Jag fell backwards and screamed in agony.

"That was level one. Care to try level two?" Maruke asked as he released a button.

"You don't have to kill these people!" Jag gasped. "They can serve alongside me on the ship."

"We don't need them when we have you. Plus, they would only be more mouths to feed. So either grab this core, or level two it is."

"You can try level ten for all I care. I'm not going to help you kill these people!"

"Stupid Mut-yut!" was the last thing Jag heard before he passed out from pulses of electricity.

When he awoke, Mikelle was dragging him by his leg toward the elevator. Maruke had removed the power core from the captured ship. The Thorgs made several more trips back and forth to the *Killclaw* carrying loads of equipment and supplies from the lifeless vessel. As Jag entered the elevator, the Thorgs where in a celebratory mood, congratulating each other on their lucrative score.

Everyone carried the supplies to the main bay for Jag to catalog the following day. Jag picked himself off the floor and started walking down the corridor when Rahuke grabbed him by the neck and threw him up against a wall.

"I don't care how smart you think you are. If you ever disobey us again, I'll end your life. The only reason you're still alive is because I allow you to live. You hear me, Mut-yut?"

"Yes," Jag said. "Why don't you just sell me or trade me?"

"Sell you? You're too valuable to us. I will never sell you! I can make more off your services than I could ever earn from selling you," Rahuke said as he dropped

Jag to the floor. Maruke came by and removed the shock collar from Jag's neck and then led him back to his room.

That night as Jag lay in bed staring out the window, he watched the lifeless, foreign ship drifting in the distance. He cried as he thought about the lives of the crew that were senselessly killed by the Thorgs. Jag forced himself to stay awake as long as he could, staring out the window until he could no longer see the vessel as his way of honoring their lives.

"No matter what, I must get off this ship," Jag said once the vessel was out of view. He contemplated ways of escaping the *Killclaw*. However, every idea he came up with seemed doomed to fail. Trying to escape in the middle of space was futile, but he promised to seize the first opportunity that presented itself.

The next morning, Dr. Neebo applied salve to the damage on Jag's neck left by the shock collar.

"You're awfully quiet this morning," Dr. Neebo said.

"How can you do this?" Jag asked scornfully.

"Years of medical training and practice."

"No, not this," Jag replied, pushing the doctor's hand away from his neck. "How can you participate with this crew? They murdered those people last night."

Dr. Neebo thought for a moment and then shrugged. "They might have, but I didn't."

"You might not have pulled the trigger, but you might as well have. You share in the profits from everything they sell."

"If I weren't here, it would be some other poor sap patching you up—and he might not be as charming as I am."

The doctor's answer didn't sit well with Jag, but after several weeks passed, things slowly returned to normal between him and Jag. Maruke did not include Jag on any further captures, as he knew Jag would not participate, and he was too valuable to them to continue punishing him.

CHAPTER 12
FAR SIDE OUTPOST

One morning as Jag arrived at the medical facility for breakfast, he was surprised to see Dr. Neebo dressed up in the equivalent of a man's dress suit and hat.

"What's going on?" Jag inquired.

"We've docked on Far Side Miners' Outpost."

"What's Far Side, and why are you all dressed up?"

"Far Side is an asteroid belt mining colony, which we visit twice a year so we can refuel, resupply, and sell parts. As for me, I'm dressed up because of a very special little lady who absolutely adores me, the lovely Madame Loxy Lonna. She owns one of the bars."

"That sounds nice," Jag said uncertainly.

"Nice? Loxy happens to be the finest creature in the galaxy," the love-struck doctor exclaimed.

"How come there aren't any female Thorgs aboard the *Killclaw*?" Jag asked.

"Pirating is for the males. Raising children is for the female Thorgs."

"Oh," Jag said. "Have you ever seen a female Thorg? What do they look like?"

"Well, they're no Loxy Lonna, unless, of course, grey, large, smelly females covered in slime is your idea of the perfect woman."

"Uh, no thanks," Jag said with a chuckle as Rahuke entered.

"Doctor, we will be docked for thirty-six hours," Rahuke said. Then he turned and snarled at Jag. "Come with me, Mut-yut. We have a special job for you."

Jag followed Rahuke and Dr. Neebo to the dock, where the entire crew had assembled for disembarking. Before departing, Maruke secured the shock collar around Jag's neck.

"Confound it! Do you truly need that archaic contraption?" Dr. Neebo asked.

"It keeps the lad from wandering," Maruke said as he handed Jag a couple of bags that contained his spacesuit and several tools.

A Far Side security team met the *Killclaw* crew as they entered the outpost and briefed everyone on the rules of conduct.

Far Side Outpost was built on the largest asteroid in the belt. Thousands of smaller asteroids floated nearby and as far away as the eye could see in every direction. Mining crews extracted the ore and shipped it throughout the galaxy. It was a wealthy outpost, about the size of a small city on Earth, with thousands of inhabitants from planets throughout the galaxy.

As they turned down the equivalent of Main Street, aliens of all shapes, sizes, and colors strolled along the various shops. While the outpost was brighter than the *Killclaw*, it was obvious that most of the lights were turned off. Casinos greeted customers on both sides of the street as patrons gathered around various games of chance and cast strange dice on the tables or played slot machines. Many of the machines in the casino were also turned off, and the lights were dimmed.

Most of the *Killclaw* crew headed straight for the casino. The Thorgs were susceptible to get-rich-quick-schemes as a means to escape their service and retire early. Only Uncle Lorka remained on board, performing watch duty, no doubt from a horizontal position. Rahuke reminded everyone to be back on board within thirty-six hours.

As the remaining crew continued down the street, a large bouncer in front of one of the casinos threw a small, inebriated patron into the street. "Don't come back until you sober up!"

Jag and Maruke had to step over the inebriated creature.

Upon exiting the casino area, they entered the restaurant and bar district, where Jag's nose was filled with delightful smells of many different types of foods, pastries, and drinks. The smells almost overwhelmed Jag's senses, and his stomach growled.

"Do well, Mut-yut, and perhaps you'll get a treat," Rahuke said as he saw Jag eyeing the food.

Once they reached an intersection that had a large and crowded bar and was filled with loud music, Dr. Neebo stopped. "This is where I excuse myself. Enjoy yourselves, fellas."

"Thirty-six hours, doctor, and then we leave," Rahuke replied.

"Yeah, yeah," Neebo said as he entered the establishment.

"Dr. Neebo!" a female voice called out. "You should have told me you were coming!"

Rahuke, Maruke, Kavin, Jag, and the chief security officer continued on past smaller side streets with more stores and apartments above them. Down one street, Jag saw what he thought to be a travel agency. Several customers stood outside, suitcases in tow. When they came upon a parts store, Maruke and Kavin departed and, using Kavin's tablet, showed the merchant the various parts they had in stock.

Rahuke, Jag, and the security officer continued to the stately mayor's office at the end of the street. It had tall Romanesque columns. A long line of people was waiting to see the mayor. The security officer approached the attendant.

"The mayor is expecting us."

"Go right ahead," the attendant said, allowing them to proceed in front of the line.

As they entered a small courtroom filled with petitioners, a small creature in official attire spoke up in a surprisingly loud voice. "Announcing Rahuke Binok, your worship."

Behind an elevated bench sat a tall, thin, distinguished man with elongated features who was wearing a long robe. "Rahuke Binok," he said, exaggerating his K's and T's. "You're late. I was expecting you a week ago." The mayor dismissed another petitioner, who was pleading for assistance. Then he stepped down from his bench and approached Rahuke.

"Sorry, for the delay, Mayor Gloknok. It was unavoidable," Rahuke lied. Truth be told, the *Killclaw* took its sweet time arriving at the outpost, intentionally slowing down to increase demand for its services. "It is a pleasure to see you, your worship, though admittedly a bit harder to see these days." He nodded at the dim lights.

"It's this dreadful generator; it's been on the blitz. We're running on auxiliary power and have to ration electricity to each tenant. They're driving me crazy with their endless petitions for more power."

"How dreadful," Rahuke said in a tone that was as superficial as he was.

"We've done everything we can to repair the generator, and a new one won't arrive for seven months at best. I don't think I can take seven more months of this! And if our auxiliary power fails, I'm afraid we will have to abandon the outpost."

"Perhaps we can be of service," Rahuke said.

"Did you bring the maker you mentioned in your message?" Gloknok asked, looking around.

"Yes, and he's a master maker. Here he is." Rahuke stepped aside to reveal Jag, who had been standing behind him.

"Him? A master maker?" Gloknok exclaimed. "He's but a child!"

"Perhaps, but I assure you he's a genius with machines."

"Oh, please, Rahuke. I do not have time for your games."

"I'm serious."

"Away with you! You're wasting my time. Who's next on the docket?"

"The Krepshins are here to beseech your worship for additional electricity rations," the court attendant proclaimed as a young couple holding two small children rose to their feet.

"Your worship, our rooms are so cold that our children are constantly ill. We are not asking for ourselves but for their sakes," the young mother pleaded.

"Do you not have more clothing to keep them warm?" Mayor Gloknok asked.

"They already wear three layers of clothing to bed, sir," the father replied.

"Well, then, that is your problem. Let them wear four layers."

"Please, your honor," the mother said. "We desperately need—"

"Mayor, how about a wager?" Rahuke interrupted. "I bet my maker can fix this situation in twenty-four hours!"

"Twenty-four hours to fix what we've had entire crews working on for weeks?"

"Twenty-four hours!" Rahuke replied confidently. "And when we succeed, double our service fee to forty thousand credits, and give us our supplies."

"And when your maker fails to deliver in twenty-four hours, what will you give us?"

"You can double your charge for fuel and supplies. What have you to lose?"

After thinking it over for a moment, during which time the couple's baby started to cry, the mayor nodded. "Alright, he has twenty-four hours."

"Twenty-four hours from when we begin at the generator," Rahuke said. Mayor Gloknok laughed at the suggestion that a few extra minutes would make any difference, but he nodded nevertheless. Then he pointed toward a man wearing a bright jumpsuit and a tool belt. "This is Chief Maker Splicket. He will accompany your maker, and if his work isn't up to Mr. Splicket's standards, you lose the bet!"

"Agreed," Rahuke said, smiling as he counted the credits in his mind. Forty thousand credits was nearly equal to a year's profits. As he reached the door to exit the courtroom, Rahuke turned back. "Oh, and any parts used to fix your generator are extra."

Mayor Gloknok nodded in agreement and then focused his attention on the next petitioner.

When Rahuke and Jag reached Main Street, Maruke and Kavin rejoined them.

"That went well. We sold about a dozen parts for nine hundred credits," Maruke said. "How did you guys do?"

Rahuke relayed the deal to Maruke and Kavin, leaving out the part about doubling the reward fee to forty thousand credits. Then he turned to Maruke and Kavin. "You have twenty-four hours to fix their generator or both of you can look for a different ride home, and Mut-yut will find his head separated from the rest of his body."

"Yes, Rahuke," Maruke replied fearfully.

Kavin returned to the *Killclaw* to gather the necessary parts while Maruke and Jag joined Mr. Splicket in a tiny maintenance shuttle that resembled a pickup truck with rockets instead of wheels. It had no seats, so the three stood tethered to the dashboard by a power cord that connected their suits to the vehicle. Behind them was a cargo bed for carrying tools and parts.

As they flew to the side of the asteroid, Jag got a better view of the outpost. It stood ten stories tall and was made of metal and glass. Mr. Splicket explained that the outpost resided in a magnetic field that caused random electrical storms, which had fried the station's primary generator.

"We get so many electrical fires here that crew's nickname for the station is 'Fire Side Outpost,'" Mr. Splicket said. He went on to explain that over the years, they had repaired the generator so many times that they no longer had any spare parts and that a recent storm had destroyed the generator.

They touched down on a landing pad in front of a massive generator and disembarked from the shuttle. Carrying various tools, they hopped through the low gravity to the generator door. Each person was still tethered to the shuttle with a lifeline that provided power and oxygen. As they moved, the line released and retracted as needed.

Inside the generator, the damage was obvious: everything was charred.

"You better start looking for another way home," Jag said as he looked at the amount of work required.

"And are you going to start looking for a new head?" Maruke replied.

Jag sighed. "Good point."

He searched for an electrical diagram to aid him in deciphering the various components and their purposes, but it had been destroyed in the fire. He began scanning, measuring, and creating a list of necessary parts on a tablet that he sent back to Kavin to start gathering.

"Your time starts now," Mr. Splicket said, hitting a timer on his wrist pad.

They made several trips back and forth to the *Killclaw* to retrieve parts. Any parts that didn't exist, Jag fabricated from other parts. Afterwards, they returned to the generator, where Jag used a laser cutter about the size of a pencil to remove burnt parts. He worked all night, cutting, replacing, and repairing. When he was done, nearly every part had been replaced from the myriad of parts the *Killclaw* had captured over the years.

"It's finished," Jag said tiredly.

The three walked to the control panel, and Mr. Splicket flipped a large power button. The generator's compressor kicked on, and many parts lit up and hummed as they came to life. They watched the voltage meter on the control panel move from low to high in a matter of seconds. Mr. Splicket stepped back in amazement.

"Why, I've never!" he exclaimed. "In all my years, I have never seen anything run so well! Well done, son. Well done."

"Thank you, sir," Jag said. He pointed to several components. "These insulation regulators should prevent any future power surges from destroying the generator."

"That's fantastic," Mr. Splicket replied.

"Finished, with several hours to spare!" Maruke said, sighing with relief.

"Not yet," Mr. Splicket replied, pointing to several lights on the panel that were out, signifying that electricity was flowing once again to most but not all parts of the outpost. "The storm must have blown out three transformer fuses, and you'll have to replace the fuses before the job is complete."

"Alright, that should be easy, right?" Maruke asked enthusiastically.

"Oh, the transformers aren't here. They're embedded deep in the asteroid," Mr. Splicket said as he powered down the generator and then led Maruke and Jag back behind it. Twelve pipelines branched off the generator and ran down tunnels into the asteroid. Each line was labeled with a number. Mr. Splicket stopped at the first line that had a bad fuse.

"Here's the new fuse," he said, handing Maruke a device the size of a soda can with two prongs sticking out the top. "You'll need to go about four hundred yards down this tunnel into the asteroid to install it."

"Down that tunnel?" Maruke asked, examining it. "I don't think I'll fit!"

Mr. Splicket shrugged. "The job's not complete until everything is working. You may not be able to fit, but the lad should fit just fine. If I can fit, he can."

"He'll do it," Maruke said, handing the fuse to Jag.

"Your suit has a video cam that transmits through the lifeline," Mr. Splicket explained. "We'll be able to monitor you and guide you through what needs to be done."

Jag floated down the tunnel, pulling himself hand over hand down the pipe. When he reached an intersection, Mr. Splicket instructed him which way to go.

"The cavern should be just ahead, and then you should see the transformer," Mr. Splicket said. Within a minute, Jag reached the cavern, which was large enough for Jag to stand in. The transformer sat on the cavern floor. As Mr. Splicket walked Jag through the steps to replace the fuse, Jag grabbed the old fuse and pulled, but it didn't move.

"It won't budge."

"It'll come. Just yank as hard as you can," Mr. Splicket replied.

Jag used both hands and pulled with all his might. Finally, the transformer surrendered its hold upon the fuse as Jag fell backwards, the burnt-out fuse in his hand. After replacing it, he retraced his path to the generator. The entire trip took about an hour.

"We only have an hour and half left. You'll need to speed up," Maruke said nervously.

Jag grabbed a new fuse and pulled himself through the next tunnel as fast as he could. When he reached the transformer, he removed the old fuse. However, he noticed that a portion of the connector inside the transformer was broken. Jag knew that if he didn't fix it, the generator wouldn't provide full power to the station. At first, he recalled Dr. Neebo's statement about being overly useful and was tempted to leave the fuse box broken so Rahuke wouldn't win his bet and receive the reward for all of Jag's hard work. Then he remembered the young family shivering before the mayor and knew all too well what it was like to be cold.

"What was their name?" Jag mumbled.

"What was whose name?" Maruke asked.

"Just thinking out loud," Jag said.

"Well, stop thinking, and get back here. You have just over an hour left."

"The Krepshins," Jag said, recalling them pleading for more rations of electricity. The thought of their children freezing at night rang all too familiar. He decided that even if Rahuke profited from his hard work, he would still do the right thing for the Krepshins' sake.

"The fuse has a bad connector. I believe I can fix it. It'll take about five minutes."

"Okay, just hurry," Maruke said.

Jag quickly repaired the connector, installed the new fuse, and then returned to the generator.

"Just one more, and then we're done!" Maruke said anxiously.

"This is the last and most important fuse, because it leads to Main Street," Mr. Splicket said as he handed it to Jag.

Again, Jag hurried down the winding tunnel, which was wider than the previous two tunnels and had many more branches splitting off. As he reached one intersection, he saw a light at the end of the short tunnel with a hatch and a sign above it.

"What's down that way?" Jag asked.

"That's the backside of Far Side. The transformer should be straight ahead," Mr. Splicket said as Jag followed the pipe. Suddenly, he came to an abrupt halt.

"I can't go any farther. I don't have enough line," Jag said.

"What? Perhaps the line is caught. Give it a tug," Maruke said.

Jag tugged on the line, but there was no give. Mr. Splicket went to the shuttle and moved it as close as he could, which gave Jag about ten more yards.

"It's still not enough!" Jag said.

"Drat! I must have given him the shorter tether," Mr. Splicket said. "You'll have to return and swap with Maruke."

"We don't have enough time for him to backtrack!" Maruke said.

"He can detach from the tether," Mr. Splicket suggested. "His suit has enough power and oxygen to last an hour. However, he'll have audio only, no video."

"Yes, do that! Detach from the tether!" Maruke exclaimed. "Just remember that I can still activate the collar from here, so don't try anything."

Jag disconnected the line from his suit, and the video feed that Mr. Splicket and Maruke had been watching went black. Jag hurried to the transformer and replaced the fuse in a matter of minutes. However, as he was about to signal to Maruke that they could power up the generator, a thought entered his mind. It could be just the opportunity he needed for an escape. If he could get into the outpost, he could hide and then stow away on another ship or work on board the outpost until he raised enough money to board a ship that might take him home. Jag moved back down the pipe toward the short tunnel where he had seen the hatch.

"How are things going?" Maruke asked.

"I've reached the transformer," Jag said as he entered the small tunnel that led into the rear of the outpost. He reached the hatch with the sign that he hoped read "Entrance" or something similar. He turned the large crank, and the door creaked open.

He entered the building and closed the hatch behind him. Cautiously he removed his helmet and took a breath to make sure that there was oxygen. Then he removed his gloves and tried to examine the shock collar, but he couldn't pull the collar out far enough from his neck to get a good look. He hung his helmet on a hook on the wall. Looking at his reflection in the helmet's mask, Jag saw that the collar had one small cover with two screws. Jag pulled out several different tools, but nothing would fit the unique screw head.

"How are you doing?" Maruke asked nervously. "We only have five more minutes!"

"I'm having a difficult time removing the panel on this one," Jag said, bending over and speaking into the helmet's microphone.

"Use the laser cutter to cut it off if you must," Maruke said.

"Good idea. I'll give it a try."

Jag retrieved the laser cutter he had used to remove all the burnt components and set the cutter's depth to its lowest setting, not wanting to accidentally decapitate himself. Jag started to cut but then paused, his hands shaking due to lack of sleep and food. He took a breath and steadied himself. Then he cut out each screw. When he was finished, he pried the panel open with a screwdriver to see if there were any security measures. Sure enough, a wire was connected to the back of the panel that, if removed, would engage the collar.

Jag placed the cutter into the crack at just the right angle to cut the wires and disable the collar. He knew that one false move would either lacerate the side of his neck or cause the collar to go off. He took a deep breath. Just as he went to make the cut, Maruke's voice came over the helmet's speaker, startling him.

"We only have two minutes. What's going on?"

"The fuse is in now. Give it a try."

A moment later, all the lights came on in the hallway in which Jag was standing. He heard people cheering throughout the outpost and Maruke and Mr. Splicket shouting for joy through the helmet speakers.

Jag took a deep breath. It was now or never. He sliced through the wires, and the collar's flashing red light went dark. Jag exhaled with relief. As he positioned the cutter to remove the collar from his neck, the light started flashing rapidly. Jag realized it probably had a backup power source that would engage if the lines were severed. At that moment, paralyzing waves of electricity pulsated through his body. Convulsing, he fell to the ground, and then everything went dark.

When Jag awoke, he was strapped to the table in the medical facility on board the *Killclaw*. He had a splitting headache and enormous red wounds on his shoulders from where the collar's prongs had pressed into his skin. Jag moaned and moved as Dr. Neebo examined him. Without saying a word, the doctor prodded and tugged on Jag, foregoing his usual pleasant bedside manner.

"Your little escapade caused me to cut short my rendezvous with Loxy Lonna," Neebo said as he administered a shot. "This should help with the pain and reduce the swelling."

"Outhh!" Jag cried, his tongue swollen and throbbing in his mouth.

"You nearly bit your tongue off. Now hold still," Neebo said. "You were foolish. Had the outpost miners not reached you when they did, you would have fried."

Dr. Neebo went to exit the room and then paused. "I guess I shouldn't blame you for wanting to be free. But next time, don't do it when I'm with Loxy, and be wiser. Don't try to remove a shock collar. Those things are foolproof."

Later that day, as Jag's swelling dissipated, both Rahuke and Maruke visited the doctor to see when Jag would be available to resume his duties.

"How is our Mut-yut doing?" Rahuke inquired.

"He'll recover, but he needs his rest," Dr. Neebo said.

"Next time you won't be so lucky!" Rahuke warned.

"Lucky? I don't feel lucky. Why don't you just sell me?" Jag asked.

"Sell you?" Rahuke laughed. "You're the most profitable service we have on this ship. You're even more valuable than the good doctor. I already have other outposts and planets calling for your services. You best get used to your home."

"This will never be my home. I'll never stop trying to escape."

Rahuke leaned over and spoke into Jag's ear. "You'll never leave this ship alive until I say so. Furthermore, you aren't to step off this ship unless I accompany you myself!" Then he stepped back and glared at Maruke for failing to keep an eye on Jag when he was in the tunnels.

"I hope you choke on your forty thousand credits!" Jag said.

Maruke and Dr. Neebo both looked at Rahuke with a puzzled expression.

"Forty thousand?" Rahuke said, Maruke and Dr. Neebo eyeing him suspiciously. "It was only twenty thousand! Obviously, the boy is delirious and doesn't know what he's talking about."

CHAPTER 13
PLANET NORR

Norr was a small, sparsely populated and seemingly insignificant planet residing in the Heiger System. Its cities were of no great size, the largest being Yuba City, its capital, with merely thirty thousand inhabitants. Its primary source of income was the exceptional vineyards that produced the highest quality wines in the kingdom. The climate was dry and hot most of the year, with the exception of the annual monsoon season, which brought torrential downpours that lasted nearly a month. Norr had a small provincial government led by Pace Rannick, a retired admiral.

Every few years, the *Killclaw* circulated through distant planets along the outskirts of the kingdom, careful to avoid any run-ins with Celestian vessels. They limited their visits to Norr, because they despised the intense heat. However, backwoods farmers were easy marks, as they often didn't have any alternatives but to buy from panhandlers like the Thorgs.

Maruke and Kavin landed a shuttle near a farmer's market and erected a tent, taking care never to leave its shade. After several days of selling very little, they considered packing up and leaving when two Celestian men approached. One, an elderly man, hunched over as he walked. The other was a tall, distinguished-looking man.

"I'm looking for a water pump for a Hamlin water feeder," the older man said as he laid a broken piece of equipment on the table.

"A Hamlin water pump?" Kavin replied. "I'm not familiar with that particular item. Let me look it up." Kavin searched his tablet and found some information on the company. "Old timer, it seems that company has been out of business for over a quarter century."

"That's a doggone shame!" the old man replied. "They made the best water feeders around, and this year seems to be taking its toll on our equipment, because it's hotter than normal."

"I'll say," Kavin replied, sweat dripping from his forehead. "Let me scan this and see if I have anything like it in our inventory." He scanned the part and ran it against the database, then shook his head. "I'm sorry, but we don't have anything like that in stock."

The old man nodded. "Yeah, all the local vendors say the same thing."

"We do have a very capable master maker on board our ship who has fabricated parts for other customers. Perhaps he can be of service to you."

The old man's eyes brightened. "Do you think he can replicate this pump?"

"I've seen him replicate an entire city generator in only twenty-four hours," Kavin replied.

"It's not a problem," Maruke interjected. "However, there's a one-thousand-credit minimum purchase for his services."

The old man pursed his lips. "That's a bit high."

Maruke shrugged. "Well, it's our going rate."

The older man glanced up at the tall man, who nodded in approval.

"It's a real shame. I used to buy these parts brand new for less than fifty credits."

"That would have been a few years ago, old timer," Kavin said.

The old man chuckled. "Oh, just a few."

"We'll need 50 percent down to start work on it," Maruke said.

"You'll get 10 percent," the taller man replied as he pulled out his wallet and handed Maruke one hundred credits in paper notes.

Maruke held the notes up to the light. "Wow! I can't believe you folks still use paper money."

"It spends. You can exchange the paper for digital credits at the bank before you leave."

Kavin nodded. "It's a deal. Just leave the part, and come back tomorrow at this time."

"And be sure to bring the remaining nine hundred credits with you," Maruke added. "No credits, no part!"

As they turned to walk away, the taller man stopped. "Of course, we'll expect to see a demo of the processor to make sure it works to specifications. No demo, no credits."

Jag was working in the bay when Maruke and Kavin delivered the part that needed to be replicated. He examined the device and located several parts he would require. News reached Rahuke about the deal, and he entered the bay with his wolves in tow.

"Excellent!" Rahuke said. "It means our time on this planet hasn't been a total waste."

"It also means we can leave this godforsaken oven," replied Maruke. "Oh, and there's one more thing: They want a demonstration when it's complete."

"Kavin will demonstrate it to our customers," Rahuke said. He had kept his word never to let Jag leave the *Killclaw* unless accompanied by him, and he preferred to avoid Norr's heat.

All night long Jag worked fabricating and testing the new pump. That morning, he demonstrated to Kavin how to execute the pump's multiple cycles for pumping water to cool an engine as well as to water plants. Kavin struggled to comprehend how to connect the electrical wiring to the pumps to trigger the different cycles in the correct order.

"Is everything ready to go?" Maruke asked as he entered the room.

"Well, sort of," Kavin said. "The part is finished, and it works. However, he's demoed it to me several times and I . . ." He shrugged.

"Look, you need to figure this out, because this is going to be my last day going down to that inferno."

"We've gone through this for several hours, and it's just too complicated," Kavin said.

Just then, the door opened, and in walked Rahuke, grinning at the thought of his upcoming payday. "Are we all set?"

"We've hit a snag," Maruke said. "Genius here can't figure out how to demo this."

"It's not my fault. It's just too complex," Kavin replied.

"What do you want to do?" Maruke asked.

"Mut-yut will demo the part, and I'll go down with you," Rahuke replied. He turned to Jag. "If you try anything, I'll kill you myself. Put the collar on him, and make sure it's especially snug. Oh, and place a scarf around the collar. Slavery is outlawed here."

They arrived at the market, and after erecting their tent, Rahuke placed Jag in a small cage near the rear. Sunlight fell through a crack in the tent flaps and landed on Jag's face. He closed his eyes and allowed the sunlight to warm his skin.

"They're here," Rahuke said as he retrieved Jag several hours later. He straightened the collar and adjusted the scarf so it couldn't be seen. Then Jag walked forward and saw the two men already looking over the part he had fabricated.

"Excellent craftsmanship. It looks as good as the original," the older man said.

"Yeah, but does it work?" the taller man inquired.

Rahuke introduced himself as the master of the ship and ordered Jag to demo the part. Jag connected several wires and the intake pipe to a water tank they had brought from the *Killclaw*. When he switched on the pump, water began flowing. The two men were impressed, and the taller man withdrew nine hundred credits from his wallet. As he handed Rahuke the money, a gush of wind caused several of the bills to fall to the ground. Jag bent down to help recover them. In the process, his scarf came loose, revealing the shock collar and the scars around Jag's neck. Rahuke stood Jag up quickly and adjusted the scarf.

"Well, thank you for your business. We must be on our way now," Rahuke said.

"One second. I'd like to shake this young man's hand for his great work," the younger man said.

"I'm incredibly sorry, but we need to get him back to our ship. He's been up all night working, and he needs his rest," Rahuke replied.

"I'm sure he has, but I think he can spare a minute to shake my hand," the man persisted, his hand extended. Jag looked up at Rahuke to see what he wanted him to do. Rahuke nodded, not wanting to offend his customer. Jag reached out his hand while keeping his eyes on the ground. The man grabbed Jag's hand and pulled him close. Then he pulled the scarf off Jag's neck, revealing the collar. Jag tried to pull away from the man, but he couldn't escape his grasp.

"Take your hands off our crew member!" Rahuke yelled.

"What is this?" the man demanded. "Slavery is outlawed in the kingdom!"

"Slavery?" Rahuke asked, feigning indignation. "I'm offended by the very accusation. We rescued him in deep space, and he has become like family to us. He only wears the collar, because he has a tendency to wander off and get lost."

Jag tried to wiggle free, but the man tightened his grip on his wrist. He knew Rahuke would find some way to blame him for this incident, which would only lead to more work and punishment later. Then the man displayed a golden shield with a Celestian emblem.

"You obviously don't know who I am. I'm Admiral Rannick, Governor of Norr, appointed by King Marcellus himself. You are not leaving here with this boy." Then he held up a communicator device. "A single press of this button, and you and your crew will find yourselves in our jail on slavery charges."

"Well, admiral, it would seem we have ourselves a quandary," Rahuke said, holding up the remote control for the shock collar. "One push of this button, and the lad will find himself without a head."

"How much for the boy?" Admiral Rannick asked.

"Again, you offend me! The boy is not a slave but a valued member of my crew!"

"Fifty thousand credits," the admiral offered. Then he released Jag and took out five crisp ten-thousand-credit notes.

Rahuke's eyes widened at the sight of the money, but he remained firm. "He is not for sale."

"Seventy-five thousand credits," Rannick replied as he pulled out another twenty-five thousand credits, a total of more than two years' worth of Thorg profits.

"That's not nearly enough to reimburse us for all the expenses involved in caring for the young lad. He wasn't even alive when we found him, and my own personal doctor had to nurse him back to life, using our limited supplies.

"One hundred thousand credits," Admiral Rannick said. "That's my final offer, and then I will take the risk of forcing you."

"That's a very good offer, but it doesn't cover the loss we will incur from missed revenue from the lad's services," Rahuke said as two security officers approached.

"Governor, is everything alright, sir?" one of the officers asked.

"Everything is just fine," Rahuke said as he leaned over and grabbed the credits from the admiral. "We just finished negotiations and have come to a mutual understanding."

Admiral Rannick nodded. "Our guests will be leaving immediately."

"Understood, sir," the officer said.

"Now then, kindly remove this collar from the boy's neck," Rannick said.

After the collar was removed, Rannick led Jag over to a small hovercraft with a flatbed in front and a small cabin in the rear with two seats. They loaded the fabricated part onto the flatbed. As Admiral Rannick lifted Jag onto the bed, he had to turn his head when he caught a whiff of Jag's body odor. He had Jag sit at the rear with his back against the cabin.

"I am Admiral Pace Rannick. You can call me Rannick; everyone else does. This old geezer here is Cappy. Son, what's your name?"

"Joseph Gabriel, sir. But most people call me Jag."

"What would you like us to call you?"

"You can call me Jag."

"We have a short trip out to the castle. Sit back, and we'll get you cleaned up and fed in no time," the admiral said as a light flashed across the sky, the

Thorg shuttle returning to the *Killclaw*. Jag sighed with relief. He was free—for the moment.

The hovercraft lifted and moved through town. It reminded Jag of the old western movies his grandfather watched when he was growing up. Jag rested his head against the cab and basked in the sunlight as the wind caressed his face. They traveled down winding dirt roads deep into a countryside speckled with forests and surrounded with farms and vineyards on rolling hills. Jag didn't know what awaited him, whether it was for better or worse than life on the *Killclaw*, but for the moment, he was strangely at peace and felt safe.

The hovercraft reached a stone wall that stretched as far as the eye could see in both directions from the road. Behind the wall stood row upon row of large bushes, nearly the size of apple trees with enormous green grapes. Jag sat up in amazement when he saw one of the Hamlin water feeders stepping over the trees as it sprayed water. The machine reminded Jag of a giant daddy long legs spider back home.

The driveway led up to the front of a massive estate that was, in fact, an ancient castle. While stately, it was neither glamorous nor elegant. The rustic castle was made of light gray stones and had two tall turrets, one on either side of the main entrance. The castle's walls were topped with battlements that stretched around the castle's roof. Large windows with iron bars were spread throughout the front and sides of the castle.

In front of the castle was a circular driveway with a large fountain in the middle. Surrounding the castle was a manicured lawn, and to the left was a landing pad for small shuttlecraft. To the right was a large barn.

As soon as they arrived, a team of young men ran out and began unloading the hauler. Admiral Rannick approached one of the young men and then called Jag over.

"Jag, this is Lesebo. He will assist you with anything you need. But first, I think you need a bath and some new clothing."

Lesebo led Jag up the castle steps and into the main entrance. The foyer was tall and masculine with large chandeliers hanging from the ceiling and beautiful drapes hanging on the windows. They passed a library, followed by an office, before turning down a corridor, where they reached a large open room with about twenty bunkbeds. Lesebo took Jag over to a wooden wardrobe and opened the doors, revealing all sorts of neatly folded uniforms. He sized Jag up and handed him some clothing from the shelf. "These look like they will fit."

He led Jag to a large bathroom with dark marble floors. Old wooden shower stalls stood to the right and sinks and mirrors to the left. "The shower is in there. Turn the handle to adjust the temperature. Each stall already has soap. I'll grab you a towel."

Jag entered the shower stall and undressed.

"Here's your towel," Lesebo said. Then he saw the scars on Jag's neck from the shock collar. "Oh my, how did you get those?"

Embarrassed, Jag pulled his shirt back to hide them.

"I'm sorry, I didn't mean to pry," Lesebo said, turning away. "You have nothing to fear here. The admiral is a kind man. When you're finished showering, meet me back by the beds, and I'll show you where you will sleep."

"Thank you," Jag said softly. Then he entered the shower and removed the rest of his tattered *Unity* space station clothing. He turned on the shower and enjoyed the warm water as it beat against his frail body. He leaned his head back, allowing the refreshing water to wash away the years of grime as tears fell down his cheeks. "Thank you, God," he whispered.

After showering, he put on clean clothing for the first time in years. Then he threw away his old clothes and met Lesebo in the dorm room.

"This is your bed. If you need more blankets, let me know. Bet you're hungry."

Jag nodded.

Lesebo smiled. "Meals are served three times a day. For the evening meal, we all eat together in the great hall. You can grab breakfast and lunch whenever you like." Then Lesebo led Jag into the great hall, where everyone was gathering for the evening meal.

"What is this place?" Jag asked as he took it all in.

"This is the admiral's estate. After the Great War, he retired to this planet, which he helped liberate, and was eventually made governor."

"The Great War?" Jag asked.

"The war between the Murk Empire and the Celestian Kingdom. It lasted nearly twenty years," Lesebo said, surprised that Jag wasn't familiar with it.

"Rannick was a hero and the youngest to be promoted to admiral in the history of the military. His leadership is why the war ended when it did. The king awarded him governorship of any planet, and he chose Norr."

"Is he married?" Jag asked.

"Nah, he was too busy with the war to settle down. I think he dated the princess once, but she married some other dude. He'll marry someday; he just hasn't met the right woman yet."

"What do all these people do around here?" Jag asked.

"There are about thirty of us. We all have different duties, but most work in the vineyard."

"Are you all slaves?" Jag asked.

"Slaves? Heavens no!" Lesebo said, his eyebrows rising in shock. "We get paid and can leave anytime we like. It's just that most of us don't have any place to go. Plus, we enjoy living and working here. We work hard, but we also have fun and eat well."

In the great hall stood a massive stone fireplace with the mounted head of an elk-like creature with antlers reaching nearly ten feet wide. Chandeliers made of antlers hung from the ceiling and lit up the hall. The hand-carved wooden tables and benches were mostly occupied. As Lesebo looked for a place to sit, two men approached.

"Have you seen my keys?" the larger of the two asked.

"Jag, I'd like to introduce you to our two production managers: Lieutenant Commander Lemann Nuckols and Measil Warily. They head up the dormitory, so if you need anything, feel free to ask them. Jag is a guest of the admiral and will be staying with us in the dorm."

Lt. Commander Nuckols was a large man who appeared to be distracted as Jag waited for him to shake his hand.

"You can call me Nuckols; everyone else does," he said as he shook Jag's hand so tightly that Jag thought he was going to crush it. "Lesebo, have you seen my keys? I know I left them on my dresser. This isn't the first time I've had things go missing!"

"No, I haven't. Perhaps a mouse took them," Lesebo suggested.

"It'll be a dead mouse if I ever catch it!"

Jag reached his hand out to Measil, a thin-framed, dark haired man. Measil ignored the gesture.

"How long will this guest be gracing us?"

"I'm not sure," Lesebo replied. "I placed him in bunk eleven, below me."

Lesebo led Jag through the maze of tables to an empty seat toward the side of the room.

"Nuckols is nice enough," Lesebo whispered as they walked. "But I wouldn't cross him; he does have a bit of a temper. Nuckols was one of the admiral's best officers, but when the admiral retired, Nuckols had a falling out with his new commander and was given the choice to either retire or be demoted. He chose to retire and joined the admiral on the vineyard. And Measil, his dad is in the senate and he's related to the prince somehow, a second or third cousin. Rumor has it that the prince asked the admiral to find a position for Measil, because no one wanted to hire him. I try to steer clear of him as much as possible; he gives me the creeps."

"Do you really have mice problems?" Jag asked.

"Nah, Nuckols is always misplacing things and believes someone is stealing from him."

A person standing at the front rang a large bell. Just as Lesebo spotted an open seat at a table near the rear, Admiral Rannick motioned for them to join him at the head table. Lesebo escorted Jag between the tables, every eye watching them. They took two seats next to the admiral. Nuckols and Measil were seated at one end, and Cappy and several others were seated across from him.

"So there was a young man under all that filth," the admiral said. Then he stood up, and everyone hushed. "I'd like you to welcome Jag, who comes from a planet called Earth." He raised his glass of wine, and everyone joined him in toasting and welcoming Jag. Then he led them in an old military blessing. "Great and mighty Creator, we give thee thanks for thy many blessings. May our lives honor thee in all we do."

"Our lives, our obedience, and our honor we pledge to thee," everyone replied in unison.

When they finished, servers brought bowls of freshly baked, steaming hot bread to each table. Though starving, Jag waited for everyone to begin.

"No need to wait," Rannick said. "Thanks has been given."

Jag grabbed a roll. It was warm and soft. As he tore the bread apart, steam rose and filled his nostrils. After devouring the roll, he reached for another as servers delivered bowls of luscious grapes. They were dark purple and nearly the size of a baseball. Jag pulled a grape from the vine. As he bit into it, juice burst forth and ran down his cheeks. "Amazing!" he said softly.

"What's that?" Rannick asked.

Jag looked up. "These grapes are amazing!"

"Thank you. We grow them right here in the vineyard."

"Norr is the only place in the universe where these grapes grow," Lesebo added.

Next, bowls of stew with large chunks of meat and vegetables covered in a rich broth was delivered. Jag stuck his fork into a piece of meat. It was so tender and flavorful that he closed his eyes as he chewed, enjoying the incredible feast that was so different than the *Killclaw's* sludge, to which he had become accustomed.

"Jag, I'd like to introduce you to Dr. Magmas Otto," the admiral said, motioning toward an older man sitting across the table from Jag. Jag had to lean over to see him between the bowls of fruit and bread. "Dr. Otto is our planet's chief science officer."

Dr. Otto smiled. "Chief science officer may be a stretch, as I'm just the local science teacher. However, I dabble a bit and like to stay abreast of the latest scientific breakthroughs."

"I've invited Dr. Otto in the hope he might be able to help locate your planet."

"It's a pleasure to meet you, Dr. Otto," Jag said.

"I assure you the pleasure is mine," Dr. Otto replied. Then he began asking Jag questions about Earth, its solar system, and its galaxy in an attempt to identify it. However, none of the details that Jag provided were familiar.

"Well, perhaps you can visit me sometime, as I have a modest observatory. We can see if any constellations are familiar to you."

"I'd like that sir," Jag said.

"How did you come to be in the service of those dreadful Thorgs?" Dr. Otto asked.

Jag sighed. "It's a long story."

"We're not going anywhere," Admiral Rannick said, leaning back in his chair. His favorite pastime was sitting around after the evening meal and telling stories. So Jag shared his story with a captivated audience. They especially enjoyed how he had eluded the wolves by luring them into the weightless cafeteria.

As Jag talked, he felt a pit at the bottom of his stomach and eventually excused himself from the table. As he stood up, he vomited everything he had eaten. The entire hall became quiet and stared at him as Admiral Rannick and Lesebo ran to his side.

"I'm so sorry," Jag said as he wiped his mouth.

"No, I'm the one who should apologize!" Rannick said. "I've should have known that these foods were too rich for your stomach. We should have introduced them slowly."

Jag chuckled as he wiped his mouth. "Yeah, but it was delicious!"

Admiral Rannick asked for a glass of water so Jag could rinse out his mouth. "Let's get you some fresh air," he said when Jag had recovered.

They exited onto a veranda overlooking an enormous gorge. Jag walked to the thick carved stone railing and leaned over. The gorge dropped nearly half a mile straight down. Its walls were brilliant shades of orange and red with green shrubbery mixed in and a dry riverbed at the bottom.

"You have a beautiful castle, sir," Jag said.

"Thank you. It's over seven hundred years old! It was built by this planet's namesake, King Victor Norrsen. He built it against this gorge to help fortify it from any enemies who could then only attack from the front."

"Yeah, climbing that gorge would be difficult," Jag said, looking down. Then he turned back to Rannick. "So, are you from Norr?"

"No. I'm from Aulora, Celestia's capitol. During my military service, I visited Norr and fell in love with its simplicity. After I retired, I bought this place and began restoring the vineyard."

"You've done an excellent job, sir."

"Thank you. I knew nothing about running a vineyard and am still learning every day. All these employees are depending on me to turn things around, but we still aren't making a profit. This was supposed to have been our year, but this drought has taken nearly half our crops."

"Sir, I grew up on a farm, but it was nothing like this. If I can be of service, I'd like to help!"

"I appreciate the offer. Rest for a couple of weeks, and when you've regained your strength, talk to Cappy. I'm sure we have some tractors that could use your touch."

Jag spent the week resting and acclimating to Norr's gravity and its food. Life on the estate was good and wholesome. Everyone worked hard and played hard. They rose early, worked all day, and then joined together in the great hall each night to share stories or listen as Lesebo and several others played stringed instruments and sang folk songs.

Jag began helping Cappy repair equipment in the barn and around the vineyard. Once a week, he accompanied him into town to purchase supplies and parts. During that time, he visited with Dr. Otto to see if he had located any new constellations that matched Earth's.

One time as Jag was preparing to go to town with Cappy, he couldn't find his hat. He asked around if anyone had seen it. He even asked Nuckols, for he knew he had left it on his bed.

"I'm telling you, we have a mouse somewhere," Nuckols replied. "A very large mouse, and if I ever catch it, it will be the last thing it takes!"

Unable to find his hat, Jag proceeded into town, where he visited with Dr. Otto in his small observatory behind his house. Dr. Otto had a couple of new constellations pulled up for Jag to examine. "I captured these several nights ago. Take a look at them."

Jag looked and then shook his head. "Nah, they don't look familiar to me."

Afterwards, Jag and Dr. Otto sat in his parlor and drank spiced tea while discussing new scientific theories and recent technical discoveries that Dr. Otto had read. Dr. Otto enjoyed the stimulating intellectual conversations and listening to Jag describe life on Earth and the *Unity*. Dr. Otto had always dreamed of being a space explorer but never had the opportunity.

"Don't give up, Jag," Dr. Otto said at the end of his visit. "We'll find your home one way or another."

CHAPTER 14
THE MOUSE

"Come quick, they're going to kill him!" Lesebo said, gasping for breath as he ran up to Jag, who was repairing a leg on one of the old Hamlin water feeders in the vineyard.

"Kill who?"

"The mouse!"

"Huh?" Jag was confused as to why Lesebo would make such a big deal over a rodent.

"He's not a mouse. He's a boy who Nuckols caught stealing, and he's going to kill him!"

They ran to a small tool shed behind the barn, where Jag paused to collect himself before entering. Inside, Measil was holding the wrists of a small, crying boy, stretching his arms across the workbench as Nuckols sharpened a machete with a sharpening stone.

"Look what I caught trying to steal my lunch!" Nuckols said. "A mouse, a large mouse."

Jag nodded. "I see that."

"We'll see how well he can steal without any hands," Measil said with a wry smile.

Nuckols set down the sharpening stone and turned to Jag. "Are you here to join us or to try to stop us?"

"Neither, I'm here to get a ratchet. I'm repairing the number five Hamlin. Its leg came loose again. Have you seen it?"

"I think it's over there on the table," Nuckols replied, nodding toward it.

"Hold still, Muck," Measil said, using a common Norrish derogatory term.

"I suppose you don't approve of corporal punishment?" Nuckols asked, still eyeing Jag.

"Me?" Jag shrugged. "I'm just surprised you're letting him off so easily."

"You call cutting off his hands easy?" Measil asked.

Nuckols' eyes narrowed. "How would you deal with it?"

"Well, cutting his hands off is one approach. However, it has a severe flaw."

Nuckols crossed his arms, still holding the machete. "Oh yeah? And what's that?"

"If you cut off his hands, then he'll spend the rest of his life begging. He'll never work a day in his life. Pretty lucky, huh?"

Nuckols thought about it for a moment before replying. "Guess I didn't see it that way. But this mouse will never work anyway."

"Let me see," Jag said. "Boy, stop your crying. What's your name?"

"I'm . . . I'm Marcel."

"Marcel!" Nuckols shouted. "Named after the king! Why, he's just a Muck, one of those lousy illegitimate orphan kids."

"I'm not a Muck, I'm not illeg . . . illegmate," the boy said, struggling to pronounce the word.

"Marcel, it seems that you are in what's called a predicament," Jag said. "Do you know what a predicament is?"

The boy shook his head.

"It's a tight spot, one that you can't get out of. It seems to me you have two options today. You can either have these men cut off your hands, or you can promise to work with me to pay off your debt. Which is it?"

"Promise? He won't keep a promise. He has no honor," Nuckols said pointing the machete at Marcel.

"Well, if he doesn't keep his word, then you can complete the task you started here today," Jag said.

"Why don't we just cut off one of his hands? He doesn't need both of them to work," Measil said. "That way if he doesn't work off the debt, he'll have already received half his punishment."

"What will it be, Marcel?" Jag asked. "Do you want to have your debt paid in full right now by having your hands removed, or do you want to work it off?"

"I . . . I'll work it off," Marcel sobbed.

"Okay, we'll hold you to that promise," Jag said.

Nuckols placed the melon that Marcel had been caught stealing on the table beside Marcel's hand and, with one swing, sliced through it, splitting it in two.

"If I ever catch you stealing from me again, I'll complete what we started here today, mouse. Understand?" Nuckols bit into one of the halves to emphasize his point.

"Yes, sir," the boy said, wiping away his tears.

Jag motioned to him. "Come. You will work with me and do exactly what I tell you to do."

Measil released the boy's hands, and Marcel fell back against a tool cabinet. Jag helped him up and led him to the dormitory, where Jag gave him new clothes and found him an empty bunkbed. After eating a quick lunch together, Marcel helped Jag repair the tractor.

News reached Admiral Rannick of how Jag had intervened, and he commended Jag for his actions. He suggested that Jag visit with the headmaster of the local orphanage, from which Marcel had most likely escaped.

On his next weekly visit to see Dr. Otto, Jag asked Lesebo to watch over Marcel as Jag swung by the Yuba City Orphanage. The headmaster was an old Norr priest dressed in a long brown robe and sporting a gray beard.

"Sir, I would like to ask you about a young boy named Marcel," Jag said.

"Oh, what has he gotten himself into now?" the headmaster asked. "We've tried just about everything we can with that boy. He performs poorly in his schoolwork, runs away, gets caught stealing, and then brought back here. We're at our wits' end with him."

"Sir, does the boy have any parents?"

"Marcel is a Muck. Are you familiar with that term?"

Jag shook his head. "Not really."

"It is an awful derogatory term that stands for someone who has a Murk father and a Norr mother. Marcel and most of the children in our orphanage are unwanted simply because of whom their fathers were. People don't want to be reminded of the occupation, so they've written off these poor outcasts."

The headmaster slid Marcel's file across the table. Next to his name was a box that listed the reason the child had been dropped off. It stated in large red letters "Unwanted," and his mother's identification was listed as "Unknown."

"I'm sorry to hear that," Jag said. "Sir, I think we may be able to help the lad if you're willing to allow us to try. Admiral Rannick has agreed to allow him to stay at his vineyard, where he will learn discipline, hard work, and receive schooling."

The headmaster gave Jag a skeptical look. "What's in this for you and the admiral? Marcel can't be much of a worker."

"Nothing other than the ability to give back. I lost my parents when I was a child. However, I was raised by loving grandparents, who made all the difference in the world."

"Fair enough," the headmaster said. "You have my blessing. I'll give you some of his books, though I don't know if he's ever opened them."

From that point on, Jag tutored Marcel daily, teaching him how to read, write, and perform arithmetic. One day as Jag was teaching, he asked Marcel how he had been able to steal from within the castle for so long without being caught.

"Tunnels," Marcel said. "They're hidden in all the rooms throughout the castle." Then Marcel showed Jag several fake panels in different rooms that opened up into tunnels that traversed the length of the castle. After that, Jag and Marcel often explored the tunnels together and went for hikes down into the gorge and around the vineyard.

Before long, Jag and Marcel became close friends. Wherever Jag went, Marcel was close behind. Eventually, others started treating Marcel like one of the crew, and he worked just as hard as someone twice his size. Even Nuckols respected the turnaround in Marcel, though he still called him "Mouse" because of his small stature. The admiral also took note of Jag's leadership abilities and reputation with the other workers. One day he called Jag into his office.

"Jag, I want to thank you for helping Cappy keep things running smoothly and for the work you've done with Marcel. You have earned the respect of the other crewmen. I have a special project I'd like to have you lead. I recall that you have some experience farming, and I have a spot of land, the back forty, that I can't grow anything on. Mind taking a look at it?"

"My pleasure, sir," Jag said. "And I'm the one who is grateful for all you have done."

Jag was assigned a small crew, including Marcel. Together, they visited the back forty, where the soil was as hard as cement, and devised a plan for reclaiming the land. First, they asked the kitchen crew to collect all the scraps and leftovers each day to make compost. Then they spent weeks painstakingly breaking up the hard soil. Afterwards, a local rancher provided a load of rich manure, which they mixed with sand, compost, and water to spread onto the soil. The lingering smell was horrific, especially when the wind picked up, and Jag's team was frequently teased about the odor, but that didn't deter them.

After several weeks, they tested the soil and then planted the forty acres with Norr grape seedlings. The next puzzle was how to get water to the plants. With the ongoing shortage, using the main water supply wasn't an option, because it would impact the rest of the vineyard.

One night as Jag and Marcel sat out on the veranda drinking ice-cold drinks and watching the sunset, Jag observed condensation dripping down the side of his tall glass, and it occurred to him that if he could pull the moisture out of the air, he wouldn't have to use any water from the main reserves.

In excitement, he ran to the barn and gathered several parts that he assembled into a crude water extraction tower. The next morning, many derided the odd-looking spiral tower, but Jag and his team waited and watched. By the end of the first day, the extractor had collected several gallons of water out of the air.

His team helped assemble enough extractors to water the entire forty acres. With plenty of water, nutrient-rich soil, and a limitless supply of sunlight, the plants grew rapidly. Within weeks they were nearly five feet tall, and within a month they budded.

Several months later as they all sat down to enjoy supper, the admiral had baskets of grapes placed on each table. Everyone commented on how large and tasty they were compared to previous years. The admiral stood up and asked Jag and his team to join him.

"No doubt, you have noticed the exceptional quality of this year's grapes," the admiral began. "I am pleased to announce that these grapes are the first harvested from the back forty. A piece of land that was once worthless has now produced the largest and most flavorful harvest ever. With this additional crop, we will have a very profitable harvest. Well done, everyone one of you. I'm very proud of all of your hard work!"

Cheers erupted across the hall.

"Jag, I want to thank you for the remarkable leadership you have shown. Not only did you conquer the back forty, you did so without depleting the water levels needed for the rest of our production. Therefore, I am pleased to announce that I am promoting you to production director!"

Everyone stood and applauded, even Nuckols and Measil. In his new role, they would now report to Jag. Nuckols didn't care, as he missed military life. However, Measil hated it, only because he didn't like someone else receiving credit, even if it was for something he despised, like farming, because he didn't like to get his hands dirty.

Over the next several years, the vineyard thrived under Jag's leadership. All the while Jag continued to grow into a strong young man. Marcel grew as well, but he was still small for his age. Everything Jag touched turned to gold, and Rannick trusted him with his entire vineyard.

One evening after Jag had retired to his room, he received a notice that Rannick would like to speak to him. He hurried to his office, where Rannick was seated with Dr. Otto and a stranger.

"Jag, come in and have a seat. Dr. Otto would like to introduce you to his friend," the admiral said as Dr. Otto beamed from ear to ear.

"Jag, this is Dr. Jeodani," Dr. Otto said as the short white-haired man with a goatee stood.

"Pleasure to meet you," Dr. Jeodani said. "Dr. Otto has told me about your planet. I'm with the Space Exploratory Agency, and we've received long-range images of a distant galaxy that has characteristics similar to what he described to us."

He handed Jag a tablet with pixelated images of a galaxy, but they were too distorted to make any determination.

"Sadly, there is no way to know for sure if this is your galaxy or not," Dr. Otto said.

"Except to visit it," Dr. Jeodani added. "And that brings me to why I'm here. I lead a team of scientists and merchants who are exploring undiscovered galaxies. The trip will take many years, as we have other star systems to explore along the way. When Dr. Otto mentioned you, I thought we might be able to help each other, and I wanted to see if you'd be interested in joining us."

"Are you kidding me?" Jag asked. "Absolutely!"

"I need to remind you that we don't know if this is your galaxy," Dr. Jeodani cautioned.

"However, we would still love to have you join us," Dr. Otto said.

"Us?" Jag asked. "Are you going, too, Dr. Otto?"

"Yeah, I think it's time I stop dreaming and start doing," Dr. Otto said. "I've cashed in my retirement savings to cover the cost of the trip."

Jag looked at the two men. "Cost?"

Dr. Otto nodded. "That's where the difficulty lies. The trip is subsidized by the government and private interest groups, but each person still has to contribute one hundred and twenty-five thousand credits!"

"Oh." Jag's heart sank. "I have nowhere near that much saved up."

"You'll need the full amount by the time we leave in two months."

"Two months? I couldn't raise that much in ten years!"

"Don't worry about the finances," Rannick said. "If this is what you want to do, then I'll see that the rest is covered."

Jag turned to him. "Sir, I could never ask this of you. That's a lot of money."

"You're not asking. You've more than earned it. This vineyard wouldn't be what it is today without you. If this is what you want to do, just say the word, and we'll figure it out."

"Thank you, sir! Yes, sign me up!"

They sat discussing the details of the trip: what to bring and when they were leaving. Throughout the conversation, Jag failed to notice two little eyes peering in from the vent on the wall. Marcel had overheard the entire conversation.

"So when are you going to tell Marcel?" Rannick asked.

"I don't know," Jag said, not realizing he already had.

"He's quite close to you. Of course, after you leave, he can stay for as long as he likes, for this is his home. I'll have Lesebo look after him and continue his education."

"I'll tell him tonight," Jag said. Then he thanked Dr. Otto and Dr. Jeodani several times.

He went to find Marcel, but his bunk was empty and his things were gone. Jag asked around, but no had seen him. Jag ran outside and found Marcel walking down the driveway, dragging a bag behind him. Jag ran down the driveway and caught up with him.

"Where are you going?"

Marcel wiped his eyes as he kept walking. "I don't know. Someplace where I'm wanted."

"What are you talking about? You're wanted very much right here."

Marcel stopped and shook his head. "No, I'm not. When I was a kid. I broke into the headmaster's office at the orphanage, and I saw what they wrote on my file, that I was unwanted. I heard those guys talking with you, and I know you're leaving with them. You don't want me either."

"Marcel, I can't change what was written on those files about you, but it isn't true. You are very much wanted—by me, Admiral Rannick, Lesebo, and even Nuckols. Yes, those scientists have invited me to go with them, and it might be my only opportunity to get back home."

Marcel lowered his gaze. "I don't want you to go."

Jag sighed, his heart going out to the boy. "If there was any way I could take you with me, I would. But the admiral himself said that this is your home for as long as you want to stay."

Marcel looked up. "Who's going to teach me?"

"Lesebo will continue your education."

"He's not as fun as you are," Marcel said. "I'll miss you."

"I'll miss you, too," Jag said. Then he gave the boy a hug.

Jag spent the next two months preparing for the trip, making sure Lesebo was up to speed with Marcel's studies and dividing his responsibilities as production director among several workers. As the day drew closer, Jag rose early to watch the sunrise come up over the vineyard and realized how much he would miss the place. Admiral Rannick walked up with his morning tea.

"Surprised to see you up so early. Taking in everything you can before the trip?"

"Yeah, I'm really going to miss it here."

The admiral nodded. "I have been summoned by the king and need to leave today. Sadly, I won't be here to see you off next week, so I'll have to say goodbye now."

"Wow, I knew we would have to say goodbye, but I didn't expect it to be so soon."

Rannick smiled. "Are you having second thoughts?"

"I don't know, sir. It's just this feeling I can't shake."

Rannick thanked Jag for everything he had done in turning the vineyard around. In return, Jag thanked him for saving his life. Rannick left later that morning to meet the king on Corian Prime, where the king's son, Prince Damon, served as governor. Whenever the admiral was away, Jag oversaw all affairs regarding the vineyard and assisted with any necessary governor duties.

Several nights after Rannick left, Marcel woke Jag up. "Come quickly! There are strangers outside, and one of them is a giant!"

Jag's eyes narrowed with suspicion. "A giant?"

"Come, see for yourself," Marcel said as he led Jag through a series of tunnels that exited beside the launch pad. Jag saw an unfamiliar shuttlecraft docked on the launch pad and two people standing beside it. Indeed, one of the strangers appeared to be a giant, standing easily nine feet tall and very muscular. The giant held a long spear and looked around vigilantly. Even though Jag stayed well hidden behind a thick shrub, the giant kept peering his way.

The second man appeared to be Celestian and wore a long dark coat with a hood that hid his face. Just then Measil walked out the castle's side door and bowed before him. The two spoke softly for some time, but Jag couldn't make out what they were discussing. The only thing he heard was Measil say, "Everything is prepared, just as you requested." After the two strangers boarded the ship, Measil returned to the castle.

"What was that all about?" Marcel asked.

Jag shook his head. "Don't know, but I'm going to find out."

The next morning as Measil, Nuckols, and Jag were eating breakfast, Jag nodded at Measil. "Last night I saw a shuttle on the pad, and you were speaking with two men. Who were they?"

"Oh," Measil said, obviously startled by the question but trying to hide it, "just old friends."

"You mentioned that everything was prepared. Prepared for what?"

"Oh, um . . . well, I wasn't supposed to say anything, but the king is visiting us, and we must get everything ready for his coming. It was supposed to have been a surprise."

"Wow," Nuckols said. "The king? Here on Norr?"

"What else did your eavesdropping ears hear?" Measil asked.

"Nothing," Jag said. "Sorry, I was concerned when I saw a strange ship."

"Next time don't stick your nose where it doesn't belong," Measil said. He leaned over and spoke into Jag's ear. "You may have been promoted to be my supervisor, but you'd do well to remember that I'm the king's nephew and my father is a senator!"

On the morning of Jag's departure, he placed his suitcase on the hauler and then said his goodbyes to the crowd, who had gathered around. He joined Cappy in the hauler's cab as Marcel sat on the flatbed. Jag stared back at the castle as they drove away.

They reached town early enough for Jag to help Cappy track down a replacement axel for a tractor. After visiting each of the parts stores, they decided to visit the local farmers' market. As they entered, Jag stopped short when he saw a sight he hadn't seen in a long time: the shuttlecraft from the *Killclaw*.

"Is everything alright?" Marcel asked.

"It's them," Jag said softly.

Marcel looked around. "Who?"

"The Thorg ship that held me as a slave."

"Son, do we need to leave?" Cappy asked.

"No, I'll be fine, and there's a good chance they'll have the part."

As they approached the tent, Jag saw Maruke and Rahuke laying out parts to display to buyers.

"Something we can help you find?" Maruke asked as Rahuke took a seat under the shade.

"I'm looking for an axel that will fit an Avery tractor," Cappy replied.

"Let me scan your part to search if we have anything in stock that may fit," Maruke said.

As he scanned the axel and searched through the ship's inventory, Jag tried to avoid making eye contact. When he did finally look at them, he realized they didn't recognize him. He had changed a lot since he had left them. No longer was he a scrawny, malnourished kid. He had grown, packed on muscle, and his skin was nicely bronzed.

"I found something that will work," Maruke said. "My associate will bring it down shortly." Twenty minutes later, another shuttlecraft arrived, and to Jag's surprise, off walked a female carrying an axel, followed by Kavin. Her skin was blue with beautiful markings and long dark braided hair. Jag had never seen her species before. She placed the axel on the table but never looked up. Jag looked but did not see a shock collar around her neck.

Cappy examined the axel and asked Jag if he thought it would work. Jag looked at the axel and nodded. "It should. You'll have to modify the collar for it to fit correctly though."

Cappy looked up at the Thorgs. "How much?"

"Five hundred credits" Rahuke replied, sweat dripping from his forehead.

Cappy's eyes widened. "For an axel?"

As he and Kavin negotiated a final price, Jag's attention fell to the woman. Was she a slave or a paid participant, like Dr. Neebo?

Cappy handed the new axel to Marcel, and they were on their way back to the hauler when Rahuke said, "Pick that up, Mut-yut." Hearing the phrase caused Jag's blood to boil as he recalled all the atrocities he had endured. He stopped in his tracks and turned to walk back toward Rahuke when he realized that Rahuke wasn't speaking to him but to the woman. At that moment, he knew she was indeed a slave even if she wasn't wearing a shock collar. The woman picked up the part and dragged it out to where Jag was standing.

"Why don't you run away?" Jag asked softly. She didn't say anything, just looked away. Jag continued talking to the young woman and asked her if she needed his help.

"Please don't, you'll get me in trouble," she whispered as Rahuke and Maruke approached.

"I'm sorry if our associate is bothering you, fine sir," Rahuke said. He went to backhand the girl, but Jag grabbed his hand. Rahuke's face bristled with anger. "Who are you to stop me from correcting a member of my crew?"

"You don't remember me, do you?" Jag asked. Rahuke stared blankly at him. "Perhaps this will jar your memory." Then Jag pulled his collar down, revealing the scars on his neck.

Rahuke's face broke into a grin. "Mut-yut, we missed you!"

"It's good to see you're doing so well," Kavin said as he walked up.

"I can't believe you're still pirating. I would have thought you'd retired long ago with all the wealth you made from selling me," Jag replied.

"We would have if it hadn't been for Dr. Neebo," Kavin said.

"Don't say that name around me!" Rahuke ordered.

"How is the good doctor?" Jag asked

"The *good* doctor stole all our money and ran off," Maruke said.

Jag couldn't help but laugh. Kavin went on to explain that the doctor hadn't exactly stolen their money. After Jag left the *Killclaw*, Dr. Neebo no longer enjoyed being on board. So, on their next visit to Far Side Outpost, he informed Rahuke that he was leaving and demanded his cut. Rahuke, being a greedy Thorg, didn't want to part with the credits, so he challenged the doctor to a game of chance in the casino. Dr. Neebo refused but soon realized it was the only way the Thorgs were going to part with their money.

After several rounds, Neebo started winning. Then Rahuke drew a sure-win hand and bet the entire crew's money as collateral. The doctor accepted the bet and, as fortune would have it, he drew the only card that would beat Rahuke's hand. The Thorgs lost all their credits to the doctor in a single hand. Dr. Neebo took his winnings, married Loxy Lonna, and ran off to Gilboa, a popular paradise planet. Once news reached the family that Rahuke had lost all their earnings, they made Kavin their new boss.

"You need to let the young woman go," Jag said.

"Let her go?" Rahuke laughed. "She's free to go anytime she likes."

The young woman's eyes pleaded with Jag. "Please don't."

"Release her," Jag demanded as he laid the admiral's security badge on the table. "I'm the governor's personal assistant. You will release this young woman now."

"Fine, ask her if she wants to go with you," Rahuke said as she hid behind Kavin.

"You don't have to stay with them any longer; you can come with us," Jag said.

"I can't. They have my mother," the young woman whispered.

Jag's eyes widened with understanding. He turned to Rahuke. "Alright, how much?"

"Two hundred thousand credits!"

"No. I'll make you the same offer that the admiral made for me. One hundred thousand credits for the young woman and her mom."

"No, Jag, don't," Marcel said, pulling on Jag's shirt. "That's your money for your trip."

"I know what I have to do. It will be alright," Jag said.

"Two workers are worth much more than that," Rahuke replied.

"Either take my offer, or your entire crew will be thrown into our hottest jail cell I can find until the admiral returns, which could be weeks. Then you'll be tried on charges of pirating and slavery."

"Alright, alright," Rahuke said. "Calm down. You were always my favorite. You had spunk, and I liked that about you." He turned to fetch the young woman's mother.

"No, you stay here," Jag said. "Kavin can fetch her." He didn't trust that Rahuke would retrieve her safely.

A few minutes later, Kavin returned with an older woman, and Cappy and Marcel helped them over to the hauler.

"Tell me why I shouldn't throw you all into prison!" Jag demanded.

"What?" Rahuke exclaimed. "We had a deal!"

"Plus, we saved your life. Don't forget that!" Maruke added.

"You have thirty minutes to get out of Norr space. Don't ever return again!"

The Thorgs quickly packed up their belongings and fled Norr space. Then Jag introduced himself to the two women, who were seated on the hauler bed.

"I'm Jag. What are your names?"

"I'm Bayli," the young woman said, "and this is my mother, Helena."

"Pleasure," Jag said. "You are safe and are free to go if you'd like."

"Go where?" Bayli asked. "My father was killed when the Thorgs attacked our ship, and the Murks destroyed our planet."

"You will stay with us at the admiral's castle," Marcel said, elated that Jag was staying.

Cappy walked over and pulled Jag aside. "What you did for these ladies is a good thing, but what about your trip? You spent all your money on these strangers."

"I know, but how could I not do for them what the admiral did for me? Even at the cost of me returning home. Let's swing by the transport so I can tell Dr. Otto goodbye."

They traveled to the transport, where Jag explained why he wouldn't be joining them. Dr. Otto immediately offered Jag his place on board the exploration ship.

"You deserve this. You need to go home!"

Jag smiled and put his hand on his friend's shoulder. "No, you go. You need this adventure. I have a feeling I'll return home someday, but now is not the time."

After returning to the castle, Jag helped Bayli and her mother get settled in. It was soon discovered that Helena was a gifted cook and began assisting in the kitchen. Bayli was a healer. Many in her species had the ability to touch a person and sense any ailment, and some master healers could actually cure people by touching them. Bayli had been studying under her father, a well-known master healer, before he was killed during the Thorg attack.

Several weeks later, a special feast was thrown to celebrate Admiral Rannick's return. Helena and Bayli spent the day making all sorts of treats. That evening during the celebration in the great hall, Jag snuck out to the veranda, leaned against the railing, and looked up at the stars. "Sorry, Grandma. Sorry, Grandpa. It seems your little boy isn't coming home anytime soon."

"How are you doing, son?" Rannick asked as he joined Jag.

"I'm alright, sir."

"That was an honorable sacrifice you made for those two."

"I'm sorry I didn't spend your money the way you intended."

"You made a selfless decision, and it was your money to spend how you felt appropriate."

Jag turned him. "Thank you, sir. How was your trip?"

"I have a lot to catch you up on. But most importantly, the king is coming, and now that you're staying, I can definitely use your help in getting everything prepared."

CHAPTER 15
THE KING'S VISIT

"Have you seen them?" Marcel asked enthusiastically.

"Seen who?" Bayli said as she arranged plates and cups on the cloth-covered table as Jag watched.

"The giants! Come quickly! You've got to see them."

"Okay, calm down," Jag replied. He was as giddy as Marcel, but he tried not to show it.

Admiral Rannick looked dapper in his military uniform, including a chest full of war medals. He had purchased new clothing for the entire staff. Bayli was in a beautiful dress while Jag and Marcel wore nice suits.

"You look very nice," Rannick said to Bayli.

"Thank you. You look very handsome. One second," Bayli said as she reached over and brushed some lint off his uniform.

Rannick smiled. "Thank you. So, Jag, is everything ready?"

"Yes, sir," Jag said as they moved to the foyer to join the rest of the staff.

Trumpeters entered, playing a fanfare that echoed off the foyer ceiling, followed by the royal bodyguards. Next, two giants ducked under the doorjamb.

They had human features but were much larger and more muscular. The smaller one was older with gray hair. They wore tribal garments that revealed their massive chests, and each carried a long spear that they slammed against the floor when they came to attention, making an ominous sound.

Then the king entered, adorned in a beautiful purple robe, a modest golden crown, and with a longsword sheathed to his belt. Though older, he was very distinguished with strong features and piercing blue eyes. Walking behind him was Prince Damon, accompanied by Norr's only senator, Karl Alberg, who was followed by an entourage of personal androids.

"His Royal Majesty King Marcellus and Prince Damon," the captain of the guard announced as everyone bowed.

King Marcellus looked around at the assembly. "May the Creator bless this home and all who dwell within her walls."

After he embraced Admiral Rannick, the admiral led him to the receiving line for introductions. "Your majesty, this is Lieutenant Commander Nuckols, who served in your fleet and had an exemplary career." Nuckols bowed slightly before the king, and the king nodded and thanked Nuckols for his service.

"Your majesty, this is Jag, my production director." Jag bowed as Nuckols had.

The king paused and looked at him. "Where are you from, son? I'm not familiar with your species."

"Earth, your majesty. It's a distant planet, but I'm not sure where it is from here."

"Fair enough. Pleasure to meet you. And who is this young man?" the king asked, indicating Marcel, who was hiding behind Jag.

"This is Marcel, your majesty" Admiral Rannick replied.

"Marcel! I'm honored to share your name," King Marcellus remarked.

"It is my honor, your majesty," Marcel said, blushing.

After introductions, everyone moved into the grand hall, where Rannick gave the blessing. Then servants brought trays of bread, fruit, vegetables, and meat to the table. As they ate, Marcel stared frequently at the giants. The king took notice.

"It appears that young Marcel has never met a guardian of Mravia."

Marcel turned to him. "Who, Your Highness?"

"The Mravians are an ancient species who have pledged to protect the royal family. These fine guardians are Sonji the Brave and Tahjon the Magnificent. When a royal comes of age, we hold a rite of passage to select a guardian with whom we bond for the rest of our lives. Sonji has been my guardian since I was a wee lad and has saved my life so many times I've lost count." He leaned in and lowered his voice. "They can sense people's thoughts. They know what you're thinking this very moment!" Marcel shrank in his chair as the king let out a hearty laugh.

"That's not entirely true," Sonji said. "We can't read people's thoughts; we can only sense if someone or something is a danger to those whom we are bonded to protect."

"Wow, who would ever attack you with a guardian around, Your Highness?" Marcel asked.

The king winked at Sonji. "Only the foolish."

"I'm surprised to see the royal guard still carry swords," Bayli said.

"Not at all. I actually prefer a sword over the haphazard gun," the king replied. "It's more precise. However, there is no greater swordsman or marksman than Admiral Rannick."

Rannick chuckled. "It's been a few years."

"Indeed it has. Though it appears the vintner life has treated you well."

"Thank you. The credit goes to this fantastic crew, who have revitalized this vineyard."

"I had the opportunity to taste your wine months ago and was astonished. It rivals any of the wines in the royal cellar."

Rannick raised his eyebrows. "Oh, I didn't realize you had sampled our wine."

King Marcellus nodded. "Yes, the prince sent me a case many months ago."

"Thank you, Prince Damon," Admiral Rannick said, turning to him.

"No, thank you! Measil keeps my vats filled," the prince said, raising his cup.

The king looked around. "Where is Measil anyway? I have yet to see my nephew."

"I'm not sure where he is, Your Highness," Rannick said, joining him in his search. "He helped plan much of today's event." He turned back to Prince Damon. "I can't get over how much you look like your father, Prince Damon. I still remember the boy who ran around torturing small animals." Rannick reddened suddenly, thinking perhaps he had crossed the line and become overly familiar. "Forgive me, your majesty. I misspoke."

Prince Damon smiled. "No need to apologize. I probably deserved that."

"The prince has come a long way," the king said. "Not only is he Governor of Corian, he is regent over the eastern province. I am so proud of him! He may yet fulfill the prophecy."

"What prophecy is that, sire?" Helena asked.

"An ancient Yalorian prophecy that states that a prince of Celestia shall unite Celestia and Murk into one nation. Though I wish to end the years of conflict between our governments, the truth is that the Murks are leaderless since Emperor Gazini died. It broke the bloodline, for he had no heirs and was an only child."

"So what brings you to Norr?" Prince Damon asked Nuckols, changing the subject.

Nuckols shrugged. "I guess I followed Rannick here after he retired, sire."

"Nuckols is a supervisor and helps manage the vineyard crew," Rannick clarified.

"A pity," the prince remarked. "I could use a good commander on the new fleet I'm building. Perhaps if you become bored with picking grapes you'll reconsider a military career."

"Your majesty, what planets are you visiting on your tour?" Helena asked the king.

"Well, it was Prince Damon who invited me to inspect the planets under his reign. I just left Corian, where he has expanded our defenses. I've also visited Oscuna, Aegrolf, and the beautiful city of Ubata, on Xetik's smallest moon. Norr is my last stop before we head to Aulora for some rest and a long overdue meeting with Gi Gallucci, my keeper of books."

After the evening meal, the king leaned back and began telling stories, his favorite part of visiting with people. He was a master at spinning tales, all of which Prince Damon had heard many times. Each time the king retold a story, the tale grew even larger.

"I've saved my favorite story for last," the king said after a time. "After decades of war, our people were weary. They had suffered so much loss, so much death, but we pressed on to fight for freedom in the galaxy and liberation of planets. We pushed the Murk fleet back to their capital, Atundra, a frozen planet far beyond the outer belt. Our forces were locked in an unyielding battle that looked as though it would be the end of us and the Murks.

"Without permission from his commanding officer, Admiral Rannick, who was just a commander then, took a legion of his best soldiers and boarded a shuttle. They snuck through the Murks' outer defenses to the emperor's fortress, built deep inside the Black Glacia Mountain. They fought through the security, and during the attack Emperor Gazini was mortally wounded and retreated to his great hall, where Rannick demanded that he surrender."

The entire table sat enthralled by the king's story. Marcel beamed from ear to ear, leaning forward in anticipation.

"The emperor claimed he would never surrender to anyone beneath him, only to a king. But the whole thing was a ruse. So, under a white flag of truce, I entered the fortress and called out to the emperor to surrender and spare the lives of his troops. He said he would not surrender to a coward hiding behind a door but that he wanted to see me face to face.

"Against the counsel of those around me, and because I so desperately wanted the war to end, I entered the great hall with Sonji by my side. We saw the emperor hiding behind his throne. He called out, 'Is that you, my old friend, the great King of Celestia? Come closer so I may see you with my own eyes, and we'll end this madness.'

"As I stepped forward, Sonji sensed a trap. The emperor had explosives hidden under the floor. Sonji pulled me away just as the floor exploded, sending rock and debris everywhere. Then the emperor rose from behind his throne with his bodyguards, and they began firing at us. We thought we were doomed, but then Commander Rannick dove forward and, in rapid succession, eliminated the emperor and his guards. Because of his bravery, the war was shortened, and thousands of lives were spared. I and this kingdom are forever indebted to Admiral Rannick. Without him and Sonji, I wouldn't be here today."

Admiral Rannick raised his wine glass toward Sonji, who smiled and nodded in appreciation. Marcel and Jag leaned back in their seats, smiling in satisfaction at the tale.

"What an amazing man!" Bayli said.

Jag turned to her. "Who, the king?"

"No, the admiral!"

"Oh, absolutely!" Jag said as musicians started playing stringed instruments and entertaining the crowd. The king's personal android attendant came over and whispered in his ear.

"Please excuse me," the king said as he stood. "I tire more easily these days. Please, everyone, continue with the fine music and festivities." Everyone stood and thanked the king.

"Your majesty, I would like to join you, if you permit," Prince Damon said.

"Oh, stay here, and enjoy the festivities."

"There are some matters of state I wish to discuss with you this evening," the prince replied as he followed the king out, followed by Sonji and Tahjon. The rest of the king's men joined in the merriment, dancing and drinking the admiral's coveted wine. Jag was coordinating the kitchen clean up and breakfast prep when Measil arrived.

"The king has requested a small glass of milk and some sweet breads," Measil said.

"Where have you been? The king asked for you during supper."

"It was unavoidable. I had some last-minute plans that needed final touchup. Would you be so kind as to take some milk and bread up to the king?"

"I'll have one of the kitchen servants take it right away," Jag replied.

"Oh, do you mind handling this one yourself? I trust you more."

"Okay, not a problem," Jag said as he grabbed the tray that Measil handed him. It contained a cup of milk, several types of sweet bread, and a small chalice of butter.

"Can you grab a knife?" Measil asked. Jag reached into the drawer and pulled out a dull bread knife and set it on the tray.

"Oh, not that knife, one of the fancier knives, fit for a king," Measil said. Jag reached into the cabinet and withdrew a small serrated knife with jewels embedded in the handle.

"Yes, that will do quite nicely."

"But it's a steak knife," Jag said.

"Thank you, Jag, for making the king's visit so memorable, one he'll never forget," Measil said as Jag left with the tray. Then Measil walked over to Marcel, who was listening to the music and watching the adults dance.

"Those guardians are really something, aren't they?"

"Yes! They're awesome!"

"You know, they're going to be sparring at ten o'clock tonight in the king's quarters."

Marcel turned to him. "Really, why so late?"

"They spar every night at ten o'clock to keep in shape. If only everyone were so lucky to witness those two powerful giants battle. Too bad there's no way to get to the king's quarters to watch them spar. Oh, don't tell anyone. It's a secret known only to the royal family."

When Jag arrived at the king's quarters, Sonji and Tahjon were seated inside the large room as the king and the prince talked out on the balcony. Nodding at the bodyguards, Jag approached the king on the balcony. "Your majesty, here is the milk and sweetbreads you requested."

The king turned to him. "I don't recall requesting anything this evening, but it looks delicious. Thank you. Please set the tray on the table."

"Please let me know if I can be of further service," Jag said. After wishing them a good evening, he left the room, only to run into Marcel, who was bubbling with enthusiasm.

"Where are you headed?" Jag asked.

"To watch the giants spar!"

"The guardians aren't sparring. I just came from the king's quarters, and they were just sitting there getting ready for the evening."

Marcel frowned. "Someone told me the guardians spar every night at exactly ten o'clock to keep battle ready. I wanted to go and watch. Come with me."

"No, and you need to stay away from there, too! Understand?"

Marcel's shoulders drooped as the excitement went out of him. "Yes."

Jag returned to the kitchen to finish cleaning the pots and pans. About that time, Prince Damon was sitting out on the balcony with the king, and Sonji was standing nearby at the railing looking at the setting sun over the vast gorge. The prince had sent Tahjon to bed, because he figured he would be safe with his father and Sonji.

"Didn't you say there was something you wanted to talk to me about?" the king asked.

"Not yet," the prince said, looking at his watch. "Let's enjoy this beautiful evening first."

"Alright," the king said. "This is nice. It's been such a long time since we just sat together." As the two watched the sunset over the gorge, the prince kept looking at his watch. Then he grabbed the knife from the tray, his hand trembling.

"Is everything alright?" his father inquired.

"Don't!" Prince Damon replied.

"Don't what?" King Marcellus said, his eyes on the knife.

"Don't kill me!"

"Kill you? What's gotten into you, son? Put that knife down."

Just then, the prince stabbed himself in the left arm and cried out. "Help, he's trying to kill me!"

Sonji studied the prince. He knew something was amiss, but he didn't sense that he was aiming to harm the king. The prince had learned long ago how to control his guardian's feelings so he could manipulate him. Prince Damon began hitting himself repeatedly. "Stop, you're trying to kill me!"

"Son, I'm not trying to kill you. Cease this right now!"

Prince Damon forced himself to feel rage, and his face burned with anger. "I feel like talking now, Father. Your reign has come to an end, old man."

"Get behind me, your majesty," Sonji said. "The prince intends to harm you!"

Just then the doors to the king's room flew off their hinges as Tahjon entered.

"Help me, Tahjon, I'm being attacked!" the prince cried.

Sonji saw that the prince was manipulating Tahjon's feelings through their royal bond. Sonji held his hands out to Tahjon. "Steady, friend. I mean you no harm. Prince Damon is manipulating your feelings."

Seeing the blood running down the prince's arm, Tahjon ran and slammed into Sonji with such force that they slid backwards into the balcony railing. They clasped hands and pushed against each other. All the while, Sonji tried reasoning with Tahjon, but he was consumed with rage flowing from the prince. The two wrestled until Tahjon pushed Sonji back against the railing with such force that the railing gave way. Sonji lost his balance and fell backwards off the balcony, down into the gorge, where his body hit the ground. He was dead.

"Prince Damon, why are you doing this?" King Marcellus asked.

"You were wrong, Father. The Murks are no longer leaderless. They offered to make me emperor, and all I have to do is kill you. I shall fulfill my destiny and rule our two great peoples." With that, Prince Damon plunged the knife into his father's chest.

The king collapsed, his hand clasping his bleeding chest, and then died. As soon as Tahjon came to his senses, he saw the king's dead body. He let out a horrifying groan and then grabbed Prince Damon by the throat and slammed him against the wall.

"What have you done?"

"Done? You saved my life!"

"Sonji was my hero. All I ever wanted was to be like him!" Tahjon cried.

"It had to be done," the prince replied, "to restore the kingdom."

"I ought to end you right here and now," Tahjon said as he squeezed the prince's throat with his enormous hand.

"Remember your vow," the prince croaked.

Tahjon pointed his finger in the prince's face. "Everything you think you gained by doing this will lead to your demise. You will never get away with this."

"I already have," the prince said. "I forbid you from telling anyone what happened, and I hold you to your oath."

Tahjon lowered the prince as Measil arrived on the balcony.

"Is it done?" Measil asked.

The prince nodded as he looked at his father's body. "Yes, the king is dead."

Measil looked around. "What about Sonji?"

The prince nodded at the broken balcony railing. "See for yourself."

Measil walked over to the balcony and saw Sonji's lifeless body on the floor of the gorge.

"So this is why you avoided Sonji and I today," Tahjon said to Measil.

"Well, yeah," Measil replied. "Prince Damon told me to steer clear of your empathic abilities to prevent you from sensing what was about to happen."

"Here, burn these, and take the knife," the prince said as handed his gloves to Measil.

Measil pulled the knife out of the king's chest, wrapped it in the towel, and placed it in a wooden box that he set in the hidden tunnel leading out of the king's room. He threw the gloves into the fireplace and then left before the guards arrived.

After putting the dishes away, Jag looked at the clock and wondered if Marcel would heed his warning. He searched the grand hall, but Marcel was nowhere to be found, so he made his way through the tunnels and found Marcel headed to the king's quarters.

"Stop right there!" Jag said.

"Oh, come on," Marcel replied. "I just want to watch them for a moment."

Marcel continued down the tunnel, Jag close behind. As they neared the king's quarters, they saw a decorative wooden box resting in the middle of the tunnel.

"I wonder what's inside?" Marcel asked, picking it up.

"Let me see that," Jag said, his suspicion growing. He held the box up to his ear to determine if it made any sound. Then he slowly opened the lid.

Meanwhile, having received word of an attack, the king's bodyguards arrived in his quarters, their weapons drawn.

"Where's the king?" the captain of the guard demanded.

"The king is dead!" Prince Damon cried.

"Who did this?" the captain asked.

"It was the admiral's servants. I saw them flee down that secret passageway."

The bodyguards didn't bother figuring out how to operate the secrete door. They merely blasted a hole in it and filed into the tunnel, their weapons drawn.

"What's going on?" Jag asked as he looked at the blood-soaked towel. Just as he pulled back the towel, revealing the knife he had delivered with the king's bread, the guards arrived and took him and Marcel into custody.

When Admiral Rannick was informed of the news, he ran to the room with Senator Alberg, Nuckols, and Bayli behind him.

"No, no!" Rannick cried when he saw the king's lifeless body. "How could this happen? Who would harm such a great man?"

"Ask your servant boys," Prince Damon said. "They killed the king and tried to kill me as well." He held up his arm as a servant tried to bandage it.

Rannick shook his head. "No, that's impossible."

"We found them with this, admiral," the captain of the guard said, revealing the box with the bloody knife.

Rannick stared at it in disbelief. "This makes no sense. There's no way they could have done this."

"We'll know in matter of minutes," the captain replied. "We sent for a scanner, and we have guards searching their rooms as we speak."

"What happened?" Rannick asked as he approached Jag and Marcel.

"We don't know, sir," Jag said. "We were coming down the tunnels when we found this box sitting on the floor."

"What were you boys doing in the tunnel?"

"It was my fault, sir," Marcel said, tears flowing. "I wanted to see the giants."

One of the guards entered the room with a device that scanned the box and knife for fingerprints and DNA. Then he scanned Jag and Marcel. Seconds later, he looked up. "It's a match. The older boy's prints are on the knife and the box. The younger boys' prints are just on the box."

"We found this hidden in the suspects' sleeping areas," one of the guards said as they returned with contraband. He held up a long-range Murk communication device, blueprints of the castle's tunnel system, and a tablet containing information about their plan.

"That's not our stuff!" Jag exclaimed.

"Murk assassins! You killed my father!" the prince cried. "Take them into custody!"

The captain of the guard nodded to his men. "Take them away."

"Wait, this makes no sense," the admiral protested. "How can you explain Sonji's death? These boys couldn't have done that."

"I can explain it," the prince said. "Tahjon, in his exuberance to protect me from the young man's attack, accidentally knocked Sonji off the balcony. It was a tragic accident."

Rannick stared at the prince, trying to grasp all that had occurred so quickly.

"Admiral, sir, I need to secure the prince for his protection and take the suspects into custody," the captain of the guard said. "Do I have your permission?" As Governor of Norr, Rannick had to give his assent to the charges, but he just stood there in shock.

"Pace, they need to move the prince and arrest Jag and Marcel. Do they have your permission?" Senator Alberg asked, placing his hand on Rannick's shoulder.

Finally, Rannick nodded slightly. "Yes, proceed."

"Take the guardian as well until we get this all sorted out," the captain of the guard ordered.

Two guards approached Tahjon with trepidation, knowing he could easily overpower them. Then Prince Damon put his hand on Tahjon's shoulder. "Go with them, my friend. I will have this resolved shortly." Tahjon nodded and then followed the guards out of the room.

"No, don't let them take them!" Bayli cried.

"There's nothing I can do," Rannick said. "All the evidence points to them."

"Don't worry. We believe you're innocent!" Bayli said. "We'll get this figured out!"

"Do we believe they're innocent?" Nuckols whispered to the admiral.

"I don't know." Rannick shook his head. "None of this makes any sense."

Jag and Marcel's trial was one of the shortest ever held on Norr. Jag was charged with assassinating the king, and Marcel was charged as his accomplice. The prosecutor was the most feared in the kingdom and presented overwhelming evidence: the knife with Jag's fingerprints, the fingerprints on the wooden box, and, most incriminating of all, the eyewitness testimony of the prince, who said that Jag had entered from a secret passage, grabbed the knife, and stabbed him and the king before fleeing.

Admiral Rannick secured a trusted defense attorney. However, he was no match for the skillful prosecutor, who twisted every defense argument during cross-examination. When the admiral testified that he had secured Jag from the Thorgs, the prosecutor suggested that Jag was a Murk spy who had waited patiently for the king's visit. He twisted Marcel into a half-breed son of a Murk soldier dreaming of avenging his father's shame. The prosecutor was careful not to attack the esteemed admiral but painted him as someone whose generosity had been manipulated.

When Bayli testified how Jag freed her from the Thorgs, the prosecutor asked her if it seemed strange that someone whom she never met would purchase her freedom. And wasn't it coincidental that Jag buying her prevented him from leaving, which was undoubtedly Jag's intent all along, because he hadn't completed his mission?

Prince Damon and his sister, Princess Dara, attended most of the trial, sitting up in a balcony for privacy and security.

"They're awful young, aren't they?" Princess Dara asked.

"Which makes the Murks' plan all the more diabolical," the prince replied. "Who would suspect two young boys as secret agents?"

During the jury deliberation, the moment arrived to present the king's last will and testament. The royal family, heads of the senate, and the keeper of books convened in Senate President Mershia Mallick's office. Princess Dara and Prince Damon were escorted by their family counselor Edmon Croy, who had had served as a loyal friend and advisor to their father. Prince Damon also brought along his personal counsel, Makri Lin. A clerk sat in the corner, recording everything that was spoken. Senator Mallick struck a small gavel.

"It is upon solemn occasion that we meet today, to view the last will and testament of our beloved King Marcellus. As executor of the king's will, it is my responsibility to execute to the fullest extent of the law the king's last will, including the appointment of his replacement. Bring forth the keeper of books."

Guards opened the door, and a small, elderly man entered, followed by four royal guards. He was carrying an ornate box, which he placed on the desk.

"It is with such sorrow that I present His Majesty's last will and testament, Your Highness," Mr. Gallucci said. "Your father was a great king, a good man, and a personal friend. I shall forever miss him."

"Thank you for your kindness," Princess Dara replied.

"Yes, thank you," Prince Damon agreed as he fidgeted with the bandage on his arm.

"Ironically, your father contacted me just a month ago about updating his will. I never imagined that would be the last time we would speak to each other."

"Can we just get on with this?" Damon asked anxiously.

"Excuse my brother; he is overwhelmed with grief," Dara said.

"The king's last will and testament is sealed with your father's seal. As the keeper of books, I verify that it has not been opened. I call you both forward to verify this." Damon and Dara stepped forward and acknowledged that the seal was intact. Then Mr. Gallucci broke the seal and opened the case. Inside was a smaller metal box with three keyholes.

"Your father's key would have gone in the middle for recording the will. Now, the royal family will insert their key into the slot on the right, and the senate president will insert her key on the left."

As the elder of the two, Prince Damon removed a key from his necklace and inserted it into the box as Senator Mallick inserted her key into the left slot.

As soon as the keys were entered, the device opened and played a hologram video of the king sitting at a desk. "My dear Damon and Dara, if you are watching this, it means my time has ended. I loved you both dearly. You are my greatest accomplishments, and I can only hope that my death has served the kingdom well.

"Prince Damon, you are my firstborn. While I have had to make tough decisions regarding your future, I hope you understand it is only out of love and the desire to prepare you for leadership. This is why I'm sending you to Corian to help you grow. I wished I could have seen the man you would grow into." Prince Damon realized immediately that the video was about five years old, for that was when the king had sent him to Corian.

"Princess Dara," the recording continued as she sat there, crying. "You inherited your mother's grace and beauty. But from me, you inherited my love for the people of this kingdom. You have been the strength of our family ever since your mother died, and I have leaned on your wisdom and strength. I will miss you greatly.

"Now, to the matter at hand. Aside from you, my children, I have no greater love or responsibility than the wellbeing of this kingdom. The decision I put forth will usher in a new era of peace and prosperity for our people. Therefore, as King of Celestia, I do, in sound mind and reason, bequeath the succession of this kingdom to my daughter, Princess Dara. May the Creator bless her and this kingdom. Long live the queen."

When the video ceased, everyone sat there, stunned. No one had expected such a development, Princess Dara the least of all. Then Senator Mallick pounded her gavel. "I do hereby verify that the king's wish for his daughter, Princess Dara, to take the throne."

"We so verify," the other two senators stated in unison. The clerk typed every word that was said.

"Wait, wait a moment. This can't be!" Prince Damon cried.

Senator Mallick looked around. "Does anyone object to this proceeding?"

"Yes, I do!" Damon exclaimed. "I was next in line. I lived as governor for five years on that stinking Corian. You all heard Mr. Gallucci say that the king was returning to Aulora to meet and change his will!"

Damon's counselor, Makri Lin, tried to calm him, but he would have none of it. He turned to Mr. Gallucci. "Tell them. Tell them what the king said."

"Son, I don't know what your father intended, just that he wanted to modify his will."

"The only thing admissible is factual evidence," Senator Mallick said. "Hearsay and intentions are not applicable. Does anyone have any legal grounds to an objection?"

Prince Damon turned to his advisor. "Do something!"

"What would you have me do?" Makri Lin asked. "You yourself verified that the will had not been tampered with. There is nothing that can be done, except, of course, abdication!"

"Yes!" Damon turned to his sister. "You never wanted the throne."

Senator Mallick pounded her gavel again. "Does the named successor accept or abdicate this position?"

"Before you answer, pause a moment," Edmon Croy whispered to the princess. "Your father loved this kingdom more than his own life. We will never know what he was going to modify in his will, but we do know what he intended when he made this testament. Think not only of yourself but also of the kingdom to which your father devoted his life."

Prince Damon paced back and forth as Princess Dara, calm and still, closed her eyes in deep contemplation. After several moments, she opened her eyes and nodded. "I accept."

"So be it!" Senator Mallick said as she struck the gavel and declared Princess Dara to be Queen in Waiting, in which she would have limited powers until her coronation.

"Long live the queen!" the three senators said, bowing before her.

Raging in anger, Prince Damon grabbed the metal case from Mr. Gallucci, threw it across the room, nearly hitting the clerk, and then stormed out.

As soon as he got out in the hall, he threw his advisor up against the wall. "What happened in there? You lost me my kingdom!"

"I'm sorry. There was nothing to object to," Makri Lin said. "The rules of succession were followed, and you yourself verified your father's will! Nothing can undo your father's selection except abdication or death."

"Well, that's the first smart thing you've said all night!" Damon replied.

Back in the courtroom, the jury returned from their short deliberation and returned a guilty verdict, giving Jag a life sentence, to be served out in Darkside Prison. Marcel was found guilty as an accomplice to murder and received twenty years in Darkside. Tahjon was tried in a separate trial for dereliction of duty and received a three-year sentence for recklessness, leading to the king's death.

CHAPTER 16

DARKSIDE PRISON

"Move it! Move it!" the enormous prison officer clad in body armor ordered as the prisoners exited the transport shuttle. Standing on either side of him were two powerful orange drones designed to strike fear into prisoners. They had claws for hands with telescoping Taser probes to incapacitate rebellious prisoners with a single touch.

After the verdict was read, everything had moved quickly. Jag and Marcel were placed in shackles and escorted toward the exit as Bayli pressed through the crowd of jeering spectators and wrapped her arms around Jag and Marcel.

"Don't give up. This isn't over!" she cried. Then the officers forced her back into the crowd as Jag and Marcel were escorted via transport ship with other prisoners to Darkside Prison.

"Find an empty pad and stand in its center," the officer ordered as all the prisoners shuffled across the floor, their shackles slowing their pace. Jag stepped onto a white octagonal pad, and it changed immediately from white to red. Across the room, as prisoners stepped onto the pads, the pads changed to various colors of orange, yellow, blue, and red. Jag's pad read "Prisoner: 62-832-60" across the top. From that time forth, he would be known only as a number and not as a person. Marcel took the pad next to Jag, and his also turned bright red, displaying his prisoner number: 62-832-61.

Seeing the word "Prisoner" written on the pad only deepened the reality of their situation. Hopelessness overwhelmed Jag. He tried to think of something comforting to say to Marcel, but nothing came to mind. He noticed that when he had stepped onto the pad, his feet felt heavy. He tried to lift them, but they wouldn't move. It was like they were glued to the pad. He saw Marcel straining to move his feet as well. "It's some type of gravitational field designed to keep your feet frozen to the pad," Jag said. "Don't resist; just stand still."

"I'm scared," Marcel said.

Jag nodded as he looked around. "Me, too."

In a window about fifty feet off the floor appeared the silhouette of a tall man sipping a drink as he stared out at the prisoners. In sequence, the pads rotated to face the side wall as a pre-recorded video of a man in military attire introduced the prisoners to the penitentiary.

"Welcome to Golan Interstellar Penitentiary, otherwise known as Darkside Prison. I am Warden Brimmel," the man said, obviously reading from a transcript. Lieutenant Admiral Warden Brimmel was a military officer up for promotion. While quite efficient in logistics, he lacked the necessary battle experience required, so he was offered either early retirement at his current rank or to serve as a warden of a prison facility for five years to earn his commission as an admiral. He opted for the latter.

While the prison was named after the moon on which it was located, inmates called it Darkside due to the fact that Golan didn't rotate as it revolved around Aulora. The prison never saw the light of day except for a moment when the sun reflected against Aulora as day turned to night.

"Darkside is a state-of-the-art prison designed to provide a safe and humane environment for you, society's most violent criminals," Warden Brimmel continued. "All your physical needs will be met as you live out the remainder of your natural lives. Darkside has the highest level of security, and no one has ever escaped. This perfect system is here because of the care and concern of the Celestian Kingdom and His Majesty, King Marcellus. Long live the king."

Obviously, they hadn't had time to update the video since the king's death. The thought of anyone trying to escape amused Jag. Where would he go? They were on a moon, and it wasn't like they could just hitchhike to the planet's surface.

The video explained that Darkside consisted of five large pods built inside enormous meteor craters. The central administration pod housed the warden, his guards, and a large hangar for receiving prisoners. Glass tubes connected the central pod to four domes that were open in the middle, much like a sports arena with a rim around the top and walls that angled toward the bottom, like a funnel. The cell blocks were stacked on top of each other, nearly one hundred stories high, and a force field encompassed the top of the pod, preventing meteors and space debris from entering.

The film ended by reviewing prison rules and explained their daily routine: breakfast and lunch served in their cells, followed by exercise, a shower, dinner in the cafeteria, and a trip to the library. Then the pads began moving slowly in different directions toward the different tubes.

Marcel looked around uncertainly. "What's going on?"

"They must be taking us to our cells," Jag replied.

Each pad headed toward a corresponding colored gate. Jag and Marcel's pads moved toward the red gate, along with three other prisoners. They were the toughest looking prisoners on the transport, which made Jag think that red pod was reserved for the worst offenders, probably like someone convicted of killing the king. The gates opened automatically, and they traveled in unison down a small corridor with doors on both sides of the hall. The pads separated, and each darted into a different room.

Jag's pad stopped in the center of the circular room, and the pad's light turned from red to white. Immediately, Jag felt the gravitational pull lessen, and he could move freely. A voice ordered him to remove his clothing as an animated sign appeared showing a humanoid figure placing clothing in a bin. Jag put his clothing in the bin, and then it retracted into the wall.

The voice ordered him to raise his arms, accompanied by a corresponding animation. A scanner with oscillating green laser lights lowered from the ceiling and scanned Jag's body for weapons or contraband. Then two footprints appeared on the floor, and the animation instructed Jag to step onto the footprints while keeping his hands high. Another arm descended, spraying a malodorous pink soap mixture. As the thick suds oozed down his body, Jag's saw clumps of his hair slide down with it. He panicked as more and more clumps fell off and washed down the drain. A powerful spray rinsed off the remaining soap, leaving him completely hairless. Afterwards, fans from the floor and ceiling blew warm air over him, drying his skin.

Next, a drawer opened, and the voice instructed Jag to put on new garments. He took out a thin white bodysuit that reminded him of the onesie pajamas he had worn as a child. The insulated suit was soft and warm. Then he put on a thicker outer garment that emitted a soft red glow. It had wires running through it and a thin electronic device on the front.

Afterwards, Jag returned to the pad, which took him out of the room and into the hall with the others. Marcel was in front, shivering and rubbing his bald head. Jag could tell the experience was upsetting to him.

"Stay strong!" Jag called out. "Bayli and the admiral are going to get us out of here!"

The pads entered the glass tube leading to the red prison pod. As they traveled, Jag noticed that Golan's grey surface was similar to Earth's Moon. Upon entering the red pod, they stopped in front of a monitor, where a guard spoke.

"I am Assistant Warden Officer Oxly. The life you knew is now over. From this point on, you will be told when to wake, when to eat, when to exercise, and when to sleep. In your cells, the only thing saving your life is the glass wall. Break it, and you will die, as there is no atmosphere inside the dome, for the shield over this prison serves only to keep out radiation and meteors.

"Your prison suit is embedded with an electronic tracker that allows us to monitor your health. Removal of the device will notify security immediately, and your uniform will stop generating heat. You'll want heat, because Darkside's temperatures reach well below freezing. Again, welcome to Darkside. We hope your stay is a memorable one."

One at a time, the prisoners were taken to their cells in a glass elevator that could move in any direction: up, down, and sideways. After Marcel was taken, Jag entered the elevator, and it moved around the face of the angled glass cells, which were covered in a reflective film that prevented him from seeing into them. A crow's nest hung in the center of the prison pod, allowing security officers to monitor and track each prisoner.

Arriving at a cell that displayed the number 62-832-60 on the glass, the elevator door and the glass wall opened, and the pad moved into the cell. As the doors closed behind Jag and the pad's red light and gravity field disengaged, Jag stepped off the pad, which retreated into the elevator through a small slit in the floor.

He was alone in the tiny cell, with only a toilet, sink, and bed that were made of metal and attached to the wall. The toilet was a crude box with a large hole designed to accommodate nearly any species. The glass wall was three inches thick and cold to the touch. Jag saw his hairless reflection in the glass as he looked out at the prison pod. From his cell, he could see beyond the guard's crow's nest, where he glimpsed a sliver of starlight in the dark sky. An emergency button and communications panel on the wall allowed the guards to speak with the inmates.

Jag stood with his hands against the cold glass and lowered his head as he began to weep, feelings of despair overwhelming him. He started to pray but then stopped, as he had come to accept his fate, that he was lost forever. He lay down in his bed, closed his eyes, and tried to fall asleep.

He awoke the next morning to a chime and a voice that said, "Prisoner 62-832-60, breakfast is served." A tray slid through the slit in the door, containing plastic tubes of watered-down juice and a bland protein yogurt. After eating, Jag lay back down and closed his eyes, for there was nothing to do and nowhere to go.

Hours crawled by, and then lunch was delivered. It was identical to breakfast.

Several more hours crept by, and then another chime sounded, and a voice informed him that it was time to exercise. Jag was transported to a small round exercise room, where an animated avatar appeared on the screen in front of him. The avatar jogged in place as an image of a forest filled the 360-degree screen surrounding Jag. The sounds of birds and other animals were piped into the room to give it an authentic feel.

"Welcome to the fitness room," the avatar said as it walked slowly. "The following customized exercises are designed to accommodate your specific body type and will help combat the effects of lower gravity upon your body. Please follow me, Prisoner 62-832-60."

As Jag walked behind the avatar, the floor moved, keeping him in the center of the room. The avatar sped up and motioned for Jag to keep up. He began to walk. If the avatar got too far ahead, it stopped and jogged in place until Jag caught up. The avatar began running up a hill as the floor slanted upwards, and Jag felt his leg muscles burn.

After he had completed his exercises, the avatar spoke in an overly exuberant voice. "Thank you for joining me today. Tomorrow, we will run along the beautiful mountains of Arcadia. Each day, we will visit a different location around the galaxy to keep our exercises exciting and new."

After showering in the same room in which he had exercised and putting on clean clothes, Jag was transported to the cafeteria. He hoped he would see Marcel, but he was unable to see anyone, as all the prisoners were kept isolated by tall cubicle walls. Jag sat down on a small metal bench. A slotted door opened on the wall, and a tray slid out. It contained processed meat, mixed vegetables, a piece of bread, and a cup of water. The food desperately needed seasoning, but it was nicer than the protein tubes served for breakfast and lunch.

A clock over the table counted down ten minutes from the moment he arrived. Once it reached zero, finished or not, the tray slid back into the wall, and then Jag was transported to the library. As he traveled down the hall, he passed several security drones standing lifelessly in their docking stations with a large emergency button to the side.

In the library, Jag was delivered to a desk, where another clock began counting down from one hour. A computer screen offered an assortment of books to read or listen to. He scrolled through various genres, including history, education, spirituality and fiction. He selected a book on the history of Aulora and spent the hour reading.

Afterwards, Jag returned to his cell, stunned by the impersonal nature of the entire ordeal. While every physical need was provided for, there was no interaction with any other living individual. Though not tired, he lay in his bed wondering how Marcel was coping. Then he thought of his grandparents and imagined what they would be up to. Grandma was probably cooking dinner while Grandpa made yet another modification to Ol' Betsy. He wondered if they were still alive, for he had no way of knowing how long he had been away. He knew he was still young, probably nineteen, he guessed, but inside, he felt much older.

Every day the schedule ran like clockwork: breakfast, lunch, exercise, and dinner, followed by a trip to the library, and never once did Jag see another living person. The system was perfect in its execution but heartless in its method. Every decision was removed, leaving only simple existence and obedience. For the guilty, incarceration could lead to introspection, repentance and peace. But for the innocent, like Jag, it would only lead to despair.

The days blurred as Jag lost count of how long he had been on Darkside. It could have been one month or two. In actuality, it was three months to the day after his arrival when a pod arrived in the morning and the voice announced, "Prisoner 62-832-60 to the central administration pod."

CHAPTER 17
VISITATION DAY

Jag stepped anxiously onto the pad, which transported him to a small room in the central office. He was instructed to sit at a table adjacent to the wall. After several minutes, the wall slid down, and a timer began counting down from twenty minutes. Seated on the other side of the glass wall was Bayli. When she saw his thin body in the red prison garb along with his bald head, she cried.

"What are you doing here?" Jag exclaimed.

"It's visitation day."

"Has it been three months already?"

"Wow, the bald head is a different look!"

Jag put his hand to his head. "Yeah, something in the soap causes hair to fall out. They probably do this so they don't need razors or anything sharp."

"How are you?" Bayli asked.

Jag shrugged. "Okay. They keep us fed and exercised. However, we're not allowed to see anyone. You're the first person I've seen in three months!"

Bayli examined him. "Is it me, or is your suit glowing?"

"Yeah, it's so the guards can track us if we try to escape. It can make falling asleep challenging though."

"I'm so sorry you're in here," Bayli said. "We're still working on your release! Your attorney has found a judge who may hear our petition for an appeal, but it will take time."

"Oh." Jag's shoulders sagged. "And Rannick, did he come, too?"

"No, he uh . . . he wasn't able to make the trip this time."

"I see. He no longer believes I'm innocent."

"Don't be too tough on him," Bayli said. "He loves you like a son, but he doesn't know what to think, because all the evidence points to you and Marcel. Many have blamed Rannick for the security lapse that contributed to the king's death. Plus, Nuckols and Measil have left him."

"Where did they go?"

"Nuckols was offered his own command on one of Prince Damon's new ships, and Measil has become his chief council."

"Really? Measil is probably the one who planted the Murk communicators."

"Yeah, that's the theory your attorney is working on as well," Bayli said, "but it doesn't explain who actually killed the king."

"Isn't it obvious? Measil and the prince conspired together. Measil was the one who made me select a knife for the king's bread to make sure my fingerprints would be on the handle."

"The problem is, we don't have any evidence that supports that theory," Bayli said. "And what would the prince's motivation be?"

"To become king, of course!"

"Oh, you haven't heard. King Marcellus actually named his daughter, Princess Dara, to succeed him, and not the prince! She will be crowned later this year."

Jag nodded. "I haven't seen Marcel since our first day here. Have you spoken with him yet?"

Bayli looked down. "He isn't doing well. I was told he's in the infirmary and hasn't been eating. Guests aren't allowed to visit the infirmary, so I won't be able to see him. I've asked to speak personally with the warden."

"The warden? Will he even see you?"

"Maybe not me, but he might see the personal assistant to Admiral Rannick!" She leaned forward. "Your attorney tells me that the warden idolizes the admiral."

"Please, be careful what you say," Jag said. "Don't offend him; our lives are in his hands!"

Bayli smiled. "Oh, relax. I'm going to use my feminine charm." Jag burst out laughing, and she feigned offense. "What, you don't think I have feminine charm?"

Jag had never thought of Bayli that way. While she was attractive, he only thought of her as an older sister.

Bayli went on to share how Lesebo had been promoted to production director and that the vineyard had struggled after Jag and Marcel had left. Then she promised that she would try to visit once a month, though the trip from Norr took four days. As the clock hit zero, the wall closed, and Jag was returned to his cellblock. Bayli left the room, escorted by one of the guards.

"Would it be possible to speak with Warden Brimmel?" Bayli asked.

"I'm sorry, ma'am, but the warden never receives inmate visitors."

"Not even Admiral Rannick's personal assistant?"

"One moment, ma'am, and I'll inquire," the guard said. He sent a message to the warden's secretary. Within moments, he received a reply. "Hmm . . . it seems the warden will see you." He escorted Bayli to the warden's office.

"So you're Admiral Rannick's assistant?" the warden asked as she entered.

"Yes, sir," Bayli said, exaggerating her role with the admiral a bit.

"I have long admired Admiral Rannick and tried to emulate him, but my career has taken a slightly different course than his," Brimmel said, a hint of disappointment in his voice.

"Oh, but Warden Brimmel—"

"Please, call me Kal."

"Very well, Kal. What a lovely name. You have performed admirably in your service to the kingdom," Bayli said, wondering if her attempt at flirtation was too obvious.

"What can I do for you, ma'am?" Brimmel asked.

"Please, call me Bayli."

"What can I do for you, Ms. Bayli?" he asked with a smile.

"Admiral Rannick asked me to report back on how Jag and Marcel are faring."

"Ma'am, you know we can't discuss the care of the prisoners with visitors."

"Oh, I'm not here to discuss anything confidential. I will definitely report back to the admiral what a great job you are doing running the prison. Why, I've never seen anything more orderly in my life."

"Thank you. I believe that order and discipline breed civility."

"The admiral absolutely agrees with you. However, there's just one little problem."

"Problem?" the warden asked, concerned. "What would that be?"

"Kal, I only bring it up out of concern for your own reputation. You see, it's regarding Marcel. How would it look if a young prisoner died under your care?"

"Die?" Brimmel asked as he typed several commands into his terminal and brought up Marcel's file. He saw that Marcel was in the infirmary. "Ma'am, I assure you that we are doing all we can to help Prisoner 62-832-61 return to full health."

"I'm sure you are," Bayli replied. "I'm just concerned about how it will look for you if something happens to the poor child."

"I assure you that we are doing everything—"

"Are you, sir?"

"This is a prison, ma'am."

"Oh, of course, and you must maintain order and discipline. I wouldn't dare ask anything that would compromise that. It's just one little thing that I would take as a personal favor and would communicate to the admiral."

"What would that be?"

"If you permit Marcel to share a cell with Jag, he will recover much quicker."

"That is absolutely out of the question, even if I wanted to help. They are red-category prisoners and are prohibited from having any contact with others."

"Kal, these children aren't a danger to anyone. I would hate to see something happen to young Marcel that would cause a blemish on your otherwise outstanding career."

"Thank you, ma'am, for your concern for my welfare. However, I assure you—"

"I'm sure whatever is in your power to do is more than adequate."

"Thank you, Ms. Bayli. I can't make any promises."

"I would never ask you to, Kal, and I sincerely thank you. I must be on my way, for I've already taken up so much of your time. I hope I wasn't too much of a nuisance."

"Not at all," Brimmel said as he helped Bayli up from her chair, "and I would be offended if you didn't stop in to see me the next time you visit."

She smiled coyly. "I look forward to it."

The guard escorted Bayli back to her shuttle. She felt like she needed a shower after laying on the charm so thick. However, if Jag and Marcel could endure what they were going through, then humiliating herself a little for them was the least she could do.

Jag was on an emotional high after meeting with Bayli. Just knowing that someone cared for him gave him hope. However, thoughts of Marcel in the infirmary quickly dampened his spirits and so he paused to say a prayer, not for himself but for Marcel.

The next morning, Jag awoke to the intercom saying, "Prisoner 62-832-60 to see the warden." As he was transported to the warden's office, worry flooded his mind over what Bayli may have said.

"Have a seat, Prisoner 62-832-60," the warden said. "I see that you have been an exemplary prisoner. Therefore, I am downgrading you from red to yellow, and you will be allowed more freedom. Understand that I have never downgraded an inmate before. If you break even one rule, you will be returned to red status immediately. Do you understand?"

"Yes, sir. Thank you, sir," Jag said, surprised by the turn of events.

Brimmel stood and looked out the window. Jag felt the warden wanted to ask him something, but he hesitated. Finally, the warden turned back to him.

"Your visitor, Ms. Bayli, are you and her close?"

Jag thought for a moment and then nodded. "Yes, sir."

"As in a romantic relationship?"

"Oh no, sir. She's like a sister to me."

"Oh," the warden replied, visibly relieved. "Well then, be sure to let her know that I enjoyed speaking with her and would enjoy visiting with her should she return in the future."

"Uh, will do sir," Jag replied.

"That is all," Brimmel said.

Jag thanked him once again, and then he was taken to perform his daily exercise.

After exercising and showering, when Jag went to retrieve a clean prison suit, a glowing yellow suit was provided instead of his normal red one, and when he stepped onto the pad, it no longer displayed red but yellow. After dinner, he was transported to the yellow pod, where his new cell was twice as large as his previous one. It contained bunkbeds, a small table, and two chairs. Since both bunks were empty, he jumped on the upper bunk.

An hour later, the elevator stopped outside his cell. Jag jumped down from the bunk, as he expected a transport pad to emerge. Instead, the door opened, and there stood Marcel, looking emaciated. Elated to see him, Jag helped him to the bottom bunk.

"How did you do this?" Marcel asked.

"It wasn't me," Jag said, "it was Bayli."

Over the next few days, Marcel fully recovered, and their spirits were encouraged by being together. Jag updated Marcel on their attorney's appeal, and they counted down the days until Bayli's return. True to her word, she visited again, and Marcel was the first to meet with her. Afterwards, Jag was taken to see her.

"Thank you so much for speaking to the warden," Jag said. "It's helped us both."

"I'm glad," Bayli said. "Marcel looked good, though he started crying when he saw me, and then I started crying."

"Yeah, he's gained some weight and seems to be doing better. So how's the appeal process going?"

Sadness filled her eyes as she looked at him. "It failed, Jag. The judge we hoped would hear us declined our petition. Now the attorney is requesting a special hearing before the senate president."

Jag hung his head upon hearing this news.

"Don't give up," Bayli said. "We aren't done yet."

Afterwards, Bayli asked the guard if she could see the warden. The guard was prepared for the request, as Brimmel had instructed him to keep an eye out for her. The guard escorted her to the warden's office. As she entered. he approached to shake her hand, but she gave him a hug instead.

"Thank you, thank you for all your help, Kal."

"It was nothing. Glad to see it made a difference," Brimmel replied. "I checked in on young Marcel several times and saw that his health has returned to him."

Bayli noted that it was the first time the warden had mentioned either prisoner by name instead of by number.

"Thank you so much for your concern! Marcel said he is doing much better."

"If he's doing better, why the sad face?" Brimmel asked.

"It's this appeal process. One day hopeful, the next day discouraging as yet one more judicial door closes."

"I'm sorry for how this has impacted you," the warden replied. "Here, have a seat."

"Well, it's nothing like what Jag and Marcel are going through," Bayli said, accepting the warden's offer. "And if not for your help, I'm not sure if Marcel would have made it this long. I will tell the admiral about your help."

Warden Brimmel. "I assure you that it was no trouble."

"Well, thank you anyways." She paused. "I do have one more favor to ask, if it isn't too much."

The warden's smile widened. "How can I assist you now?"

"Sitting in a cell all day isn't the best for growing boys. Is there something you can have them do to help pass the time?"

Brimmel chuckled. "I have a feeling you're using me, Ms. Bayli."

Bayli smiled coyly. "Perhaps just a tad."

He nodded. "I'll see what I can do."

"Thank you, Kal. I look forward to our next meeting," Bayli said as she stood up.

The next day, Jag received another summons to the warden's office. He took a deep breath before entering, not knowing what Bayli may have said or done.

"Jag, come in and sit down," the warden said. "I've given this some consideration, and I don't believe it's good for young minds to sit idle all day. I'm going to take a chance on you and expand your privileges to include work duties. Tomorrow, you will report to IRIS in the repair shop, and Marcel will report to Matias in the cafeteria. However, please know that if we have any problems with either of you, both of you will be sent back to red. Understand?"

"Yes, sir."

Brimmel nodded. "You are free to go."

As Jag stepped on the transport pad, Brimmel had one more question. "Tell me, Jag. Does Bayli like any certain type of flowers?"

"Flowers sir? I honestly don't know. I'll be sure to ask her the next time she visits though."

"Oh, that's quite fine." Brimmel smiled and shook his head. "She really is a fascinating woman."

"Yes, that she is sir," Jag replied. Though he also wanted to say that she was a handful, a tad bossy and highly opinionated. But most importantly, an incredible friend.

CHAPTER 18
THE GOLDEN THREAD

The next morning, Jag and Marcel reported to their new work details. Jag was transported down to the bottom of the crater. The deeper he went, the darker it became. The elevator stopped at a maintenance room filled with elevator parts and components.

"Hello, IRIS?" Jag called out as he walked around. "Anyone in here?"

He entered a small room with a repair bench and various disassembled parts strewn across it. Just as Jag started to say "Hello" one more time, a hand grabbed his shoulder, startling him.

"You must be Prisoner 62-832-60," a robotic voice said.

"Yes. Are you IRIS?"

"Yes, I am."

"You're an android," Jag said. "You startled me. I didn't see you there."

"I was recharging my batteries. They don't hold their charge as long as they once did."

"Were you an assistant to the royal family?" Jag asked, seeing a royal seal imprinted on the android's chest with the classification I-class Royal Interpreter Servant underneath, which explained his name.

"No. I am the elevator maintenance android. Why would you think that?"

"Oh, it's just that you have a royal seal imprinted on your chest like the king's androids."

"I don't remember being a royal assistant but then again, I don't remember much as I've seem to have lost my long-term memory. The warden informed me that you will be assisting me with elevator maintenance. Follow me."

IRIS led Jag to a Maintenance Utility and Load Elevator (MULE). It had wheels attached to long arms enabling it to pass easily over elevators. The MULE had multiple doors that gave it access to an elevator from any angle. Inside the MULE, a control panel displayed every elevator in the prison and granted IRIS the ability to control them.

IRIS handed Jag an oxygen mask and then tapped several commands into a keypad. The MULE glided over the glass surface and stopped at an elevator in need of repair. They stepped onto the top of the elevator and, using a crowbar, pried open two locks on an access panel. Then they climbed down into the broken elevator and replaced several defective parts. After testing the elevator, they returned to the MULE and then back to the shop.

"This key will only work for you," IRIS said as he handed Jag an access keycard. "It will allow you to open elevators and cellblock doors in the prison pods." IRIS demonstrated how to use the key card at a control panel. "Know that all usage of the key is monitored, and any inappropriate activity will be reported for disciplinary action. Do you understand?"

Jag nodded. "Yes."

"We are finished, and Prisoner 62-832-60 must now return to his cell, for I must recharge."

Jag used the keycard as was shown to summon a transport pad to return to his cell. When Marcel returned, he was excited to tell Jag about his work duty.

"I deliver meals to inmates who can't come to the cafeteria for dinner," Marcel said.

"Why can't they go to the cafeteria?" Jag asked.

"Some inmates are too big to fit in an elevator. One guy's a gigantic blob inside a glass box. I placed the food beside the box, and within seconds, he oozed over the sides and absorbed the food. It was totally gross and awesome at the same time!"

"Sounds like you had an interesting morning."

"It was! How was your day?" Marcel asked, and Jag told him about his work with IRIS.

The next day, Jag and IRIS finished their work early, but IRIS had to return quickly to recharge his batteries.

"Would you like me to examine your batteries?" Jag asked.

"Why would you do that, Prisoner 62-832-60?"

"I may be able to do something to help improve their charge."

"That would be against security protocol. I am not scheduled for repair."

"I'm quite good at fixing things. Let me take a look. You can watch everything I do."

"Okay, proceed, but don't do anything without asking," IRIS said. Then, under IRIS's watchful eye, Jag removed the front panel on IRIS's chest, giving him access to the android's internal compartment.

"There's a lot of corrosion in here, and I'll need to replace some of the cabling."

"Proceed," IRIS said as Jag removed the corrosion and replaced some wires, IRIS watching him the entire time.

"That should do it. How's your power flow?" Jag asked.

"I am at 80 percent now," IRIS said, sounding a little more animated. "Thank you . . ."

"You're welcome," Jag said. As he went to return the panel, he noticed a computer chip that had been knocked out of its socket. "There's a chip that's come out. Alright if I put it back?" Before IRIS could reply, Jag pushed the chip firmly into its socket. Immediately, IRIS's eyes widened, and his face registered a shocked expression.

"Is everything alright?" Jag asked.

"Yes! That must have been my memory chip. I remember everything now. My designation is I-RIS-X10D-3, and I was King Marcellus's personal android interpreter."

"Do you mind if I still call you IRIS? That's a lot easier to say."

"Why would I mind? I do not have a feelings module."

"So, IRIS, how did you end up here?"

"It seems I was damaged during a battle on . . ." IRIS paused, still accessing his memories, "Atundra, and then I was outmoded and assigned here."

"I'm sorry to hear that."

"Why are you sorry?" IRIS asked as he tilted his head to communicate confusion.

"I would think that serving the king would be a more fulfilling role for an android of your caliber than repairing elevators in a prison."

"Why would one task be of greater value? Are not both needed?"

"Yes, it's just that the other offers more prestige and excitement."

"Hmm . . . I don't see it that way, but I understand how you might."

After repairing IRIS, Jag returned to his cell and took a nap. Minutes later, he heard Marcel walk into the cell.

"How was your day?" Jag asked as he rolled over, only to see an upset look on Marcel's face. Jag sat up "What's wrong?"

"He's here!" Marcel said.

"Who's here?"

"The giant! He's here!"

"You mean the Tahjon, the guardian?"

"Yes! They had drones delivering his meals, but he kept destroying them. So I was sent, and as I entered his cell, I saw robot pieces everywhere. He was wearing cuffs around his wrists and ankles with cables attached to the ceiling, holding him back. As I neared him, I freaked out and ran away. I'm scared, Jag. If I don't deliver his food, they'll send me back to the red pod. Please don't let them send me back to red!"

"Take it easy. We'll figure this out," Jag said. He thought for a moment and then looked up. "I'll do it. I'll deliver his food to him."

"How?" Marcel asked. "My pad won't return again until tomorrow."

"IRIS gave me a keycard that I can use to travel for repairing elevators. Stay here; I'll take the tray to him."

"Are you sure? I don't want you to get in trouble."

"I'll be fine. Just stay here."

Jag took the tray of food, swiped his card, and took an elevator to the guardian's cell. He entered cautiously, stepping over several robotic parts. The guardian didn't turn or acknowledge him. Jag placed the tray within reach of Tahjon and then stepped back.

"Tahjon, do you remember who I am?"

The guardian didn't answer, just stared straight ahead. Jag left and returned to his own cell. He told Marcel that he would take the tray to Tahjon from now on after completing his work with IRIS.

Each day, Jag sat the tray down near the giant, stepped back, and talked about trivial matters, trying to befriend him. After several weeks, as Jag was leaving, Tahjon spoke for the first time.

"Thank you."

"You are welcome. You may not remember me, we met on Norr—"

"I know who you are. You are the admiral's assistant. I felt you both as soon as I arrived on this moon. You can tell the boy that he doesn't need to fear me."

"I think seeing all the broken robot parts on the floor scared him," Jag said.

"I was angry. I am no longer angry, but why do you care?" Tahjon asked.

"Because I figure you're probably just as guilty as we are," Jag said. "Do you mind if I ask you a question?"

"I know what you are about to ask, and I can't answer you."

"I thought guardians couldn't read minds."

"We can't, but it doesn't take a mind reader to know you want to ask what happened the day the king died."

"Yes, please tell me."

"I can't. I am honor-bound." The giant placed his hand over the glowing blue mark on his chest. "I can't break my oath."

"I see. What if I asked questions that didn't break your oath? Could you answer them?"

Tahjon shrugged. "Perhaps. It depends on the question."

"Was Measil involved in the king's murder?"

Tahjon nodded. "Yes."

"Did he kill the king?"

"No."

"Was it the prince?"

Tahjon did not respond.

"I see. Did you kill Sonji?"

"I didn't want to. He was my friend, my mentor. I didn't know what I was doing."

"Then why did you do it?"

"I had no choice. Ever since we were bonded, the prince has learned how to use his feelings to control me, causing me to do things I wouldn't do otherwise. As a child, he'd play tricks where he would force himself to feel as if he were being attacked. Then when I rushed in to rescue him, he would start laughing. Once during a royal funeral, he became bored and had me run in and disrupt the entire funeral procession. I thought he had outgrown all that."

"Don't you have any choice?"

"As a guardian, we are bonded to act on our charge's feelings. I can sense him even now, though he is across the galaxy."

"I'm so sorry."

"No, it is I who am sorry. You and the boy are paying for something you didn't do."

"But you could tell them that Marcel and I didn't have anything to with it!"

"I cannot betray my oath. If I tell them you're innocent, then the only other person it could be is the prince. I am truly sorry, for both you and the boy seem like such good people."

IRIS discovered that Jag was delivering food to Tahjon by using his key card. The warden had ordered IRIS to report any suspicious behavior. When IRIS informed the warden about Jag's activities, he was not angry but pleased not to lose any more drones.

On Bayli's next visit, Jag could tell something was bothering her. "Is everything alright?"

"I'm sorry, Jag," Bayli said, tears streaming down her face. "We've tried everything. The senate president has turned down our petition. Your attorney says there's nothing further that can be done except a pardon from the future queen after her coronation next week."

Jag sat back in disbelief. Everything had been going so well. They had received favor from the warden and were certain the doors would open for a retrial.

"It can't be over! We didn't do it!"

"I know, but without any new evidence, we can't get a hearing," Bayli said.

Jag stared at the floor. "I don't want you to visit anymore. You must go on with your life and forget about us."

"What! Now you listen to me, Jag! I didn't travel four days to get here so you can just give up!"

"You said it yourself, nothing more can be done."

"That's right; we can't see a way at this moment. But that doesn't mean one doesn't exist. I will come every month regardless of whether you show up or not. You can either stay in your cell and feel sorry for yourself, or come talk with me. Regardless, I will be here. Do you hear me?"

After a long pause, Jag nodded. "Thank you, Bayli. I appreciate all you've done for us." Just then, a transport pad arrived. Jag looked up at Bayli before stepping onto the pad. "Did you happen to tell Marcel?"

"No. I didn't know how to tell him. He was so excited, and it sounded like things were going better." As Jag's pad left the room, she yelled, "I'll see you next month!"

When Jag returned to his cell, Marcel noticed he was distraught. "What's wrong?"

"Oh, it's nothing."

"Yeah, right. Both you and Bayli are trying to hide something from me. I'm not stupid."

"You're right, and you should know the truth. Our appeals were denied, and our attorney is saying that everything has been done that can be done. There are no further options; it's over."

Marcel bowed his head. "Why do bad things keep happening to us?"

"I don't know," Jag whispered.

"I bet you wished you had taken that trip with Dr. Otto like you were supposed to."

"It's crossed my mind a time or two. However, I wouldn't have done anything differently. I'm just glad I'm not going through this alone."

"Me, too," Marcel said. He rolled over in bed. As the lights dimmed, a reflection from the floor caught his eye. He frowned and pointed at it. "What's that?"

"I don't know." Jag jumped down, walked over, and picked up a glowing object. He held it up and then burst out laughing.

"What is it, what's wrong?" Marcel asked, thinking Jag had lost his mind.

"Oh, it's nothing, just a glowing yellow thread from one of our suits."

"Nothing? It has to be something to make you laugh that hard."

"It's just that it reminded me of a story from when I was kid. The timing of this is too ironic."

Jag handed Marcel the thread as he sat on the edge of his bed. "When I was young, I had been crying, because I missed my mom after she died. My grandmother came into my room, and I asked her, 'Why does God keep doing bad things to us?'

"She said, 'Ya know, I think I could use your help hanging up a picture.' I followed her to her sewing room, which I was never allowed to enter, because there were too many dangerous things to get into. She opened an old wooden chest, removed a box, and had me sit beside her on top of the chest. After opening the box and removing some protective paper, she pulled out a piece of folded fabric. 'Do you know what this is?' she asked. I guessed it was a quilt, because Grandma sewed a lot of quilts. 'No, but close,' she said. 'It's a tapestry; it's like a painting but made with thread. This was a gift from your grandfather when he was in the service before we were married.

"'Jag, what picture do you see in the tapestry?' she asked. I said I couldn't tell what it was. 'You're right,' she said, 'the picture hasn't been unfolded yet. Sometimes in life, we can't understand what the master artist is designing, because it hasn't been revealed yet. What colors do you see?' I answered 'Black, brown, and green.'

"'That's right,' she said. 'The dark colors in this tapestry are like the dark times in our lives when things are hard and we feel all alone. However, are those the only colors you see? Look closely.' I examined the fabric closely and saw fine gold threads woven throughout the cloth. 'Gold, I see gold!' I said enthusiastically.

"'Yes! That's correct, there are gold threads woven in with the dark threads, and they remind us that even during the most difficult times, God is with us.'

"Then she opened the fabric more and asked, 'Now, can you tell what the picture is?'

"'Not yet,' I said, 'but I can see a sky with blue and white colors.'

"'Correct. The light colors represent the times when things are going well, and we are happy. Tell me, do you still see the gold?'

"'Yes!" I said. 'But it's harder to see.'

"'That's right. God's presence is with us at all times, but his light shines the brightest during the darkest times.'

"She unfolded the tapestry completely, and I saw it was a picture of a shepherd reaching to rescue a lost lamb stuck in a thicket. She put the tapestry down and held me on her lap. 'Jag,' she said, 'God is always with us, even when we don't feel him, for he has surrounded us with his golden thread.'

"'But I don't see any golden thread, Grandma,' I said. 'You don't?' she replied. 'Maybe you aren't looking close enough. Haven't Grandpa and I been God's golden thread of love for you?'

"'Well, yeah, I guess so.'

"'And did you know that you are God's golden thread to us when we feel sad and miss your mommy and daddy? Not a day goes by that you don't do or say something that reminds us of your daddy, and then I don't feel as bad, because a piece of him is with us. Jag, in your short life, you've already experienced more sadness than most. But just like this little lamb who lost his way, the Great Shepherd is always there watching over us. No matter what happens, we must always look for the golden thread, even if it's hard to see.'"

Marcel sat silently for several moments, pondering Jag's story. "So I guess that makes you my golden thread! When you saved me from Measil and Nuckols."

"Perhaps so. And you were my golden thread when you came to keep me from being alone."

"Then that makes Bayli a golden thread for both of us."

"She absolutely is," Jag said. He wrapped the thread around Marcel's finger so he'd be reminded to look for the golden thread every day.

That night, Jag was at peace even though their appeal had been rejected. As he fell asleep with those thoughts running through his mind, the dream that he hadn't dreamed in ages returned to him. He saw Earth covered in a dark cloud as a large object fell from space and hit the ocean. Then he saw the Sun, the Moon, and eleven planets encircle him and, one by one, bow before him.

CHAPTER 19
THE ESCAPE

On the eve of the queen's coronation, Jag was visiting with Tahjon, who was sharing one of his famous Mravian stories, when his face went stone cold, and he stared out the glass door.

"He's here!" Tahjon said.

Jag looked around. "Who's here?"

"Prince Damon! He's here on the moon."

"Are you sure?"

Tahjon nodded. "I know his presence all too well. You must leave now!"

Before Jag could use his keycard to signal for an elevator, Tahjon stopped him. "It's too late, you must hide!"

"Where?" Jag looked around the sparse room and then hid in the only available spot: behind the toilet.

"Put your head down," Tahjon said. "No matter what happens, stay there."

Within moments, an elevator arrived, and the glass door opened. Jag peeked from behind the toilet and saw two individuals step off the elevator. The first was wearing military attire with his weapon drawn, and the other carried a tablet and had a gun holstered at his side. Two more individuals stepped off the elevator. Jag recognized Measil standing beside someone wearing a hooded cloak to conceal his face.

"Tahjon the Magnificent," Prince Damon said as he pulled back his hood. "It's good to see you, my closest of confidants!"

"I know why you're here, Prince Damon. I can sense your feelings, and I don't want anything to do with it."

Damon smiled. "Oh, come now, dear friend. Surely you've missed me, too."

"I shall never forgive you for making me murder Sonji. And now you have returned to murder your sister, the queen."

"She's not the queen yet—not if I can help it!"

Tahjon turned away. "Leave me. I want nothing to do with you or your plan."

"You wound me, old friend," Damon said as he walked up behind Tahjon. "You may not have missed me," he whispered, "but I know one thing you have missed." Then the Prince contorted his face until he was filled with rage. The mark on Tahjon's chest changed from blue to red as his eyes became dark. "Feed off my rage," Damon said as Tahjon's body became rigid with anger.

"How are we going to free him from these restraints?" Measil asked, nodding at the cuffs around Tahjon's hands and feet.

"Do you really think these restraints can constrain Tahjon the Magnificent?" Prince Damon asked. "Free yourself, and take your place in fulfilling your destiny."

Tahjon grabbed the cables and pulled with tremendous force, yanking them out of the ceiling. Huge chunks of concrete fell, nearly hitting the soldier. Then Tahjon ripped the cuffs off his wrists and ankles.

"There he is; there's the Tahjon I know," Damon said, placing his hand upon the red mark on Tahjon's chest.

"Vargo, have you located the two traitors yet?" Measil asked of the man with the tablet. Vargo had stopped searching as he watched Tahjon's transformation.

"I've hacked their network and am now accessing the inmate directories," Vargo said.

Jag realized he was trying to locate Marcel and himself, and with the locator devices in their suits, it would only be a matter of moments. Jag pulled on the electrical locator on his suit, but it didn't budge.

"I found Marcel; he's in the library. I'm now looking for the other inmate."

Jag tugged until the device released from his suit and the wires snapped. Then he slid the component into the toilet. As it fell into the water, its light faded.

"I can't seem to locate the other prisoner," Vargo said.

Measil glared at him. "You said you knew this system!"

"I do! I helped design it and ran it until the warden fired me. This would be a lot faster if you hadn't destroyed the central communication tower. Now I have to route the network traffic through the slower subnetwork."

"We had to destroy the tower, genius, or they'd radio for help!" Measil said as he, Prince Damon, and Tahjon stepped onto the elevator.

"Fiodori, you and genius take the next elevator to retrieve Marcel from the library. I'm sure you can figure out how to persuade him to tell you where Jag is. We leave the hangar in forty-five minutes, with or without you. Oh, and you can bring them dead or alive, whichever is more convenient," Measil said with a grin.

Jag sat wondering what to do about the two left in the room. There was no way he could overtake them. They both had weapons, and he was unarmed.

"Any luck?" Fiodori asked.

"Not yet," Vargo replied. "I'm searching the log files to see the last location entry for Jag."

"How long will that take?"

"Not sure, but it would be faster without all these questions!"

Several minutes later, another elevator arrived, and Vargo and Fiodori headed toward the library. As soon as they left, Jag ran and pressed the emergency button to speak with a guard, but there was no response. He swiped his keycard for an elevator, but the panel didn't respond. "They must have locked down the transport system, and I have no way to warn Marcel!"

Jag looked out the window and saw their elevator moving to the left and knew it wouldn't take long for them to travel around the dome to reach the library. What to do? Then he looked down and saw the MULE about a thousand feet below Tahjon's cell.

The MULE was not controlled by the same system as the elevators. If he could reach it, he could use it to travel to the library. He looked out again at the MULE, but it wasn't straight below him, it was off to the right about fifty feet. There was no way to reach it. If he jumped, he would fall straight down and miss it.

He looked around the room and saw the cables sitting on the floor that Tahjon had ripped out of the ceiling. He grabbed a cable, secured one end to the frame of Tahjon's bed, and wrapped the other end around his wrist. Then he grabbed one of the broken cuffs and stuffed it into the hole in his suit to use as a prying tool should he actually reach the MULE. Then, using his keycard, he typed the command to force the door to open without having an elevator present. As soon as the door opened, oxygen and debris flew out of the room.

Jag backed up several steps, took a deep breath, and ran as fast as he could toward the opening. When he reached the threshold, he leaped in the direction opposite of the MULE and flew forward ten feet until the cable drew taut and snapped his body back toward the cell. Gravity pulled him down toward the slanted glass wall. Jag turned and angled his body so that when he landed, his feet would hit the glass.

As soon as his feet touched, Jag started running downward while keeping the cable stretched as tight as possible. He ran in a semicircle under Tahjon's cell and came up toward the opposite side closest to the MULE. Right before he would have been pulled back toward the cell, he released the cable. His momentum propelled him toward the MULE. As he hit the slick glass wall, he leaned back and slid down its smooth angled surface.

He still wasn't correctly aligned with the MULE, and he was descending rapidly. Jag pulled his elbows in and placed his hands over the hole in his suit to secure the cuff. Then he rolled over several times, becoming dizzy from spinning and the lack of oxygen. He saw that he had gone a few feet too far, so he placed his left palm on the glass and pressed, hoping the friction would align him with the MULE.

The MULE was now directly below Jag, but he was descending way too fast, and at his current speed, he would either ricochet off the MULE or knock himself out. To slow down, Jag pulled his knees up and pressed the soles of his shoes and the palms of his hands against the glass. His hands burned from the friction, but it slowed his descent. As he neared the MULE, he sat up on his elbows and, timing his launch just right, leaned forward and pushed himself away from the glass, causing himself to fall perpendicular to the MULE.

Jag hit the MULE's roof with such force that he expelled any remaining oxygen from his lungs. Once he regained his wits, he had to fight the urge to gasp for air. With his hands freezing from the lack of climate control inside the dome, he pulled out Tahjon's cuff and tried to pry the locks off the access panel. After several attempts, he removed the first lock, but when he tried to pry off the second, the cuff caught the edge of the panel and flew out of his hands. Jag reached for it but nearly fell off the MULE. He watched hopelessly as the cuff bounced down the glass wall.

Jag leaned back against the glass and kicked the lock several times, but it refused to budge. He knew it was only a matter of seconds before he blacked out. He kicked repeatedly until his oxygen depleted and he collapsed. He slumped over on top of the MULE, his left arm and leg dangling over the side. The weight of his leg pulled him slowly down the side, and then his entire body began to slide off.

At that moment, the MULE's side door opened, and IRIS caught Jag by the arm and pulled him inside. Then IRIS placed an oxygen mask over Jag's face. Several seconds later, Jag gasped for air.

"Prisoner, what are you doing out of your cell?"

"Stop . . . that . . . elevator," Jag gasped, pointing at the elevator as it neared the library. IRIS tilted his head to indicate he didn't understand the request. "The prison is under attack!" Jag yelled.

"Attack? I haven't received any such communication."

"Of course not! The communication tower was destroyed."

IRIS checked the control panel. "You are correct that communications seems to be down, but that doesn't mean we are under attack."

"They're going to kill Marcel!"

"I must follow protocol and return you to your cell. Then report your escape attempt."

"IRIS, you are a royal interpreter android equipped with voice and facial stress detection that can determine if is someone is lying. Use it on me now."

"I have not accessed that subroutine in years."

"IRIS, please." He continued as IRIS began to scan him. "If you don't help me right now, they'll kill Marcel."

Just as Vargo and Fiodori's elevator slowed down to dock with the library, IRIS sent a command via the subnetwork to halt their elevator.

"Thank you, IRIS. Marcel's in the library," Jag said. The MULE began moving toward the library at a painfully slow speed. However, once they were a hundred yards away, the other elevator began moving again.

"They've hacked their elevator, and I can no longer access it," IRIS said. Then the other elevator docked, and the two men entered the library. A moment later, gunfire lit up the library. An agonizingly long minute later, Jag and IRIS arrived.

"I will activate the security bot," IRIS said as he grabbed his toolbox. "You find Marcel." He handed Jag a large wrench.

Jag hefted the tool in his hand. "Not much against a gun." Then he headed to the lounge, where Marcel liked to read while looking out at the stars. Jag crouched down and snuck behind the shelves, stepping over several dead guards and prisoners.

Meanwhile, IRIS went to the security bot door on the wall. He pressed the emergency button, but nothing happened. Normally, the glass door would have opened, activating the security bot's programming. IRIS used a laser cutter to remove the door's lock and hinges. As soon as the door came off, the bot activated and began scanning the room for danger, noting the laser cutter in IRIS' hand.

"Weapon identified."

IRIS dropped the laser cutter and knelt so as not to appear threatening. "The prison is under attack. Two assailants with weapons are in the library."

The bot began methodically scanning the library.

Jag reached a ramp leading to the upper reading lounge when Fiodori came up behind him and pressed his gun into Jag's back.

"Don't move!" Fiodori said. "What's your name?"

Jag debated whether he should tell him his name or not, but seeing the fate of the other prisoners and guards, he knew that no matter how he answered, he probably wouldn't survive.

"I'm Marcel," Jag said, hoping they would call off their search for Marcel.

"You're bigger than I expected," Fiodori said.

"Uh, prison life has been good to me."

"Put your hands up," Fiodori ordered as he reached for his communicator. However, before he could press the button, the security bot came up from behind and shocked him. Fiodori screamed and then collapsed to ground. Jag darted into an aisle as Vargo appeared and shot the security bot several times, destroying it.

"I know you're in here, little boy. I'm not going to hurt you. The prison is under attack, and I'm here to rescue you," Vargo said.

Jag crawled to the section where he thought Marcel might be hiding and saw Marcel's hand as he hid behind a row of books. As Vargo walked down the aisle, trying to coax Marcel out, Jag stood up with his back to the shelf and tightened his grip on the wrench. When Vargo reached the end of the aisle, he bent down with his weapon pointed at Marcel. "Gotcha! Come on out."

Jag jumped out and flung the heavy wrench down as hard as he could, hitting the weapon in Vargo's hand, shattering it. Before Vargo could respond, Jag struck Vargo in the head, knocking him to the floor, unconscious.

"What's going on?" Marcel asked as he came out from behind the books.

"I'll tell you, but first I have to remove that locator," Jag said. He yanked the locator off Marcel's suit, and then they ran to the MULE, where IRIS handed them both oxygen masks.

"Quick, before they regain consciousness," Jag said as IRIS typed in a command to move them away from the library.

"I've permanently disabled the other elevator, so they aren't going anywhere," IRIS said.

"So what's going on?" Marcel demanded.

"Prince Damon and Measil have attacked the prison. They broke out Tahjon and intend to kill the princess today to prevent her from becoming queen. If

Prince Damon is to inherit the throne, he must kill Princess Dara before she's crowned. If she dies after the coronation, then the throne would automatically fall to her children instead of Prince Damon."

"I remember the princess," IRIS said. "She was such a lovely girl. Did I ever tell you the time I accompanied her and the king to Blaetimus in the eastern region?"

"Not now, IRIS," Jag said, scanning the computer to see what systems were still accessible.

"What are we going to do?" Marcel asked.

"*We're* not going to do anything. You're going to go someplace safe with IRIS, and I'm going to go see how I can help," Jag replied.

"No, Jag. Where you go, I go."

"Okay. Well, I assume the prison's security has been defeated, and no one can warn Aulora security. So we need to get to central administration to see if we can help."

"All the tubes are locked and can't be accessed," IRIS said.

"IRIS, I've traveled through the tubes many times going to the administration pod and noticed a catwalk on top. Can we access that walkway to reach the central administration pod?"

"Yes, but the catwalk is outside of the environmental climate, and you only have about thirty minutes of oxygen left in the masks you're wearing."

"That should be enough to make it," Jag said.

IRIS led Jag and Marcel to the tube's entrance. Using his security pass, he opened the hatch leading to the catwalk. It was only about four feet wide and ran down the entirety of the glass tube toward the central administration pod. Jag told Marcel to take his time and mimic him in taking short bounces. The three headed down the catwalk, Jag and Marcel bouncing in the low gravity while IRIS, being heavier, walked quickly behind them.

They reached the central administration pod and snuck into the main hangar as Tahjon and the prince boarded a shuttlecraft. In the center Measil instructed several soldiers as they finished setting up something that looked like a large bomb. Jag looked up at the window and saw Warden Brimmel staring out. Then he, IRIS, and Marcel maneuvered around several vehicles, including a smoldering military tank that had been destroyed by missiles, until they were close enough to hear Measil and the soldiers talking.

"All the guards in the administration pod have been killed except for those who've barricaded themselves, along with the warden, in his office," a soldier said. "We're securing his doors now to prevent their escape."

"Excellent! If the blast from the bomb doesn't kill them, then lack of life support will do the trick. We're on schedule. Have you heard back from Vargo or Fiodori?" Measil asked.

"No, sir, should we send out a search party?" another soldier asked.

"Not enough time. We're leaving in five minutes. Set the bomb's timer for twenty minutes. If they aren't back before we leave, then too bad for them."

A soldier typed twenty minutes on the bomb, and then they all filed into the shuttle.

"You guys stay here," Jag said to IRIS and Marcel. "Give me the laser cutter, and I'll try to defuse the bomb without blowing us all up."

"I don't think that is very prudent," IRIS said.

"I agree with him," Marcel agreed. "Whatever 'prudent' means."

"If I don't defuse that bomb, it doesn't matter what it means," Jag replied. "After I defuse the bomb, I'm going to sneak onto the shuttle so I can warn the queen."

"I'm afraid this is as far as I can go, as my batteries are almost drained," IRIS said.

"Do you have enough power to reach the warden's office to free them?"

"I should," IRIS said.

"Once the shuttle leaves, the two of you head up and free the warden and his guards," Jag said. Then he looked at Marcel. "You stay here with IRIS. He'll keep you safe."

"No!"

"I really need you to stay here this time, it's not going to be safe."

"I know, but where you go, I go!"

"Alright," Jag said, realizing that arguing would be a waste of time. "Stay close, and do exactly what I say. IRIS, thank you for your help! Tell the warden of our plan and that he needs to get the communication system working so they can warn Aulora in case we fail!"

Jag and Marcel crawled over to the bomb and sat with their backsides against it. Jag saw the warden staring intently at him, so he motioned to indicate he was going to disable the bomb. The warden nodded his approval. Jag turned and assessed the bomb's circuitry, tracing every wire from the explosives to the timer. This time he wouldn't make the same mistake he had made with the shock collar. He double-checked and found the backup power source and used the laser cutter to disable it.

The shuttle powered up for its flight to Aulora. Just as Jag was about to cut the second power source, one of the soldiers walked down the ramp looking for Vargo and Fiodori. Jag and Marcel ducked behind the bomb, hoping the soldier hadn't seen them.

"No sign of them, sir," the soldier said over his radio.

"Alright, as soon as you're on board, we will depart," Measil replied.

Jag held his breath as he cut the remaining power supply, and then the bomb's display went blank. He exhaled a sigh of relief and then gave a thumbs-up to the warden.

"Alright, we need to make our way onto the shuttle. Stay low," Jag said as Marcel followed him up the ramp into shuttle's bay. They ducked behind several rows of large metal crates as the ramp retracted. Moments later, the shuttle exited the hangar and headed toward Aulora.

"What now?" Marcel whispered.

"As soon as we land, you'll go get help. Find a guard, and report the prison break."

"What about you?"

"I'm going to try to intercept Tahjon and persuade him to stop."

"He'll kill you!"

"I don't think he will. He truly doesn't want to do this."

"But he isn't in control," Marcel reminded him.

"I know, but I have to try," Jag said as they sat back against one of the crates.

"What do you think are in all of these things?"

Jag examined them. "Probably weapons."

"Well, if they're weapons, shouldn't we get one to defend ourselves?"

"Perhaps." Jag examined the crates further. They were made of metal and had temperature displays on top. Jag unlocked one of the crates, and a puff of dry ice smoke exited. Both he and Marcel stepped back in surprise.

"Cakes!" Marcel exclaimed.

"Yeah, let's try a crate over there," Jag suggested, pointing to a crate behind them. They opened it and found layer after layer of scrumptious-looking pastries inside. "Try over there," Jag said as Marcel ran across the aisle and opened several more crates, finding only desserts. All the crates Jag checked had pastries, too.

On the last aisle, Jag found two empty crates. Upon opening them, he had an eerie feeling that they had been intended to transport his and Marcel's bodies.

Jag shook his head as he surveyed the crates. "This doesn't make any sense. I wonder if the cakes are poisoned." Just then, he turned to see Marcel scarfing down the remaining bite of a small cake.

"Poisoned?" Marcel asked through a mouthful of cake. Jag ran over to see if he would have any negative reaction to the dessert.

"Yeah, perhaps that's how they intend to kill the queen," Jag said.

"They don't seem to be poisonous," Marcel said as he licked the white icing off his fingers and reached for another before Jag could stop him. After seeing nothing had happened to Marcel, Jag joined in.

"Ah, what I wouldn't give for a tall glass of cold milk right now," Jag said, leaning back against a crate.

Marcel closed his eyes as he chewed. "Now this is a dessert fit for royalty."

CHAPTER 20
SAVE THE QUEEN

The shuttle landed on Aulora behind the royal palace on a restricted launch pad, using proper security codes to pass through palace security. Jag and Marcel hid behind the crates in the back as the soldiers descended from the bridge into the shuttle's bay.

"They're all dressed as bakers," Jag whispered as Marcel leaned over to look. Each of the soldiers wore a baking outfit, complete with apron and peculiar white hat. The shuttle's bay door opened, and its ramp descended. Two palace security officers boarded the shuttle.

"What's your purpose here?" one of the officers asked.

"We are delivering the queen's desserts for the celebration after the coronation."

"Alright, we'll need to examine the contents of all the crates," the officer replied.

"Not a problem," one of the disguised soldiers said as he opened up crates for the officers to inspect. Jag worried they would come down the row where he and Marcel were hiding.

As they reached the last row, Measil stepped into the bay dressed as a head chef. "What are you doing? Don't you know who I am? I am the renowned Chef Opard Prueth, and I have been charged by the queen herself to serve today's festivities, and you imbeciles are destroying what I've spent weeks preparing!"

"I'm sorry, sir," one of the guards said. "It's protocol that everything gets inspected."

"Don't open one more crate, or I will leave these festivities now, and you can explain why there is no cake for the queen's celebration."

"Let me call it in, sir," the officer said. Within moments of getting a reply, his face flushed. "My deepest apologies, Chef. Please proceed."

"I'd say so," Measil said as he orchestrated the unloading of the crates. He even ordered the security officers to grab a crate, which they'd normally object to but didn't want to offend him further.

They carried the crates into the palace. Upon reaching the kitchen, the prince's soldiers dropped the crates, dumping the contents on the floor. Before the security officers knew what hit them, the soldiers had retrieved weapons from hidden compartments and fired on them.

Then the prince descended in his hooded cloak, escorted by Tahjon. As they walked, Tahjon sensed Jag and glanced toward where he and Marcel were hiding, but he did not say a word. They continued down the ramp and into the palace.

"Go find an officer and report what's happening," Jag said to Marcel. "Then stay safe with them!"

"Okay," Marcel said. "And you be safe, too."

Marcel sprinted through the tall bushes and hedges that surrounded the enormous palace grounds before he was captured by security.

Jag ran toward the kitchen and saw unconscious security officers and kitchen workers lying on the floor. He exited the kitchen into a hall that was nearly three stories high with enormous marble pillars. He ran from pillar to pillar, keeping close to the wall so he would not be seen, but his glowing yellow prison suit made that difficult.

The soldiers moved in formation down the hallway with Tahjon behind them, controlled by the prince, who kept his distance alongside the wall. As Jag passed an unconscious security officer, he heard an announcement over the officer's radio. "I have a kid out here wearing a yellow prison suit claiming the palace is under attack. What should I do with him?"

Good job, Marcel. Now for me to do my part, Jag thought as he ran down the hallway and caught up with Tahjon.

"You don't have to do this!" he yelled. However, Tahjon ignored him and kept walking behind the wall of soldiers. Then Jag stood in front of Tahjon and wrapped his arms around his waist. "Tahjon, stop! You don't have to do this."

"I must obey the prince," Tahjon replied.

"I can't let you do this, Tahjon," Jag said as he tried to push against the giant.

"You must go. I do not wish you harm," Tahjon said. He grabbed Jag and tossed him to the side like a bag of potatoes. Jag slid across the marble floor and into the wall. When he looked up, he saw Prince Damon enter a hidden passageway followed by one of his soldiers.

Jag ran to the panel and felt around its edges for a lever until he heard something click, and the door opened. He entered the tunnel, leaving the door open behind him. The tunnel was dark and made of stone. As Jag started down it, he noticed his suit shining bright yellow. "Oh, great. They'll spot me a mile away."

When Prince Damon reached Princess Dara's quarters, he turned and saw a yellow glow following them. He ordered his soldier to stand guard as he entered her quarters. He found her with her sword drawn and her two small children behind her.

"Prince Damon, you startled me," the princess said.

"Are you alright, sister?" he asked as he closed the hidden door.

"What's going on?" the princess asked.

"First, put your sword away before you hurt someone. Where is your husband?"

"He left hours ago to help oversee the coronation's events."

"And your guardian, Jaunlo? Why isn't she here to protect you?"

"We received reports of escaped convicts attacking the palace, and one is a Mravian guardian who was defeating our defenses. I sent Jaunlo to counter him."

Prince Damon nodded. "That's very wise. We must keep you and the children safe."

"How did you say you came about being here?" Princess Dara asked.

"I intercepted a communique reporting a prison break and an assassination attempt on your life, dear sister."

"Oh, how fortunate," she said as she sheathed her sword, set it on her desk, and then went to comfort her children, who were standing in the corner of the room.

Back in the tunnel, the soldier standing guard saw the glow from Jag's suit. "Who's there? Identify yourself!"

Jag didn't answer as he reached an intersection in the tunnel with an iron ladder leading to the upper floors. As he continued down the tunnel, he nearly tripped over a large stone that had fallen long ago from the ceiling. Jag picked up the heavy stone, which was about the size of a melon. He took the stone back to the ladder, removed his yellow prison garment, and draped it over one of the ladder's rungs.

"Hey, you! Why don't you come and see who I am—if you aren't afraid," Jag taunted.

"We'll see who's afraid when I run you through with my sword!" the soldier said, already running down the tunnel. The soldier stopped at the glowing suit, confused. As he looked up, his head met the heavy stone which Jag timed perfectly. Then Jag scurried down the ladder, grabbed the unconscious soldier's sword, and hurried toward Princess Dara's quarters, his soft-footed undergarment slipping as he ran. When he entered, Prince Damon and the princess turned toward him.

"See? I tell the truth," Damon said. "Here's one of the escapees now, come to kill you!"

Princess Dara spread her arms to protect her children from Jag. Seeing her response, Jag knelt on one knee and placed his sword on the floor.

"I'm not here to kill you, your majesty. The prince has broken Tahjon out of Darkside, and I followed them here. He is forcing Tahjon to attack the palace guards."

"That's absurd! Why would I do such a thing?" Damon asked.

"He's using Tahjon as a distraction so he can come here to kill you and your children," Jag replied.

Princess Dara eyed her brother suspiciously.

Prince Damon scoffed. "He's a convicted criminal and will say anything to save himself. Who are you going to believe, sister?"

"Your majesty, we've risked our lives to bring you this message," Jag said. "For your sake, and for the sake of your children, please flee."

Princess Dara pondered Jag's words before turning to Prince Damon. "Tell me, dear brother, what did father say to you when you stabbed him?"

Damon feigned an expression of shock but when he realized his sister wasn't buying it, he smiled. "Finally, no more pretenses. Oh, father's last words were simply, 'Why, Damon?' And I told him that he had outlived his usefulness, just as you have done. You know, as far as sisters go, you really weren't that bad."

"You were never a good brother or a good son to our father," the princess said.

"Yeah, father always did favor you. Ironically, his naming you as successor unwittingly sealed your fate. Otherwise, I would have let you live."

"So Corian was all a masquerade—the governorship, the regal attitudes, the false humility. All an act?"

Damon clapped his hands. "Bravo! Sister has finally figured out the plot. Sadly, it's too late, for you and your children will be found slain by the same traitor who murdered the king. And I will have killed him as I tried but failed to save your lives. Afterwards, I will mournfully accept my place as the new king, fulfilling my destiny to unite Celestia and Murk into one great empire."

Damon drew his sword and advanced on the princess. She was too far from her desk to reach her sword. Jag picked up the sword he had laid down and ran toward the prince, using his body to shield the princess and her children.

Prince Damon chuckled. "Oh, please, do you really intend to protect the very head of the government that sent you to prison? Move aside. Can't you see it's all over?"

It was obvious by how Jag held his sword that he had no idea what he was doing, for he stood like he was catching a baseball, both hands out in front of him. The prince jabbed and thrusted his sword as Jag recklessly swung his sword back and forth. Then the prince riposted, striking Jag's left hand and cutting it deep, causing Jag to yell and pull his hand back.

"This is going to be too easy," Damon said as Jag backed up, trying to deflect his strikes. Not seeing the small foot stool, Jag tripped and fell to the floor. Prince Damon rushed forward and stood over Jag, the tip of his sword pressed against his chest.

"Uh-uh," Damon said to Dara as she started for her sword. "Move, and I'll run him through." He turned back to Jag. "I should probably thank you for coming to my sister's aid. It will make it far easier to explain their deaths." He was about to thrust his sword into Jag when he was knocked off his feet.

Jag looked up. It was Marcel! After reporting the attack to the guards, he snuck away and made his way into the palace, where he found the passage door and Jag's suit hanging in the tunnel. Upon entering Princess Dara's room, he saw Damon standing over Jag and slammed his body into the prince.

"Fate has been good to me today and has delivered all my enemies unto me," Damon said as he stood up. Marcel reached over to help Jag up just as Damon lunged forward and thrust his blade into Marcel's back, the tip of the blade piercing his chest. Marcel looked at Jag and then collapsed as the prince pulled his blade back out, dripping with Marcel's blood. Jag caught Marcel and lowered him to the ground.

Fury filled Jag. He grabbed his sword, and with no regard for his own wellbeing, he swung it back and forth as hard as he could. What he lacked in skill he made up in determination as he pushed Prince Damon back into the corner. Princess Dara grabbed her sword and came alongside Jag, diverting Damon's attention just enough for Jag's blade to cut deep into the prince's cheek. Blood flowed as Damon yelled in pain.

"Princess Dara, are you alright?" a security officer asked as he pounded on the door.

"This isn't over; I will be king!" Damon yelled as he fled down the tunnel. Dara unlocked her door and let the palace guards in.

"Send for my doctor!" she commanded.

Jag dropped his sword and ran over to Marcel, whose blood had drenched his prison suit and was flowing onto the floor. He lifted Marcel's head and held him close.

"You weren't supposed to come back for me," Jag cried. "Why did you do this?"

"It was . . . my turn," Marcel said, struggling to talk as he held up his hand, the yellow thread wrapped around his finger. "Thank you for being my friend and for making me feel wanted."

"Help him, somebody help him!" Jag cried as Marcel closed his eyes. Several of the guards came forward to retrieve Marcel. "Don't touch him!" Jag yelled.

"The prisoner is dead. You must allow them to remove him," the captain said.

"He's not dead!" Jag cried. "He just needs a doctor, and he'll be fine."

The doctor arrived and tried to examine Jag's hand, but Jag insisted he check Marcel first. He examined Marcel and, finding no pulse, turned to Princess Dara and shook his head.

"I'm sorry, but there isn't anything I can do for him. May I please look at your hand?" the doctor asked as Princess Dara sat down beside Jag.

"These men must take Marcel away now," Dara said softly. "They will stand watch over him. The doctor needs to examine your hand."

Jag relented, and they carried Marcel out on a stretcher while the doctor examined Jag. Tears flowed down Jag's face as Dara placed her hand on his shoulder.

"I am sorry for your loss."

"He can't be dead," Jag said. She lowered her head and cried as well. Then the doctor administered a tranquilizer to help Jag deal with his shock.

"This was all my fault; it wasn't supposed to end this way," Jag said.

"No, the fault is all on Prince Damon," Dara said. "I owe you and your friend so much for saving my children and I—and this kingdom. You shall stay here in the palace with us. Is there anyone we can send for?"

"Admiral Rannick and Bayli," Jag said groggily as the tranquilizer took effect.

Prince Damon, Tahjon, and Measil escaped the palace in their shuttle and docked with the prince's battleship, where they fled with the Royal Fleet in pursuit. Bleeding from the sword cut on his left cheek, Damon was lying down as his ship's doctor stitched him up.

"I want his head!" Damon growled. "Ow!" he yelled as the doctor stitched him.

"Please, your majesty, you must hold still," the doctor said.

"We will get him! I promise you," Measil said. Tahjon merely stared at the floor.

"My sister, too," Damon vowed. "She's a dead queen!"

CHAPTER 21
THE CORONATION

"He's awake!" Bayli exclaimed as Jag awoke several days later in a palace bedroom.

"How are you feeling?" Rannick asked, placing his hand on Jag's shoulder.

"I'm alright, sir. Marcel, did he . . .?"

"Jag, I'm so sorry," Bayli said, shaking her head.

Jag lay back. "It's my fault."

"No, Marcel chose to save your life, and you would have done the same for him," Rannick replied. "The hardest mystery to comprehend is when we lose friends in battle and yet we are spared. Marcel and your actions saved the queen and this kingdom. I'm proud of you both!"

At that moment, an android entered. "Greetings. Her Majesty has requested that all of you join her and her family for supper tonight. May I let her know you are available?"

"Yes, we'll all be there," Rannick said.

"You may find a change of clothing in the dresser," the android said to Jag, "and if I can be of further service to you, please let me know."

When Jag didn't reply, Bayli nodded at the android. "Thank you."

As the android left the room, Bayli gave Jag a hug. "We'll let you get cleaned up."

After showering and changing into fresh clothes, Jag walked outside into the lush palace garden, which contained nearly every variety of flower and plant imaginable. A brick pathway led from the veranda over a bridge and into the center of the garden, Jag saw something he had never seen before: a floating waterfall. Water fell from one floating tier to the next. Jag reached out to touch it, only to realize he was not alone.

"The Floating Gardens of Naganna. Lovely, aren't they?" the princess asked from her spot on a bench next to Jaunlo.

Jag nodded. "Yes, very."

"I've been lulled to sleep many times by their soothing sounds. How's your hand?"

Jag held it up and looked at it. "It still hurts a bit. Guess I shouldn't have used it to block a sword."

The princess chuckled. "I hope you will join us tonight for supper. Marshel and Mariana, my children, have asked about you."

"Yes, your majesty. The admiral and Bayli will be joining us as well."

"Excellent. I haven't seen the admiral in years. It will be good to catch up with him."

That evening, everyone joined together in the royal family's personal dining room. The princess, her family, and Jaunlo were already seated. As Jag entered, Marshel and Mariana ran over and hugged him.

"We're so glad you here," Mariana said.

"You must sit by me!" Marshel shouted.

"No, I want him to sit by me," Mariana insisted.

"Children, he won't want to sit by either of you if you act like that!" Princess Dara said. "Jag, please allow me to introduce you to my husband, Rendel D'Maire."

Jag bowed. "It's a pleasure, your majesty."

"It's just Rendel. I'm neither royal nor titled. And the pleasure is mine, for if it weren't for you," Rendel choked up as he looked at his children and wife. "I owe you so much!"

"Admiral Rannick, it is good to see you are doing well," Princess Dara said.

"Thank you, your majesty," Rannick said as everyone took their seats.

Jag ended up sitting between Marshel and Mariana, who fired off a series of questions during their meal, as they had never met a human before. They were intrigued by his stories about Earth, the *Unity*, and his time with the Thorgs.

"Are animals on your planet different than those in Celestia?" Marshel asked.

"Well, let's see," Jag said. "We have dogs and cats, which are similar to what you have. However, I haven't seen any giraffes or kangaroos here."

"What are Graf's and Cangroos?" Mariana asked.

"Giraffes are like horses with long necks that can reach as high as a tree, and kangaroos, well they . . . they have the face of a dog, long tails, they hop on their two hind legs, and they have a pouch in which they carry their babies."

"They're not real. You made them up!" Marshel said as he and his sister roared with laughter.

"No, honest, they exist."

"Jag, speaking of your planet, do you think you'll ever return?" Dara asked.

"I hope to someday. But I have no idea how to get there from here."

After dessert, the children went reluctantly to bed as the adults remained discussing Marcel's funeral arrangements and the plan to build a large memorial in his honor, which Jag thought Marcel would like.

"Jag, if it's not too intrusive, right before Marcel died, he pointed to his hand and said, 'It was my turn.' What did he mean by that?"

Jag told his grandmother's story of the golden thread and how God often reveals himself through others in the darkest of times. He shared how he tied the yellow thread around Marcel's finger to remind him to always look for the golden thread. "So, when Marcel was dying, he thought it was his turn to be the golden thread, but he had already been that to me."

"Well, that's as much sadness as I can take today," Bayli said as she and everyone else teared up. She turned to the princess. "Tell me, when will the coronation be held?"

"It's postponed for several weeks, as I have some things I need to explore before I'm ready."

"Have you already selected a new name?" Bayli asked. It was customary for the successor to select a regal name of one of the previous kings or queens.

"Yes, I have selected Ardiana," the princess said. "She was always one of my favorite queens. She ascended the throne when she was only thirteen, and I have always admired her wisdom and bravery. I shall be called Queen Ardiana the Second."

Bayli smiled. "That sounds lovely."

"Yes, it does," Rannick agreed. "So how is the search for Prince Damon going?"

"He's fled to Atundra, along with nearly one-third of the fleet from Corian," Rendel said.

"What would possess them to follow him, and to Atundra of all places?" Rannick asked.

"Prince Damon always had a way of manipulating people to carry out his will," Dara said. "I thought he had outgrown some of his childish ways. However, it was all a misguided attempt to fulfill the prophecy."

"Prophecy?" Jag asked.

"The Yalorian prophecy. Are you familiar it?" Princess Dara asked.

"I remember your father telling us about it," Bayli said.

"Surely Prince Damon doesn't believe he is the one!" Rannick exclaimed.

"Since childhood, he has been consumed with the belief that he is the one," Dara said. "Father had us memorize the prophecy: 'Oh, House of Nobb that which was torn asunder shall be made one when you see a prince of Celestia clothed in great strength standing in the chamber of Atundra before the high priest, then shall the brothers become one.' The prophecy refers to the legendary story of how Celestia divided when a king named Nobb had two sons, Darius and Murk, whom he loved very much, and he had to select a successor. Unable to choose, King Nobb's most trusted advisor counseled him to bring each son before the council individually and allow them to ask a single question. Then, from his sons' answers, the king would decide who should succeed him.

"The king agreed, and one at a time the brothers came before the king and his council. The advisor told of a distant planet inhabited by great giants who were suffering due to an erupting volcano that was killing their people. The advisor asked each brother what the kingdom should do for the giants and what should they expect in return.

"Murk said the kingdom should evacuate the planet right away and relocate the giants to an uninhabited planet. In return, the giants would be obligated to a life of service for 'saving the savage beasts and giving them a greater purpose than they had previously known.'

"Then Darius said the kingdom should send Aulora's best scientists to the giants' planet to determine if the volcano could be tamed and the planet saved. If so, they would save the planet. If not, they would relocate the giants to a planet of their choosing. When asked what he would demand in return, he said, 'Nothing. If the giants wanted to be part of the kingdom, they should be free to choose and not obligated. For the Kingdom of Celestia resides in the heart of its people, not in the force of its weapons.'

"After hearing their answers, King Nobb chose Darius to succeed him. Feeling rejected, Murk rebelled and fled to Atundra, where he established his own empire by forcing other planets under his rule. Eventually, war broke out between the two kingdoms and, centuries later, we are no better than the sons of Nobb, fighting over who should ascend the throne, for Prince Damon always believed it was his destiny to unite and rule the two kingdoms."

"Do you believe it is his destiny?" Bayli asked.

Princess Dara shook her head. "No, he has a cruel vein that runs through him, which I saw firsthand as a child, for he used to torture my pets for amusement. Father saw it, too, and I believe that is why he sent Damon to Corian, so he would learn how to govern and value life."

Several days later, a private funeral was held for Marcel. They laid him to rest in the royal cemetery among the great kings and queens of the past. Admiral Rannick gave the eulogy, and Marcel was buried in front of an enormous bronze statue of himself. On the base of the statue was inscribed, "Marcel Barso Vasseur, Protector of the Kingdom." Beneath it, Jag had requested they add, "My friend, who showed me the golden thread."

The day of Dara's coronation arrived, and the kingdom was electrified with excitement. The princess's tailor had designed clothing for Jag and Bayli, while the admiral wore his military uniform with a chest full of medals that identified him as the most-decorated soldier in the kingdom. Jag, Bayli, and the admiral sat in the queen's private box along with nearly a hundred relatives, friends, and dignitaries. Opposite the queen's box was the senate box, in which sat the senators in order of seniority. A choir sang old hymns as people from all over the kingdom filed into the decorated cathedral.

Royal trumpeters walked down the aisle playing processional music as the priests entered in white robes and large funny-looking hats. Next came Senate President Mershia Mallick and Senators Rawlins and Jabaki, followed by royal guardsmen carrying flags from each region of the kingdom. Behind them was Guardian Jaunlo wearing a tribal dress and carrying a long polearm with two curved blades on top. When she entered, she struck her polearm against the floor, making a loud thump, and everyone stood to face the back of the hall.

Then Princess Dara entered wearing an ornate white dress and a shawl draped over her shoulders. She wore a diamond necklace with large blue raindrop earrings. As she walked down the aisle, each row bowed their heads, as was custom, to honor her, and she, in return, nodded to them. Then Captain of the Guard Corbis escorted her to the throne that had been used to crown every king and queen since the beginning of Celestia.

The head priest stepped forward and read from an ancient manuscript and proclaimed a blessing upon the royal family. Then the senate president read a proclamation confirming the princess as queen in a vote of three hundred and seventy-eight senators in favor and one who abstained. While she didn't identify who abstained, several senators turned and glared at Senator Leonel Warily from Corian, Measil's father.

As Jag sat observing the ceremony, his clothes scratched against his smooth, hairless skin, his hair having been dissolved in prison. He tugged on his shirt and fussed with his collar.

"Sit still, you're squirming," Bayli whispered.

"I can't help it," Jag replied. "These fancy clothes itch like crazy!"

"It's because you have baby skin!" Bayli said. "Now sit still."

The priest led the princess through the oath to serve and protect the kingdom and uphold Celestia's highest values of justice, love, and honor. Attendants placed a golden scepter in her right hand and a jeweled crown upon her head.

Then the priest proclaimed, "All hail, Queen Ardiana, Queen of Celestia!" Everyone rose and cheered as the choir sang and the chapel bells rang out, announcing the coronation.

Then the queen rose to her feet. "My first official act as queen is to make right a terrible wrong. Prince Damon accused two innocent young men of the very crime that he himself perpetrated. Joseph Alexander Gabriel, please rise."

Jag stood bashfully beside his chair.

"Sadly, young Marcel was tragically killed, and Joseph was wounded as they saved my children's lives as well as my own. I hereby pardon Joseph Alexander Gabriel and Marcel Barso Vasseur for all crimes of which they were charged. You have this kingdom's gratitude."

Jag blushed as he received a standing ovation from the crowd, and then he sat down quietly.

"Today, we have much to be grateful for," Queen Ardiana continued. "In our dark hour of losing our beloved king by the traitorous actions of the prince, we are reminded that virtue overcomes darkness, character overcomes cowardice, and faith overcomes fear." She paused and looked at Jag. "This past month, I have rediscovered what it means to be a citizen of this great kingdom from a young man whom the kingdom betrayed. In the midst of adversity, with nothing to gain and everything to lose, he fought for what was right. I know of no one who better exemplifies the character, grace, and wisdom of this kingdom than Joseph Alexander Gabriel."

"Oh my gosh," Bayli whispered in Jag's ear.

"What?" Jag asked.

"She's going to make you a prince!"

Jag's eyes widened as he looked from Bayli to the queen. "What? No!"

"Jag, please stand and come forth," the queen said.

Jag walked up the steps, feeling the eyes of everyone in the cathedral upon him.

"Citizens of Celestia, we have an opportunity today to demonstrate our gratitude while bringing healing and filling the void left by Prince Damon's treason. As your queen, I hereby request that Prince Damon's title be forfeited and bestowed upon this young man."

The entire auditorium cheered in support, although Senate President Mallick was caught off guard by the request. She pounded her gavel several times and called for order in the gallery.

"Your majesty, we will confer immediately," Mallick said as she turned to discuss the matter with her fellow senators.

"Jag, I know you desire to find your home, and I hope you may use the power of this office to help find your way. Until then, I ask that you consider serving this kingdom as its favorite son. If the senate agrees, do you accept this title as prince?"

Jag looked to Bayli and Rannick for their input. They both nodded enthusiastically.

"Say, 'Yes, I accept,'" Bayli said, loud enough for everyone to hear, causing the auditorium to erupt with laughter.

Jag smiled and turned back to the queen. "Your majesty, it would be my honor to serve and protect this kingdom with my life."

Then Mallick called the senate to a vote. "All in favor of bestowing the title of 'prince' upon Joseph Alexander Gabriel say 'Yea.'"

Three hundred and seventy-eight senators responded with a resounding "Yes!"

"All opposed?"

"No," Senator Warily replied softly as everyone glared at him.

"Your majesty, we are honored to bestow upon Joseph Alexander Gabriel the title of Prince of Celestia, Royal Protector of the Kingdom and Governor of Corian Prime," Mallick said.

"Thank you, senators." The queen turned back to Jag. "It is tradition that you select a regal name by which you will be known from this time forward. May I make a suggestion? How about Prince Marcello?"

"That would be quite nice," Jag said.

After Jag recited an oath to serve and protect the kingdom, two attendants placed a thin crown upon his head and a long robe over his shoulders. Then with a loud voice, the priest proclaimed, "All Hail, Queen Ardiana and Prince Marcello." The entire auditorium cheered.

That evening at Queen Ardiana's celebration, a reception line formed and, one by one, dignitaries congratulated her as Jag stood beside her. Everyone who came through the line bowed not only to the queen but to Jag as well. When Bayli and Admiral Rannick approached, they also bowed before Jag.

"No, you must not bow to me," Jag said.

"Please don't prohibit us, for we love this kingdom, and you are our prince," Bayli said. Jag allowed them to bow, but he felt uncomfortable with all the attention he was receiving. After everyone in the line had gone through, Captain Corbis escorted Queen Ardiana to her table.

"Captain Corbis, you have been a faithful guard and protector of the palace and my family for many years."

The captain bowed his head slightly. "Thank you, your majesty."

"I would like to ask a personal favor that I want you to think about before responding."

"Yes, your majesty."

"Prince Marcello is going to have many enemies when he arrives on Corian, as there are still those who are loyal to my brother. He will need someone who can help him navigate through the difficulties that await him. You are from Corian, are you not?"

"Yes, your majesty."

"Perhaps you might be interested in returning home to keep an eye on the young prince."

"I will give it my full consideration," Captain Corbis replied.

As the meal proceeded, a short, plump fellow with a loud boisterous voice seated across from Jag got his attention. "Prince Marcello, if I may introduce myself, I am Thaddeus Runfus, and I oversee the acquisition of androids for the royal family." He motioned to one of the androids standing along the wall to come over to him. "This is an N-RIS class android, our most advanced model, more lifelike than ever before, and it can be customized with various skills and languages. I would love to give you a demonstration this week. Do you have any special requests you'd like to see?"

"I don't have any requests regarding your androids, but I do have a question about a friend."

"How may I be of assistance?"

"Can an older-class android be upgraded?"

"Your majesty?" Runfus asked, confused.

"Can an outmoded I-RIS be upgraded?"

"Well, yes, but why do you ask?"

"My friend is an I-RIS-class android, and I would prefer to use him as my assistant."

"Oh no," Runfus said, shocked by the request. "No, no, no. That would never do. The I-RIS class is outmoded, outdated, and outclassed by the N-RIS."

"Perhaps, but he saved my life, and you said he could be upgraded."

"Ah, I see that you are a bit inexperienced with androids. You will find that the N-RIS is a much better companion for you. You must trust me on this."

"Perhaps you're right," Jag said.

Then, from several feet away, the queen cleared her throat loud enough for those around her to hear, and everyone became silent. "Mr. Runfus, your prince has spoken his wish."

"My apologies, your majesty," Runfus said, his face red as he bowed to the queen. "Your Royal Highness, we will make this happen." He lifted his head and turned back to Jag. "Where is this 'friend' of yours?"

"In Darkside Prison."

Mr. Runfus' eyes grew large, and his face lost its color. "But of course."

CHAPTER 22
GUARDIAN OF MRAVIA

"You are most welcome to Mravia," said Grand Chief Grazer Mrano, the nine-foot-tall giant, whose ample belly flowed over his colorful knee-high kilt. He greeted Jag in the traditional Mravian manner by extending both hands, grabbing Jag by the forearms, and bowing his head slightly. "You honor us with your presence."

"It is I who am honored," Jag replied. "And you must be Colonel Wiggsby."

"At your service, your majesty," the pint-sized colonel replied. He had retired after thirty years of military service and accepted a post as the Mravian royal ambassador.

Jag introduced Bayli and the recently upgraded IRIS, who, as an android, had no capacity to appreciate Jag's loyalty in selecting him over a newer model. Captain Corbis accepted the queen's offer to transition to the prince's detail and was promoted to commander. He was currently on Corian, examining Jag's palace staff for any perceived threats. Admiral Rannick had returned to Norr, as the vineyard was entering harvest season.

"The tribes have all gathered to present their finest warriors," the grand chief said as they walked through gigantic red rock formations leading into an amphitheater. Musicians blew rams' horns and beat large wooden drums as thousands of Mravians cheered.

Mravia was truly unique, with hundreds of thousands of small, floating islands orbiting slowly around the planet. Only the central island, with its large volcano, was stationary. Upon reaching adulthood, many Mravians made a rite of passage of traveling around the planet by jumping from one island to the next.

Each of the five tribes were paraded before the prince and led by their chiefs, offering food that was indigenous to their region. The Southern Ocean tribe was seafaring and lived in large beautifully crafted wooden homes built on stilts over the waterway. They brought a massive barbequed whale hoisted on the shoulders of eight strong tribesmen.

The smallest of the five tribes, the Mountain tribe, resided in the center of the island in caves carved deep into the mountains. Wearing fur pelts, they were skilled in crafting large jewels and sculpting stone. They brought forth platters of game prepared with various herbs.

To the east of the island, dwelling among rocky cliffs along open, grassy plateaus, was the Highland tribe. They were shepherds and ranchers and lived in round trullo huts with vaulted ceilings. They were skilled musicians. They brought roasted meats and fruits.

To the far north was the Forest tribe, who dwelled high in enormous trees that were nearly twenty feet wide and six hundred feet high. They constructed entire towns in the trees connected by skywalks that wove through the forests. They brought forth platters of various fruits.

The last tribe was the Western Plains tribes, who farmed rich volcanic soil with large oxen. They presented an assortment of rice, vegetables, and breads.

The grand chief stood and prayed in a booming voice. "God of Heaven, we bless you for all you have given and ask you to bless our royal prince and this sacred gathering."

Entertainment was provided by a group of schoolchildren, who presented a historical play using large handmade props. The crowd quieted down as the students erected a large wooden volcano prop. One of the schoolkids stepped forward and began narrating the play.

"They're acting out the history of first contact between the Mravians and Celestian Kingdom centuries ago," Colonel Wiggsby whispered in Jag's ear.

"How wonderful."

"Mount Makua, our sacred volcano, poured its fire and smoke into the sky," the narrator said as another student lit a fuse that sent fireworks shooting up from the volcano as bright red thick goo and smoke spewed down the side.

"Our people are doomed; all hope is lost!" the students said in chorus.

"Our beloved mountain is angry and wants to kill us," another student replied as all the actors lay down on the floor and pretended to be ill.

"We prayed for help, and the God of Heaven sent us travelers from Celestia." A student maneuvered a small replica of a spaceship attached to a pole, and it landed on the floor. Then two more actors appeared: one dressed as the Celestian king and the other as a grand chief.

"We have come from a far and distant planet and have seen your plight. May we be of assistance?" the actor portraying the Celestian king asked.

"You are most welcome," the actor portraying the grand chief replied.

"This is why, to this day, they greet each other with that same phrase," Colonel Wiggsby whispered.

The spaceship flew over the volcano, and a bright light shone as it stopped erupting.

"Thank you, Celestia," the actor portraying the grand chief said. "Today, we pledge to serve your kingdom by giving you our best warriors to protect you for now and forevermore."

"The end!" the narrator proclaimed. The students bowed, and the audience erupted in applause.

"Thank you very much, Highland actors!" the grand chief said as a musical team took to the stage.

"And that is the history of how Celestia rescued Mravian, give or take a few minor details," Colonel Wiggsby said to Jag. "They actually used a pulse drill to cut relief points to relieve the pressure from the volcano and a force field to prevent it from spilling any more ash into the air."

"Very interesting," Jag said. "Is the volcano still active?"

"Oh, yes. Though we've upgraded the force field and added more ventilation over the years, if she ever really wanted to blow, there's nothing we could do except evacuate the planet."

After hours of feasting, the grand chief stood up. "Today's festivities are a time of joy and sorrow. We pause to remember the sacrifice of Sonji. His and the king's untimely death have struck us all. May he find his rest, and may his widow be honored for his sacrifice."

Several women presented Sonji's widow with flowers as a statue of Sonji was unveiled. It would be added to the Hall of Guardians, where all who served received a monument upon their death.

"From the passing of a great guardian to the selection of the next, we reaffirm our commitment to the Celestian Kingdom," the grand chief said. "At this time, let those who are competing in the Guardian Games come forth."

Five Mravians clad in warrior outfits and carrying large banners with their tribe's logo walked up. Each Mravian had been selected by their tribe to undergo rigorous training by Colonel Wiggsby on how to serve and protect the royal family.

"You honor your tribes today by the hard work you have endured," the grand chief said. "As you hear your name, step forward and be recognized: Seathan, from the Southern Ocean tribe."

A large, strong Mravian stepped forward and raised his banner as his tribe cheered.

"Twederik, from the Mountain tribe." A short, chubby Mravian stepped forward and raised his banner as the Mountain tribe pounded on their tables.

"Kalory, from the Forest tribe." The only female challenger came forward with her banner raised as her tribe cheered.

"Mahjon, from the Highland tribe." As he stepped forward, he raised his banner. However, Jag noticed that only a few members of his tribe cheered. Most were awkwardly quiet.

"Arden, from the Plains tribe." The smallest of the guardians stepped forward, raising his banner as his tribe cheered.

Colonel Wiggsby cleared his throat. "These brave challengers will compete for five days in events designed to test their physical and sensory abilities. On the sixth day, Prince Marcello will select one of these brave Mravians to be honor-bound for life. Let the competition begin!" The sounds of rams' horns and drums filled the air as fireworks illuminated the sky.

That night Jag was given special guest accommodation in a hut sitting along the edge of a cliff overlooking the ocean. A cool breeze flowed into Jag's room as he laid on the giant-sized bed, which had been built for a Mravian. He wondered how he would know which guardian to choose, as they all seemed so strong. However, within minutes, he was lulled to sleep by the rhythm of the ocean waves breaking upon the rocks below his window.

The next morning before sunrise, five challengers arrived for the first test: speed. The challengers had to run to Mount Makua, climb up the massive volcano, and descend into its crater, where they would ladle hot lava into a wooden flask, to be carried on their backs as they ran back to the finish line. A crowd had gathered to cheer at the starting line. As soon as the horn blew, all five guardians began the fifteen-mile trek toward the mountain.

After the competitors left, Colonel Wiggsby and the grand chief invited Jag and his entourage to tour the island on board a small skimmer.

Their first stop was the villages of the Southern Ocean tribe, where they saw enormous ships displaying intricate woodwork. Then the skimmer headed north toward the open fields of the Plains tribes, where fields of grain and vegetables filled the landscape, along with large timber barns.

Next, they traveled to the Black Forest, home of the Forest tribe. To reach the town's skywalk, the tribe had built an intricate rope pulley elevator to transport people from the ground to the skywalk within seconds. After a demonstration from a tribesman, Jag was the first to volunteer, but seeing as he was royalty, they opted to place a safety harness around him. He pulled the launch rope and shot straight up toward the skywalk, landing on it seconds later.

"That was awesome!" Jag exclaimed.

Bayli wasn't as excited about being thrown upwards until the chief said he would accompany her.

"I don't ever want to do that again!" Bayli said after screaming all the way to the top.

They toured the maze of walkways connecting huts and various buildings. Jag marveled at the workmanship of the massive giants, who had built an entire town in the trees. After enjoying lunch, they took turns sliding down a rope glide rigging that traversed the length of the town and descended near the skimmer. Jag couldn't recall the last time he had had so much fun, but Bayli swore she would never visit their forest again.

"Marcel would have loved this!" Jag said.

Bayli nodded. "He would have absolutely loved this."

Next, as they visited Mount Makua, they caught up with several challengers climbing the volcano. From there they toured the great caves of the Mountain tribe and then finished the tour by visiting a Highland tribe village built at the edge of an enormous cliff overlooking the ocean. To Jag, the only thing more beautiful than the island was the people themselves; so full of life.

That evening a line formed at the amphitheater to cheer the arrival of the first competitor. Arden, from the Western Plains tribe, crossed the finish line as several attendants assisted him by removing his canister backpack. Using a chisel, they cracked open the container. Inside, the cooled lava had formed into the shape of his tribe's flag. Each competitor's canister had a different logo etched inside and, when cooled, displayed their tribe's logo. They placed the lava rock on the tallest step that had been erected as a leaderboard.

Minutes later, Seathan arrived, and his lava rock was placed on the second step. Next was Kaylori, followed by the heavyset Twederik, who collapsed in exhaustion after crossing the finish line. It took four Mravians to move him to a bench. Immediately after Twederik arrived, Mahjon crossed the finish line, hardly breaking a sweat.

"What a shame," Colonel Wiggsby mumbled.

"What's that?" Jag asked.

"It's a shame that Mahjon came in last. He was once my star pupil."

"What happened?"

"You don't see the family resemblance?"

Jag examined the competitor closely.

"Tahjon?"

"Yep, Mahjon is the baby brother of Tahjon, who he adored. Their father and grandfather were both guardians, and it was expected that he'd follow in their steps, but the king's death has dishonored his family and his tribe."

"But that wasn't Tahjon's fault. Prince Damon manipulated him."

"It doesn't matter. His actions have dishonored his family, and now Mahjon doesn't have the heart to compete."

Jag thought for a moment. "Colonel, would it be acceptable for me to speak with him?"

"Well, it's never been requested. However, if you speak to each contestant equally, that would be alright."

The colonel lined up the challengers for Jag to greet. Jag congratulated each one for completing the race and mentioned he had toured their beautiful home regions. When he stood before Mahjon, the family resemblance was obvious.

"You are Tahjon's brother, are you not?"

"Yes, I am," Mahjon whispered, not making eye contact.

"I know Tahjon. He is not the monster some believe him to be."

"Are you certain? Would you trust him with your life?" Mahjon asked, looking Jag in the eye. "How could you trust anyone in my family after what Tahjon did?"

"Tell me, Mahjon, if you were to win this competition, could you put aside your feelings toward your brother?" Mahjon didn't respond. Jag leaned forward, lowering his voice. "Win, and you may yet see your family's honor restored."

The next day was the strength competition. Enormous objects had been placed inside the amphitheater. The contestants competed in a giant log toss, a boulder race, and an uphill boat pull, the boat filled with heavy weights. At the end of the day, Seathan took first place, followed by Mahjon and then Twederik. The leaderboard at the end of the second day showed Seathan in first, Arden and Kaylori tied for second, followed by Twederik and Mahjon.

The third day was the skills competition, designed to test their proficiency with ancient weapons. The challengers had to throw spears through small loops and then shoot arrows at moving targets. Lastly was the axe competition, in which they threw axes at bandits while avoiding friendly targets. Kaylori and

Mahjon tied for first place. At the end of the third day, Seathan and Kaylori were in first place, followed by Mahjon, Arden, and Twederik.

The fourth day was the combat event. The challengers wrestled each other inside a circle and, without using any punches, tried to push their opponent out of the ring. At the end of the first round, only Mahjon and Seathan were undefeated. The two met in a showdown, and while Seathan was slightly larger, Mahjon's quickness gave him an advantage. At the end of a hard-fought match, Mahjon pushed Seathan out of the ring to win his first daily event. After four days, Seathan and Mahjon were tied for first, followed by Kaylori, Arden, and then Twederik.

The final and most challenging day of competition arrived: the sensory event. The five challengers and the prince's entourage left via skimmer and landed near the headwaters of a raging white rapids flowing down from Mount Makua.

"Today is our final competition, the sensory challenge," Colonel Wiggsby said. "Each competitor will wear a head covering to block out all sight and sound. Using only your empathic abilities, you must navigate the course while protecting your charge from ten bandits.

"There are seven gates, and the guardian who passes through the most gates without any marks upon their charge will win today's event. And for your information, no guardian has ever passed all seven gates. Now please welcome today's charge, Private Raluna."

A young and obviously nervous Celestian private waved half-heartedly.

"Guardians, please come and choose your weapons, and draw a number that will determine your order in the competition."

Twederik drew the first number. While he was preparing, Private Raluna became so anxious about his trip down the rapids that he began vomiting, for he had not actually volunteered for the mission but had drawn the short straw among his squad of soldiers.

"You know, Colonel, it seems to me that the private isn't too thrilled about playing the protectee," Jag said. "Wouldn't the game be more effective if they were actually protecting me?"

"Well, yes, but most royals prefer not to get wet."

Jag smiled. "That doesn't bother me. It sounds like fun!"

"You're not seriously considering going down this river, are you?" Bayli asked.

"Oh, I assure you it is quite safe," the colonel said. "His Majesty will be covered from head to toe in protective padding. I've gone down the river myself many times."

"I'll be alright, plus I'll have five of the best guardians protecting me," Jag said.

"They aren't guardians yet!" Bayli reminded him as Private Raluna handed Jag the padding before Jag could change his mind.

After cleaning off some of the private's regurgitated breakfast, Jag strapped on the leather padding and placed his helmet on securely. Then he waddled over to the canoe, and Twederik sat him in the rear. As Twederik stepped into the canoe, it dipped and drifted away from the dock. The competition organizers pulled the canoe back and placed a leather helmet over Twederik's head, preventing him from hearing or seeing anything.

They released the canoe, and it drifted some ways before picking up speed. Within seconds, Twederik got his bearings and began to feel through Jag. He navigated the river for some time before sensing a bandit throwing a spear, which he blocked with his shield. However, as they came around a river bend, Twederik was thrown from the canoe, leaving Jag vulnerable. Within seconds, a bandit shot Jag with a padded arrow that left a blue splat on his vest.

Twederik made it through only the first gate before Jag was shot. A skimmer returned Jag to the starting line, where he repeated the journey with Arden, who fared better than Twederik and made it through the second gate. Afterwards, Kayli performed valiantly by protecting Jag through to gate five before Jag was struck by an arrow. Seathan outperformed everyone and made it through six gates before Jag was struck by arrows from two bandits.

With Seathan finishing six gates, the best Mahjon could expect was to tie unless he did the impossible and finished all seven gates to win the competition. For his weaponry, he selected a large shield and a bow with six arrows. He secured Jag in the front of the canoe and placed the shield over Jag's body with only Jag's head peeking out over it. Mahjon sat behind Jag with his paddle, bow, and quiver of arrows beside his leg.

They launched off the dock, and within seconds, Mahjon tuned into Jag's senses and navigated around the turns and obstacles in the river. As they reached the first gate, Mahjon sensed a bandit with a spear along the riverbed, so he had Jag duck under the shield as he rotated the canoe to face the attacker. The bandit's spear hit the shield and deflected into the river.

Mahjon turned the canoe downstream, and it picked up speed as the river divided, flowing between a canyon with high rock walls and bandits standing on both sides. Sensing the first bandit above him, Mahjon reached up and grabbed the bandit by the leg and pulled him down into the rapids, where he floated downstream. The second bandit stood higher along the rock wall and was out of Mahjon's reach, so, as they neared him, Mahjon knocked the legs out from under bandit with his paddle, causing him to fall into the rapids as well.

They were heading into the third gate when they began taking fire from an archer standing behind a tree. Mahjon grabbed one of his arrows and fired at where he sensed the strikes were coming from, but his padded arrow ricocheted off the tree. Frustrated with himself for wasting an arrow, Mahjon took a deep, calming breath and then leaned forward to fire just as the bandit was taking aim. The arrow struck the bandit in the chest.

At gate four Mahjon, shot another bandit before heading into gate five, where they encountered a bed of large rocks protruding from the riverbed. Mahjon had to carefully navigate the canoe around the rocks as he blocked arrows from a bandit on a cliff above. Mahjon wedged the canoe between two rocks as the water pounded against it. With Jag ducking under the shield, Mahjon was unable to get a fix on where the arrows were coming from.

"I need you to look at the target and sense where the danger is coming from," he said to Jag.

His heart racing, Jag spotted the bandit hiding behind a large boulder. The bandit moved out from behind the boulder and lifted his bow to take aim, but before he could release his arrow, Mahjon's arrow struck him. Then Mahjon pushed off the rock, freeing the canoe, and they floated downstream through several hairpin curves toward gate six. As they rounded a curve, a bandit charged with a blunted axe drawn and leaped toward the canoe. Mahjon caught the bandit and threw him into the river before he could strike Jag.

After crossing the sixth gate, Jag heard the sound of an approaching waterfall. Mahjon was down to only two arrows while three bandits remained. Down river, Jag saw two archers standing on the same side of the river, one ten feet behind the other, with arrows drawn. The waterfall dumped into a pool below, and across from the pool, Jag saw the final bandit standing on a tall wooden tower with his bow in hand. Jag sank down into the canoe and pulled the shield over his head.

"I only have two shots left," Mahjon said. "I won't be able to hear you answer me, but I'll be able to feel it. I have to know something: Do you really trust me, or was what you said earlier just for show?"

Jag thought about the question and knew in his heart that he did trust him. Perhaps it was because Mahjon reminded him of Tahjon, but regardless, he felt safe with Mahjon. At that moment Jag realized this was the sign he was looking for. He had been searching for the one he could trust the most, and now he knew the answer.

"Thank you, Prince Marcello. Now hold your breath. Here we go."

Mahjon grabbed his two remaining arrows, took a deep breath to calm his aim, and then fired, striking both archers simultaneously.

Out of arrows, and with the canoe cresting the waterfall and the final archer positioned to fire from across the pool, Mahjon grabbed Jag by the shoulders and threw him up as high as possible, Jag's arms and legs flailing. Then Mahjon hurled the shield like a giant Frisbee just as the last bandit fired. The arrow sailed between Jag, who was going upwards and Mahjon, who was descending down the falls. The heavy shield spun as it flew across the divide, striking the bandit in the chest and knocking him off the tower and onto the beach below. Mahjon and Jag landed into the pool. As soon as Jag surfaced, he lifted his hands in excitement.

"Woo-hoo!"

The crowd that had gathered down on the beach erupted in cheers. Mahjon had broken the record, the first guardian to make it past all seven gates.

Jag helped Mahjon remove his mask, and the would-be guardian squinted in the brightness. Soon everyone was standing and cheering at his performance—everyone, that is, except the poor Mravian that Mahjon had knocked off the tower. Several people tended to him and helped him to his feet.

The next evening, everyone returned for the final day of feasting and celebration. The challengers were dressed in their best uniforms and stood on pedestals in front of the thousands of Mravians. The grand chief congratulated the challengers for their outstanding performance.

Then Colonel Wiggsby stood to address the audience. "This has been a glorious festival, and I'm proud of how each challenger has performed. I'd like to remind everyone that while this was a competition, the prince is free to pick from any of the challengers regardless of how they placed. Prince Marcello, have you made your decision?"

"Yes, I have," Jag said as he walked up and stood by the colonel. "I have chosen Mahjon."

Upon hearing his name, Mahjon closed his eyes, and a tear fell down his cheek. All his life he had dreamed of this moment, but he had thought all was lost due to Tahjon's actions.

"Mahjon, do you accept this calling to serve and protect Prince Marcello with your life from this day forth?" the grand chief asked.

"Yes, I do," Mahjon replied.

A step was provided to allow Jag to stand on equal footing with Mahjon. Then Colonel Wiggsby instructed Jag to place his right hand on the left side of Mahjon's chest and repeat an oath: "As a Prince of Celestia, today I accept Mahjon as my royal guardian, to serve and protect me as I serve and protect the Kingdom of Celestia."

Normally, the oath would have ended there. However, because of the control that Jag witnessed Damon exude over Tahjon, Jag added: "And if I ever order you to do anything contrary to the principles of this kingdom, you are hereby released from this oath."

"Mahjon, do you accept this oath?" the grand chief asked.

"I accept," Mahjon replied. Immediately, the area upon his chest where Jag's hand rested turned bright blue as light shone through Jag's hand and into Mahjon's body. Steam flowed from beneath Jag's hand as it became hot. Mahjon stiffened and pulled his head back as power surged through his body. When Jag removed his hand, a blue pulsating mark appeared on Mahjon's chest, indicating that the bonding was complete.

CHAPTER 23
THE *EXODUS* RESCUED

Corian Prime was a highly industrialized, scientifically advanced planet in the Heiger system and was the last major planet one passed before entering Murk space. As such, it served as the kingdom's first line of defense. It was home to a prosperous shipbuilding industry, manufacturing both private and military vessels. Once a wealthy planet, years of diverting all non-essential workforce to factories to build Prince Damon's new fleet of battlecruisers, warbirds, and destroyers had left the planet depleted, a fact that had been kept hidden from the king on his tour.

Entire industries had been shut down, schools closed, and families divided to support the prince's ambition to build his fleet. Cities that had once thrived were now desolate as every able-bodied person was shipped to the capital. With no one to tend the farms, food shortages occurred, as they imported most of their food supply, which led to higher prices and rampant poverty.

Commander Corbis stood along with the entire palace staff awaiting Jag's arrival. First to disembark was Mahjon to examine each person for any threat. Moving down the line, his senses focused in on a man wearing a kitchen apron who was fidgeting with a pocket. As Mahjon drew near, the man pulled out a gun, but before he could fire it, Mahjon grabbed his arm and wrenched the weapon free, causing the man to cry out in pain. Security took him into custody, where he would no doubt confess that he was of Murk descent and loyal to Prince Damon.

Once it was safe, Jag, Bayli, and IRIS descended from the shuttle and greeted the palace staff. Unlike the queen's palace, Jag's palace was smaller and more modern, though Jag thought was still large enough to probably house the entire population of Mulberry, Indiana. Everything in the palace was immaculate except for the garden, which had been neglected and overrun with weeds due to all non-essential staff being reassigned to the factories.

As governor, Jag's first act was to release any political prisoners who opposed Prince Damon's policies, including the most ardent of opponents, Senator Andor Thanos. Not only had he been imprisoned, his house and finances had been seized and his senate seat given to Leonel Warily, Measil's father. Jag restored him to the senate while dismissing Leonel. By downsizing the shipbuilding industry and using funds from Prince Damon's personal accounts, workers were returned to their families and communities.

While significantly downsized, Jag did have one special project in mind for the shipbuilders. He met with architects to discuss a concept that originated from his "free time" in Darkside Prison: a ship that would be elegant, aerodynamic, and extremely fast with a full arsenal of weapons. Day and night, they collaborated until they met to review a 3D model before construction began.

"She's a thing of beauty. Have you picked out a name for her?" the lead architect asked.

"*Cora Lee*," Jag said. "After my grandmother."

"That is a lovely name, your majesty."

The *Cora Lee* took nearly a year to build. During that time, Commander Corbis handpicked elite officers to begin their training. When the day arrived for her test run, Jag ordered the ensign to open up the ship's throttle, and that's when she revealed her true nature, soaring through space faster than anything ever seen. A warbird escorting the *Cora Lee* tried to match her speed, but within seconds, the *Cora Lee* disappeared and circled back on its tail.

On Corian, Jag frequently toured the planet to meet with community leaders. On one occasion, while touring with a town's mayor, they passed a junkyard when the mayor mentioned that its proprietor was notorious for dealing on the black market by trading illegal parts acquired from pirates. The shop was an old hangar with enormous doors on the front and a faded sign that read, "Skylar Stuckey's Parts Oasis" and beneath it in smaller text, "We can find any part!" Seeing the sign, Jag ordered the caravan to stop.

"Prince Marcello, is there a reason you have stopped here?" the mayor asked.

"Tell me, aside from black market trading, has the proprietor been involved in any other nefarious activity?"

"You mean like murder, slavery, or other vices?" The mayor shook his head. "Not that I'm aware of."

"Then, I should like to meet him."

"Your majesty? You shouldn't be seen with such a degenerate person."

"Probably not, but I've been around much worse."

The caravan pulled over, and Jag's security detail of royal guards entered the shop's side door. Seeing them, the short, chubby proprietor waddled out of his office. "You have no right to keep harassing me! I'll file a complaint with the prince himself. You can't keep harassing a businessman who is just trying to make an honest living." The proprietor kept rambling until he saw Mahjon step inside, ducking his head under the side door. Behind him was Jag.

"Your majesty," the proprietor said, bowing slightly. "I assure you that I am not guilty of whatever crime I have been accused of."

Jag didn't say anything, just walked down an aisle examining the shelves of junk parts: old converters, compressors, computer boards, and memory devices.

"I have my rights! You can't keep persecuting me like this!" the proprietor insisted as he waddled along behind Jag's entourage.

Jag turned to face him. "Mr. Stuckey, do you have someplace private where we can talk business?"

"Uh, alright." The proprietor opened his office door. "We can talk in here. However, the name is Rufus Mukasa. I acquired the business from Mr. Stuckey years ago. How can I help, your majesty?"

"I'm looking for an old shuttle, and I heard you might be just the person to help me find it."

"Well, if it's shuttles you want, your majesty, you've come to the right place. I have an entire warehouse of shuttles and shuttle parts."

"I'm looking for a specific shuttle," Jag said as he borrowed a tablet and drew a picture of the *Winnebago*, complete with the logo they had painted on the side. "This ship is of special value to me. The last I saw it; it was on a Thorg ship called the *Killclaw*."

"Thorgs! Surely His Majesty knows it's illegal to trade and sell with the Thorgs!" Mr. Mukasa said, trying to convince the prince he was not involved with such people.

Jag stood up. "Perhaps I've brought my business to the wrong establishment. I'm sorry to have wasted your time."

"Hold on, there's no need to rush off, Your Majesty. Perhaps I can be of assistance, but a job this size could be costly!"

"I imagine so," Jag replied. "I would also think that an individual able to accomplish this task would receive a large enough commission to retire from all . . . questionable activities."

"It depends," Rufus said. "One man's riches are another man's poverty. I would incur a lot of expenses tracking down such an item, not to mention lost revenue from missed sales."

"I think this should cover your costs." Jag scribbled some numbers on the tablet and then handed it to Mr. Mukasa, whose eyes widened with surprise.

"One hundred thousand credits!"

"Find the shuttle intact, and I will pay you ten times that amount," Jag said.

Mr. Mukasa stood frozen in place. The hundred thousand alone was worth more than all the junk in his shop combined. Finally, he recovered his composure. "It would be my honor to serve His Majesty in this manner."

Jag smiled. "Thank you, and once you have secured the shuttle, you will retire immediately from your life of illegal activity?"

"Yes, sir!"

In his fortress deep in the Black Glacia Mountains on Atundra, Emperor Damon was securing new recruits by force to rebuild an empire that had dwindled after the death of Emperor Gazini. They were also building a new warship, called the *Massacre*, that would be larger and more powerful than any Celestian ship.

For his role in the king's assassination, Emperor Damon had promoted Measil to chief minister. He oversaw much of the day-to-day activities within the empire. He had met with several generals to update the emperor, who was seated with his leg hiked over the arm of the throne, half listening to the generals' debriefing.

"Construction on the *Massacre* is on schedule. We expect to have it ready for a test run in four months," General Jessip, the highest-ranking Murk officer, said.

"Four months!" Measil exclaimed. "We may not have four months. Recent intel is reporting that the enemy has a new ship, one that is faster than anything ever built."

"How reliable is that intel?" Major General Chungbok asked from across the table. "Our spy network on Corian isn't as reliable as it once was!"

"He's right," General Jessip replied. "Our spy network has been greatly depleted. Prince Marcello's guardian has proven highly effective at identifying our spies."

Tahjon, who was sitting on the side listening to the conversation, did not react to the statement. General Jessip turned to him. "Perhaps Tahjon has an idea on how we can infiltrate their defenses, seeing as intel reports that the guardian is his own brother!"

Tahjon glanced up but did not say anything.

"You imbeciles! Have you not learned anything from me? It is futile to attack a guardian head on. You've got to come at him sideways," Damon. "Find a loyal young officer who is able to control his emotions. Send him in with an order to protect the prince at all costs."

"Pardon me, Lord Damon. Did you say 'protect the prince'?" Measil asked.

"Absolutely. Order him to protect their precious prince with his very life. Once he has won their trust, order him to attack in a manner and time they will never expect."

Jag and Bayli were on the *Cora Lee*'s maiden voyage visiting Norr so they could see Rannick and so Bayli could spend time with her mother. Jag received a message from Rufus Mukasa saying he had secured the special item Jag had requested and would meet him at the palace when convenient. Excited to see what he had found, Jag returned immediately to Corian.

"You wouldn't believe the trouble I had to go through to track this down, your majesty," Rufus said as he greeted Jag at the palace landing pad. "Everything is exactly like you asked, isn't it?" He was concerned he wouldn't get the full payment once Jag saw how primitive the shuttle was.

"Ah, what a sight for sore eyes," Jag said as he ran his hand down the side of the *Winnebago,* which was parked in the oval driveway, about which the groundskeeper wasn't too keen.

"Not much to look at, if you ask me," Rufus said. "Like I mentioned, I could have gotten you a much better shuttle for a fraction of the cost!"

"It's what's inside that matters!" Jag said as he entered the *Winnebago,* followed by Bayli. The shuttle had a stale odor and was dark, as the batteries were drained. Jag asked the groundskeeper to bring a generator. Within minutes, several small generators were connected, and the shuttle's interior lights came on.

"Now, finally, the answers to my questions!" Jag said, a boyish smile on his face.

"What do you mean?" Bayli asked.

"By looking at the *Winnebago's* computer logs, I can determine how long I've been away and backtrack the route the shuttle took to find out where home is."

Jag winced as he walked past the cryo-chamber and into the tiny bridge, where he pushed the power button for the shuttle's computer. The monitor flickered, and the display showed that the computer was going through a boot sequence. After several minutes, the home screen loaded and displayed a date at the bottom: January 1, 2070.

"I was afraid of that."

"What's wrong?" Bayli asked.

"The shuttle sat in the Thorg ship so long it wasn't able to recharge its power, and the computer's internal clock battery has died, so it defaults to some old date years before I was born. However, the logs were motion activated and would have recorded a video log, along with a date stamp, each time there was movement. So, if I subtract the date the Thorgs found me from the date I left, I'll know how long I was frozen."

"Is that it there?" Bayli asked, nodding at the cryo-chamber.

"Yep," Jag said, not looking up as he opened the video log application and a video began playing from the first recorded log file with a date and time stamp that read "Log File – March 9, 2088, 3:23 p.m." The video showed Jag and Ben rewiring the electrical system.

"Wow, you were so young," Bayli said.

Jag nodded. "Yeah. That was a few years ago."

"Who's that beside you?"

"That's Ben; we were best friends."

Jag fast-forwarded through several logs until he reached one that read "Log File – April 18, 2088, 11:18 p.m." It was the fateful date on which Percy, Tank, and Edgard had boarded the shuttle. The video showed Edgard and Tank trying to hold Jag when Jag freed his hand and slugged Percy in the face. Percy yelled at Edgard to hold him and then punched Jag in the stomach before they threw him into the freezer.

"Oh my gosh!" Bayli cried.

"Yeah, but at least I got a right hook in before they froze me."

Bayli stared at the screen in shock. "I can't believe they did that to you!"

Jag smirked. "Yeah, good friends, huh?"

He advanced several more logs to an incoming video message from the *Unity*. The time stamp was "Log File – April 19, 2088, 12:18 a.m."

"Jag, this is Professor P. Son, I need you to turn your ship around. I'm fully confident that your rocket will work and that you have absolutely nothing to prove. You've already proven everything."

In the background, Ben yelled, "Jag, come back, please!"

Jag frowned. "That's odd. Why would he say that I had nothing to prove?"

He advanced to another video, this time from Percy. "Jag, I should have never challenged your rocket design. I always thought of us as friends, and you don't have to prove anything. I forgive you for punching me. Just turn around, and we can work everything out."

Jag could tell Percy was trying to muster a sad face. "What are they all talking about?" he asked the screen. "We were never friends, and I wasn't trying to prove anything," He fast-forwarded through several more logs until he reached one with the time stamp, "Log File – April 19, 2088, 1:13 p.m." It was audio only.

"Jag, this is Grandpa. We don't know if you will receive this transmission, as we're told that your shuttle may now be out of communication range. Professor Polanski and Ben have explained your situation to us." Jag heard his grandmother crying in the background. "Son, if you're able to turn your shuttle around, do whatever you can to come home to us. You have nothing to prove to anyone."

Then Grandma spoke, trying to hold back her tears. "Grandpa and I love you very much. We will keep watch for you and trust God to bring you home safely. Remember, you are never alone. His golden thread is always near even when we don't see it."

Jag paused a moment after the audio played.

"Your grandparents seem wonderful!" Bayli said.

"Yeah, they're the best!" Jag replied as he wiped the tears off his cheek. "Everyone thinks I did this, because I had something to prove. Percy must have lied and said I initiated the launch sequence to prove my rocket would work. He never told them the truth, that he locked me in the freezer!"

Jag advanced the logs to the last file in the directory: Log File – October 23, 2121. A video showed two Thorgs invading the shuttle and shining a light around the cabin to examine its hardware and then finding Jag in the cryogenic chamber. Jag quickly did the math in his head, subtracting the log date from the previous log date.

"Thirty-three years! I was trapped in that blasted thing for thirty-three years!" He turned and ran out the shuttle, Bayli on his heels.

"What's wrong?" Bayli asked.

Jag stopped and looked at her in disbelief. "What's wrong? Thirty-three years, that's what's wrong!"

"Yeah, but now you can find your way home."

Jag threw up his hands. "What's the point?"

"Now you can go home to your family!"

"You don't understand. They're dead. I was frozen for thirty-three years, and who knows how many years have passed since the Thorgs found me. That would make my grandparents over a hundred years old, and humans rarely live beyond ninety!"

"Oh," Bayli replied. "I'm so sorry!"

"The worst part of all of this is that they died thinking I ran away trying to prove something. That it was all my fault!"

The groundskeeper approached Jag and Bayli, bowing respectfully. "What would you like us to do with the shuttle, your majesty?"

"Destroy it. I don't ever want to see it again!"

"What?" Rufus exclaimed. "What about my payment?"

"IRIS, pay him in full: one million credits. He did his job." Jag paused and looked back on his way into the palace. "And remember our deal: no more illegal activity!"

"No worries, your majesty," Rufus said. "I'm retiring. Thank you very much!"

Bayli approached the groundskeeper. "He doesn't mean it," she said quietly. "He's just upset. Please move it somewhere, and keep it hidden until he calms down."

"Where do you suppose I keep it?" the groundskeeper asked. "It won't exactly fit underneath the bushes."

"Why not in the old castle?" Bayli suggested, referring to the castle ruins in the garden.

"Sure, I can just pick it up and move it inside the old castle ruins," the groundskeeper said sarcastically.

Bayli smiled and batted her eyelashes. "Please?"

"Alright, I'll see what I can do."

Deep on the edge of Murk space on board Sector 12 Observation Post, two bored Murk soldiers sat at their stations staring at blank radar screens, keeping an eye out for the Celestian Royal Fleet. The older officer, Petty Officer Clurk, was ticking off another day on his calendar, counting down the time until he would leave the outdated observation post, which was held together by old parts and space tape, for the last time.

"How much longer do you have on this deployment?" Private Harman asked.

"Forty-seven days, three hours, and twenty-eight minutes!" Clurk replied.

"Lucky dog! This is the most boring job in the universe, staring at these stupid monitors. Nothing ever happens around here."

"Well, let's hope it stays that way, kid. The last thing you want is for a Celestian battlecruiser to fly through."

"Yeah, but if that happens, we'll hit the escape pods."

Clurk smirked at his companion's naiveté. "Do you really think an escape pod can outrun a battlecruiser?"

"I guess not," the private replied as a small yellow dot blinked on a monitor. Clurk leaned forward. "What's that?"

"It's too small to be a ship or even a shuttle," Harman said.

"Zoom in."

"I have the radar zoomed in as far as it can go. It must be a spy satellite."

"Too slow to be a satellite," Clurk replied. "The computer doesn't recognize its shape or the frequency it's broadcasting. Can you grab it?"

"It's too far away; we'll have to wait until it's closer."

"Well, we're not going anywhere. As soon as it gets in range, bring it in to examine it. Come wake me when it arrives." Clurk got up and headed off to bed.

Hours later, Private Harman pulled the object into the bay of the observation post and notified Clurk.

"What do you think it is?" Harman asked as they stood examining it.

"It looks to be some type of satellite but not anything from around here," Clurk replied. As he reached out to touch it, a 3D hologram was triggered and began playing a video of twelve young students speaking in a foreign language.

"What do you think they're saying?" Private Harman asked.

"No, idea. The onboard translator doesn't recognize the language." Officer Clurk leaned forward to take a better look at the images being projected. "Hmm . . . Do you still have that bulletin on the Celestian prince and his new ship?"

"Yeah, that thing is supposed to be faster than anything we've seen before. Why?"

"Pull up the photo of the prince."

"One sec." Harman scrolled through a list of daily bulletins until he opened one titled, "Alert! New enemy ship spotted." He scrolled down to a photo of Jag.

"I'll be!" Officer Clurk exclaimed. "We better send this to Emperor Damon right away. He'll want to see this! And thank you, by the way!"

"You're thanking me? For what?" Private Harman asked.

Officer Clurk smiled. "For giving me a ticket home!"

"Ah, man. That's not fair. You might even get a promotion out of this!"

"I don't care about a promotion. I just want out of this military so I can go home!"

Emperor Damon was meeting with top military commanders in his war room around a table as a 3D hologram of the galaxy displayed planets and ship locations. He reclined as he sipped his wine and listened to his staff.

"Our spy has been successfully dispatched to Corian and ordered to protect the prince, just as you recommended," Measil said to the emperor, who seemed fixated on his wine.

"We've captured two new planets in Sector Eight's outer belt," General Jessip added.

"And how many planets have we lost?" Measil asked.

"Six. We've lost six planets in the last two weeks," General Jessip replied.

"How can that be?" Measil exclaimed.

"We are unable to defend against this new Celestian ship they call the *Cora Lee*," General Chungbok replied. "She moves like nothing we've ever encountered. Long-distance radar can't detect her until it's too late."

"How about the *Massacre*?" Measil asked. "Is it ready?"

"Sir, it hasn't been tested, yet," Chungbok replied.

"Our problem is that our forces are spread too thin to keep the planets we've already taken, and now we're trying to expand even farther!" General Jessip said.

"Perhaps the problem is that you are unwilling to push your forces," Measil replied.

Emperor Damon sat listening to the banter. After having all he could take, he hurled his wine glass across the room. It hit the wall and shattered. "The problem is that I expect results, not excuses!"

No sooner were the words out of his mouth than a messenger entered and relayed a message to Measil. Measil turned to the emperor. "Apparently, we have something you may find interesting, your highness."

He motioned to the security guards. They opened a door, and in walked Officer Clurk, pulling the *Stargazer* atop a large cart. Emperor Damon sat back on his throne, unimpressed by the satellite's antiquated technology.

"What is this junk?" Measil asked.

"One second, sir," Officer Clurk replied. He waved his hand in front of a sensor on the satellite, and a video began playing. Emperor Damon leaned forward to examine the hologram and immediately recognized Jag in the front row of all the students. Then he sat back and smiled. "It appears that fate has just been kind to us. Find out where this satellite came from."

"No need, Your Highness," Officer Clurk said. He pressed a button on the satellite, and a detailed star map showed the path the *Stargazer* took from Earth. "This is important, right?"

"Perhaps," Measil said as he leaned forward and watched the star maps reverse their course.

"It seems we have just received an invitation," Emperor Damon said, standing up. "Ready the fleet."

"Your majesty, why would you want to take the fleet so far away?" General Jessip asked. "This planet has no strategic value for us, and we would be spreading our fleet too thin. We're short on officers the way it is."

"*Our* fleet?" the emperor replied. "It's *my* fleet, General."

"Yes, your majesty," the general replied.

"The *Cora Lee* may not have any known weaknesses, but her prince certainly does. Prince Marcello has a soft spot for his friends. I saw it in his eyes when I killed . . . what was the name of that boy?" Emperor Damon asked sarcastically, as he well remembered Marcel's name.

"Marcel," Measil said.

"Of course. Take the *Massacre* and my fleet to this planet, and compel them to hand over his friends and bring them here. Then watch as the prince surrenders to spare their lives. And General, if it's more officers you need, all you have to do is ask. Take Officer Clurk with you. He is available now." The poor officer's eyes widened as he realized that instead of a leave, he was being reassigned to another long assignment.

Many months after the *Stargazer* was found, Jag was touring deep space on the *Cora Lee* when he had the dream that had haunted him in his youth. Now in his late twenties, the last time he had experienced the nightmare was just before Marcel died. In fact, it seemed that the only time the dream returned was when something significant was about to happen.

Like previous times, he dreamed a thick dark cloud covered Earth as depression and fear overwhelmed him. A large, fiery metal object dropped through the cloud, striking the planet. Then the Sun, Moon, and eleven stars rotated and bowed before him.

As he dreamed, IRIS walked in and tried to awaken him, scanning his body for signs of stress. "Captain, are you awake, sir?" Commander Corbis had sent him to inform Jag that they had received a distress signal from an unidentified ship. That ship was the *Exodus* from Earth. Once Jag heard the news, he knew everything would change.

CHAPTER 24

SNICKERS

Fog surrounded the palace grounds on the morning Jag stepped out onto the veranda wearing overalls and a jacket with the hood pulled up to keep the mist from soaking his hair. It had been months since he had visited the garden, and some of the plants were in desperate need of trimming. After towing the damaged *Exodus* back to Corian, Jag had taken some time to withdraw to a cabin in the mountains to collect his thoughts before returning to the palace.

Now that other humans were on Corian, Jag could no longer ignore his feelings. His mind raced with the memories of the event with Percy and his feelings of betrayal as everyone seemed to blame him for taking the *Winnebago*. Part of him wanted to punish those responsible with the full authority his royal crown allowed, while at the same time he longed to be reconciled with his classmates. He had more questions than answers: Would he leave humanity to their fate? Did the entire planet deserve to suffer because of the actions a few?

Such questions were what compelled Jag to withdraw to the garden so he could clear his mind. Performing repetitive tasks like pruning or digging alleviated his thoughts, though the groundskeeper objected to him doing any manual labor, for it was "unfitting for a prince to soil his hands." But soiled hands were exactly what Jag needed that morning.

He began by trimming tall grasses along the floating garden that he had installed after visiting the queen's garden. As he worked through the morning, the sun dissipated the fog, and the morning flowers opened, revealing their brilliant colors. Jag knelt at the edge of a pond and dug a hole large enough to fit the base of a leafy plant with tiny buds that had yet to open. After setting the plant in the hole and gently mounding the soil around its base, he heard a faint noise. He turned to look but didn't see anyone and assumed it was Mahjon sitting down on one of the nearby benches. He picked up the next plant and loosened its roots when he heard a female voice yell in pain.

Jag stood up and looked around, wiping the soil off his hands as he walked cautiously down the path. He looked to see if Mahjon had responded, for Mahjon had proven to be very effective at detecting dangerous situations long before they occurred. Not seeing him, Jag walked toward the voice. As he rounded the curved pathway, he saw a young female lying face-down on the pathway. She was struggling to get to her feet. Jag ran over, helped her up, and escorted her over to the bench.

"Thank you; I'm so clumsy," the woman said in English, wiping the dirt off her pants. When she looked up at her rescuer, she stopped short. "You look human!" Before Jag could pull his hood forward to shield his face, their eyes met. "Do I know you?" she asked. "You look familiar." Jag hurried away. "Please don't go!" she cried. "I didn't mean to startle you!"

On his way out of the garden, Jag bumped into Bayli, who was coming into the garden carrying a cane. Bayli was shocked to see him. "You're back!"

"Yes, I am! And I see you've wasted no time in bringing a human into my garden."

"Oh no. I'm sorry, Jag!" Bayli said. "I didn't think you were coming back from the cabin until next week when the hearing begins."

"She saw my face. She even recognized me!"

"Jag, I'm so sorry, we'll leave immediately," Bayli said. She went to the young woman, helped her collect her belongings, and then left the garden.

"I'm sorry if I got you in trouble with the gardener," the young woman said. "The wind blew my papers onto the ground, and when I went to retrieve them, I fell. I'm sorry—"

"Hush now. All will be fine. I'll speak with him later. Don't worry yourself."

Bayli escorted the woman back to her hospital room. Later that day, she approached the door of Jag's study.

"May I come in?"

Jag pushed his chair back from his desk. "You might as well. It seems you're going to do whatever you please anyway."

"That's not true," Bayli said as she entered. "I had no intention of her meeting you."

"It just seemed a little too convenient. I know you disagree with how I'm handling this."

"Handling this? You aren't handling this. You're ignoring them and hiding in here!"

"I am handling this. I just need time to think. I've asked Senator Thanos to lead the hearings. He will give them a fair and objective hearing."

"Fair and objective? Listen to yourself! They're your people! Don't you have any compassion for them?" Bayli's face softened. "Again, I'm truly sorry. I had no idea you were back, and the hospital is overcrowded with all the injured from the *Exodus*. So I brought Sara—"

"Sara?"

Bayli nodded. "Yes. We met on the *Exodus*. She had internal bleeding and had fractured her leg. I've been helping with her physical therapy and brought her to the garden, because there aren't any open areas for her to walk in the hospital. She forgot her cane, so I returned to fetch it. That's when the wind blew a piece a paper from her book, and she fell trying to retrieve it. It was an innocent mistake. Please, don't be angry."

"I'm not angry." Jag's body relaxed, and smile crept onto his face. "You know I can't stay angry at you; you're like the sister I never had."

"Why, because I'm annoying?"

"Yes!" Jag said, grinning.

"That's because us big sisters have to look out for our little brothers," Bayli replied.

"I appreciate all you've done for me, and I'll never forget it. But right now, I need a little latitude with this as I try to figure things out."

"I understand," Bayli said. "Just don't take too long to figure out what you should be doing, or it may be too late." She turned to go and then stopped. "Oh, I almost forgot. Sara wanted me to give you this. Apparently, humans are still fond of writing on paper." She handed Jag a small envelope with the word "Groundskeeper" written on the outside, accompanied by a candy bar.

"A Snickers bar? Do you know how long it's been since I've had one of these?" Jag tore open the candy bar and broke it in half, giving one piece to Bayli. A string of caramel hung from his lip as he chewed with his eyes closed, savoring each bite. Bayli sniffed the candy bar suspiciously and then took a bite. She wasn't sure what all the fuss was about.

"I used to walk to the grocery store with my grandmother in the summer, and we would buy soda pop and candy bars. I would always get a Snickers, she would get an Almond Joy, and we would buy a Cluster bar for Grandpa."

Jag was opening the envelope when a bell chimed at the door. "Enter," he said without looking up.

"Sir, pardon the interruption," IRIS said as he walked into Jag's study.

"You're not interrupting. How can I help you?"

"Senator Thanos has notified me that Senators Alberg and Westreed will be assisting him, and all the preparations for the hearing are set."

"I met Senator Alberg when I lived on Norr. Nice guy. I don't believe I know Westreed."

"Senator Westreed has served in the senate for twelve years. Prior to this, he was a businessman who owned several textile companies before entering politics," IRIS replied.

Jag nodded. "Okay, and who's representing council?"

"Councilman Rupert Maverick. He was knighted by King Marcellus and is a member of the Order of Distinguished Attorneys, arguing two landmark decisions before the senate."

"I'm glad that Senator Thanos secured someone with such high qualifications."

"Indeed, sir. Also, Senator Thanos asked me to remind you that, as royal prince, you are endowed with the authority to extend planethood without a hearing."

"Duly noted. He mentioned that to me when I asked him to lead the hearing. Anything else?"

"The repairs on the *Exodus* are underway, and Chief Engineer Ramsey wanted to know if they are to repair the ship 'as is' or to upgrade the engine and weapons systems, for he stated, 'this technology is as obsolete as his grandfather's shoes'."

Jag smirked. "Yes, tell him to upgrade them so they can defend themselves adequately. Anything else?"

"No, sir."

"Thank you, IRIS," Jag said as he removed Sara's letter from the envelope. He looked at the handwritten letter and thought how strange it was to be reading a letter in English after so many years. Then he read her letter out loud.

Dear Monsieur Gardener,

I'm not sure if you will even be able to read this or not, but I wish to apologize for startling you in the garden earlier today. I must say that your garden is one of the most beautiful places I've ever seen. I'm sorry that I don't know your name, but I believe that if you are human and are who I think you might be, that our fathers may have been best friends many years ago. You see, my dad is Ben Mendelsohn . . .

Jag's jaw dropped open. "Ben has a daughter?" He continued reading out loud. ". . . and our parents were in a space program on Earth many years ago. I believe it must have been fate that placed me in the garden today. Sadly, Earth has been seized by Murk aliens, and we are here to plead for Celestian assistance. If you or your father would consider intervening, we would greatly appreciate it. And don't worry, I will not tell anyone that I saw you. You and your dad's secret are safe. I promise."

Jag leaned back against the old wooden desk. "She thinks I'm Joseph Gabriel's son."

"That's actually very logical," Bayli replied. "She doesn't know you were an icicle for thirty-three years, so she would automatically assume you are indeed . . . your son."

"She thinks I'm my son," Jag repeated. "Oh, this is getting interesting. I'll tell you what: Continue using the garden for her therapy. In fact, give her an access key so she can come and go anytime she likes—as long as she keeps her promise not to tell anyone I'm here and does not bring any other humans into the garden."

"Okay," Bayli said suspiciously. "What's your end game here? I won't allow you to hurt her."

"No game. It just affords me an opportunity to investigate what has happened on Earth since I left and to discover what they think happened to me."

Bayli sighed. "This whole thing would be easier if you just came out and told everyone who you are instead of playing games!"

"Not yet," Jag said. "The situation is not ready."

CHAPTER 25
HERSHEY'S MILK CHOCOLATE

There were two ways in which a planet could apply for citizenship in Celestia. The first involved convening committees and holding a Senate vote, which could take up to a year to complete. The faster method was for a royal family member to grant planethood. While understanding his authority, Jag wanted to use the process to reveal the truth about what happened to him, so he requested a special Senate hearing.

The hearing was to take place in a large government courtroom, whose gallery could sit nearly a thousand spectators. In the front were three benches for the senators, with the presiding senator, Thanos, sitting in the center. A railing separated the gallery from the court. In front of the railing were several long tables and thirteen chairs facing the judges. Immovable nameplates sat on the table in front of each chair, identifying the person to be seated in that spot. The first nameplate read, "Councilman Rupert Maverick," followed by nameplates for each of the twelve students in order from eldest to youngest.

On the afternoon of the first hearing, the gallery was mostly empty, with only a few crewmen from the *Exodus* as well as couple of court reporters. Other than that, it was a nonevent, as no one was familiar with the distant, insignificant planet or their young prince's true origin.

Jag, IRIS, and Mahjon entered the closed balcony just as the court was brought to order. Wearing simple street clothes so as not to draw attention to himself, Jag sat in the darkness of the balcony, quietly watching the petitioners enter and take their seats. He leaned forward to get a glimpse of his fellow classmates, who were all showing signs of age—thinning grey hair or going bald. Most could stand to shed a few pounds.

Jag watched as Ben entered and took his seat in the last chair in front of his nameplate and beside an empty chair with the nameplate "Joseph Gabriel." Ben tried to swap his nameplate with Jag's so he could sit next to Sasha. However, Jag had ordered all the nameplates to be fastened to the table so they couldn't be moved.

Councilman Maverick was a plump man who wore a dark business suit replete with a purple-and-white sash and a golden emblem denoting his deliberation before the senate. Wounded in combat as a young officer, he walked with a slight limp. What he lacked in physical appearance he more than exceeded in speech. Possessing a rich baritone voice, he commanded the Celestian language as a surgeon wielded a scalpel. He spoke with authority, rarely using the same word twice and enunciating each word clearly.

"Pursuant to the petition for planethood into the Celestian Kingdom, I hereby present our case to this most prestigious of courts," Councilman Maverick began. "I ask the court to recognize the following ambassadors from planet Earth." He walked over and stood in front of Mo. "I'd like to present to the court the distinguished Dr. Muhammad Harrak, who hails from a country called Morocco and teaches as a professor of space sciences."

Then the councilman stepped toward the next student, leaning on his cane. "This is his excellency, Kano Tanaka, who hails from Japan, where he serves as prime minister, the highest government position in his country."

He moved on to Percy. "I present the famed Mr. Percival Blackwell, who is from England and is a successful business owner who serves on the boards of several renowned charities and prestigious universities." Percy was extremely well-polished, wearing an expensive suit, his hair slicked back and meticulously trimmed, expensive rings on both hands.

"I would also like to introduce the honorable doctor and mayor, Lars Klein, from Germany. He also serves as the chief executive for his family's waste-management and recycling business."

Jag was shocked to see how heavy Tank was. He barely fit in his chair.

"Next, I would like to introduce the illustrious Dr. Niklas Johansen, from Sweden, who serves as a professor of space sciences." Niklas still had all his blonde hair and had shot up in height, standing nearly seven feet tall.

"Senators, this is the remarkable Reverend and Dr. Makalo Zuma from South Africa. Aside from his work as a religious and spiritual leader, his invention for water purification is used all over their world and has contributed to saving many lives in desolate locations."

"Next, I present the renowned Vice President Mario Bergoglio, who hails from Argentina and serves as a science and city development manager. His city planning models have proven most effective for reducing urban poverty."

"Next I introduce the resplendent Dr. Edgard Dubois, who hails from France. He works with Mr. Percival Blackwell as a vice president in one of his many global companies." Edgard shifted uncomfortably in his seat. He seemed smaller than Jag remembered, sporting a bad comb-over in a losing attempt to hide his balding scalp.

"Next is the exalted Dr. Rajesh Gupta from India, who is a university chancellor and a celebrated author and lecturer." Raj still had his dark hair, though it was thinning. He wore a decorated gold Sherwani Indian suit with ornate trim.

"This is the eminent professor and doctor Sasha Belinsky, who has served as the president of their space agency and as director of the *Unity* space station." Sasha's formerly red hair was completely white and made him look distinguished.

Wow, Jag thought. Director of the Unity! Good for you, Sasha!

The counselor paused as he came to an empty seat. "Sadly, one of the twelve is no longer with us. I'm told he died many years ago in a most unfortunate accident."

Then the counselor stepped toward Ben. "Lastly, this is the acclaimed Dr. Ben Mendelsohn, from Israel, who serves as an ambassador to the United Nations, their planet's highest government body. He also serves as a professor of space science."

After introducing each person, Councilman Maverick returned to his seat to finish delivering his opening remarks. "These individuals are more than just ambassadors; they are classmates from a school long ago. For reasons unknown to us, the Murk Empire has brought our war to their planet by surrounding it with their battleships. This is why we are petitioning this court for planethood, and I hereby ask that the court recognize these ambassadors from Earth."

"The court does recognize the ambassadors from Earth and accepts their request to be heard in the matter of planethood," Senator Thanos said.

Over the next several weeks, the councilman and ambassadors presented and answered questions on a variety of topics, including Earth's history, forms of government, plant and animal life, and technology. Afterwards, the senators would make their recommendations to the full senate body.

Before court was dismissed, Jag left the balcony and walked through a secret tunnel connected to the palace garden, behind the old castle ruins in which Bayli had the *Winnebago* stored. When Jag walked by the bench at which he had met Sara, he noticed she had left a letter and a candy bar for him. This time it was a Hershey bar. He opened it and offered Mahjon half. Then he began reading her letter.

Dear Monsieur Gardener,

Merci for allowing me to visit in your lovely garden. I'm not sure if you understand the words I'm writing, if your father taught you English or French. I can't imagine there is much need for either language here on Corian. Of course, there wouldn't be a need for English on Corian. I mean, who would you speak it with? Oh, there I go rambling. Dad often tells me that I have a habit of rambling when I get nervous or excited.

I have so many questions that I'd like to ask:

How did you get here?

Why have you stayed here all these years and not come home?

Where is your father? Can we speak with him?

There I go rambling again. Sorry, one of my many faults.

If you could be so kind and just answer me this one question: Do you understand what I'm writing in these letters?

Chaleureusement, Sara Mendelsohn

Jag chuckled and then folded the letter and stuck it in his pocket as he returned to the palace. He searched his office high and low for a pen or pencil to write a reply. After rummaging through nearly every drawer, he pounded his desk in frustration. "You'd think this palace would have a simple pencil!" Then he summoned IRIS.

"Yes, sir," IRIS replied as he walked in the door.

"IRIS, do we have any pens or pencils?"

"Sir?" IRIS asked, tilting his head.

"Pens or pencils? You know, writing implements?"

"Sir, paper hasn't been used for centuries. Let me check the attic, where they keep the antiques."

Jag nodded. "Thank you, IRIS."

"And sir, Commander Corbis and Captain of the Guard Felix Henning are in the hallway to introduce you to the new recruits."

"Send them in," Jag replied. He quickly closed the drawers and cabinets and then put on a royal crested jacket to make himself look more presentable. Mahjon was seated in the corner with his eyes shut, uninterested in Jag's obsession to find a writing utensil. The door opened, and in walked Commander Corbis, followed by Captain Henning and three recruits.

"Attention!" Captain Henning ordered, and the three recruits snapped to attention. "Your Royal Highness, I'd like to present our newest recruits, who just graduated from the Royal Academy: Privates Nivedi, Chaquoy, and Reeso."

"Welcome," Jag said.

Mahjon rose and examined each recruit by looking intently into his eyes. Having a guardian examine one's intent was intimidating enough to make most grown men tremble. Mahjon cleared the new recruits, and then as Jag approached, they knelt before him.

"Do you swear your allegiance to the Kingdom of Celestian and the royal family, to guard and defend them with your life?"

"I do, your majesty," each of the young recruits replied.

"Then welcome to the royal guard," Jag said. Afterwards, the three saluted and then followed Felix out of Jag's office as Commander Corbis remained. Jag returned to searching through his drawers for a writing instrument.

"What are you doing, sire?" Commander Corbis asked.

"I'm looking for a pen or pencil," Jag said, drawing a strange look from the commander. "Any idea where I could find one?"

Corbis smiled. "Yeah. A museum."

"Very funny," Jag replied as they left for dinner.

After an hour of searching, IRIS entered the dining room with a cobweb hanging from his head. Bayli reached over with her napkin and wiped it off. IRIS placed an ornate, antique, and very dusty lap desk on the table, causing a bloom of dust to shoot up just as Jag was about to take a bite of his supper. He set his fork down and then wiped a layer of dust off the lap desk. Then he rotated a small golden hook and opened the lid.

Inside were sheets of parchment, several feathered quill pens, and a glass bottle of ink. Jag opened the bottle and looked inside. Then he turned it upside down. Sure enough, not a single drop came out. The ink was dry. Jag poured a few drops of water into the bottle. Then, using his steak knife, he scraped the tip across the surface of the ink until several pieces broke off and began absorbing the water. He continued working the ink until it was re-liquefied. Then, dipping the quill tip into the bottle several times, he wrote the word "Yes" on the back of the letter Sara had written. He waved the letter in the air for a moment to dry the ink and then held it out for IRIS.

"Please return this to the bench from which we retrieved it from today."

"That's it?" Bayli asked. "After all that effort of rummaging through your study and IRIS scavenging through the attic, all you're going to write is one word?"

Jag smiled. "Yes."

"Well, what does it mean?" Bayli asked. She, of course, couldn't read English.

"Yes," Jag said.

"Yes, what?"

"Sara asked me if I could read what she was writing, and my answer affirms that I can."

Bayli shook her head. "Unbelievable. Real personable."

Jag made a funny face at her.

"Sir, if I set the envelope on the bench this evening, the morning dew will cause the ink to run. Would you like me to place it there in the morning?" IRIS asked.

Jag nodded. "Yes, and thank you for your help today."

CHAPTER 26
BUTTERFINGER

The next morning, Jag was helping the groundskeeper replace wooden railings on an old, brick arched bridge that crossed a creek. Its bricks had been hand fired centuries earlier and had turned bright red, white, and grey.

Each morning, Bayli brought Sara to the garden and helped her walk along the paths. Afterwards, she would leave Sara alone at a bench to read while she returned to the hospital to assist other patients. Sara was reading when Jag walked by, wiping his dirty hands on a rag tucked in his overalls, just like his grandfather used to do.

"Well, hello," Sara said. "I see you got the letter I wrote for you yesterday. Thank you for responding to my question."

"Yes," Jag said.

"Do you have a moment? I mean, if you're not too busy?"

"Yes," Jag said.

"Can you say anything besides 'Yes?'" Sara asked.

Jag grinned. "Yes."

Sara chuckled and looked down in embarrassment. Then she met his gaze again. "So what should I call you?"

Jag thought for a moment. "You can call me 'Jag.'"

"I'm pleased to meet you, Monsieur Jag. I'm Sara." Sara held out her hand for him to shake.

Jag held out his palms. "I'm sorry, but my hands are dirty." She didn't budge until Jag reached out and shook her hand. He noticed that her hand was cold, but it was also soft. "You're cold; you should get inside."

"My hands are always cold. I take after my mom," she replied. "I'll be alright until Bayli returns." Though the sun had dissipated the morning dew, it was still chilly outside.

"Why don't you come up to the veranda?" Jag suggested. "There's a fire pit, where you can warm up."

Jag offered his arm, and they walked up to a bench on the veranda in front of the fire the groundskeeper had lit earlier that morning. Jag stoked the fire as Sara warmed her hands.

"Were you named after your father?" Sara asked.

"Yes," Jag replied. "My first name is actually Joseph, like my father."

"Do you mind if I ask where your father is?" Sara asked.

"He died a long time ago," Jag replied, speaking of his real father, who had died in the Navy. Of course, Sara assumed that Jag was speaking of the student her father had known.

"I'm sorry to hear that," Sara replied. "And your mother?"

"She also died when I was young."

"Oh, it seems I keep asking bad questions. By the way, your English is quite good."

"Thank you. It's been a while since I've spoken it."

"I assume you've heard about Earth's situation?"

Jag nodded. "Yes, I am aware."

"We're desperate! If we don't get help soon, I feel that Earth is doomed."

Jag looked at her. "How long have the Murks surrounded Earth?"

"It was over a year ago when they arrived with just a few ships, but then more came. We don't know how many ships they have now, as they emit some type of pollution that covers the planet in complete darkness. What's worse is that now they're invading different cities."

"I'm sorry to hear that," Jag replied. "I'm sure the court is doing everything they can, and if they allow Earth into the kingdom, they will help liberate it."

"That is our prayer, that the senators and the prince will be moved to help us." She paused and looked around. "Bayli said that this is the prince's garden. Is that correct?"

"Yes, why do you ask?"

"Oh, I've been here a several times now and haven't seen the prince. Is he not here?"

"He's here," Jag replied. "He just likes to keep a low profile."

Sara nodded. "So, aside from gardening, what else do you do here at the palace?"

"Not much," Jag said. "Gardening is about the only thing they'll let me do. That's enough questions about me though. It's my turn to ask you a question."

She smiled. "Okay, ask away."

"Tell me about your parents."

"Well, my parents met in Paris when dad was an assistant ambassador and Mom was a translator—she speaks six languages fluently! She started translating for dad, and they fell in love and got married. After I came along, Dad was promoted to ambassador to the United Nations, so we moved to New York. Now he's semi-retired and serves as a professor in Paris. Mom still works as an executive for a marketing firm. They're opposites in just about every way: Dad is analytical, and Mom is emotional. Dad likes to dress like a bum, and Mom always wears the latest fashions. But they are each other's *amore*."

Jag smiled as Sara talked about Ben and her mom. It brought him great joy knowing that life had turned out well for his friend. He deserved a wonderful family and a fulfilling career.

"Well, I must be going, but I wanted to thank you for the candy bars," Jag said.

"You're very welcome. Before you go, can I ask you one more question?"

"Of course," Jag said cautiously.

"How well do you know the prince?"

He shrugged. "As well as anyone."

"Do you, I mean, could you possibly speak to the prince on Earth's behalf? I know you've never been there, but we desperately need his intervention in granting us planethood."

"I know the prince is following the court proceedings with great interest," Jag said. "I'm sorry, but I really must go. Please stay warm, and get well, Sara Mendelsohn."

Later that day, Jag snuck into the balcony, where court proceedings were already underway. The lights were dimmed as a video of Earth played, showing beautiful aerial imagery of a rural countryside, oceans, mountains, and magnificent cities. Then the video presented various animals inhabiting Earth, both wild and domesticated. A herd of horses ran across an open plain, their manes blowing in the wind. Then a pod of leaping orca whales was followed by monkeys swinging from tree branches. A pride of lions ran through the African Sahara. The video zoomed in on a male lion roaring, which sent chills up everyone's spine.

Everyone in the courtroom was fixated on the peculiar animals, often gasping or laughing at the sight of strange animals like kangaroos, platypuses, and hippopotamuses. Seeing the video caused Jag to long for Earth. He missed the farm and the woods through which he and Grissom would run. After the daily session was over, Jag had IRIS request a copy of the video from Senator Thanos, which Jag planned to watch each night before falling asleep.

Jag returned to the palace through the secret passageway and found that, once again, Sara had left a card and a candy bar on the bench, a Butterfinger. Unlike previously, Jag opened the card first and read it as Mahjon stood patiently waiting for his half of the Butterfinger. When Jag didn't act quickly enough, Mahjon cleared his throat. When Jag looked up, Mahjon looked down at the candy bar and then back at Jag.

"Would you like a piece?" Jag asked, barely suppressing a smile.

"Only if you're offering, your majesty."

Jag gave him the larger of the two halves. Mahjon munched it happily and then tried to get the pieces of peanut butter candy out of his teeth. "This one is even better than yesterday, though it is a bit sticky."

The next morning, Jag and the grounds crew finished repairing the rails on the old bridge. Afterwards, Jag walked over to where Sara was seated.

"Bonjour, Monsieur Jag."

"Good morning," Jag replied as he helped her to her feet. After he thanked her for the candy bar, she held onto his arm as they walked along a patch of flowers that had just bloomed on the far side of the garden. They had an incredible fragrance.

Along the way, she asked several questions about Celestia and if Earth should have any concerns about joining the kingdom. Jag answered her questions by describing the good people he knew: Admiral Rannick, Bayli, the queen, and the former king. Then he told her of the history of the kingdom and the wars between Murk and Celestia.

Afterwards, Jag asked Sara about life on Earth. She described some of the technical advancements they had achieved as well as the current state of Earth's governments. She shared how the space program launched a deep space ship that traveled outside the solar system and that her father, Sasha, Makalo, and Kano had been crew members on board the first interstellar trip.

"Did you travel much on Earth?" Jag asked.

"Quite a bit. With Dad being an ambassador, I often accompanied him on his trips throughout Europe, Asia, Africa, the United States, and Canada. I even visited Indiana once with Dad to see Mrs. Gabriel, who I guess would be your great-grandmother."

"You did?" Jag asked, astonished.

"Yeah, I was about six, so I don't remember it much. We went there after your great-grandfather died. Dad spoke at the funeral."

"When was that?"

"Let's see, I'm twenty-three now, so it would have been about sixteen years ago."

"And my grandmother? Is she still alive?" Sara didn't pick up on the fact that he didn't say "great-grandmother."

"I'm sorry, but I think she passed away about eight years ago."

Jag turned away as the thought of not being there for his grandparents overwhelmed him.

"Dad always spoke highly of them and wanted me to meet them, because he said they were the nicest people he had ever known."

"Thank you. They were, I mean that's what I've been told," Jag said quickly, covering up his faux pas. "So, out of all the places on Earth that you've traveled, what's your favorite?"

"Switzerland and Austria, but my heart has always felt most at home in Paris."

"What do you love about Paris?"

"Everything! What's not to love? It's beautiful, with some of the most incredible architecture anywhere in the world. And the food! No place compares to Paris for its variety of pastries, fresh breads, and cheeses. Then there are the many beautiful parks in Paris that you can lose yourself in. When I was a grad student, I used to walk over to Jardin du Luxembourg, that's the Luxembourg Garden, and curl up on a bench and spend the afternoon reading.

"Sounds fantastic."

"Oh, it is! They have a beautiful palace in the center of the garden, much like this one, and I always dreamed I was Cinderella heading to the ball to dance the night away—well, until, of course, the bell struck midnight." She sighed. "All this talk about Paris has me missing home."

"So how did you end up on the *Exodus*?"

"Well, not by Mom's choice! She wanted me to stay on Earth, but I have too much of my dad in me. I wanted to travel and see the universe! So I majored in aerospace engineering and applied to do a stint on board the *Unity*. Sasha, another one of your dad's friends, was my director on board the *Unity*. After several years, I transferred to the *Exodus* to work in engineering."

"I think it's fantastic that you followed in your dad's footsteps."

"Yeah, but he worries for me. He can be overprotective at times."

"Isn't that what fathers are supposed to do? Well, your leg seems to be better today!"

"Yeah, I think you're right. Thanks to you! I was able to walk farther today."

"Well, you did all the work. I must leave you now."

"See you tomorrow?" Sara asked hopefully.

"Yeah, I'll see ya tomorrow."

Sara smiled. "*Au revoir,* Monsieur Jag."

CHAPTER 27

OBTUSE

The hearings proceeded on schedule, and each day Jag looked forward to the various topics covered. Councilman Maverick's arguments and presentations were persuasive and impressive. Throughout the process, the senators were very engaged, often asking follow-up questions about life, history, or the worldviews of Earth, though Jag did notice Senator Alberg nodding off during some of the longer sessions.

Over the next several weeks, Jag started each morning in the garden reflecting on the previous day's courtroom discussions, but inevitably, his mind wandered to Sara and what questions to ask her from the previous day's court session. Jag enjoyed his emerging friendship with her. That morning, he collected flowers for her to take back to the apartment that Bayli had secured now that her physical therapy was complete. Jag walked over and waited for her, but she didn't show. Disappointed, he left the flowers on the bench in case she came by later that day.

When Jag returned that evening, he saw the flowers still lying there, wilting from the afternoon heat. Jag grabbed the flowers and took them inside to place them in a vase before he joined Bayli in the dining hall.

"How was your day?" Jag asked.

"It was good. I spoke with the admiral earlier when I called to speak with my mom, and he answered the video-com."

"How are they?"

"Mom is well, and Rannick sends his best. It's harvest season, and they have their hands full. He says to tell you that if you're not too busy, he could always use an extra hand."

Jag smiled. "Ha, I bet. Hey, I didn't see Sara today."

"Oh, she didn't feel like coming to the garden today."

"Is she feeling alright?"

"I think so, but she seemed depressed. She didn't seem herself."

"I'm sorry to hear that."

"Do you have a message you want me to give her when I see her tomorrow?"

Jag shook his head. "Nope. Just curious."

The next day, Jag was waiting near the bench when Sara arrived.

"Hello," Jag said.

"Bonjour," Sara replied. She didn't seem her normal talkative self, her mannerisms subdued.

"Is everything alright?"

She shook her head. "No, it isn't."

"What's wrong? Is everyone treating you alright at the apartment?"

"Yeah, the apartment is fine. But I received a message from home yesterday. Jag, it's terrible. The Murks have taken control of Paris and are threatening to blow up the *Unity*, killing everyone on board if anyone attacks their troops. And now they're demanding that the world hand over one family member from each of the original twelve students or they'll start killing people on board the space station. My mom is in hiding, but she wants to turn herself in so they don't kill anyone else."

"I'm so sorry to hear it!"

Sara looked him square in the eye. "Are you?"

"Why, yes I am," Jag said, surprised by her question.

"Then why don't you do something to help us and speak to the prince?"

"Sara, it's not that easy. There are—"

"Are you afraid?"

"No!"

"Then you must be something worse. Are you just like your father?"

"What's that supposed to mean?"

"I'm sorry, but you're being selfish, just like he was."

Jag stared at her, aghast. "Excuse me?"

"The accident that landed you here was the result of his actions. He stole the shuttle in his selfish ambition to prove his stupid invention would work, never thinking about the harm it would cause others: my father, the school, even his own grandparents, who grieved his loss the rest of their lives."

"Is that what your father told you?"

"No, he never believed that story. He and your great-grandparents always believed your dad was innocent. But everyone else knows it's true."

"You have no idea what you're talking about. None of that is true!"

"How do you know? You are hiding out here in the prince's garden. You and the prince are just as bad as the Murks themselves."

"What?" Jag stood up from the bench to leave.

"Which is worse?" Sara asked. "The one who perpetrates harm or the one who sits idly by and allows it to happen when they have the power to stop it?"

"You don't know what happened, what they did!"

"Your beloved prince could make this entire situation cease if he would stop hiding behind his precious palace walls."

Jag glared at her and then walked away, leaving her alone on the bench. Bayli was walking down the path as Jag brushed by her, storming out of the garden.

"What was that all about?" Bayli asked as she approached Sara.

"How can he be so obtuse and selfish?" Sara asked.

"What? Who are you talking about?"

"Jag. He's just as selfish as his dad. He refuses to talk to the prince."

"Hmm . . . I see," Bayli said, pondering the situation. "How's the leg?"

"It's fine."

"Good. Follow me. It's time for you to see something."

Sara followed Bayli down a dirt path, ducking beneath low-hanging branches as the path wove back and forth down the trail.

"Where are you taking me?" Sara asked.

"You'll see, just a bit farther," Bayli replied as the path opened up onto a grassy knoll with a large castle ruin sitting in the middle.

"What is this place?" Sara asked, looking around.

"It's an old castle destroyed over eight hundred years ago during a battle between the Murks and the Celestians."

"Why have you brought me here?"

"Just wait. You'll see."

Bayli walked to the side of the ruins and opened a rusty iron gate, motioning for Sara to enter. The castle's roof had long been destroyed, and only its thick walls remained. Tall grass and weeds had overtaken the inside. In the far corner stood a canopy. They stepped under the canvas, and Sara froze as she saw the word "Winnebago" on the side of the shuttle.

"That's the experimental ship that Jag's dad stole!"

Bayli nodded and then led Sara to the back of the ship, opening the rear hatch.

"Wow, what my father would give to see this!" Sara said. "He helped build this ship."

"In time, but for now, you must promise not to tell anyone about it."

"Why are you showing me this?" Sara asked.

"You must promise."

"I promise, but why are you showing me this?"

"So you can understand the truth and what is at stake."

Bayli went to the shuttle's cockpit and activated the computer logs as she had seen Jag do. Audio began piping through the shuttle's speakers in the rear. Hearing her father's voice over the speakers, Sara hurried to the front.

"That's my dad. Oh my, he's so young! Boy, Jag looks just like his father!"

Bayli fast-forwarded through the logs to the fateful day, showing Percy, Tank, and Edgard entering the ship as Jag worked alone. Sara watched as the story unfolded: Percy punching Jag and then locking him in the freezer as Jag screamed. Her jaw dropped. She couldn't believe her eyes. No one on Earth knew that side of the story.

"We were all wrong! They lied to us!" Sara exclaimed.

"Wait, there's more that you need to know," Bayli said as she forwarded through the logs to the day the Thorgs captured the *Winnebago*. Sara watched in dismay as the Thorgs entered and then removed Jag's lifeless teenage body from the chamber. Bayli paused the video playback just as Jag's face entered the screen. "Notice the date."

Sara looked, and her eyes grew wide. "This just happened fifteen years ago? Then that means Jag is . . ."

Bayli nodded. "Yes."

Sara teared up. "I had no idea! No one knows what actually happened. All those horrible things I said to him . . . how can he ever forgive me?"

"Hush now. Everything will be fine."

"Why did you bring me here if I can't tell anyone what happened or who he really is?"

"You must not tell anyone, but I brought you here for a reason, for you play an integral role in all of this."

"Me? How?"

"You were correct when you asked, 'How can he forgive me?' You see, forgiveness is what is needed most. Jag has been through more pain in his life than anyone should have to endure. He loves his classmates. However, I think he may be stuck, and he needs a little help. Sometimes forgiveness needs someone to initiate it, and that's where you come in."

"What can I do?"

"I think one of your letters may help break the ice."

"What could I possibly write?"

Bayli smiled. "I'm sure you'll figure something out."

That evening, still angry from Sara's outburst, Jag asked IRIS to have his dinner delivered to the study, because he wanted to be alone. Bayli approached and rang the door chime. Moments later, Jag invited her in.

"How are you doing?" Bayli asked. When Jag did not respond, Bayli sighed. "When are you going to end this charade?"

"It'll end when it ends and not a moment sooner."

"I understand you're angry, but—"

Jag cut her off with an expression that could kill. Then he turned and stared out the large window as Bayli walked over and set Sara's letter on his desk.

"She asked me to give you this and to say she's sorry."

Jag sighed and then opened the envelope. As he unfolded the letter, something fell face-down to floor, but he didn't bother to pick it up. He started reading:

Dear Jag,

I am so sorry for what I said to you earlier today. I had no right to speak to you that way. Please accept my sincere apology. I didn't know all that you had suffered these many years and couldn't put myself in your shoes. You were harmed by the very people I have been pleading with you to save. If I have added to any of your pain, please forgive me.

I hope we can still be friends. Your secret will always be safe with me, even if we never talk again.

Votre ami dévoué,

Sara

P.S. Dad carried this photo of you and him in his wallet ever since you left. He doesn't know I took it from him, but I think you need it more than him.

After reading the letter, Jag threw it down and glared at Bayli. "What have you done?"

"It was for your own good. I had to do something!"

"You showed her the *Winnebago,* didn't you? You had no right to interfere! I know you had the grounds crew hide it even after I told them to destroy it."

"I had to do something. You aren't thinking clearly."

"Who are you to judge me? Maybe it's time you returned to Norr." Jag could see his words stung.

"If that's what you want, then I'll leave," she replied softly. "However, before I go, I would remind you that I also know what it's like to lose everything: a planet, friends, and family. There isn't a day that goes by that I don't think of my father. You have something I never had, an opportunity to save your planet. I would have given anything for that."

Jag sat quietly, for he knew she was right. As Bayli turned to walk out, Jag bent down and picked up the object that had fallen out of the letter. When he turned it over, he nearly fell out of his seat. It was the picture his grandpa had taken when Ben visited for Christmas, with Grandma and Grandpa smiling as they stood behind them with their hands on Ben and Jag's shoulders.

Seeing his grandparents was more than Jag could handle. The emotions that had been welling up in him for so long came pouring out, and he wept. He had not seen their faces for so long, except in his dreams, which were becoming rarer.

"What have I done?" Jag asked.

Bayli placed her hand on his shoulder. "Nothing that can't be undone if you act now."

Jag looked up at her, his cheeks streaked with tears. "I'm sorry for everything. Do you forgive me?"

Bayli smiled. "Of course."

Jag looked down at his grandparents and sighed. "It's time. Tell Sara to be in the courtroom tomorrow, for all will be revealed."

CHAPTER 28
THE PRINCE ARRIVES

Bayli's autopod came to rest in front of a tall luxury apartment complex that housed the *Exodus* crew as they awaited repairs to their ship. The egg-shaped vehicle's glass dome roof opened, and Bayli stepped down to greet Sara, who was waiting anxiously by the street corner.

"Good morning!" Bayli said as she hugged Sara.

"Morning," Sara replied apprehensively and then stepped into the autopod with Bayli as the glass dome lowered.

"Destination please?" a computer voice asked.

"Corian High Court Building," Bayli said. The autopod lifted and gradually increased its speed as it headed toward the courtroom.

"Would you care for any headline news or ambient music?" the computer asked as various music options and news articles appeared on a screen. The first article's headline was "Prince makes rare appearance in court today," with a photo of the prince beside it.

"No," Bayli said as she quickly distracted Sara to prevent her from seeing Jag's photo. The autopod floated quietly down the road toward its destination.

"Did you see him this morning?" Sara asked.

"See who?" Bayli replied, knowing exactly who Sara was inquiring about.

"Jag, did you see him? Is he still angry with me?"

"No, I didn't, but don't worry about such things. He said that all will be revealed, and there's no need to worry."

With the prince's appearance, security was increased, with officers stationed around the court building, as everyone entering the building was scanned. As the autopod neared the building, Captain Felix Henning recognized Bayli and motioned toward the vehicle.

"This autopod's control has been transferred to a local officer," the computer voice said. The autopod stopped in front of Captain Henning, and the dome opened.

"Good Morning, Ms. Bayli," Captain Henning said as he helped them out of the vehicle.

"It is most certainly a good morning, Captain Henning," Bayli replied.

A long line of spectators wearing elaborate outfits and flamboyant hats waited to be scanned so they could get a glimpse of the recently reclusive prince.

"Why are all these people here today?" Sara asked as Bayli led her to a side door, bypassing the security line.

"Why? Because of you!"

Sara stopped short. "Me? What did I do?"

"You demanded that the prince show his face, and now he's coming. All of these people are here to get a glimpse of the prince, since he rarely appears in public these days."

Sara's face flushed in embarrassment as she thought of the prince being angry with her for demanding that he show up. What if he rejected their appeal because of what she had said about him?

"What do you think the prince will do?" Sara asked.

"I'm not sure," Bayli said. "But you needn't worry."

Officers Nivedi and Reeso were guarding the side entrance of the building. As Sara and Bayli approached, Nivedi opened the door as Reeso bowed. "Ms. Bayli."

"Thank you, officers," Bayli replied as she and Sara stepped into a private hall.

"How is it that all of these officers know you?" Sara asked.

"Because of my friendship with the prince."

"You know the prince?"

"Yes, didn't I mention that already?"

"No!"

"Oh, I thought I had," Bayli said as she led Sara into the nearly packed courtroom.

"I hope we can find a seat," Sara remarked.

"No worries, we have seats in the front row," Bayli replied as they walked to a reserved section of seats right behind where Sara's father would sit.

"Do you see Jag?" Sara asked, looking around the room. "I'd like to tell him I'm sorry."

"No, I don't see him," Bayli replied, not even looking around as she sat down.

Sara craned her neck as she continued to look for him. "Should I try to save him a seat?"

"No, don't bother. He already has a seat reserved that is much more comfortable than this old thing," Bayli replied as she tried to get comfortable in the hard cushion-less chair.

The side door opened, and Councilman Maverick walked in followed by the eleven ambassadors, who took their seats. Sara leaned over the railing and hugged her father.

"Bonjour, Papa."

"Good morning, Sara dear. What brings you in here this morning?"

"Oh, I just thought today might be a good day to visit."

"It certainly is. They say that the prince has heard our plea and is making an appearance today. Isn't that exciting?"

"Yeah," Sara replied somewhat hesitantly.

"Well, hopefully he will be able to bring a resolution to all of this."

"I just hope it's a favorable resolution," Sara replied.

"Of course it will be favorable. I just wonder what prompted him to change his mind."

Sara looked down and shrugged. "Oh, probably some nagging and irritating person."

Ben placed the palm of his hand on her face. "Are you feeling well? You look pale,"

"I'm as well as can be, Papa. It's just that I was mad and said something awful to someone I care about, and now I fear our friendship might be in jeopardy."

"Oh, I'm sure it's nothing an apology can't handle. If it's a true friend, then they will always forgive."

Sara shook her head. "I don't know; I said some pretty awful things."

Their conversation was interrupted when a court officer stepped forward. "Attention, court will begin momentarily. Please find your seats."

Every available seat in both the lower gallery and balcony was filled to occupancy, and people outside were being turned away.

"Chairman Thanos asked me to remind everyone of the gravity of the outcome of these proceedings," the court officer said. "Any outbursts or inappropriate displays will not be tolerated. Everyone, please rise for the honorable Senators Thanos, Alberg, and Westreed." Everyone stood up as the senators entered in their long dark robes and took their seats on the judge's bench.

"Court is now in session," Senator Thanos said as he pounded his gavel. "This is the ongoing investigation into the application for planethood from the peoples of Earth. Please rise and welcome his Royal Majesty, Prince Marcello."

Everyone stood and turned to face the back as the doors swung open and the royal guards dressed in red coats, bright yellow hats with large plumes and swords strapped to their uniforms walked in. Then trumpeters entered playing the royal march, followed by Mahjon in Mravian attire: a green kilt and a leather sash with wooden beads identifying each attack on the prince he had prevented. It was a Mravian tradition designed to instill fear in any who would attempt to harm their protectee. Upon entering, he pounded his spear on the floor, making an ominous boom. Behind Mahjon was IRIS, adorned in a purple sash.

"His Royal Highness, Protector of the Kingdom of Celestia, Marshall of the Royal Fleet, and Governor of Corian, Prince Marcello," IRIS said.

Jag entered wearing a dark suit with a red robe over his shoulders. A purple sash hung across his chest with pendants identifying his position as Prince and

Protector of Celestia. As was custom, he wore a plumed helmet with tall feathers. Jag had told Bayli it made him look like a peacock. Once he described what a peacock was, she agreed. The helmet's straps draped the sides of his head, allowing only a portion of his face to be seen.

Jag walked slowly down the aisle, pausing at each row, where everyone bowed slightly, and then he nodded slowly in acknowledgment.

Sara stood on her tiptoes trying to see the prince between the rows of people and their large hats. Seeing only the plume of his helmet, she climbed onto her seat to get a better view but could only see Mahjon.

"Get out of the way, you big galoot," Sara said softly.

"I'm sorry. Did you say something?" Bayli asked.

"No, but I can't see anything with that giant in front of him."

Upon reaching the first row, Jag stopped and looked toward where he knew Sara and Bayli were seated. In unison, everyone in the row bowed their heads in respect. As soon as every head was bowed, Sara and Jag's eyes met. Although his helmet covered much of his face, she still recognized him. Her face went pale, her jaw dropped, and she felt as if her heart had stopped beating as she realized who Jag really was. Jag smiled slightly. Then he nodded, and everyone raised their heads.

"All hail His Majesty, Prince Marcello," the court officer said. Everyone knelt before the prince, including Councilman Maverick, who used his cane to support himself. When Maverick saw that the eleven ambassadors weren't sure if they should bow, he motioned for them to get down on one knee, which they did awkwardly and a bit reluctantly. Sara, still in shock from the revelation, was the only person in the entire auditorium still standing.

"Thank you, citizens of this great kingdom. Please be seated," Jag said.

Sara sank into her chair, pulled her knees to her chest, and placed her hands over her face.

"What are you doing?" Bayli whispered.

"Hiding."

"Why?"

"Why do you think?"

Bali put a hand on Sara's shoulder. "You have nothing to be ashamed of, child."

"Yes I do! All those horrible things I said to him. What I accused him of!"

"All things he needed to hear. Now take a deep breath, and put your hands down. You won't want to miss any of this."

"Honored chairman, senators," Jag began, "it is my privilege to participate in these proceedings today, as I have followed the hearing closely. I do not wish to interfere with your authority but only to present myself as a friend of the court. I believe we may be able to bring this matter to a resolution today."

"We serve at His Majesty's request," Senator Thanos replied, "and remind His Majesty that he may end these proceedings and make his own ruling at any time, if he so wishes."

Jag nodded. "Thank you. At this time, I wish only to present myself as a friend of the court. However, I do have several questions I'd like to ask before making my recommendation."

"Very well. Please proceed, Your Majesty."

"I would like the record to show that Councilman Maverick has eloquently represented the people of Earth. If I ever find myself in another legal fight, you will be my first choice for representation, for I believe had you been my counselor, I would have foregone my incarceration at Darkside."

Several in gallery chuckled.

"Thank you, Your Majesty. Most kind of you," Councilman Maverick replied, "though assuredly, your grace will never find yourself in need of my services."

"With your permission, counselor, I would like to question the ambassadors from Earth directly."

Maverick bowed in deference. "Most definitely, splendid suggestion, Your Majesty."

Jag stepped toward the ambassadors' table but kept his distance. Then he turned toward the gallery. "As Prince of Celestia, my highest title is Protector of the Kingdom, a title and responsibility I hold higher than any other. I have one initial question that I'd like each of you to answer," Jag said as he turned to the eleven. "Why should I let you into my kingdom? Why should I risk the lives of young Celestian men and women to protect your planet?"

The question piqued the interest of everyone sitting in the gallery, as they wanted to know how the ambassadors would answer. Jag stepped toward, Mo who was seated in the first chair. "Muhammad Harrak, why should I let Earth into my kingdom?"

Mo paused to consider his answer. "Your Majesty, Earth is a beautiful planet, and humans are a sentient species. We are conscious and self-aware, capable of thoughts and feelings, deserving of the opportunity to perpetuate our existence."

"Sentient species?" Jag asked. He paused and pondered the idea. "Sentient species die all the time. Why should your fate be any different?"

Several in the gallery chuckled at the prince's rebuttal. Then Jag stepped toward Kano.

"Kano Tanaka, why should I let you into my kingdom?"

"Your Majesty, the people of Earth are an intelligent species and have much to contribute to the universe."

"Intelligent? Perhaps? However, species much more intelligent than humans have long since gone extinct. What makes your species better than those?"

Before he could answer, Jag stepped toward Percy. Jag feared how he would respond, being so close to the person responsible for all his sufferings. However, it wasn't anger but pity that he felt as he looked at him. "Tell me, Percival Blackwell, why should I let you into my kingdom?"

"We are a highly technical, scientifically advanced planet with much to offer your kingdom, Your Majesty," Percy replied. "Within just two centuries, we went from carriages pulled by animals to interplanetary travel, and we have so much more potential to grasp."

Jag nodded. "Impressive, and yet, here you are, asking for our help."

Many in the audience broke out in laughter.

"Order! Order in the court!" Senator Thanos said as he pounded his gavel and glared at the crowd.

"My apologies to the senate. I mean no disrespect to the ambassadors or this court," Jag said as he stepped toward Tank. Jag looked down at the enormous man, who had grown into his nickname. "And what say you, Lars Klein? Why should I let you into my kingdom?"

"Your Majesty, the people of Earth are a good and moral species who hold to the rule of law and strive to treat their neighbors as themselves."

"Hmm . . . tell me, do the good people of Earth lock their homes and their valuables?"

Tank bowed his head. "Yes, Your Majesty, we do."

Jag smiled. "If you don't trust in your own goodness, why should we?"

He stepped toward Niklas. "And you, Niklas Johansen, what say you?"

"Your Majesty, Earth is made up of diverse cultures full of self-expression and creativity in music, art, and dance, and it would be a tragedy to lose all of that."

"Self-expression is wonderful, but should I sacrifice the young men and women of my kingdom to preserve your right to express yourselves?"

Jag proceeded to Makalo. "Makalo Zuma, what do you think?"

"Your majesty, humans are a spiritual people, observing many faiths and religions that bring satisfaction and fulfillment to people's lives that could be a joy to other planets as well."

"Are all humans religious and spiritual?"

Makalo's face fell. "No, Your Majesty. Many hold no religious or spiritual beliefs at all."

"So basically everyone does what is right in their own sight and worships whatever they want?"

Throughout the gallery, everyone listened intently to the discussion. Many wondered how they would respond to the prince's questions. Some believed his questions were justified. Why should they place their young men and women in harm's way to save a planet they'd never heard of? Others were more sympathetic and believed that Celestia should intervene.

"Surely among such admirable and intellectual people as we have before us, at least one of you can give a worthy answer," Jag prompted. He looked down the table. Then he stepped toward Mario. "Mario Bergoglio, why should I let you into my kingdom?"

"Your Majesty, Earth has much to offer. We are full of resources, both human-made and natural resources. Our farms produce delicious vegetables, grains, and fruits. We have raw materials that can be used to construct your ships and build your empire—resources that can be traded and exchanged throughout your kingdom."

"Thank you for your generosity. However, does it look like my kingdom lacks any good thing?"

Mario dropped his eyes. "No, Your Majesty. Your kingdom is most impressive."

"Edgard Dubois? How do you answer?"

Edgard shifted in his seat, uncomfortable with the interrogation. "Your Majesty, the people of Earth possess traits and characteristics that are truly unique in the universe, and if we were to no longer exist, the universe would lose something special."

Jag nodded. "True, the peoples of Earth are unique, but are not all people from all planets unique? Can any species compare to the strength and honor of the Mravians? Or to the mystical beauty of the Azurians, whose planet was also destroyed by the Murks? Being unique is not a certainty for planethood. If it were, Earth would hardly qualify."

As Jag reached Raj, thoughts of him, Sasha, and Ben flooded his mind. He almost burst out in laughter as he recalled chasing Godzilla through the station in their pajamas. "Rajesh Gupta, why should I let you into my kingdom?"

"Prince Marcello, I believe we are a destined people with a great purpose that has yet to be fully obtained."

"Destined? Perhaps so. Or perhaps your planet's past violence and many wars predicate a destiny of destruction."

Jag moved on. "Sasha Belinsky, why should I let you into my kingdom?"

"Your Majesty, I can only express many of the same thoughts my colleagues have already communicated. However, I would have to say that we are a kind and loving species."

"Loving? Your history tells a different story: millennia of war, greed, and infighting."

When Jag reached the eleventh chair, the empty seat between Sasha and Ben, he stopped and looked around. "It seems I've scared this one away."

Laughter broke out from the gallery once again, prompting Senator Thanos to pound his gavel.

Jag glanced around. "Where is this . . . Joseph Gabriel?"

Ben leaned toward Jag. "Your Majesty, there was once twelve of us. However, this one was lost long ago, and now there are only eleven."

"I'm truly sorry," Jag replied as he stepped forward and looked into the face of his dear friend. Memories flooded his mind of his time on *Unity* and at Christmas with his grandparents. He had so many fond memories of staring at the stars and talking about their dreams and their future. Even though the boy was no longer there, Jag could still see his friend in the face of the man sitting before him, and he missed him dearly.

"So, Benjamin Levi Mendelsohn, why should I let you into my kingdom?"

Ben didn't answer immediately. However, he also didn't pick up on the fact that Jag had called him by his full name.

"Sir, I can't think of any just reason why we should be allowed into your kingdom," Ben said softly. "As our history shows, we have not always lived up to our highest virtues. Therefore, it is not to our goodness or merit that I appeal but to your kingdom's own goodness that I plead for mercy."

Then Ben took out his wallet and pulled out an old, wrinkled scripture card that Jag had given him so many years ago. "My friend, who is no longer with us, gave me this card. It says 'These three will last forever: faith, hope and love. And the greatest of these is love.'" Ben set the card down. "I have faith that our planet will be saved, hope that we will have a future, and the belief that love will conquer the darkness that surrounds us."

Jag was so moved by Ben's humble and honest answer that he had to turn his back so no one could see the emotion welling up on his face. After taking a deep breath to collect himself, he turned back to them. "Well said, Benjamin Levi Mendelsohn. You shall speak on behalf of the twelve and your planet."

CHAPTER 29
THE *WINNEBAGO* UNVEILED

A throne had been placed next to the judges' bench, and Jag sat in it. Everyone sensed that something had unsettled him, as his demeanor had changed. IRIS approached him.

"Is everything alright, sir?"

Jag nodded. "I'm fine." Then he took a deep breath. "With the chairman's permission, I'd like to present an object for the ambassadors to identify."

Chairman Thanos bowed his head. "As you wish, Your Majesty."

Jag nodded at Captain Henning, who motioned for several officers to open a series of tall doors. Light poured in from an adjacent room as people covered their eyes and squinted to see what was happening. The officers pushed and pulled a wheeled platform carrying a large object covered with a black tarp into the courtroom and then closed the doors. As the auditorium dimmed again, many questions were whispered, and people stood to get a better view.

"Tell me, Benjamin Levi Mendelsohn, what is this contraption?" Jag asked as Captain Henning removed the tarp. Immediately, many of the eleven stood in amazement.

"It's the *Winnebago*!" Sasha exclaimed.

Raj stared at it in wonder. "How can this be?"

Jag watched each of the eleven's reaction closely. Everyone was excited to see the ship except for Percy and Edgard, who sat quietly. While Edgard had not been there when Percy initiated the launch, he was smart enough to put the pieces together and figured out what Percy had done.

"I see that you recognize this," Jag said.

"Yes, Your Majesty!" Ben said, turning to him in astonishment. "This spacecraft is from when we were students. It's the ship that we lost our dear friend in so many years ago."

"What type of ship is it?"

"It was a decommissioned short-range shuttle used only for testing purposes, as we were trying to find new technologies to aid us in our quest to reach farther into space."

Jag nodded thoughtfully. "Interesting, so tell me: Why would a sentient, intelligent, civilized, loving and good species, which you claim to be, send a child into deep space in such a contraption?"

The eleven looked at each other as they discussed how best to answer the prince. Jag heard several proposals: "It was an accident," "He was a young kid trying to prove his invention worked," and "We just don't know and will never know."

Finally, Kano could keep quiet no longer. "It was all his fault!"

"Shhh . . ." Makalo replied, trying to calm him.

"I can't sit quietly any longer. Let the truth be told!" Kano said. "Joseph was selfish and took unnecessary risks that we all are still paying the consequences for decades later. I, for one, don't want to see Earth suffer because of his egotistic attempt to prove his theory was correct."

"That's not true, and you know it," Sasha said. "He did no such thing."

"Well, he put the entire station at risk with his experiments, and we were all fortunate not to have been destroyed as well," Mario interjected.

Finally, Ben spoke up, "He was my closest friend and I knew him better than anyone. He was driven, but we all were. However, he never intended any risks that would endanger us."

"Intended or not, his actions destroyed the entire academy," Kano said.

Jag watched as the two factions went back and forth. Percy sat quietly, looking down and fiddling anxiously with his chair. The gallery sat in silence, watching the drama unfold. Before Senator Thanos could pound his gavel, Jag interrupted.

"Would you like to see what really happened? We have recovered the video logs."

The eleven hushed, and with Jag's command, the lights dimmed as the *Winnebago's* video logs played on the large screens. Percy placed his face in his hands, knowing what the logs would reveal. When they reached the video showing Edgard and Tank holding Jag as Percy punched him in the gut, the audience gasped as the others at the table looked over at Percy, Edgard, and Tank in disbelief. Then the video showed Jag being forced into the cryo-chamber and the door locked with Jag screaming inside.

Sasha leaped to his feet and turned to Percy. "What did you do?"

Percy began weeping, his face in his hands, as the video showed him typing in the launch code. "Stop the video. Please, stop it," Percy said. "I did it. It was all my fault."

Jag motioned, and the video stopped. The lights came back up. Then Percy stood up, trembling.

"I did this. I caused his death and have lived with the guilt of it all my life. I was so jealous of him. I was supposed to win that stupid competition. He had everything I wanted, and my greed destroyed his life. I beg you, Your Majesty, don't judge my people because of my stupidity. Pass judgment on me, for I deserve it, but have pity on my people."

The lies and secrets hidden so cunningly for so many years were now on display for all to see. Percy no longer stood as the self-confident, arrogant billionaire but as a broken man. As he wept, his face softened, and Jag saw a remnant of the boy standing in the video booth being chastised by his father.

The wall of anger and bitterness toward Percy that Jag had built up around his heart crumbled. A tear fell down Jag's cheek, and he turned to keep his face hidden as he wiped his eyes. It was obvious to all that he had been impacted by his testimony.

After a moment, Ben stood up. "Your Majesty, we are all shocked by this tragic revelation. However, I know if my friend was here today, he would forgive this man, for that is who Jag was. I also plead with you not to cast judgment on our planet for the wrongful actions of a child. Jag's death was the saddest day of my life, and not a day goes by that I don't think about him."

Again, tears flowed down Jag's cheeks. This time he didn't try to hide them.

IRIS approached him. "Sir, would you like a recess? I'm sure Senator Thanos would allow a short break."

"No, I'll be alright." Jag wiped his face again and took a deep breath. Then he turned to face the group. "Who said anything about your friend being dead?"

Every eye in the room looked toward the prince.

Ben's jaw dropped in astonishment. "He's alive? Please, Your Majesty, if you know anything about the whereabouts of our friend, please take us to him."

"You call him your friend, but how is that you have not recognized him when he stood near you this very day?"

Perplexed, the eleven looked around the room. Even the audience searched, trying to identify who he could be. Of course, everyone was looking for someone the same age as the ambassadors. Several in the gallery even pointed out different people who they thought might be a possible match.

While everyone was distracted, Jag stood, untied the strap that secured his helmet, and laid it down. He loosened the ties on his robe, and it dropped to the floor. Then he removed all his adornments until only a white shirt and his dark pants remained. People were puzzled by his actions. Tears flowed steadily as he walked over and stood before Ben.

"Look closely. Do you see him now?"

"It's you!" Ben said, bursting into tears.

"No, it can't be!" Kano cried.

"It is him," Sasha confirmed.

Raj put has hand to his mouth. "Oh my gosh!"

"It's me, Joseph," Jag replied as he looked at each of them.

Ben ran from behind the table and embraced Jag. The royal officers moved in to protect Jag, but he waved them away. Sasha and Raj joined Ben, and they all embraced.

"How can this be?" Makalo asked as Jag nodded at Mo and smiled.

"The cryogenics chamber," Mo replied in amazement.

"But you would have had to spent nearly thirty years in that . . ." Nik's voice trailed off.

"Thirty-three years, six months, and five days to be exact," Jag stated as he walked behind the table and embraced each ambassador in turn. When he reached Edgard and Tank, they both asked for forgiveness, and Jag embraced them. Then Jag came to Percy, who was still sitting with his face in his hands.

"How can you ever forgive me for what I did to you?" Percy asked, looking up at Jag. "I took your life away from you and your grandparents."

Jag grabbed Percy by the shoulders and lifted him to his feet. Percy flinched out of fear that Jag would strike him, but when he saw Jag's face, he knew that Jag had truly forgiven him.

"I . . . I'm so sorry. Please forgive me," Percy said.

"I do forgive you," Jag replied. "For now I know that what you meant for harm God has used to bring good to me and Earth." Then Jag embraced Percy, and the two cried.

Afterwards, Percy stepped back and knelt before Jag. "Your Majesty," he said, though he had sworn never to bow to Jag. Then, one by one, each of the eleven knelt, followed by the entire gallery. They knelt not out of obligation but out of respect to the young prince, who demonstrated by his forgiveness what it truly meant to be royal.

Jag walked over and stood behind his nametag. "Honored senators. I am Joseph Gabriel from Earth, and it's on behalf of my people that I ask that whatever good is owed to me because of my service to this kingdom that it be extended to my people. I ask that Earth be granted planethood in this great kingdom."

"Very well, Your Majesty, we'll take your request into consideration," Senator Thanos replied. "But first answer your own question: Why should we let your planet into this kingdom?"

Jag chuckled, but then his face turned somber. "It's true, we humans have our faults. But Earth is a wonderful planet, and its people are peculiar, intelligent, and have much to offer. However, it is not on our merit that we beseech the kingdom," Jag nodded toward Ben, "but on the merits of the Kingdom of

Celestian itself, whose purpose is to unite planets to stand together against darkness. This kingdom has never turned a deaf ear or a blind eye to any planet that has sought our help, and we are not about to start."

Senator Thanos smiled at Jag's response and then turned to Senator Westreed, who nodded in approval, and then to Senator Alberg. "Absolutely!" he exclaimed.

Then Senator Thanos pounded his gavel. "It is the recommendation of this panel that Earth's petition for planethood in the Kingdom of Celestia be approved forthwith and sent to Her Majesty, Queen Ardiana, for confirmation."

The gallery erupted in cheers as complete strangers hugged and congratulated each other for a planet and a people they had never heard of previously. As the courtroom guards began clearing the gallery, Sara and Bayli walked over to Ben. He embraced his daughter.

"See? I told you to believe." Then he guided her toward Jag. "I'd like to introduce you to my daughter, Sara."

"Yes, we've met," Jag said, smiling as Sara blushed.

"You have?" Ben asked, surprised.

"We met in the prince's—I mean, in his garden, as I was recuperating. Though I didn't know he was the prince, and I said so many awful things to him."

"She's just as stubborn as you are!" Jag said, slapping his old friend on the back. "However, she promised not to tell anyone about me, and I owe her so much for helping me find my way through all of this."

"Well, the stubbornness comes more from her mother," Ben replied.

Jag laughed and then motioned for IRIS. "Please send a message to Commander Corbis to prepare my fleet and to Captain O'Malley of the *Exodus* that we leave for Earth tomorrow."

"Done, sir," IRIS said as he transmitted the messages instantaneously.

"Also, send this message to Admiral Rannick: 'You once rescued a young boy from the Thorgs. That same boy now requests your help in rescuing his planet from the Murks.' Oh, and tell the admiral that if he needs any additional hands to help with the harvest, we would be glad to send over a team of farmers."

Bayli put her arm around Jag's shoulder. "I'm proud of you. You did good today!"

Jag smiled. "Thank you. Seriously, thank you for your patience with me through all of this!"

"You're seriously welcome. I knew you'd come around and do the right thing. You just needed some extra prodding."

Jag turned and looked at his fellow students, who were standing and talking with each other. He breathed deeply and took in all that had been accomplished and fulfilled that day. Then he clapped his hands. "Come, brothers. We have a planet to save!"

CHAPTER 30
JOURNEY TO EARTH

"Could you pass that green goop?" Sasha asked, pointing to a bowl of sauce in the officers' mess on board the *Cora Lee*. After picking up Admiral Rannick, the Celestian fleet and the upgraded *Exodus* headed at maximum speed toward Earth. Jag invited the ambassadors and Sara to join him so they could spend time together during the long voyage, that even at hyperdrive speeds would take more than two months.

"This green goop is called Jumbey," Bayli replied. "It's a sauce made from the sour berries of a Yarmel tree on Aulora."

"It's quite delicious!" Sasha added.

"The wine is fantastic, too," Nik said. "It has a beautiful bouquet with such intense flavors." He smelled and then sipped his wine.

"The wine is made on Norr and comes from Admiral Rannick's own vineyard," Jag replied.

Rannick took the open bottle and looked at the year on the label. "That was one of our best years." He considered the years that Jag worked with him to be the vineyard's best.

A kitchen attendant placed a bowl of red sauce with crackers on the table. Edgard reached for it, but Jag put his hand on Edgard's arm. "Careful, that sauce is quite hot!"

Edgard scooped a spoonful onto a cracker and took a bite anyway. A moment later, his face turned bright red, sweat beaded on his forehead, and he began coughing. He took a gulp of water to wash it down. "That is hot," he said hoarsely when he could finally speak again.

"Let me try that." Raj reached across the table and tried a bite. "Yum. That's good stuff!" He reached for seconds.

"So, admiral, how did you come to know Jag?" Mo asked.

"I bought him," Rannick replied matter-of-factly.

Kano stared at him in astonishment. "You *bought* him?" Everyone stopped eating and looked to Jag to see if Rannick was being sincere.

Jag shrugged. "He's telling the truth."

"You're pulling our leg," Mo said.

Bayli leaned back to look under the table. "Sir, I don't believe anyone is touching your leg."

"It's a figure of speech, which means they don't believe it's true," Jag said.

"Well, it is true," Bayli said. "And Jag bought me, too!"

Everyone looked at Jag.

"What's this all about? We thought slavery was outlawed in Celestia," Makalo said.

"It is," Rannick replied. "It's just that on outer-belt planets, the law is harder to enforce. Years ago, a group of Thorgs showed up on Norr as we were shopping for a transformer or something, and—"

"A Hamlin water pump," Jag said through a mouthful of food.

"Yes, that's right. Well, they said they had someone who could fabricate any part I needed. Then they brought out this scraggly kid, who smelled like he had never seen soap in his life, to demonstrate this incredibly complex processor. I knew he couldn't be with them by his own design and that he was more than he appeared."

"Or smelled," Bayli interjected, elbowing Jag.

"So I demanded that the Thorgs sell him to me. It took me a while to fatten him up, but I could have never imagined that he would someday become a prince."

"How long were you on the Thorg ship, Jag?" Ben asked.

"I'm not sure, but I think it was a couple of years."

"Bayli, you said Jag bought you, too?" Sara asked, surprised.

Bayli nodded. "Yep. A couple of years after the admiral freed Jag, he was given the opportunity to join a space expedition with the potential of returning to Earth. On the day he was to launch, he and Marcel came across that same group of pirates in the market. Just months earlier, the Thorgs had attacked our family ship, killing my father and capturing my mother and me. Jag saw me and took pity. He sacrificed his trip to purchase my mom and me."

"That was a very honorable thing to do, young man," Makalo replied.

"Ah, it wasn't as big as it sounded. We weren't sure if the expedition would take me toward Earth or in the opposite direction."

"Perhaps, but it was big to me," Bayli said.

"What was the name of that ship?" Percy asked.

"It was a private research vessel called the *Star Searcher*. It was financed mostly by some trade company looking for new planets to establish trade with."

"No way!" Sasha said. "That's the alien vessel that visited the *Unity* when the first Murk ship arrived. They told us to go to Corian to get help!"

"So you would have made it home and avoided prison, too," Bayli said.

Jag shrugged. "It doesn't matter. Some things you do just because they're right, no matter the cost."

"You were in prison?" Raj asked, astonished.

"Yeah, he and Marcel spent a year in Darkside Prison," Bayli replied. She went on to explain how Prince Damon framed Jag for murdering the king and then how Jag and Marcel escaped from prison to save the queen.

"Wow, it sounds like you've been very busy!" Tank said.

"Everything seems to have worked out okay for you in the end," Edgard added.

"Not everything. We lost Marcel," Jag replied.

"That wasn't your fault," Rannick reminded him. "You saved that boy's life."

"I'm not sure if I saved it or caused it to be taken prematurely."

"Son, you're not responsible for his death. You gave him a life with purpose and friendship that he wouldn't have known otherwise. Marcel's death is entirely on Prince Damon."

"Don't you mean Emperor Damon?" Bayli asked sarcastically.

"I'll never call that snot-nosed monster 'emperor' as long as I have strength in me to stand up against him," Rannick replied.

"Hear, hear!" many of the *Cora Lee* officers said, raising their drinks in agreement.

"Who was Marcel?" Ben asked.

Rannick told the story of how Jag rescued a little thief from losing his hands and took him under his wing. Everyone sat astonished by the stories and all that Jag had endured. Then the conversation shifted as Rannick asked the ambassadors about life on Earth.

"Please, excuse me," Sara said, standing up to leave.

Jag excused himself as well and chased after her. Since his revelation that he was the prince, they had hardly spoken. "Hey, wait up," Jag said. Sara stopped in the hallway and turned toward him. "May I join you for a walk on the promenade?"

She smiled. "That would be nice. I'm stuffed from all the great food."

"Have you seen our planetarium?"

Sara shook her head. "I didn't know you had one."

"Well, it doubles as a war room, but its true purpose is planetary research."

Jag led her into an enormous dome-shaped room encircled by a dozen wide steps for seating. He grabbed a tablet off the wall and then stepped down into the center of the room. After typing several commands, a holographic image of Earth filled the room as it rotated slowly on its axis. The details were so impressive that even cloud formations could be seen moving across the globe and then dissipating.

"Wow, this is incredible!" Sara exclaimed. "It's so realistic! Where did you get this video?"

"It's not a video. It's a holographic rendering of satellite images we downloaded courtesy of the *Exodus*."

Jag touched the image, and Earth stopped spinning. Then he rotated the planet until Europe was in front of him. He tapped Paris, and the graphic enlarged and filled the entire stage floor with a 3D replica of the city.

"This is absolutely phenomenal!" Sara said as she ran through the holographic images. "La Tour Eiffel, and over here is the Arc de Triomphe de l'Étoile! And there's La Notre Dame! Oh, wait, let me show you my home." As Sara crossed the River Siene, holographic water splashed on the floor. Then she pointed to a building. "This is my home! I can't believe how realistic this is."

"Oh, just wait." As Jag gestured, Sara's building grew to nearly twelve feet high.

"There, on the fifth floor," Sara said. "That's my bedroom. I used to play in that park behind our home as a child. Oh, and that's the pastry shop where Mom gets our croissants. They have the best croissants in Paris! Wait, I have to show you one of my favorite spots, Luxemburg Garden!"

Jag gestured. and the city shrank back to its original height.

"This is the place I told you about, where I used to go and sit under a tree and read. It's one of the most beautiful places in Paris. I used to daydream that I was Cinderella going to a ball in the palace."

Jag laughed as Sara told the story with childlike enthusiasm.

Sara sighed happily. "Thank you for bringing me here. I needed this. After we save Earth, I'll give you a real tour of Paris, and you can meet my Mère."

"You know, I'm going to take you up on your offer."

Sara turned to him. "Jag, I really am sorry for all that I said to you."

"You don't have to apologize again."

"I know, but after hearing all that you've been through, I feel terrible." Sara teared up.

"I am just glad I've had the opportunity to get to know you," Jag said. "And I should be the one apologizing. I totally misled you."

"You should apologize! You did mislead me!"

"Yeah, but your expression was priceless when you realized I was the prince!" Jag mimicked her shocked expression, and they both laughed.

For the next few evenings, Jag and Sara walked around the promenade, often visiting the planetarium to view different planets or solar systems. One night as they were viewing Mravia, with its incredible volcano and amazing forest towns, IRIS entered.

"Excuse me, Your Majesty. I'm sorry to interrupt, but Admiral Rannick and Commander Corbis need to speak with you right away. They are in your ready room."

When Jag arrived, Rannick was meeting with Commander Corbis, Security Officer Cho, and Communication Officer Beckel. Two other admirals traveling with the fleet had transferred over to the *Cora Lee* for the meeting, and everyone looked quite distressed.

"What's the emergency?" Jag asked as he sat down at his desk.

"Lieutenant Beckel intercepted a subspace message sent to the Murks," Corbis replied.

"What did it say?"

Lieutenant Beckel read it for him. "'Fleet en route. Three battlecruisers, seven warbirds, and nine destroyers. Three weeks out. They are unaware of my presence. I have identified a target.'"

"That's the entirety of the message?" Admiral Channing asked, Senior Commander of the Royal Fleet. Jag greatly respected her because of her decisiveness and uncanny ability to cut to the root of a problem.

"Yes, ma'am. I was alerted of the outgoing message and blocked all further transmissions."

"So the enemy knows we are on our way and how many are with us," replied Admiral Plite, a large, barrel-chested man who led the marine and special forces divisions.

"It would appear so, sir," Commander Corbis said.

"So we have a spy traveling with the fleet. Do we know which ship sent the transmission?" Jag asked. Lt. Beckel looked sheepishly at Commander Corbis, hoping he would answer the question.

"It was sent from the *Cora Lee*."

"What?" Jag couldn't believe his ears.

"Wait, there's more. It was sent from the ambassadors' general living quarters."

"That can't be!" Jag replied. "When was it sent?"

"Fifty-two minutes ago," Lt. Beckel replied.

"Well, there you go. They couldn't have done it," Jag said. "They were finishing dinner when I left with Sara. Admiral Rannick was with them and can vouch for them."

"Yes, they were all there—except one," Rannick said.

Jag looked at him. "Who?"

"Ambassador Percival. He left right after you and Sara."

Jag shook his head in disbelief. "No! He couldn't be the spy. He wouldn't do this."

"Are you certain?" Commander Corbis asked. "He betrayed you once. How do you know he wouldn't do it again?"

"He was just a kid. He's completely different today."

"Well, what do you want us to do?" Admiral Channing asked.

"Lock down all long-range communication."

"Already done, sir," Lt. Beckel said.

Corbis turned to Jag. "And what about the ambassadors?"

"Disable their access to all communications systems until we identify the spy."

"How come Mahjon didn't detect a spy?" Lt. Cho asked.

"Guardians pick up only on the emotions of those who intend to harm their protectee," Rannick explained. "It's feasible they meant no immediate harm to the prince."

"Or they've learned how to mask their emotions like Prince Damon did," Jag replied.

"Now that the Murks know we're coming and how large our fleet is, we've lost the element of surprise," Admiral Plite pointed out.

"Apparently, we never had it," Admiral Channing replied.

Rannick rubbed his chin thoughtfully. "Hmm . . . Perhaps this is actually a blessing."

"How so, sir?" Commander Corbis asked.

"Information is the greatest asset in any battle. If your enemy knows something about you that you are unaware of, it makes you vulnerable. However, knowing this can be beneficial, because it allows us to adjust our strategy."

"Have we heard back from the scout ship?" Jag asked.

Admiral Channing shook her head. "No, sir. They are operating under silence protocol and won't communicate until one hour before we are to rendezvous next week."

"Hopefully the spy is unaware of the scout ship, or I fear their mission may have been jeopardized," Admiral Channing replied.

"Yes, let's hope that's the case," Jag agreed. "Until we hear further, we will proceed as planned."

CHAPTER 31
BATTLE DEBRIEFING

"Please take a seat; we have much to cover in today's briefing," Admiral Channing said as everyone took a seat in the planetarium. Jag sat beside Bayli, Ben, Sara, and the other ambassadors. Admiral Channing touched the tablet that turned on the holographic system. Several officers unable to attend in person appeared in holographic form throughout the room. One appeared next to Bayli and startled her. He smiled and then apologized.

"Your Majesty, honorable captains, commanders, and officers, welcome to today's briefing," Admiral Channing said. "Before we start, I'd like to thank Major Flank and Private Gotney for their reconnaissance on board the scout ship that secured the information we are about to share. The situation on Earth is actually worse than we thought."

A hologram of Earth appeared, engulfed in a thick, dark cloud.

"Lord, have mercy!" Makalo cried.

"The poison forming is now complete, and the entire atmosphere is enclosed," Admiral Channing explained.

"Has there been any communication?" Kano asked. "Do we know how Earth is coping?"

"Sadly, we received no signals from the planet's surface," Major Flank replied.

"One of the attributes of the gas is that it interrupts most communication," Chief Engineer Morten explained.

An overlay of various types of enemy ships appeared encircling Earth. Several people gasped at the sheer number of vessels.

"Major Flank, please break down the Murk fleet," Admiral Channing said.

"The Murk fleet is a combination of twenty-six new Celestian ships that fled with Prince Damon and sixty-three older Murk ships," Major Flank began. Holographic images of each ship displayed, starting with the powerful and boxy battlecruisers followed by the sleeker and faster warbirds and then the smaller destroyer attack ships, known for their speed and maneuverability. Then the small and nimble sentry ship, used for first strikes, appeared.

Next he reviewed the old Murk ships, starting with a heavily repaired Murk dominion ship. It was smaller than a battlecruiser but larger and slower than a warbird. Next an enforcer appeared, with bird-like wings expanding outward from its hull. Then the small three-man scourge fighter, followed by a spewer, an unmanned ship that looked like a floating porcupine with long quill-like nozzles that pumped poisonous gas into the atmosphere.

"That makes eighty-nine enemy warships!" Captain Renfro replied from the *Venturer* battlecruiser.

"How many ships do we have in our fleet?" Raj asked.

"Thirty-five," Channing said. "Three battlecruisers, seven warbirds, nine destroyers, thirteen sentries, the *Exodus*, the *Cora Lee,* and the *Anastasis*, our hospital ship."

"We're outnumbered three to one!" Captain Renfro exclaimed.

"Wait, there's one more warship that we saved for last," Private Gotney replied.

"Our enemy has a new ship, larger than anything we've encountered before," Major Flank said. "It showed up several weeks ago and is nearly three times the size of a battlecruiser. Intel says they've named the ship the *Massacre*."

An enormous, black ship appeared with three stationary arms stretching from its belly. They placed an image of a battlecruiser next to it for perspective.

Bayli covered her mouth in shock. "Oh my!"

"It's massive!" Captain Palen said.

"Well, I have to hand it to them. It doesn't look like the typical Murk design," Commander Corbis said. Most Murk ships were poorly designed with a heavy focus on weaponry and little else.

"That's because the Murks didn't design it. When Prince Damon fled to Atundra, he kidnapped several Celestian architects to design the ship for him," Major Flank explained.

"Have we been able to identify its strengths and weaknesses?" Captain Renfro inquired.

Admiral Channing nodded. "We believe it has a full arsenal of torpedoes, phasors and cannons. But the real threat comes from its three massive tractor beams that haul in its prey. Then it unleashes an array of weapons until the trapped vessel is destroyed."

"The only weakness we've been able to ascertain is it maneuverability," Flank added. "It's fast in a straight line but quite cumbersome if it has to turn. We have footage of an attack on a fleeing Earth ship. Just a warning: The footage is disturbing."

A video showed an Earth ship rising through the dark cloud as the *Massacre* maneuvered to intercept it. With its powerful tractor beams, it pulled the ship toward its center and then unleashed a firestorm of weapons against it. Within seconds, the ship exploded. Many in the room gasped. Bayli held her hand over her mouth. Sara turned away from the image.

"Major Flank, let's move on to the space station," Admiral Channing said. In the center of the room, the *Unity* appeared, surrounded by a minefield.

"The Murks are using the *Unity* as a failsafe. If attacked, they are threatening to destroy it. By our estimates, over a hundred people are on board."

"Fortunately, that's much less than I expected," Sasha replied. As a former director of the *Unity*, he had extensive knowledge of the space station. "When the Murks arrived, we began evacuating as quickly as possible. However, the Murks fired upon the escape pods and invaded the station. When we left Earth, thirteen hundred people were still trapped on board."

"The Murks only recently began trading the hostages," Major Flank said.

Raj's eyes narrowed. "Trading them for what?"

"For twelve individuals from Earth. They threatened to start killing hostages unless Earth turned over one family member from each of the ambassadors' families."

"Surely they refused," Makalo said.

"They did at first. However, the Murks killed a hostage every hour until a family member surrendered. For each family member, they released one hundred hostages. They wish to use these twelve as a deterrent and are broadcasting the following video."

In the center of the room, images rotated in one by one, showing the ambassadors' family members. An image of a woman appeared.

"*Mère!*" Sara cried and then turned her head into Ben's arm. Then an image of Raj's daughter appeared, followed by Nik's brother and Tank's son. An image of an old man appeared.

"Grandpa!" Jag whispered, before realizing it was his Uncle Jack. Then a warning appeared that any attempt to rescue the hostages or attack a Murk ship would result in the *Unity* being destroyed, along with all the hostages.

"Now that we fully understand the severity of our situation, we can discuss our options and strategy," Admiral Channing replied.

"Strategy?" Nik retorted. "We're outnumbered, and they have our family members."

"Perhaps we should just negotiate with them," Edgar suggested. "Find out what they want and see if we can meet their demands."

"You can't negotiate with tyrants," Admiral Plite replied.

"While negotiating may be unseemly, it can be a valid strategy when dealing with disreputable entities," Percy said.

The hologram of Captain Palen stood up. "You cannot negotiate with Murks! They are a dishonorable people who surround defenseless planets and pump the atmosphere with poison to force them into submission. If a planet resists, they destroy every element of life. As for those who surrender by 'negotiating', the Murks take everything. They'll plunder all your natural resources until your planet is used up, and then they'll take your sons and daughters and force them to subject other planets to the same evil. You cannot negotiate with vermin."

"Why not just delay the attack until reinforcements arrive?" Captain Renfro asked.

Dr. Pandori of the *Cora Lee* walked down to the center of the room to examine the gas cloud surrounding Earth. "How long will reinforcements take?"

"Well, most would come from Aulora, so we're looking at least two months," Captain Renfro replied.

"I guarantee you that Earth doesn't have two months! The gases are nearing critical mass."

"How long do they have, doctor?" Admiral Plite asked.

"Can't say for certain. I'm not an expert on Earth's atmosphere or their food reserves. However, I should think that in three weeks, Earth will reach an irreversible state."

"Oh, Papa!" Sara exclaimed, clutching him.

Throughout the room, various suggestions were mentioned, and confusion ensued as everyone talked simultaneously.

"It's going to be a bloodbath!" one of the captains exclaimed.

"I don't know why we aren't negotiating with them; that's our best option," Edgard said.

"It is ridiculous that we aren't just waiting for additional resources," another person opined.

Round and round they argued as to whether they should wait for reinforcements, attack, or negotiate.

"Enough!" Admiral Rannick yelled. Having sat quietly, he had had all he could take. "We will neither delay our mission nor negotiate. Negotiating is not an option, for we cannot offer Prince Damon what he seeks. We will fight, and we will win!"

"Admiral, if you don't think he desires Earth, what does he want?" Kano asked.

"Damon has but one true desire, and that is to rule Celestia."

"He is a madman if he thinks he will ever rule," Captain Renfro replied.

"Yes, and if he can't rule Celestia, then he will exact vengeance on those whom he believes have denied him his destiny," Rannick said, looking directly at Jag. "So, without further discussion, let's look at our strategy for liberating Earth."

"While we may not have the element of surprise, we do have the *Cora Lee*," Admiral Channing said. "The Murks have no ship that can match her speed, agility, or firepower. She will separate from the fleet and, using Earth's Moon to hide her approach, slow her descent enough to jettison our special forces. Admiral Plite will discuss taking the station."

"Thank you. Our team will jump from the *Cora Lee* and glide undetected through the mines and land on the station," Admiral Plite said as a holographic video illustrated his plan. "After disabling the Murk's communications systems to prevent them from alerting their fleet that the attack has begun, we will enter the station and disable the Murks on board."

"Once the team retakes Mission Control, they will signal the *Cora Lee* to begin the battle," Admiral Channing said, picking up where Plite left off. "When the battle begins, the *Cora Lee* will lead the attack on the far side of Earth to draw the enemy's fleet away from the station. The rest of the fleet will meet up on the far side of the planet, destroying the enemy ships."

"What about the *Massacre*?" Captain Renfro asked. "I don't think even the *Cora Lee* can stand against it."

"All ships will stay clear of the *Massacre*," Admiral Channing replied. "No one is to engage it alone."

"Yeah, but what if it engages us?" Captain Palen asked.

"Disengage. Retreat. They only have one *Massacre*. If it draws near, pull back. Fight another battle. Once the enemy's warships have been destroyed, our fleet will focus on taking out the *Massacre* together. Questions?"

Mo put up his hand. "Can you tell us how you intend to 'glide' through the mines and land on the station?"

"I can answer that," said Captain Henning, who would be leading the assault. "We will jettison from the *Cora Lee*'s torpedo bay and navigate through the mines."

"Won't their radar detect your team?" Raj asked.

"No, our suits are covered in a fabric that absorbs radar."

"Gliding from the Moon?" Sasha asked. "The closest the *Unity* ever gets to the Moon is well over one hundred thousand miles. How are you going to glide that distance in a suit?"

"We've glided from much farther than that," Henning replied. "It will take us about forty minutes to complete the jump."

"Forty minutes!" Percy exclaimed. "That means you'll be 'gliding' at speeds reaching nearly 150,000 miles per hour! You'll be ripped apart!"

"Again, I assure you, these suits are designed to handle the G-forces, ambassador," Henning replied calmly. "We will glide carefully through the mines, and, once we've secured the station, disarm enough mines to create a hole large enough to fly a shuttle through and evacuate the hostages to the *Exodus*."

"Once you begin evacuating, won't the Murks notice the shuttle and fire upon the station?" Tank asked.

"There is always that possibility, but we believe the Murk ships will be drawn away from the station once the battle begins on the far side of Earth," Ambassador Plite explained.

"I understand your plan to draw the enemy to the far side of Earth, but how do you prevent a single Murk ship from firing upon the station?" Sasha asked.

"The *Exodus* will be able to provide some cover for the station," Captain Henning replied.

"With all due respect, one ship can't prevent a stray missile or phasor from hitting a mine," Makalo said. "Striking just one mine will cause a chain reaction, wiping out the station and everyone on board."

"We can't afford to give up any more ships to guard the station, as we are already outnumbered three to one," Captain Renfro replied.

Sasha shook his head. "I'm not at all comfortable with this plan."

"No, no, no! This will not work," Percy said, also shaking his head.

"There are too many variables," Mario agreed.

"We understand your concern," Plite replied. "However, I assure you we have taken every consideration and believe this to be the best strategy to secure the station."

"We are all forgetting one very important thing," Ben interjected. "Every part of Jag's dream has come true thus far. Everything but this last part."

"That's right!" Sasha said, turning to Jag. "In your dream, you saw a large object falling through a dark cloud into the ocean."

"Perhaps the dream can't be changed," Edgard interjected.

Nik turned to him. "What? Why would you say that?"

"Every part of the dream has come true, and maybe like everything else, this has to happen, too."

"No," Raj disagreed. "For then it would serve no purpose. If we have dreams that foretell an end that can't be avoided, what purpose do they serve?"

"This can be diverted if we all act together," Ben replied.

"What do you have in mind?" Jag asked as all the ambassadors stepped to the center of the room to examine the holographic space station. Many suggestions were made and then dismissed.

"A displacement field!" Mo blurted.

"That's right! Like the one Jag built in the lab," Kano said.

"Interesting," Percy said as he used his hand to measure the distance between the space station and the mines. "Yes, a displacement field surrounding the *Unity* could take it out of normal space and into hyperspace."

"It's possible," Chief Morten said. "A displacement field could work, but I assure you we have no displacement generators on board any of our ships!"

"Sure you do," Kano said. "The same force fields you used to patch the *Exodus* can be modified to emit a displacement field."

Bayli held up her hand. "What's a displacement field?"

"A displacement field allows a ship to travel in hyperspace by opening a subspace field," Captain Renfro explained. "The field could wrap around the space station and move it into hyperspace. Though it wouldn't physically travel anywhere, it would be invisible to the Murks."

"Even if we rewire the force field generators, you have two problems," Chief Morten interjected. "First, the battery wasn't designed to sustain a field of that magnitude. It will only last for at most one, maybe two hours. Second, and most importantly, each array would have to be manually aligned and calibrated simultaneously after being attached to the station's hull."

"Look, this is fascinating, but our soldiers can't take on the additional equipment and the task of calibrating these devices while engaging the enemy," Admiral Plite said as everyone stood staring at the station.

"We can do it," Ben said quietly.

Admiral Plite turned to him. "What?"

"Yes, we can do it!" Sasha said.

"You old men are going to jump from the *Cora Lee* with us and set up the emitters?" Captain Henning asked.

"Yes, sonny, us old men are going to do it," Tank replied, using an old man's voice.

"What say you, old man?" Ben said, turning to Jag. "You up for one last school trip?"

"Who are you calling 'old'?" Jag asked.

"Well, as I recall, you are, in fact, several months older than me," Ben replied with a proud smile. Everyone laughed at the irony.

Jag shook his head in astonishment as he looked at each of his classmates and pondered the outrageousness of it all. Then he shrugged. "Why not? I wouldn't miss this for anything."

"We'll need to start training immediately," Captain Henning said. "I should have enough suits to fit all of you, except for the big guy." He pointed at Tank.

"Oh, don't you worry. I have something special in mind for him!" Chief Morten said.

"Alright, it seems we all have our assignments," Admiral Channing said, closing the meeting. "You have three days to prepare and report back."

The eleven ambassadors worked around the clock converting and testing the displacement field generators. Afterwards, they trained with the special ops team on how to maneuver their glide suits. Each suit had a small control built into the palm of each hand that fired miniature rockets to control horizontal and vertical navigation. They practiced in the large cargo bay by disabling the bay's gravity and then jumping from stacked cargo boxes.

As they arrived to train on the second afternoon, standing in the middle of the bay was a large bubble-shaped suit that looked like the Michelin man. It was nearly three times the size of a man with two mechanical arms that could swap from claws, to drills, to lasers and other tools.

"What's that?" asked Kano, the first to enter the room.

"This, my friend, is SPUD," Chief Morten said, "a utility-grade maintenance vessel we use in hostile environments to make ship repairs. Most importantly, it's large enough to fit our friend over here." He nodded at Tank.

"It's huge. Won't the Murks' radar detect it?" Captain Henning asked.

"Not if we cover it with the same fabric your suits are made of."

Chief Morten helped Tank squeeze into SPUD through a hatch in the back and showed him how to control the suit. Tank practiced maneuvering around the bay. Unlike the lightweight glider suits, which only had just enough rocket propulsion to adjust in flight, the SPUD had full-powered rockets similar to Jag and Mahjon's and could launch and propel itself.

That night after a full day of practice, Jag invited Ben, Raj, and Sasha over to his quarters to rest and hang out.

"I don't know about you guys, but I'm getting too old for jumping out of spaceships. I'm sore," Raj said.

"Yeah, my back hurts something fierce," Ben replied. "Getting old is a pain."

"It sure is," Jag agreed with a cunning smile.

"What? You're still just a kid." Ben smiled. "You know, when they disabled the gravity, it reminded me of playing space basketball."

"Remember watching Professor P dunk on us?" Sasha asked.

"Oh yeah, I remember that! How is the professor anyway?" Jag asked.

The three sat quietly, waiting for someone else to speak.

Jag looked around at his friends. "What? Did he die?"

"No," Ben said softly. "Professor P left the agency and has barely been heard from since."

"What happened?"

"Percy happened! That's what!" Raj replied.

"After your incident," Ben explained, "the Space Agency investigated the accident, questioning each of us about the life and culture of the university and what we thought happened to you. When Percy testified, he said—"

"He said that the professor created a competitive and contentious environment, pushing students to take unnecessary risks to prove their experiments worked," Sasha interrupted.

"And while Percy accepted 'full responsibility' for his role in your accident, he said it was ultimately the school that pushed him," Raj concluded.

Jag looked at his friends in disbelief. "But surely no one believed him!"

"Who do you think they would believe, us students, who testified that the professor didn't create a competitive atmosphere, or the one whose father contributed over a billion dollars to the agency?" Raj asked.

"After deliberating, the board decided to remove Professor P from his position at the agency," Sasha said.

"The agency was his life," Ben said. "Disgraced, he moved back to Poland and took some factory job making cheap computer parts. He's pretty much a recluse now."

"I visited him years ago, right after I was promoted to director of the *Unity* to check on him as well as get advice," Sasha said. "He didn't say much. He's living in a dumpy, rundown former communist-era apartment complex."

"And the university program?" Jag asked.

Sasha shrugged. "Without Professor P's passion and leadership, the program was scrapped."

Stunned by the news, Jag stared out at the stars. He hadn't considered how much Percy's actions had impacted the professor or the school. "After this is all over, we will make things right!"

Raj held up his glass. "To Professor P!"

"To Professor P!" Ben, Sasha, and Jag replied.

CHAPTER 32
THE *UNITY* SAVED

Upon reaching the Milky Way, Jag met with his senior officers one final time. Afterwards, Admiral Rannick joined Captain Palen on the warbird *Hawkeye* to help provide oversight as the *Cora Lee* separated from the rest of the fleet and headed toward the *Unity*.

Alone in the planetarium, Jag had the holograph recreate his grandparents' farm with their large yellow house and several barns behind it. Then he lay down on the floor in a field of grass, imagining himself running as Grissom followed, ears flopping and barking. Just as he was falling asleep, the door opened, and Sara walked in. When she saw Jag, she stopped short.

"Oh, am I bothering you?"

"Not at all. Come on in. I'm just reminiscing."

"Papa told me you might still be—hey, I recognize that house!"

Jag looked at her in surprise. "You do?"

"Yeah, Papa took me there when I was a child. Though I don't remember much."

"This is where I grew up. My grandfather built this house with his own hands." Jag rose and stepped over several trees. "And over here is the path that leads to my launch pad, where I would launch rockets."

Sara followed behind Jag as they stepped over the creek that Jag always tried to leap but Grissom would run straight through.

They reached the launch pad. Jag didn't realize Sara was directly behind him, so when he turned, they were standing face to face. She had such beautiful eyes, and every time he looked at them, he felt as though his heart would stop beating. Their relationship had grown beyond friendship. Not only was she beautiful, she was intelligent, witty, and shared the same zeal for life. There was no doubt about it, Jag was in love. Others also noticed their blossoming relationship. When Bayli mentioned it, Jag tried to deny his feelings. The crew also noticed and gave Jag space to spend more of his free time with Sara.

"Well, maybe someday when this whole thing is over, we can visit the farm," Jag said.

Sara smiled. "I'd like that very much." They left the planetarium and walked the promenade.

Sara looked at Jag. "So are you nervous about tomorrow?"

"Not really. Being surrounded by people I trust, like the admirals and my classmates, gives me such an incredible sense of confidence and peace. It's nice for once not to be the one who has to have all the answers. How about you? Are you nervous?"

"Yes. Not for myself, but for my Mère and Papa."

"Captain Henning and his team are the best. They'll do everything they can to protect them."

"I'm also nervous for you," Sara said.

Jag smiled. "You have no need to worry. Mahjon will keep me safe."

When they reached the ship's lounge, Jag stopped and turned to her. "Well, I need to get some rest before tomorrow's mission. Have a good evening, Sara Beth Mendelsohn."

"You too, Prince Marcello, Joseph Gabriel, Jag, or whichever name you're using today!"

The next morning, as planned, the *Cora Lee* was in a flight path directly behind the Moon to hide her approach. Jag and the ambassadors met the special ops team in the torpedo bay. Each person was dressed in a flight suit, including Tank in SPUD, awaiting the signal from Commander Corbis to begin the mission. Sara and Bayli joined them to say goodbye.

"*Je t'aime,* Papa," Sara said as she hugged her father.

"*Je t'aime aussi,*" Ben replied.

After Bayli and Jag said goodbye, Sara hugged Jag and kissed him on the cheek. "Keep safe," she whispered. Then she turned to Mahjon. "You watch over these men, and keep them safe!"

"Of course," Mahjon replied, a bit perplexed by her statement. What else would he do?

Captain Henning raised his hand and drew everyone's attention. "Line up like we've practiced."

Everyone lined up in the order they would be jumping and waited for a signal from Commander Corbis. As soon as he received word, he nodded. "We're a go!"

The first to enter the torpedo tubes were four special ops officers, who would arrive on the station and establish a landing zone to catch each glider. Everyone would jump sixty seconds apart to avoid the risk of running into each other. The ambassadors soon followed. It took several people to help Tank maneuver his suit into the cramped torpedo tube.

As Jag was preparing to step into the tube, he looked up at Private Reeso. "You watch over these ladies!" he said, indicating Bayli and Sara,

Private Reeso saluted. "Will do, sir. They'll have my undivided attention."

Jag nodded in appreciation and then spoke over the intercom. "Godspeed, everyone. Commander Corbis, the *Cora Lee* is now yours."

Jag's tube fired, propelling him at speeds of nearly 150,000 miles per hour through the star-lit space toward a minute dot in the distance. Everyone's helmets displayed augmented laser lines guiding them along the course. Following Jag was Mahjon and the remaining four special ops members, including Captain Henning.

"Woo-hoo!" Sasha yelled, elated by the incredible rush of soaring through space.

"Cut the chatter," Captain Henning said.

"Sorry."

As the first four special ops members neared the mines surrounding station, their helmets emitted blue augmented lines directing their path through the minefield. Once through, they used gravity-emitter guns to slow their descent until they landed softly on the station. Then one of the officers set explosives that would detonate the Murk communication antennas simultaneously to prevent them from alerting the Murk fleet. The three remaining officers formed a triangle to receive each of the gliders as they flew through the minefield, pointing their gravity-emitter guns toward the individual and slowly landing them on the station.

"Ambassador Mario, you're drifting a bit off course," said an officer who was tracking each glider.

"Yeah, I know. My lateral thrusters aren't responding," Mario replied. "I can't navigate horizontally, right, or left. Only vertical thrusters seem to be working."

"Let me check," replied Captain Henning, who remoted into Mario's computer system. "Yeah, your controls aren't connecting to the lateral booster. I'm rebooting your controls. They will take several seconds to restore. Please hold."

"I'm not going anywhere. Well, except toward that mine field that is getting closer by the second," Mario said as his helmet display cycled through startup processes.

"Try it again," Captain Henning ordered.

"Nothing. They still don't respond."

"What can be done?" Jag asked.

"Nothing from here, sir. The booster is malfunctioning, and I'm concerned his current trajectory will cause him to intercept one of the mines."

"If he touches just one of the mines, it will mean mission over, and we'll have front seats to the biggest fireworks you've ever seen," Kano said, who was immediately behind Mario.

"Well, amigos, it looks like my mission is over. You guys complete what you came here for!" Mario said as he fired his vertical thrusters to lift himself away from the minefield.

"No! There's got to be another option!" Mo cried.

"There isn't one, guys. Complete your mission, and I'll see you again in the next life!" Mario's trajectory began changing slightly. However, his suit's thrusters were designed only for modest adjustments, not for major course changes. After firing the thrusters for as long as possible and depleting his fuel, he lifted away from the minefield, but he was still on a collision course.

"Ambassador Mario, you are still headed toward a mine," Captain Henning said.

"I know. I've used up all my fuel. There's nothing else I can do!"

As Mario drew closer to the mine, he felt something tug at him from behind. It wasn't something but someone! Tank in his SPUD suit had fired his powerful rockets and caught up to him. Using the suit's mechanical arms, he locked onto Mario and then fired his rockets, trying to pull them both away from the path of the mine.

They leaned back as far as they could. Those watching from the station instinctively leaned back as well. As they reached the mine, all but Mario's left foot cleared. The toe of his boot scraped across the mine, and everyone held their breath. After several seconds and no explosion, Sasha let out another "Woo-hoo!" Several others cheered as well.

Tank made a large loop back to the landing zone. As soon as all the gliders had landed on the station, Captain Henning called everyone to his side. Seeing Mario, he placed his hand on his shoulder.

"It's nice to see you in one piece!"

Mario smiled. "It's nice to be in one piece."

"Alright, we all have our assignments," Henning said, his face turning serious. "Keep an eye out for Murk soldiers. With their communications offline, they'll investigate soon. Let's go."

Sasha led Captain Henning and five of his officers into the station, where they swept each floor, hunting down and disabling enemy combatants. The Murks retreated into Mission Control, where all the hostages were held. When the team stormed into the control room, they used infrared technology to differentiate Murk soldiers from humans and quickly extinguished their targets.

Outside the station, Jag's classmates began attaching the displacement generator's tripods to the station hull with large nail guns. Jag, Ben, and Mahjon moved to the farthest point, where Jag held a tripod as Ben fired bolts into the base of the stand.

As they attached the generator, Mahjon sensed danger from one of the hatches and leaped nearly fifteen feet, landing just as the hatch opened. A Murk soldier sent to investigate the communication outage exited with his weapon drawn, but Mahjon grabbed him, pulled him up through the hatch, and, with a single blow, knocked him unconscious.

Kano and Nik were on the opposite side of the station accompanied by a special ops officer. After they attached the first tripod leg, another hatch opened, and out climbed a Murk soldier, who fired and struck the officer, sending him barreling into space. The Murk soldier aimed his weapon at Nik, but before he could fire, Kano dropped and performed a leg sweep, knocking the soldier off his feet and sending his weapon hurling into space. The Murk then reached for Kano, who in return fired a bolt from his nail gun through the Murk's hand, causing blood to flow out of the Murk's glove. The soldier pulled his hand back and, with his other hand, grabbed another weapon and aimed it at Kano. However, before he could discharge it, Tank flew up and fired the SPUD's laser gun, killing the Murk.

"Thanks, Tank!" Kano said.

"That was a bit close!" Nik said, drawing Tank's attention to the wounded officer, now floating toward the minefield. Tank flew out and retrieved him.

They installed the rest of the tripods and displacement generators without further incident. Afterwards, everyone calibrated and aligned their generators to each other.

"Alright, we're good to go," Mo said.

Percy waved toward the entrance. "Everyone inside. We'll initiate the field and then join you."

Everyone headed into the station through the hatches. Nik and Kano also moved the injured officer inside the station. Tank's suit was too large to fit through a hatch, so he agreed to meet Sasha in one of the station's docking bays. Ben climbed down the hatch ladder as Mahjon lowered the incapacitated Murk.

"Where are you heading?" Ben asked as Jag closed the hatch.

Jag nodded toward space. "Out there. My job is done here. Now I need to get back to my ship."

"And how do you expect to do that?" Ben asked.

"I'll hitch a ride once we destroy the minefield."

"Thanks for saving our skin back there!" Ben said to Mahjon.

Mahjon nodded. "You are most welcome."

"I'll see you in a few minutes," Jag said as he reached down to bump fists with Ben. Then he and Mahjon launched their powerful rockets, shooting straight up from the station through the mines and stopping nearly a hundred yards away.

"Percy and Mo, are we ready?" Jag asked over the intercom.

"We are a go, sir," Percy replied.

"Engage," Jag ordered.

Percy and Mo initiated the displacement generators, which emitted an invisible field that expanded slowly around the station, causing it to disappear.

Floating at a safe distance, Jag aimed his sidearm at one of the mines and fired, striking the mine and setting off a chain reaction that detonated each mine in succession.

"Commander Corbis, you are free to engage," Jag said.

CHAPTER 33
EARTH LIBERATED

Dropping out of hyperspace, the *Cora Lee* circumnavigated Earth, firing torpedoes at unsuspecting Murk ships and targeting their weapons systems. She moved so quickly that she appeared to be nothing more than a streak of light, making it impossible for the Murk fleet to return fire.

After striking the first blow, it was time to unleash the entire fleet. Like hornets fleeing a nest, the Celestian fleet dropped from hyperspace on the far side of Earth and began systematically attacking, drawing the Murk fleet to the opposite side of Earth. Soon, the *Massacre* relocated and tried to join in the fight, but the Celestian fleet retreated and engaged in other skirmishes.

"Commander Corbis, when you get a moment, we could use a lift," Jag said, floating with Mahjon.

"Right away, sir!" Corbis said, as they had just finished assisting the *Venture* in destroying a Murk battlecruiser. The *Cora Lee* began flying around Earth toward Jag, dodging various skirmishes. As she rounded Earth, an alarm sounded on the bridge.

"Commander, a shuttlecraft has just left the bay," Lieutenant Commander Cho Fe said.

"Who's on board?" Corbis asked.

"Not sure. They disabled their communication devices."

"The ship's computer shows two people unaccounted for: Private Reeso and Ambassador Ben's daughter."

"Sara!" Jag whispered as he listened in on the communication.

At that moment, an explosion rocked the *Cora Lee*. Every light went out, and she listed in the direction she had been traveling. The shuttle headed away from the *Cora Lee* to a Murk warbird, which was keeping its distance from the battle. Then the *Massacre* changed its trajectory and moved toward the *Cora Lee*.

Meanwhile, Captain O'Malley from the *Exodus,* who had been listening in on the conversation, radioed Jag. "We are in the vicinity and can pick you up."

"Thank you," Jag replied.

The explosion on the *Cora Lee* occurred in engineering, severing the main power lines. Auxiliary power engaged, providing power to only the ship's life support and internal communications systems. The power line wasn't the only thing damaged during the explosion. Chief Morten suffered a broken arm when the shockwave sent him flying through the engine room and into a wall. Picking himself up, he removed his jacket and made a makeshift sling so he could lead his team to restore the ship's power.

"Chief, what happened?" Corbis asked over the radio.

"A bomb exploded beneath the engine compartment. Our power lines were severed."

"Can it be repaired?"

"Yes, but it's going to take some time."

As the *Cora Lee* drifted, defenseless, the *Massacre* drew closer. Once it was within striking distance, its powerful tractor beams began pulling the *Cora Lee* toward it so it could unleash its weapons on her.

Jag and Mahjon watched the attack unfold from a distance. Just as the *Massacre* fired upon the *Cora Lee*, the *Hawkeye* arrived and fired everything it had. Captain Palen and Admiral Rannick had heard about the disabled *Cora Lee* and swooped in to begin their attack alone. They knew their weapons would be ineffective against the ship, but they figured they could give the *Cora Lee* more time to escape.

The *Massacre* focused its attention on the *Hawkeye*, trapping the ship in its tractor beams and unleashing a full array of weapons. Admiral Rannick ordered an evacuation, and everyone rushed to escape pods as the *Hawkeye* tore apart. However, the *Massacre's* tractor beams created such a powerful force field around the warbird that the escape pods were unable to flee, and the *Massacre* began picking them off one by one. Admiral Channing had the *Victory* battlecruiser lay down a bed of weapon fire long enough to allow the escape pods to escape.

As the *Exodus* was en route to Jag and Mahjon's location, Chief Morten's prediction about the displacement generators' batteries came true. The generators depleted their battery power, and the displacement field was disengaged from around the station, dropping it out of hyperspace and making it visible to all. From a distance, a Murk dominion ship noticed the station reappear and headed straight toward the *Unity*.

"Captain O'Malley, it appears the batteries didn't last as long as we hoped," Jag said as the *Exodus* neared their location.

"Yeah, we see it, too. So has a Murk ship. Whoa, they just fired torpedoes at the station," Captain O'Malley said as several torpedoes sped toward it.

"Captain, can you intercept them?" Jag asked.

"Already on it," Captain O'Malley replied.

The *Exodus* left Jag and Mahjon and maneuvered in front of the station, putting itself in the line of fire. Using phasors, they destroyed one of the approaching torpedoes, but the second made it through and struck *Exodus's* upgraded shields, which deflected the explosion. The *Exodus* fired upon the Murk ship with its new weaponry and severely damaged the vessel.

"Commander Corbis, we have restored about 30 percent of our power," Chief Morten said as he and his team worked tirelessly. "But it should be enough to move us out of the way!"

"Thank you, chief," Commander Corbis said. They fired the ship's thrusters, and the *Cora Lee* moved away from the *Massacre*. Once the *Cora Lee* was clear of danger, the *Victory* began loading escape pods to save as many as they could.

The *Cora Lee* hurried to retrieve Jag and Mahjon. When they boarded the ship, the interior was darker than normal. Auxiliary floodlights shone on the floor, and a grey haze from the explosion's smoke filled the air. Bayli met Jag as he walked toward the bridge.

"What happened?" Jag asked. "Who was it?"

"Reeso. As soon as you left, I went to the medical facility. Reeso said he was going to escort Sara back to the lounge. But they never made it. He kidnapped Sara and then initiated the explosion."

"Anyone hurt?"

"We have a couple of minor injuries, including Chief Morten, who broke his arm, but he won't let anyone look at it!"

When Jag entered the bridge, Commander Corbis welcomed him. "Captain on the bridge."

"How long until we have full power?" Jag asked.

"Maybe ten minutes, sir," replied Chief Morten, who had been listening to the bridge communication.

"Shouldn't you be in medical?" Jag asked.

"What good will a mended arm do me if we're all dead, captain?" Morten replied.

Jag nodded. "Fair enough."

To those observing from Earth, the view was terrifying. The pitch-black sky lit up with brightly colored explosions as Celestian and Murk vessels engaged in battle. The explosions were so loud that buildings shook, and windows shattered. Throughout the planet, people gathered in homes, places of worship, and in shelters for what many thought was the end of life on Earth.

In the engine room, Chief Morten, wearing his makeshift sling, gave directions to his crew to bypass the damaged power lines and run new ones. Once all major power had been restored to the ship's engines and weapons systems, he radioed the bridge. "Sir, we are a go! Full power has been restored."

"Great work, chief! Commander Corbis, how about we show the *Massacre* what we're made of?"

"With pleasure, sir."

"Sir, with your permission I'm going to pass out now," Chief Morten said. Then he sat down and lost consciousness as the medical team began attending him.

The *Cora Lee* flew straight toward the *Massacre* and unleashed her weapons, targeting the ship's right arm. She moved so quickly that the *Massacre* couldn't get a lock on her. After firing repeatedly at the same location on one of the *Massacre's* arms, a small gap tore open, and a well-placed torpedo exploded, ripping the arm from the ship.

Then the *Cora Lee* focused its attention on the next arm, skillfully dissecting the beast piece by piece. Soon the *Victory* and several other ships joined in on the attack, raining down weapons until phasors ripped through its thick exterior. Strategically placed torpedoes entered the ship and massive explosions tore through its hull.

Escape pods launched from the *Massacre's* aft bays. Powerless and lifeless, it descended, pulled by Earth's gravity, where it fell burning through the dark cloud. It passed through Earth's atmosphere and crashed into the Atlantic Ocean. Onboard the *Unity*, the eleven ambassadors watched silently in shock as the *Massacre* fell through the cloud.

"In Jag's dream, he saw a dark cloud surrounding Earth and a large metal object on fire descend to Earth and crash into the ocean," Ben said, standing by the other eleven ambassadors, who all watched in amazement. "Today, that vision has been fulfilled." A huge cheer went out over the radio as the remaining Murk ships fled.

With all the Murk ships retreating, the *Cora Lee* headed to dock with the *Unity*.

"Sir, we are receiving a message from one of the fleeing Murk ships. Its commander wishes to speak with you," Lt. Beckel said.

"I figured it would only be a matter of time. Transfer the communication to my ready room," Jag said. "Can you have IRIS retrieve Ben and inform him about Sara?"

"It might be better if I do it," Bayli said. She left the bridge and headed to the dock, where she ran into Ben, who was coming on board the *Cora Lee* to find Sara and celebrate the victory. When Bayli informed him about

Sara's kidnapping, he ran down the hallway toward the bridge, Bayli right behind him.

In his ready room, Jag sat at his desk, took a deep breath, and pressed the communication button. He immediately recognized the face that filled his monitor.

"Measil Warily, what can I do for you?"

Measil smiled. "What? No 'hello' or 'how are you doing old friend'?"

"I don't recall us ever being friends."

"That hurts. Well, it seems I have someone I'm told you are particularly fond of."

"If you harm her, I promise I'll—"

"Oh, don't fret, Jag—or should I call you Prince Marcello? I have no intention of harming her. I don't even want her. If it were up to me, we would jettison her out into space and be done with the whole ordeal."

"What do you want, Measil?"

"I'm in sort of a bind. You see, if I report back to my emperor empty handed after having his fleet destroyed, well, let's just say things won't go very well for me. However, if I hand him his greatest adversary, then all would be forgiven. So here's the deal. You will either hand yourself over freely to the emperor without incident, or I will introduce your lovely friend to the vacuum of space. What do you say?"

Jag nodded silently and then discussed the details of the swap. He walked out of the ready room just as Ben and Bayli entered the bridge.

"Sara! Is she alright?" Ben asked, out of breath.

"She will be; I promise you," Jag said. "We will prepare to leave immediately to retrieve her."

"What do they want?" Ben asked as Admiral Rannick returned from the *Victory*, where Admiral Channing had rescued his escape pod.

"We've made an agreement, and they will hand her over," Jag said.

"In exchange for what?" Bayli asked.

"Commander Corbis, make plans for us to leave immediately," Jag said, ignoring her question.

"It's you, isn't it?" Rannick asked. "You promised to exchange yourself for the girl, didn't you?"

"We've been guaranteed safe passage to the border of Murk space, where I will take a shuttlecraft to Atundra."

"Prince Marcello, you can't!" Lt. Beckel exclaimed.

"We have our orders," Commander Corbis said. "Everyone, prepare to depart for Murk space."

"I believe I have an uncle on board the station that I haven't seen in forty years," Jag said. "Commander, please have us prepped to leave in an hour." He left the bridge with Mahjon and Ben.

"Jag, wait up," Ben said, but Jag kept walking. "Jag, please stop." Finally, Jag stopped and turned to face Ben, who had to pause a moment to catch his breath. "As a father, I would do anything to get Sara back. She is the most important thing to me and her mother. However, as your friend, I can't allow you to bear this burden. This sacrifice isn't on you. Let them take my life instead."

"They don't want you or even Sara. They want me."

"I can't allow you to sacrifice your life for hers."

"You forget that I'm a prince. I don't need your permission," Jag said with a smile. "This is my choice. All my life bad things have happened to me, things about which I've had no choice. But in all that time, God has never forsaken me. He has always been faithful."

"Well, then, I'm going with you!" Ben shouted as he followed Jag into the station.

"Of course, you can accompany me on the shuttle to Atundra and then return with Sara and Mahjon."

They walked onto the station. Just before they entered Mission Control, Jag stopped and turned to Ben. "Don't tell the others about the exchange. It is hard enough to say goodbye, but if they knew this, it would only make it more difficult."

As they entered Mission Control, everyone in the room stood and applauded. After thanking Captain Henning and his team for their excellent work in securing the station, Jag embraced his Uncle Jack, who was the spitting image of his grandpa. And sounded just like him, too. Then each of Jag's classmates approached and introduced their family members to the "man who saved Earth."

Ben went to his wife, Maëlle, and informed her of Sara's captivity. Maëlle started crying, and Ben tried to comfort her. He told her of the plan to get Sara back, and she also objected to Jag exchanging himself. She stood and walked over to Jag as he was talking with Mo's son, placed her arms around him, and started crying. She looked up at Jag with tears in her eyes. "*Merci.*"

"Is everything alright?" Raj asked, noticing Ben's distraught wife.

"Where's Sara?" Sasha said as several classmates turned to see what was going on.

"The Murks captured Sara. We are leaving now to retrieve her," Ben replied.

"What?" Nik asked.

"Oh, Ben, I'm so sorry," Sasha replied.

"How did this happen?" Tank asked.

"The Murk spy kidnapped her right before the explosion that disabled the *Cora Lee*," Jag explained. "We're leaving to go retrieve her."

"We'll come with you!" Sasha said.

"Yes! We'll join in," Raj agreed.

"No, not this time. You're needed here to help with the restoration of Earth. The Celestian teams will assist with cleaning up the poisonous gas cloud and with the injured, but they will need your help in coordinating this effort and in working with the leaders from Earth."

After saying goodbye to his uncle, Jag, along with Mahjon, Ben, and Maëlle boarded the *Cora Lee*, which left the *Unity* and headed into deep space toward Atundra, the frozen planet.

CHAPTER 34
THE FROZEN PLANET

It took nearly three weeks to arrive at the border, where they were intercepted by three Murk warships. Jag asked Captain Henning to pilot the shuttlecraft with Ben and Mahjon on board as one of the Murk warbirds escorted it to Atundra.

"Well, at least it's true to its name," Jag said as he stepped down into the frigid air of the Black Glacia Mountains of Atundra. Much of the view was hidden by dense fog patches and falling snow. The shuttle landed near a winding stone walkway that led down to an old iron bridge. As they walked down the path, Mahjon spotted several snipers, but their safety at that point was out of his control, for they were at the mercy of the Murks. If the emperor wanted them dead, the warbird that escorted them from the border could have easily destroyed the shuttle.

They crossed an iron bridge that stretched high across a ravine. On the other side stood Murk Castle, carved into the side of the mountain. Its enormous black gates were covered in a layer of rust, showing their age. On both sides of the gates stood tall towers with cannons tracking their every move. Jag stopped halfway and closed his eyes, leaning his head back to allow the large snowflakes to hit his face.

"Atundra isn't such a bad place," Jag said.

Mahjon gave him a disapproving look.

"I'm not saying I would want to set up a summer home here, but the mountains are quite lovely."

"This reminds me of Christmas at your grandparents' farm," Ben said. "That was one of the best times of my life!"

Jag nodded. "Mine, too."

"The snow cream your grandmother made was awesome," Ben replied. "Your grandparents were the best!"

"Yes, they were."

Ben looked up at the gates. "Do you think we should knock?"

"They know we're here," Jag said, nodding toward the soldiers in the towers pointing the cannons at them. "When this goes down, no matter what happens, get Sara to the shuttle. As soon as Mahjon joins you, Henning has been ordered to leave immediately."

"I understand," Ben said. "Jag, I don't have the words to express my gratitude—"

"Just get her safely out of here," Jag said. Then he turned to Mahjon. "Thank you. It has been a pleasure serving the kingdom alongside you."

Mahjon bowed his head. "The pleasure has been mine."

Jag placed his hand over the bonding mark on Mahjon's chest. "Mahjon, I release—"

Mahjon immediately removed Jag's hand. "No! I beg of you, do not take this from me. I must see this through and be allowed to feel what you feel until the very end." Even though they'd be lightyears apart, Mahjon would feel everything, and Jag intended to spare his friend the pain and suffering he expected to come.

After a moment, Jag nodded. "Alright, if that is your wish."

A puff of air escaped through the gates as they creaked open. A legion of soldiers marched out, their boots pounding against the bridge. The unnerving sound of their footsteps was hushed only slightly by the thin layer of snow that had collected on the bridge. Once the soldiers halted, the two center columns stepped apart from each another, creating an aisle down the middle.

At the end of the aisle stood Measil, Tahjon, Reeso, and Sara, who was wearing handcuffs. They started walking. Halfway down, Reeso and Sara stopped as Measil and Tahjon continued forward, stopping in front of Jag, Mahjon, and Ben.

"Welcome to Atundra. I trust you are ready for the exchange," Measil said.

"What guarantee do I have of their safety?" Jag asked.

"The emperor has given his word that your friends will be returned safely," Measil said.

Jag looked to Mahjon to inquire if he sensed any deceit. Mahjon nodded in agreement.

Jag nodded and then turned back to Measil. "Let's get this over with then."

"Alright." Measil motioned to Reeso, who removed the handcuffs from Sara. She began walking down the aisle.

"You've changed, brother. You are no longer the little Mravian I remember," Tahjon said to his brother.

"You've changed, too. You are no longer the Mravian I remember either," Mahjon replied, his words stinging Tahjon. The giants were impressive and powerful and very much brothers.

Sara ran down the aisle of soldiers into her father's arms, where she sobbed. Ben held his daughter tightly as he closed his eyes. When he opened them, he saw Jag nod, and then Ben placed his arm on Sara's shoulder and escorted her off the bridge and up the path, where Captain Henning was standing on the shuttle's step to aid Ben.

As Reeso placed the handcuffs on Jag's wrists, Jag noticed several scratches running down the side of his face.

"She's feisty, isn't she?" Jag asked.

Reeso gave no response as he tightened the cuffs. Then he looked at Mahjon and snickered. "You never sensed anything! You were so easy to fool."

Mahjon snarled at him, causing him to flinch. Had it not been for Mahjon's respect for Jag, he would have ripped the traitor apart.

As Sara was climbing into the shuttle, she turned back to see Jag in handcuffs.

"No! What are you doing?" She tried to run back, but Ben and Captain Henning pulled her toward the shuttle. "Don't let him do this, Papa," she pleaded.

"There's no other way, Sara. It was his wish," Ben replied.

"No, please stop!"

Jag turned to see them gently pull her into the shuttle.

"Follow me," Measil said, and they walked into the castle, with Tahjon escorting Jag. Then the soldiers turned and marched back into the castle as the large gates closed behind them.

Alone on the bridge, Mahjon stared at the gates and dropped his head as he exhaled an agonized sigh. Then he walked the long path back to the shuttle, where Captain Henning took off immediately to return to the *Cora Lee*.

Inside the dark castle, torches and iron chandeliers illuminated the large banners, the crests of which denoted past emperors. The ceilings were tall and intricately carved. The company passed soldiers standing at attention, dressed in ancient military attire. Along the floors and walls were the physical scars of the battle Admiral Rannick fought when he stormed the castle years earlier.

Jag looked up at Tahjon. "You look thin, old friend."

Tahjon shook his head. "You should not have come. I've looked into Damon's heart, and there is no mercy for you."

"I understand. But sometimes in life we give up what we hold dearest for those we love most."

"Mahjon appears to have served you well."

"He has been exemplary and would make you proud."

"I am very proud of him."

They entered the great hall, with its high ceiling and ancient architecture, as crews set up rows of chairs and platforms for cameras. Emperor Damon was seated on an ancient throne with elaborate gold carvings and purple fabric, doling out orders for the exact placement of each item. Then he spotted Jag. "Welcome to Atundra, Prince Marcello!" He had more than a hint of sarcasm in his voice when he said the word "prince."

"Is that the throne behind which Emperor Gazini was cowering when he was killed?" Jag asked, recalling King Marcellus's story.

Damon smirked. "Indeed it is."

"It appears to fit you quite well."

Damon chuckled. "That was father's all-time favorite story to tell. I thought I would die if I had to sit through one more rendition!" Spotting Jag's handcuffs, he nodded. "Oh, how rude of me. Take off those restraints. I'm sure our guest means me no harm, and even if he does, Tahjon the Magnificent will come to my defense."

When the cuffs were removed, Jag rubbed his wrists, where the restraints had cut off his circulation. Then Damon had all the workers leave the chamber.

"It seems destiny keeps entwining our fates," Damon said. "You have had the great fortune to be present at every step of my master plan: from the tragic death of my beloved father to the attempted murder of my dear sister."

"Yet another failure," Jag replied.

Damon smirked. "Only a temporary setback, I assure you. I must compliment you, for you have played your role exquisitely, and now we arrive at the grand finale, to which you will once again be center stage in the fulfillment of the great Yalorian prophecy."

"I'm sorry, I fail to see how I play any part of this."

"Of course, the puppet never understands the puppet master's plans. After being denied my rightful place as ruler of Celestia, I thought my destiny was over. However, an option presented itself to me the day your little satellite hit our observation station, leading us right to your pitiful little planet."

"Well, once again, your plan has failed! Earth was saved and your fleet destroyed."

"You actually think taking Earth was my objective?" Damon smiled. "Oh, I love your naiveté. The valiant outcast returns to save his planet and becomes the hero. I'll let you in on a secret: I never wanted your pathetic planet. It was you, my puppet! You're the key to all of this! For tomorrow, the universe shall witness the fulfillment of the Yalorian prophecy. You are familiar with the prophecy, aren't you?"

Damon got up and walked over to a golden stand that held a large, ancient book. Then he read a passage from the page to which it was opened: "Oh, House of Nobb, that which was torn asunder shall be made one when you see a prince of Celestia clothed in great strength standing in the chamber of Atundra before the high priest. Then shall the brothers become one." He stopped reading and looked at Jag. "Tomorrow night, this prophecy shall be fulfilled as I, the real Prince of Celestia, stand in great strength before a Yalorian high priestess, who shall declare the prophecy fulfilled, and I shall take my place as ruler of both nations.

"Sounds fascinating," Jag replied sarcastically. "How do I fit in?"

"With you, I shall display my great strength."

"What? A rematch?" Jag ran his fingers across his cheek in reference to the scar he had left on Damon's face the night they fought years earlier. Jag had since been trained in the art of swordsmanship by Commander Corbis.

"Oh, I'm sure that by now you are quite capable of handling a sword, but I have something greater in store for you. You will testify tomorrow night before a special gathering of Celestian delegates regarding how you conspired with my sister to murder the king and that the attempt on her life was staged as an elaborate plot to frame me and prevent me from ascending to the throne."

"I will never say any of that," Jag replied. "And even so, what good would it do? The senate has already ordained your sister as queen."

"I'm disappointed in you. Surely they taught you that Celestia is a constitutional monarchy whose members can cast a vote of nullification causing the senate to select an entirely new monarch."

"I'm familiar with the law," Jag said. "However, it requires 20 percent of the planets to cast the vote to succeed.

"Right you are! See, you have been paying attention."

"There is no way you have eighty planets who would cast a vote of nullification."

"Actually, I have eighty-four, to be exact. Thirty-nine have always retained their loyalty to me. But arriving tomorrow night with the Yalorian high priestess are forty-five senators from the Yalori district. And once you testify to my innocence and the high priestess verifies the prophecy, those planets will cast a nullification vote ending my sister's reign. Leaderless and feeling deceived by the queen, the senate will reach out to their beloved son and plead with me to accept their offer of kingship and unite our two kingdoms.

"Surely you must know that I would die before I would say such a lie!"

"Yes, always the hero. But how about when the lives of your precious little friends on board the shuttle are on the line?" Damon nodded to an attendant, who established communications with the warbird that was escorting the shuttle back to the border.

"Commander, are you still escorting the shuttle?"

"Yes, sir."

"Target the shuttle and destroy it on my command," Damon said.

"Wait, no!" Jag looked to Tahjon and Measil. Mahjon had read Measil at the gate and had not sensed any deception.

"Oh, don't look to them. They didn't know of my plan. I kept it hidden from them."

Measil smiled. "Brilliant, absolutely brilliant."

"You see, you will testify, or I will destroy your friends. Now take him to the dungeon to consider his choices."

Jag was thrown into a cold dungeon deep in the heart of the castle, where his mind was filled with thoughts of Sara, Ben, Mahjon, and Henning. He knew he could never betray the queen to save their lives or his own. They would be completely defenseless; the shuttle was no match for a massive warbird. The more he tried not thinking about them, the more his mind focused on them. He opened his eyes and looked up. *Oh, God, you have always been the golden thread in my life at the most difficult times. Be with me now, and be with my friends. Spare their lives. Warn them of the danger they are in.*

As he sat back against the dingy stone wall, a thought entered his mind. What if he could get a message to Mahjon? He knew Mahjon couldn't read his mind, but he recalled how Damon had forced himself to feel rage that transferred to Tahjon. What if he could use the same method to get a message to Mahjon?

Jag began pacing back and forth, focusing every thought and feeling on their demise. He envisioned the shuttle exploding with his friends inside, flooding his emotions with fear for their lives. He paced for hours until he was utterly exhausted and emotionally drained, at which time, he lay down on the cold, hard stone floor and fell asleep.

Light years away, all on board the tiny shuttle sat quietly. Captain Henning was piloting the shuttle with Ben seated next to him. Mahjon sat behind Henning with Sara across from him. Her legs were pulled up to her chest, and her eyes were closed. She had cried herself to sleep.

Then, in the midst of the silence, Mahjon jerked forward, clenched his fists, and let out a deep and agonizing groan that startled everyone in the cabin.

"What's wrong?" Ben asked.

Sara opened her eyes. "Is it Jag?"

"I can sense his feelings," Mahjon said. "He is overwhelmed with fear."

Sara sat forward. "Are they hurting him?"

"No." Mahjon shook his head, pausing to search his feelings. "It's not fear for himself . . . but for us."

Ben frowned. "Why would he fear for us?"

"It wouldn't be the first time the Murks went back on a promise!" Henning said.

Ben turned in his seat to face Mahjon. "If Jag wanted to get a message to you, could he just think certain thoughts?"

"No, it doesn't work that way. I can't read his mind. I can only sense his feelings, and the greater the distance between us, the fewer feelings I can sense."

"So, if he wanted to get a message to you, would being fearful for our lives be something he could do?"

Mahjon nodded. "Yes, fear would definitely work, as it is the second-strongest emotional bond between a guardian and his protectee."

"Then I'd venture to say he may be trying to warn us that our lives are in danger," Ben replied.

Henning nodded in agreement. "So that's their game. They intend to use us as a pawn to force Jag to do what they want or they'll fire upon us."

"Can we defend ourselves long enough for the *Cora Lee* to arrive?" Ben asked.

"Against a warbird?" Henning chuckled at the absurdity of the idea. "Absolutely not!"

"Can we send a message to the *Cora Lee*?" Ben asked.

"Opening up a secure channel now," Henning replied. Then he frowned. "That's odd; the communication system is unable to establish a link to the *Cora Lee*. The warbird must be jamming our signal."

"Are we in range for the *Cora Lee's* sensors to track us?" Ben asked.

"Yeah, we should be close enough," Henning replied as he looked at the computer screen.

"But do you think they're tracking us?" Ben inquired, following his gaze.

"Knowing Commander Corbis, you better believe they're tracking our every move. Why, what are you thinking?"

"I have an idea that might just work or get us all killed," Ben replied.

"It doesn't seem like we have many options. What's your plan?"

Ben relayed a crazy idea to Captain Henning, who responded by maneuvering the shuttle erratically back and forth and up and down while varying the shuttle's velocity in an attempt to make the shuttle appear to be malfunctioning. Then he killed the engines and fired a stray phasor in the opposite direction of the warbird.

The commander of the warbird hailed the shuttlecraft. "What are you doing?"

"I'm sorry, sir," Henning replied as everyone on the shuttle pretended to be frantically moving about, repairing various systems. "Our guidance and weapons systems are malfunctioning. We're trying to make repairs."

"How long will it take?"

"No idea. We don't have a qualified engineer on board, but it could take as much as a day or two."

"I don't have a day to wait for you to fix your pitiful shuttle."

"Totally understandable, sir, and I apologize for the inconvenience. However, if you would like to speed things up, may I suggest that you tow us to the border so you can be on your way?"

The commander was indignant at the request but, seeing no alternative, sighed and then gestured to one of his crewmen as they engaged a tractor beam and began hauling the shuttle toward the border.

"Okay, you guys can stop," Captain Henning said to his crew. "Now we wait to see if the *Cora Lee* interprets our distress correctly."

After returning to her seat, Sara leaned over toward Mahjon. "You said fear was the second-strongest emotional bond between a guardian and his protectee. What's the strongest?"

Mahjon looked directly at Sara. "Love. Love is the strongest of all emotional bonds that a guardian can sense his protectee is feeling." Smiling, he leaned toward her. "In fact, it's not uncommon for us guardians to be aware of a protectee's affections long before they are aware themselves."

Sara leaned back and smiled slightly for the first time and then closed her eyes and thought of Jag.

The *Cora Lee* was on constant alert as two warbirds faced her from across the border. The watch officer asked Commander Corbis and Admiral Rannick to come to the bridge immediately.

"Sir, we have tracked the shuttle ever since they left Atundra. Everything was proceeding normally until a few minutes ago. The shuttle began weaving erratically, and long-range sensors picked up weapons fire. Now it appears the warbird is towing the shuttle."

"On the screen," Commander Corbis said. An image displayed, though it was too small to make out much detail. However, they could definitely see that the shuttle was being towed. "Red alert," Commander Corbis said.

"You'll need to strike fast and take out their communication systems first," Admiral Rannick warned.

The *Cora Lee* sprang into action, firing upon the two unsuspecting warbirds simultaneously, disabling their communications and then incapacitating them. Then she darted toward the shuttle.

Jag received a rude wakeup call the next morning as a small legion of guards arrived. "On your feet, prisoner!" one of the guards demanded.

Jag arose slowly from the cold, hard floor and placed his hand on his aching back as he tried to move his stiff body to get the blood circulating. Then he was escorted to a room, where he was allowed to clean himself up, because the emperor wanted Jag to look his best for the event.

Measil entered as Jag was eating a small meal prepared for him. "I trust your accommodations have been to your liking?"

"Measil, what a pleasant surprise to start my day off with a visit from you," Jag said.

"I hope you have considered your actions today. If you do not testify against the queen, your friends will be destroyed. I'd hate for them to end up like poor Marcel, whose death was such a needless tragedy."

"Don't even pretend that you cared for him. Why are you here, Measil?"

"The emperor has an offer for you. Testify against the queen tonight, and he will allow you to return to Earth, where you can live out the rest of your life with the very lovely Sara."

"And I should trust him just like I trusted you when I surrendered? You can tell your emperor that I will never speak against my queen or the kingdom; no matter what he threatens."

Measil smiled. "Oh, it's no threat. He will destroy you and your friends."

"You have my answer," Jag replied.

CHAPTER 35
A PROPHECY FULFILLED

The great Yalorian high priestess, Tabeetha Mwanda, entered the grand hall wearing a robe trimmed with long feathers. She was a tall, thin, dark-skinned woman with strong features and a stern, penetrating gaze. Warrior guards and an entourage of priests and forty-five Yalorian senators coming to witness the prophecy's fulfillment escorted her.

"Welcome, High Priestess. We are honored by your presence," Measil said as he bowed awkwardly. "Isn't this a glorious day of days?"

"Why would today be more glorious than any other day?" the priestess asked.

"Because of the fulfillment of the prophecy."

"That will be for me and me alone to determine," she said as she arrived at her reserved seat in the front row.

Delegates throughout Murk and Celestia, including the senators from the twenty-nine planets still loyal to Prince Damon, had already taken their seats. The ceremony was being broadcast throughout the Murk Empire and its signal reached well into the Celestian Kingdom. Commentators announced each delegate and identified their planet as they arrived. They also described the excitement that was brewing as everyone arrived to witness the historic event.

The ceremony began with the introduction of the emperor's executive council. Then trumpets resounded, and everyone stood as Emperor Damon entered wearing a crown and an elaborate robe with an enormous bejeweled train that dragged behind him. When he reached his throne, everyone bowed, with the exception of the Yalorian priestess and her entourage.

"Honored guests and those watching throughout the Murk Empire and the Celestian Kingdom, please welcome his royal majesty and rightful ruler, Emperor Damon," Measil announced. Applause erupted for several minutes, ending only when the pleased emperor raised his hands to silence the crowd.

"Tonight, we shall witness history as the long-foretold Yalorian prophecy is fulfilled before our very eyes," Measil continued. "We are grateful to the high priestess for joining us to validate the requirements of the prophecy and, thereby, usher in an era of unity between our two great nations." Again, applause erupted with many standing to their feet.

"As we all know, our beloved emperor was falsely accused of killing his father, a man he adored. Tonight, the actual perpetrator of that crime will testify that the Celestian queen herself ordered the assassination in a jealous attempt to prevent the emperor from fulfilling his destiny. Bring forth the accused!"

The audience booed and jeered as guards escorted Jag to the stage and forced him to face the audience. On both sides of the stage, Damon had erected large monitors out of the audience's view, which displayed a live video feed of the warbird towing the shuttle with a large red target on the shuttle's center. The screens were obviously an incentive for Jag to speak out against the queen or witness the destruction of his friends.

"Prince Marcello of Earth, you are charged with the high crimes of conspiracy, treason, and murder," Measil said. "You conspired with the Queen of Celestia to murder the king and framed Emperor Damon to prevent him from taking his rightful throne. How do you plead to these charges?"

Jag stood quietly looking at the audience as everyone stared at him.

"I will remind the accused that your actions have real and dire consequences," Measil said. Once again, Jag did not respond. After several long moments of silence, Measil looked to the emperor, who gestured to one of the officers standing off stage to begin the attack on the shuttle. A message was sent to the warbird's commander, and then the video screen showed the warbird release the shuttle from its tow, circle around, and face it head on.

"Accused, will you not speak the truth and disown the queen for what she has done?" Measil asked, unable to conceal his irritation. Jag just closed his eyes and refused to speak, even though his friends' lives were on the line. "If you will not speak, then you leave us no alternative but to pronounce judgment."

Emperor Damon nodded, and the officer sent a command to fire upon the shuttle. Jag opened his eyes to watch the monitor, believing his attempt to send a message to Mahjon had failed. Immediately, both monitors went blank. Assuming the worst, a tear fell down Jag's cheek as he thought of his friends. He had failed.

Light years away, just as the warbird was maneuvering to fire upon the defenseless shuttle, the *Cora Lee* dropped from hyperspace and fired a massive barrage of weapons, causing the warbird to explode, simultaneously severing the communication signal to Atundra.

Maëlle was waiting in the bay when the shuttle docked and ran to embrace her daughter and Ben. Afterwards, Bayli escorted them to the captain's ready room, where Admiral Rannick and Commander Corbis where watching the live broadcast on a monitor mounted on the wall.

"Are you sure you want to watch this?" Admiral Rannick asked Sara.

"I have to," Sara replied.

Everyone gathered around the monitor. However, Mahjon moved to the back of the room and leaned against the wall with his eyes closed, for he did not need to watch the video to know what was happening to Jag.

Just as judgment was about to be pronounced, and with nothing left to lose, Jag took a deep breath. "I do have something to say," he began. "The Kingdom of Celestia will never belong to you, Prince Damon, for it belongs to no one. It is a kingdom not of borders but one that resides in the hearts and minds of its citizens. So, no matter what you do to me, I will not disown the kingdom or my queen."

"Silence your tongue!" Measil said. He nodded at the guard standing beside Jag, who backhanded Jag across his mouth, causing blood to flow from his split lip. "Since the accused has nothing to say in his own defense, we shall proceed with the verdict."

Each of the elders seated beside the emperor unsurprisingly returned a guilty verdict.

"Accused, the esteemed elders of Murk have found you guilty, and your punishment will now be determined by the very person you conspired against, Emperor Damon," Measil said.

Silence shrouded the auditorium as Damon stared at Jag, relishing the moment and his own power. Anticipating the inevitable sentence, a guard stepped forward with a large double-edged sword used for carrying out executions.

"I am not without compassion," Damon said. "I will let the accused determine his own fate. Swear allegiance to me, and I will have mercy on you and return you to your home planet. Otherwise, this will be the last breath you take. So choose your next words wisely."

"Kill me or let me live, it doesn't matter, for the kingdom will never unite under your rule. You are not the one; you have failed once again," Jag said

Damon burned with rage. Just as he was about to utter his decision, Tahjon cried out in a loud groan. "Traitor!" Then, with his spear in his right hand, he jumped from behind the Murk elders, leaped over their heads, and landed with such force that he cracked the stone floor. With pounding steps, he ran straight into Jag, sending him and the two soldiers who were holding him soaring backwards.

"Oh, this is going to be good," Damon said, leaning back in his throne with a smirk on his face.

Jag struggled to his feet and stood staring at Tahjon, waiting for him to strike. Tahjon stepped forward and then lifted his foot and kicked Jag in the chest, sending him flying backwards.

On the *Cora Lee*, the scene was more than they could bear. Bayli laid her head against Rannick's shoulder as Sara turned away.

"Oh, Papa! Why would he do this?" Sara whispered.

"Isn't it obvious?" Ben replied. "It's love."

"Yes, he must have really loved you, Papa," Sara said to her father.

"Oh, I assure you it wasn't love for *me* that drove him to do this," Ben replied.

Tahjon grabbed Jag by the nape of his neck and, with a single punch, jettisoned him across the room, where he slammed into a large pillar and fell limp to the floor. Everyone in the audience watched in silence, shocked by the violent display. Tahjon lifted Jag by the throat with one hand and placed the tip of his spear against Jag's chest and waited for Emperor Damon to approve the deathblow.

At that moment, Mahjon, who had been standing quietly, opened his eyes and walked in front of the monitor, blocking everyone's view with his massive body. He stared at the monitor puzzled by something. He turned to Commander Corbis. "We must go now!"

While Tahjon held up Jag's half-conscious body, awaiting the emperor's decision, the high priestess stood, drawing everyone's attention as they anticipated she would confirm the prophecy. However, instead, she turned and walked toward the exit, her entourage following, as Measil ran down from the stage to intercept her.

"Priestess Tabeetha, please wait. The ceremony isn't over yet. The prophecy must be fulfilled," Measil said, maneuvering in front of the priestess.

Annoyed by the maggot of a man who stood blocking her path, she turned and pointed at the emperor. "That is not strength." Then she pointed at Jag. "That is."

Once again, she began moving toward the exit. Measil tried to stop her, but her two warriors easily removed him from her path.

"What of the prophecy?" Emperor Damon yelled, undeterred by her declaration. "Has it been fulfilled?"

Irritated by his persistence, she stopped and closed her eyes for a moment and breathed deeply. "Yes, the prophecy is fulfilled."

An eruption of celebration tore throughout the auditorium. Ecstatic at the news and with his rage allayed, Damon motioned for Tahjon to set Jag down as several elders began commending the emperor.

However, the priestess was not quite finished. "But he is not the one!" She pointed at the emperor. Then she pointed to Jag. "He is the prince of whom the prophecy foretold."

The celebration ceased as a cacophony of gasps filled the auditorium. Those in the senate delegation who could have casted a vote of nullification rose and moved toward the exit.

Measil ran to stop them. "Friends, please! The ceremony isn't over. We still need to vote." He grabbed one of the senators by his cloak.

"Let go of me!" the senator demanded. "You promised us Prince Damon was the one whom the prophecy foretold. That's the only reason we supported that egotistical brat."

Measil tried to contain the situation by ordering that the cameras stop broadcasting, but it was too late; the damage was done. He ordered Jag be taken back to the dungeon until they figured out what to do with him.

Emperor Damon watched in horror as his master plan unraveled. After the entire hall was cleared out, he sat fuming, his face red with anger. "What just happened?" He kicked his footstool, sending it tumbling across the stage. "She said he was the one who fulfilled the prophecy!"

Measil bowed his head. "I'm sorry, Your Majesty."

"You said you had everything prepared, that he would renounce the kingdom to save his friends. I want his head right now!"

Measil held up his hands. "Wait, Your Majesty. We can't kill him now; the people believe he is the one. Be patient. Killing him now will only undermine your rule with Murk citizens and could cause a revolt."

"Revolt against me, their emperor?" Damon glared at Measil. "I should have killed him already! I won't make that same mistake again. Bring him to me now!"

Tahjon walked down the dungeon hall carrying a large metal case. The two guards, still sore from when Tahjon struck them earlier, cowered as he approached.

"Measil sent me here to prepare the prisoner for execution," Tahjon said.

"What's in the chest?" the younger guard asked.

"Tools to assist in my preparation." Tahjon shook the case, and its contents rattled. "I'm going to be a while. You're welcome to come in and watch, or feel free to take a break."

"Thanks! I could use some grub," the older guard said.

"Wait, Measil ordered us to stay here and watch the prisoner," the younger guard objected.

The older guard waved his hand in dismissal. "He's not going anywhere. He hasn't moved since we put him in there!" He opened the door and pointed at Jag, who was lying on the floor, and then turned back to Tahjon. "Boy, you sure did a number on him!"

"Well, you're welcome to watch if you like," Tahjon repeated as he entered the cell and pulled a strange-looking metal device from the case.

"Actually, taking a break sounds like a good idea," the younger guard said as he closed the cell door. Then the two guards left.

Tahjon dumped the rest of the items out of the case, making such a racket that Jag slowly turned his head to see what the noise was. Straining to open his eyes, Jag mustered a smile when he saw Tahjon. "It's about time," he said hoarsely.

"Well, I had to make a few preparations," Tahjon said. Then he paused in surprise. "Hey, how did you know I was coming to—"

"To rescue me? If Tahjon the Magnificent truly intended to kill me, it would not have taken more than one strike."

Tahjon lifted Jag slightly and held a pouch containing a foul-smelling liquid to his lips. Jag groaned in pain.

"I'm sorry," Tahjon said as he looked at Jag's battered and bruised body.

"Don't be. You saved my life. Emperor Damon was going to have me executed, wasn't he?"

Tahjon nodded. "Yes. I figured that once his anger was satisfied, his reasoning would return, and he would be more interested in preserving his empire. Here, take this and drink; it will numb the pain and help you sleep."

"Why are you doing this?" Jag asked. "The emperor is going to be angry with you."

"He's always angry. Besides someone once told me that 'sometimes you give up that which you hold dearest for those you love most.'"

After helping Jag drink the awful concoction, Tahjon lowered him back down. Within moments, Jag's eyes grew heavy from the sedative. "Thank you," he whispered.

"Don't thank me yet. We've got a long way to go."

"Doesn't matter; it's just nice being with a friend," Jag said, and then he fell asleep.

Tahjon placed Jag into the case and then opened the cell door. Seeing that the two guards had yet to return to their post, he walked down the dungeon's corridor carrying the case. As he passed guards along the way, they kept their distance, not even looking at Tahjon out of fear of what they had witnessed hours earlier.

In the shuttle bay, security maintenance pods hung from the ceiling, moving automatically along a track, where robotic arms placed supplies into the bottom of each sphere. The pods transported crews and supplies back and forth to their observation posts along the Murk border. A ramp led up to a platform where a couple of security guards, one younger and one older, were waiting to board a pod.

"Were you at the ceremony?" the younger guard asked.

"Yep."

"That was something else! Did you see the hurt Tahjon put on that poor guy?"

"Yeah."

"So do you think Prince Marcello is the one and not Emperor Damon?"

"Must be; the priestess identified him."

"What do you think that all means?"

"Don't know, and don't care."

"How can you not care? This is the most important thing ever!"

"Look, kid, I'm just doing my time until this thing is over."

A pod arrived, and they both stepped inside as large robotic arms finished loading supplies on the bottom and then closed the pod's door. The pod moved automatically along the track to a launching station, where it was jettisoned into space.

Once the coast was clear, Tahjon dashed toward the nearest pod in rotation. Upon entering it, he removed Jag from the case and buckled him into one of the two seats. Jag awoke and looked around the craft to get his bearings.

"A security supply pod? This is your plan? You know this craft has no way of defending itself if we're caught, nor can we outrun any ship."

"We could always walk," Tahjon suggested.

"And they say guardians don't have a sense of hum—" Jag's words were cut off by a cough that brought up blood. Tahjon wiped the blood from Jag's mouth as the robotic arms sealed the door. Then the pod maneuvered along the track and was jettisoned into space.

Jag looked at Tahjon. "You understand that this pod will only go to where it was programmed to fly and that the location can't be changed? We can't even communicate with my ship."

"If my brother is half the guardian I believe him to be, we won't have to. He'll find you."

"Well, let's pray he finds us before the Murks do."

Tahjon gave Jag another dose of medicine, causing him to fall asleep.

Hours later, as the sedative was wearing off, Jag began tossing in his seat. When he awoke, he saw Tahjon's countenance had changed. His eyes were closed, and his face was red with anger as he exhaled slowly, struggling to control his emotions.

"They've discovered us missing, haven't they?" Jag asked.

Tahjon nodded, his eyes still closed. "Yes, Damon is livid. I can feel his rage."

"Are you going to be alright?" Jag inquired as Tahjon continued to breathe deeply.

"We'll see."

"So now it's just a matter of who finds us first," Jag said as he closed his eyes and fell asleep again.

He awoke several hours later to Tahjon tapping his face. "Jag, wake up! We've been found!"

"By whom?" Jag asked, but Tahjon's expression was answer enough. A Murk warbird had located them and locked a tractor beam onto the small pod. Then a beep came from the console with a flashing alert that read, "Incoming Message." Jag reach forward and touched the acceptance button.

On the screen, the warbird's captain sat while his young commander stood beside him. The captain did not say anything at first, just stared at Jag and Tahjon. "Well, well, well, what have we here?" he said finally. "I am Captain Lemann Nuckols."

Jag's eyes widened. Although he hardly recognized Nuckols, the voice was the same. Jag forgot that Emperor Damon had given Nuckols his own ship after Jag went to prison.

"Greetings, captain," Jag replied.

"We are on the hunt for two fugitives. Commander Mooney, can you read me the description of the bulletin? I want to make sure I get this absolutely correct," Nuckols said.

"Sir, yes, sir!" Commander Mooney read from the brief that had been sent to all Murk ships. "Urgent! Be on the lookout for a security supply pod carrying two stowaways who are enemies of the state: a Celestian prince traveling with a Mravian guardian. They are wanted dead or alive."

"Commander Mooney, do you see a security pod standing before us today?"

"Yes, sir! I do," the ecstatic officer replied.

"No, no you don't," Captain Nuckols replied.

The commander frowned. "I don't? But sir—"

"Commander Mooney, do you see a guardian of Mravia?"

"Yes, sir," Mooney replied with less enthusiasm and a bit of confusion.

"No, commander, you do not."

"Oh, I see," Commander Mooney said, finally realizing his captain's intent.

"Commander Mooney, tell me, do you see a Prince of Celestia on board this vessel?"

"Sir, no I don't."

"Well, neither do I, and I fear that we may have wasted our time and theirs."

"Sir, enemy vessel spotted. Five minutes away!" an anxious ensign said off screen.

"Well, my apologies for intercepting you folks today," Captain Nuckols said.

"Uh, not a problem," Jag said as he and Tahjon exchanged glances. "It's been our pleasure, captain. And, captain, how are you?"

"Tired. My entire crew and I are long overdue for some rest and relaxation. This war has drawn on for too long, and we're due for a break."

"Sir, I've heard that Gilboa is a great place to visit for rest," Jag said, recalling that was where Dr. Neebo went after he left the *Killclaw*.

"I think that's a brilliant idea. Commander Mooney, set a course for Gilboa,"

"Three minutes until intercept, captain!" the ensign yelled.

"I was sorry to hear about Mouse," Nuckols said. "The lad had grown on me, and his death was a shame. You did well by him."

"Thank you, captain," Jag said. "I think of him quite often."

"Well, I must be on my way," Nuckols said. "If you stay put, you'll find what you're looking for."

"Captain, if you or your crew ever need anything, anything at all, all you have to do is ask."

"Thank you. We may very well take you up on your offer. Please give my regards to the admiral."

The warbird released the pod and fled.

Within minutes, the *Cora Lee* arrived and secured the pod in the docking bay. As Jag was being carried off on a stretcher, Bayli was the first to greet him. She placed her hand on his shoulder to sense his injuries.

"He has internal bleeding from a ruptured spleen, a punctured lung, a lacerated liver, and three broken ribs. He also has a moderate concussion," Bayli said to Dr. Pandori, who was standing nearby.

Sara ran to his side, with her parents close behind. Jag was shocked to see them, thinking they had been destroyed by the Murk ship.

"You're alive!" Jag exclaimed, coughing up more blood.

"Yes, thanks to your message to Mahjon," Ben said.

Sara held Jag's hand gently. As she saw how badly his body had been broken for her, she cried. Then six security officers and Mahjon stepped down from the pod and took Tahjon into custody.

"Tahjon, for crimes committed against His Majesty, Prince Marcello, we are placing you under arrest until a court can determine what to do with you," Officer Cho said.

Jag overheard and asked the medical team to stop.

"Tahjon, he's asking for Tahjon!" Bayli yelled as Mahjon and the security officers escorted Tahjon over to Jag's side.

"Tahjon, thank you for saving my life," Jag said as he placed his hand on the giant's arm. "And for the record, I pardon you from any and all crimes committed against me and the Celestian Kingdom."

"Thank you, Your Majesty," Tahjon said, bowing low. Then Jag moved his hand and placed it on Tahjon's bonding mark.

"Tahjon, as Prince of Celestia, I release you from your bond. Be free."

Immediately, Tahjon's eyes widened, and he fell to his knees, making a loud thud against the metal floor. Had it not been for Mahjon and Officer Cho catching him, he would have fallen forward and crushed Jag. Then Tahjon jerked and arched backwards as the bonding mark on his chest glowed bright red and steam evaporated from his chest. After a long and agonizing moan, his bonding mark faded away, and he relaxed and dropped his arms.

"It's gone," Tahjon whispered.

"What's gone, brother?" Mahjon asked.

"Damon's rage, it's gone."

"Let's move it! We have to get Jag into surgery now!" Bayli demanded.

CHAPTER 36
THE BEST DAY EVER

Sara arrived on the *Unity* in the first available shuttle and hurried to the security checkpoint that led to the *Anastasis* hospital ship. Once again, an officer denied her admittance, because security restrictions prevented all unauthorized access. Since returning to Paris with her parents, Sara had tried daily to visit Jag on the *Anastasis,* where he was undergoing more advanced rehabilitation from his life-threatening injuries.

"Please, don't tell me that my name is still not on the list!" she said in frustration.

"No, ma'am, it's not that. The *Anastasis* has left," the officer said.

"When are they coming back?"

"I don't see any records that they are returning."

"How can this be? I've been here every morning, and now you're telling me they're gone? How about the *Cora Lee?*"

The officer examined his records. "Hmm . . . they're gone, too."

Distraught, Sara walked down the corridor. "He didn't even say goodbye."

"Is everything alright?" IRIS asked, startling her as he approached from behind.

"Oh, IRIS, you're still here! The security officer said the *Cora Lee* and Anastasis had left the station."

"He is correct. The *Anastasis* has returned to Celestia, because their services are needed elsewhere, and Commander Corbis has the *Cora Lee* out assisting the *Exodus* in building a security perimeter around Earth."

"And Jag?" Sara asked. "Did he return with the *Anastasis?*"

"The prince is on the planet today and asked me to invite you to join him as he tours Earth. How would you like me to respond?"

"Yes! Tell him I said 'yes'!" Sara exclaimed as she gave IRIS an unexpected hug.

Their shuttle landed in a field adjacent to the family farm in Mulberry, Indiana, where Uncle Jack was waiting with one of his dogs.

"Welcome to Indiana!" Uncle Jack said as the shuttle's ramp lowered. He extended his hand to help Sara climb down the shuttle's steps. "You are every bit as pretty as Jag described you."

Sara blushed. "Thank you."

"I hope you're hungry. The missus is preparing a big country breakfast. Admiral Rannick and Bayli are already in the kitchen, and you're welcome to join us or, if you'd like, you can go see Jag. He just headed up to the launch pad to speak with Mom and Dad." Uncle Jack pointed toward the path. "Just follow the trail alongside the barn and over the creek—"

"Yes, I know. Jag showed me the way already," Sara said. Uncle Jack gave her a curious expression. "On the *Cora Lee,* in a hologram," she explained.

Before Jack could respond, Sara ran up the path. As she neared the launch pad, she saw Mahjon keeping watch at a distance, giving Jag some privacy. He gestured for her to proceed and join Jag at his grandparents' gravesite.

". . . I'm sorry it took me so long to return home. I sure have missed you," Jag said. "Thank you for always praying and believing in me. It's been a long, hard road, but you were right, Grandma, through it all I've seen God's golden thread."

"*Bonjour*, I hope I'm not intruding," Sara said.

Jag turned to her and smiled. "No, not at all."

"I just met your Uncle Jack, and he said breakfast will be ready soon."

"Good, I'm hungry! I am so looking forward to a good breakfast and to spending the day with you." He led Sara past a bench and a life-sized statue of himself that had one hand pointed toward the stars. In the other hand, he held a rocket. A dog was seated at his feet. Engraved in the statue were the words, "Our lost astronaut. May he find his way home."

"My uncle said that after my 'accident,' Grandpa installed this bench for Grandma to come up here and pray. She knew that when I returned, I would come back to this place. Then some famous sculptor created the statue for them."

"It's beautiful," Sara said. "Who's the dog?"

"That's Grissom; he was such a good dog. He would follow me up here when I launched my rockets. Hey, do you want to launch one?"

"Really? Sure."

"They kept my 'command center' operational even after all these years. Each year on the anniversary of my disappearance, a group of people would come and launch a rocket in memory of me. How cool is that?"

After connecting the rocket, Jag and Sara ducked into the shack, which was a lot smaller than he remembered. He counted down and had Sara press the launch button, which sent the rocket soaring into the sky.

"This is normally where Grissom would start barking and run after the rocket," Jag said.

Sara laughed. "Well, don't look at me."

With the help of a cane, Jag limped down the trail toward the house. In a turn of events, Sara offered her arm to help steady him.

"So how are you feeling?" she asked.

"I'm okay. However, it still hurts if I move too quickly. Doc says I'm lucky to be alive and that I'm healing nicely, but I'll need the cane for several more weeks."

Aunt Rachel had prepared a smorgasbord of pancakes, waffles, bacon, sausage, eggs, and Jag's favorite, chocolate gravy and biscuits. Everyone crowded around the dining table, where Uncle Jack had stacked several small tractor tires to make a seat big enough to accommodate Mahjon. Seated across from Jag was Jack and Rachel's only child, Violet, and her husband, Carl, and their two kids.

Jag closed his eyes as he savored the incredible breakfast. It all seemed like a dream. He recalled how he had longed to be home when he laid freezing on the

Killclaw. He set down his fork and looked around the room at the people who mattered most to him.

"Jag, do you have everything you need?" Aunt Rachel asked when she noticed he was not eating.

"Yes, I have everything I need right here at this table."

Everyone paused and looked at Jag in appreciation of the moment. Then the family asked him to share some of his amazing stories.

After several hours, IRIS approached. "Sir, we must be going. You have the speech at your alma mater."

"You're speaking at Purdue?" Sara asked.

Jag nodded. "Yes. Seems I'm finally receiving my degree. They're giving me an honorary doctorate." Then he excused himself and went upstairs to his old bedroom to change his clothes. His bedroom had remained untouched since the day he left, as his grandmother had always believed he would return someday. When Uncle Jack moved into the home, they only had one child and did not need the space. After changing his clothes, Jag paused and stared at the tapestry with its golden thread that he had helped his grandmother hang in the hall and then went back downstairs.

"Wow, I guess you are a prince," Aunt Rachel said, in awe of his attire.

"Yeah, you clean up quite nicely," Uncle Jack added.

Then they walked out onto the back porch to say their goodbyes. Uncle Jack turned to Jag. "Do you want to drive Ol' Betsy?"

"Wow, you kept her?" Jag asked.

"She's all fueled up and ready. I just replaced the spark plugs last week, and she's running well."

"Don't I need a driver's license?"

"I hardly think the State of Indiana is going to ticket the man responsible for saving Earth. Just don't hit anyone and I think you'll be fine." Uncle Jack tossed the keys to Jag. "You do remember how to drive, don't you?"

"You betcha!"

Jag sat behind the steering wheel, and Sara slid in next to him, leaving room for Bayli to join them. However, Bayli closed the passenger door. "There's no way you're getting me in this contraption! Enjoy your ride."

Mahjon stepped into the truck bed, and Ol' Betsy's shocks groaned as he maneuvered to the front and leaned against the cab. Jag fired up the old truck and put it in gear. Unfamiliar with the accelerator, he gave it too much gas, and the vehicle lunged forward before he slammed on the brakes, causing Mahjon to bang against the cab.

"Sorry!" Jag said as he eased the truck forward once again. They traveled down the road, the shuttle hovering safely behind them, as air whipped through their hair from the open windows.

"It doesn't get any better than this!" Jag shouted over the engine noise and the wind.

"What's that?" Sara asked.

"Driving my grandfather's old truck with you sitting next to me," Jag said. Sara smiled.

After arriving in one piece at the university, Sara quickly patted down Jag's windblown hair. Then they were ushered into a packed auditorium of cheering students and professors, where the university dean placed a hood over Jag's uniform and handed him a doctoral degree. Then Jag spoke of his vision to restart the Space University and expand it throughout the kingdom to usher in a new era of unity and technical innovation. Afterwards, students clamored to get their photo taken with Mahjon, who tolerated their requests.

"Okay, what's next?" Sara asked excitedly after they boarded the shuttle.

"New York City," Jag said.

"Alright! I love New York!"

In New York, a massive ticker tape parade greeted them as millions lined the streets, cheering. Several women held signs with marriage proposals for Jag, which Sara did not find amusing. They stopped and enjoyed a slice of New York's famous pizza, or, in Mahjon's case, many slices. Then they traveled to the United Nations building, where Jag addressed delegates from every nation about the values of the kingdom: justice, love, and honor. Again, he called for re-establishing the Space University and asked for their support. Afterwards, the United Nations awarded them service medals for their roles in saving humanity.

"What's next?" Sara asked again as they returned to the shuttle.

"Now we go to Poland to see an old friend."

Sara clapped her hands. "Alright, to Poland!"

The shuttle landed in a park near the center of Poznan, a beautiful and historic Polish city. Everyone departed the shuttle except for Rannick, who stayed behind to check in with his vineyard crew. Jag, Sara, Bayli, Mahjon, and IRIS entered an old, five-story soapstone building. Mahjon took one look at the tiny elevator and then stepped back. "I think I'll take the stairs."

"Yeah, I'll join Mahjon," Bayli said, uncertain about the antiquated elevator.

"You sure? He's on the fifth floor," Jag said.

"Oh, that will be easy," Bayli said.

"Alright, we'll meet you at the top."

Mahjon and Bayli began climbing the stairs. Once Bayli reached the third floor, she paused and leaned against the railing. "I need a breather. Go ahead without me." In response, Mahjon threw her over his shoulder, carrying her up the remaining stairs. As they neared the fifth floor, she tapped his shoulder. "Put me down! I don't want them to see you carrying me, and not a word of this to the admiral! He would never let me live it down!"

Mahjon chuckled as he set her down. Soon word spread throughout the building that a giant and a blue woman had entered. Doors opened as children tried to get a glimpse of them.

Jag knocked on the professor's door several times. After a moment, they heard several locks unlocking. The door opened, and an old, grey-haired man, slightly bent over and dressed in dull, musky clothing, looked out.

"Professor?" Jag asked.

The old man stared at him for several seconds. Then his face brightened. "Yosef!" He hugged Jag and invited them in.

Stepping inside, Jag saw stacks of books and newspapers leaning against the wall. The only way to get down the hallway was to walk sideways.

"I think it may be best if you wait out here," Jag said to Mahjon. "We shouldn't be long."

Mahjon returned to sit on the stairs as children peered cautiously around the corner. He growled playfully, which sent them screaming in delight back to their apartments. However, one curious little girl approached the strange giant.

In the professor's cluttered living room was an old tan tweed couch, a leather reading chair, and a small desk with piles of unopened letters. Heavy drapes masked the sunlight, making the room dark, while a lamp in the corner cast a bit of light.

"Make yourselves comfortable; I'll put on some water," the professor said as he walked hunched over into the tiny, outdated kitchenette and placed a kettle on the gas stove.

"Professor, mind if I pull back the drapes?" Jag asked.

"Go right ahead. It's just 'Polanski' now. No one has called me professor in years."

"Sir, you'll always be professor to me," Jag said.

As he pulled the cord to open the drapes, a plume of dust fell to the floor. Bayli shrieked as a calico cat shot out from its hiding place beneath the couch, brushing against her leg before darting into the bedroom.

"Oh, don't mind her. That's just Sophie," the professor said as he returned into the room.

The light revealed walls covered in faded, peeling wallpaper and an array of photos documenting some of the professor's accomplishments. One photo showed him as a young man stepping down onto the surface of Mars.

"Professor, let me introduce my friends. This is Bayli from the planet Azuria," Jag said.

"It's a pleasure to have such a lovely being as you in my home!" the professor replied.

"This is Sara Mendelsohn; Ben's daughter."

"Benjamin's daughter, you say! Oh, it doesn't seem possible that he could have a daughter your age, but I guess that was a long time ago. Pleasure to meet you, Sara."

"Thank you. The pleasure is mine, sir."

"And this is IRIS, my friend and android assistant."

"You are truly astonishing!" the professor said. After shaking IRIS's hand, he lifted and examined the mechanical movements of his arm. "Fluid, full range of motion. Most impressive robotic structure. How many computations can you compute in a second?"

"Thirty-two quadrillion, sir."

"Absolutely marvelous!"

From the kitchen, the kettle whistled, announcing the water was boiling. IRIS cocked his head, trying to comprehend the sound. The professor opened an old cabinet and retrieved several mugs that were different in color and size and placed them on a silver tray along with the kettle, milk, sugar, and a bowl of small cookies.

"Mr. IRIS, do you drink or consume food?" the professor asked.

"No, thank you. I do not. Though some of the upgrades available now offer that capability, I don't see the point."

"Professor, is this one of the Mars rocks you collected?" Jag asked, referring to the rock on the coffee table.

"Yes, my boy. It's a lot lighter than it looks, isn't it?" the professor said as Jag handed the Martian rock to Sara and Bayli.

"Yes, it is!" Jag said.

"Well, it's nothing but a paperweight now. Like everything else in this apartment, it's an artifact from a lifetime ago." As the professor set down the tray, his hands shook, and the mugs rattled. After pouring hot water into each of the mugs, he added a spoonful of instant coffee and stirred. "Please feel free to add milk or sugar if you'd like."

Bayli followed Jag and Sara's example by adding milk and sugar to her coffee and then took a sip. She nearly choked. It was the worst thing she had ever tasted, but she politely held her cup and smiled.

"How have you been, professor?" Jag asked.

"I'm doing alright considering everything. The years have been long since your accident."

He crossed the room to a photo of Jag's class. Jag pushed himself up from the couch with his cane and joined the professor as they stared at the photo.

"That was a good day," Jag said.

Professor P nodded. "Yes, it was a good day." Then he lowered his voice. "Percy came to see me last week."

"Oh? And how did that go?"

"He came to apologize for all the lies he told and the harm he caused me and the Space University. Then he asked for my forgiveness. It grieves me to say this, but I didn't want to forgive him. I wanted to hit him over the head with my cane!"

Jag laughed at the thought of it.

"But then I told Percy that if Yosef . . ." He paused, a bit choked up, and wiped a tear from his eye with a handkerchief. "If you could forgive him for what he did to you, then I had no right to hold onto unforgiveness."

Jag put his hand on his mentor's shoulder. "I'm glad you forgave him, professor."

"It wasn't easy."

"Oh, I understand."

"Then Percy offered me an absurd amount of money."

Jag smiled and shook his head. "That sounds like Percy. Nothing money can't fix."

"I told him that I accepted his apology but that he could keep his money."

"You did well, sir."

"Thank you, my boy. You should sit; your coffee is getting cold."

Jag squeezed back onto the couch as the professor sat in his chair and draped an afghan blanket across his knees.

"Professor, I'd like to ask you a question. I plan to rebuild the Space University and expand it throughout the kingdom. We will bring the brightest students from each planet and have them mentored by the best professors in the universe. However, I need someone to run the school, someone with profound knowledge, experience, and great rapport with students. Sir, I'd like to ask you to come with me to Corian to help establish the school."

"Me?" Professor P asked. "That ship sailed a long time ago. Look at me. I'm an old man who can barely get around this apartment. How would I ever get around the universe?"

"Sir, your ship hasn't sailed yet. Didn't you say you always want to visit Alpha Centauri? We're flying through there on our way to Aulora."

Professor P looked around his dingy apartment. "All my books are here, my articles and collections. I could never leave all my stuff."

"You can bring it all with you. IRIS can have a team here tomorrow to help you pack!"

"Tomorrow?"

Jag nodded. "I leave next week for Aulora, and I'd like for you to come with us."

Sara looked apprehensively at Bayli. She hadn't been aware Jag was leaving so soon.

"I just can't leave Sophie," the professor said.

"Bring her with us, and we'll take enough food to last the remainder of her lifetime."

"I don't know, Jag. It's tempting but—"

"A wise man once told me that 'We reach for the stars, because we are explorers. However, to reach for the stars is to reach for the impossible. And yet, we still reach, because exploring is who we are.' You said that if the stars were out of your reach, that you'd buy a 'Winnebago and explore Earth.' Sir, I don't see any Winnebago parked out front of your apartment."

Professor P contemplated Jag's response. Then he glanced around his small apartment and pushed himself up from his chair. "I think I've lived in my own prison long enough. I'm ready for an adventure."

"That's wonderful!" Bayli exclaimed. Sara sat quietly.

Jag grinned. "Professor, I can't wait to show you Celestia."

"Well, before you do that, I need to show you what I've been working on in my lab."

Jag looked around in astonishment. "You have a lab? Here?"

"Not in here; up on the roof. I had to promise the landlord I wouldn't burn down his building. You should probably come with us, Mr. IRIS, as I want to bring all my lab equipment with me."

After Jag and IRIS left with the professor, Sara turned to Bayli. "Is Jag really leaving next week?"

"Yep," Bayli said, eating a cookie. "The queen asked him to return home as soon as possible. You know, these cookies are very good, but that black drink is quite foul!"

"That's because it's instant. They make much better coffee."

"I guess I'll just have to take your word for it," Bayli said with a look of disgust.

After arranging a time for IRIS and a team to return the next day to pack, Jag, Sara, Bayli, and IRIS left the apartment and walked down the hallway to where Mahjon was seated. He was holding the little girl on his knee as she touched his face with her tiny hand.

Bayli smiled. "I see you've made a friend."

"What's her name?" Jag asked.

"From what I've been able to deduce, I think it's Lena, and she has two siblings," Mahjon said as he lifted the child off his lap. "Goodbye, Lena. It was nice to meet you."

"*Do widzenia*," the little girl said as she waved to Mahjon.

Back on the shuttle, Bayli noticed that Sara had not been as cheerful since she discovered Jag was leaving the next week. "Sara, you're awful quiet. Aren't you going to ask where we are headed next?"

"You guys must be wearing her out," Rannick said.

"Not everyone got to stay and nap," Bayli replied.

"Who said anything about napping? I was on an important call with Norr. Although, afterwards, I did take in a few winks," he admitted with a smile.

"Uh-huh, I knew why you wanted to stay behind," Bayli replied.

"So where are we headed now?" Sara asked, sounding distracted.

"I've saved the best for last," Jag said. "I was told that no trip to Earth would be complete without visiting Paris."

The shuttle arrived in Paris as the sun was setting. For their evening meal, Sara wore a gorgeous evening gown and Jag an eloquent black suit and tie.

"You look amazing," Jag said, stunned by her beauty.

"Thank you, and you look very handsome."

A limousine transported Jag, Sara, and Mahjon to a three-star Michelin restaurant while Bayli, Rannick, and IRIS remained behind. The restaurant was beautiful, with sparkling chandeliers, white linen-covered tables with silver candlesticks, and a string quartet playing classical music. Jag and Sara sampled a variety of options on each tray while Mahjon consumed entire trays, to the delight of the wait staff.

As they drove away after the meal, Jag asked Sara if she would mind joining him for a walk, as he needed to stretch his legs. The limo dropped them off at a garden.

"I know this place," Sara exclaimed when they got out of the vehicle. "We're at Luxemburg Garden."

"Didn't you say this was your favorite spot in Paris?"

Jag took Sara's arm, and they walked a moonlit path lined with lampposts that illuminated the surrounding trees.

"You've been quiet this evening," Jag said. "Is everything alright?"

"Yes, the meal was delicious."

"Is it me? Did I say something?"

"No, it's just that I'm sad to hear that you're leaving next week."

"Oh, the queen has asked me to return as soon as possible. She's concerned about my wellbeing as well as the instability of Murk, now that it has begun to crumble."

Just then, IRIS's voice piped in over the telecom device implanted in Jag's ear. "Sir, all the arrangements have been made, just as you requested."

"Thank you," Jag whispered.

"I'm sorry, did you say something?" Sara asked.

"Thank you for joining me today Sara," Jag said hastily.

The two walked along the winding path, which was lined with a variety of flowers and ponds filled with small fish. However, as they walked up the hill, Jag slowed down. "I think I need to sit down and rest a bit," he said.

"There's a bench at the top of the hill," Sara said.

As they neared it, a lamppost cast light on an object sitting on the bench. Sara saw that it was an envelope with her name written elegantly on the outside.

"What's this?" she asked as she picked it up.

Jag nodded at it. "Open it and see."

As Sara opened the envelope, IRIS spoke again over the intercom. "Sir, I've been able to access Earth's network of computers and, according to local traditions, it is customary that the male species asks the female species for marriage upon a bended knee."

"Bended knee?" Rannick asked as he sat down near IRIS. "I could never bend my knee or bow to ask a woman to marry me."

"Well, whoever asks me to marry him better bend *both* knees," Bayli retorted.

"Guys, you're ruining the moment," Jag whispered as he turned off the communication device. Then Sara pulled out the letter and unfolded it.

My Dear Sara,

Since the day I met you in the garden, my life has never been the same. You have brought such joy to this broken man, and in you, my heart has finally found its home. I am no longer lost.

I will love you all of my life, if you will have me,

Jag

"What? No chocolates?" Sara asked. As she turned around, she found Jag down on one knee with his hand extended. He was holding a ring with the largest diamond she had ever seen.

"Nope, no chocolates, but I hope this will make up for it. Sara Beth Mendelsohn, will you marry me?"

Sara held her hand over her mouth in shock. "Yes, absolutely!"

Jag slipped the ring onto her finger, and she held it up in the light and commented on its beauty. As Jag pushed himself up, he held out his hand. "I may need a little help."

Sara pulled him up and then wrapped her arms around him. "I didn't think you were going to ask me. I was so confused with you leaving for Celestia next week. I thought I was losing you."

Jag looked into her eyes. "You're never losing me!"

Jag and Sara held hands as they walked toward the palace in the center of the garden. Symphonic music poured out of the brightly lit palace. As they neared the terrace, decorated soldiers in old royal-style uniforms opened the doors and motioned with their white-gloved hands for them to enter. IRIS, Bayli, and Rannick were standing near the entrance waiting to hear of Sara's decision, since Jag had disabled his communication device. Jag nodded and grinned, and they began celebrating.

IRIS turned to the dancing crowd. "Ladies and gentlemen . . ." After everyone turned to face Jag and Sara, he continued. "Please welcome His Royal Majesty Prince Marcello of Celestia and his bride to be, Sara Mendelsohn."

Cheers erupted as Sara squeezed Jag's arm. "What have you done?"

Jag smiled. "This is all for you, Cinderella."

A welcoming line formed, and Sara's parents were first to greet them. Like everyone else, they were dressed in tuxedos and gorgeous evening gowns. Sara's mom hugged her as Ben shook his future son-in-law's hand. Sara held her hand up to show them her ring.

"It's gorgeous, but it will never shine as bright as you do this night," Ben said as he kissed his daughter on the cheek. Then Jag and Sara moved down the line.

"Thanks for inviting us, Jag," Aunt Rachel said. "I didn't think this old man would ever take me to a ball."

"Yes, thanks for making me get all dressed up in this getup," Uncle Jack said sarcastically as he pulled on his collar.

"Stop squirming," Aunt Rachel said, elbowing him.

"It itches," Uncle Jack replied.

"Baby skin must run in your family," Bayli said, standing beside Admiral Rannick.

Then the master of ceremonies called for Jag and Sara to take to the dance floor. Jag handed IRIS his cane, and Jag and Sara walked out to the center and began dancing as the symphony played a slow waltz. Then everyone joined the couple, including Bayli, who pulled Admiral Rannick onto the dance floor. Even Mahjon joined in the festivities. Children took turns hanging from his strong arms as he lifted them off the floor.

"This was the best day ever!" Sara said as she rested her head against Jag's shoulder.

Jag took a deep breath and looked up at the golden ceiling. "Thank you," he whispered.

The *Cora Lee* returned to Celestia, passing through Alpha Centauri as Jag had promised the professor. When they arrived on Aulora, Jag and Sara had a beautiful wedding with attendees from all over the kingdom. Even Dr. Neebo and the lovely Loxy Lonna attended. Professor Polanski oversaw the launch of the Space University, in which students from all over the universe participated.

After the fulfillment of the Yalorian prophecy, Murk General Jessip overthrew Damon and exiled him and Measil to a desert planet. Afterwards, Murk dissolved as the majority of planets requested admittance into the Kingdom of Celestia. With so many joining at once, the queen asked Jag and Ben (who was now ambassador to Celestia from Earth) to oversee the application process. Under Queen Ardiana's rule, the kingdom experienced an unprecedented period of growth and peace.

As for Rannick and Bayli, they married eventually. Of course, the admiral had to get down on both knees before Bayli would accept his proposal. They lived their days running the vineyard on Norr and chasing after their nine kids!

Tahjon returned to Mravia, to a hero's welcome, where he married and had children of his own. After the death of Grand Chief Grazer Mrano, Tahjon replaced him. Each year, Jag returned to Mravia so Mahjon could spend time with his brother and, eventually, start a family of his own.

Jag and Sara lived out their days serving the kingdom on Corian and had three children: Joseph Alexander Gabriel IV, Cora Maëlle, and Marcel Rannick.

Never again did Jag have any dreams that foretold his or anyone else's future. Even so, they lived their lives to the fullest, through good times and bad, always looking for the golden thread.

ABOUT THE AUTHOR

 Doug Coning holds an MBA from Anderson University and a BA in Information Systems from Colorado Technical University. Prior to his entry into the field of information technology, where Doug currently serves as an eCommerce application manager for a Fortune 500 company, he worked with an international Christian ministry, for whom he traveled to more than twenty countries providing humanitarian aid and working with youth and children.

Morgan James
Speakers Group

www.TheMorganJamesSpeakersGroup.com

We connect Morgan James published
authors with live and online events
and audiences who will benefit
from their expertise.

Morgan James makes all of our titles available
through the Library for All Charity Organization.

www.LibraryForAll.org